D0047660

A FAMILY TORN BY LOVE AND LOSS

STEPHEN NOWELL: A Loyalist, drawn to the English cause by his vision of a mighty empire. A man haunted by tragic loss and bitter regret.

KATHERINE NOWELL STIEGLER: She had learned the terrible price of war and violence. It had cost her both the men she loved.

AMY NOWELL: Living in the shadow of her mother's pain, she swore she'd never make the same mistake—until love left her no choice.

ANTOINE GINGRAS: A proud, wary French Canadian, how could he choose between his passion for Amy and his country's cause.

LOUIS JOSEPH STIEGLER: Torn between his mother's need and the rebel call, he became a man on two battlefields.

AARON BRANT: A Loyalist, a proud leader of the Iroquois, he was a man of peace, yet formidable in battle. Through him the drama begun in BLACK-ROBE would be drawn full circle.

THE CANADIANS

A PEOPLE TORN BETWEEN A DESIRE FOR INDEPENDENCE AND THEIR LOYALTY TO THE CROWN

Bantam Books by Robert E. Wall
Ask your bookseller for the books you have missed

THE CANADIANS
by
Robert E. Wall

III
BIRTHRIGHT

BANTAM BOOKS
TORONTO · NEW YORK · LONDON · SYDNEY

BIRTHRIGHT: THE CANADIANS III
A Bantam Book/February 1982

ISBN 0-553-20277-4

Bantam Books are published by Bantam Books, Inc. Its trade-
mark, consisting of the words "Bantam Books" and the por-
trayal of a rooster, is Registered in U.S. Patent and Trademark
Office and in other countries. Marca Registrada. Bantam
Books, Inc., 666 Fifth Avenue, New York, New York 10103.

Antoni i Marijanna Wróbel
Niech żyją nam:

A GENEALOGY

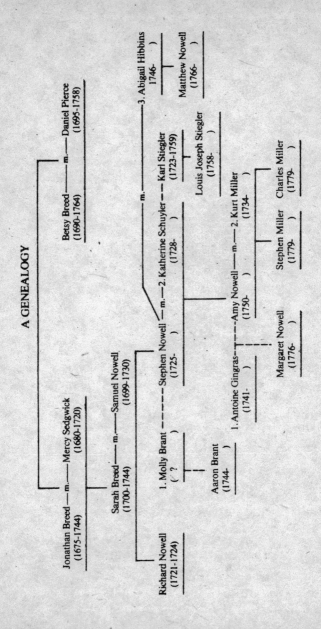

BIRTHRIGHT

PROLOGUE

Among his people a nineteen-year-old was a man, and Kenonranon had been taught by his uncle and his grandfather to behave like a warrior. But mostly it was his mother who had taught him what it meant to be a Mohawk. She said little but he could see the pride in her eyes and in the way she straightened her shoulders when he brought game to the longhouse or honor to the clan. It mattered little to him, or to her for that matter, that her husband was white and that Kenonranon's own father was a white man. She had rejected his father, the blackrobe, because his ways were the ways of the whites, but her husband, the white man Johnson, was in his heart as much a Mohawk as his mother or his uncle.

Kenonranon was tall, almost six feet. His legs were short but his chest was deep and his shoulders broad. His golden skin was darkened by the sun and by the bear grease with which he covered his body to ward off insects. It was his eyes that made him different from the others who surrounded him. They were a striking light blue.

He had come to the land of the Inland Seas at the request of his stepfather and his uncle. He was to observe the western Indians and to report back to Johnson and his uncle, Joseph Brant. Johnson had heard the stories that even the Seneca, a people of the Longhouse and cousins to Kenonranon, were restive. The tribes of the west had always loved the French and had never accepted their defeat in 1759 and their expulsion from Canada in 1763.

The council fire grew brighter as warriors heaved great logs upon it. In the rear of the dark clearing, drums began to beat softly to summon the tribal leaders together. The council members entered the clearing and then parted to allow a pathway for their leader to join them.

The chief of the Ojibwa was named Minavavana. His people dwelled near the English fort at Michilinackinac, which guarded the straits connecting Lake Michigan and Lake Huron. Although he was only about fifty years old, his face was lined with wrinkles and his long, braided hair was streaked with grey. He spoke a language that Kenonranon did not understand, but an Ojibwa who had known his uncle Joseph Brant at Dr. Wheelock's English school translated the speech for him.

Minavavana held the long wampum belt of war in his hand. It had come from Pontiac of the Ottawa earlier in the week. The great council of the tribes near Detroit had decided on war. All the English forts were to be attacked and their garrisons destroyed. Then the Indians would fall on the English settlers and destroy every man, woman and child.

The Ojibwa sat in council to decide the fate of the English garrison at the fort on the straits.

The fire was now large, and yet Kenonranon could barely make out the outline of the elders and warriors who sat around it. The intense heat had driven the council members into the shadows to escape it. But Minavavana could be heard.

"You know that the French king promised to be father to the Ojibwa," he shouted. "We became his children, and we have been his loyal sons." He paused until the grunts of assent that came from the shadows stopped. "The English made war on our father. Our father was old and tired. While he slept, his treacherous enemies got up and stole Canada from him. But now our father's sleep is over. I can hear him stirring and stretching as he awakens. He asks aloud for us: 'Where are my children?' When he awakes fully he will call on us to destroy his enemies—the English.

"The English have conquered the soldiers of our father. Canadians are docile and accept the foreign yoke. But the

Ojibwa are unconquered. We still own the forests and the lakes. These we cannot allow the English to take from us. The spirits of our people killed by the English must be avenged. We must kill the English. We must drive them from our land. We must dig up the bones of their dead. They can have no peace in the soil of our fathers. It is war now. It is war until the English are gone forever."

Minavavana threw off his blanket. His torso glistened in the firelight. His body, painted red and black, was naked except for the cloth that covered his loins. The drums began to beat loudly. The chief took the belt of wampum and carried it to each elder and each warrior. One by one they touched it. When all had signaled acceptance of Pontiac's war of extermination, Minavavana gave a great yell and picked up his war ax. He raced to the pole beyond the light of the fire and struck it with a great blow. The ax sank into the wooden post. It would take an arm stronger than most to retrieve it. It would remain there as long as the Ojibwa made war on Louis XV's enemies.

Kenonranon studied the scene carefully. He would have to repeat these words for his stepfather. Johnson would want to know all. But if he did not leave the camp tonight, it would be too late. Tomorrow the Ojibwa would attack the English at Michilinackinac. He stepped more deeply into the shadows. When he was sure that he could be seen by no one, he began to move quietly away from the council site.

He must exercise all the care and stealth that his uncle Joseph Brant had taught him. He moved noiselessly through the underbrush. He knew there would be a scout posted, but the scout would be more interested in keeping strangers away from the council than in stopping someone who came from the fire. Kenonranon saw the Ojibwa hiding in the brush by the stream that flowed into the Great Lake. The scout had not covered his back and was fully visible in the moonlight. Kenonranon crept up behind him. He raised his tomahawk and brought the flat face of it down on the back of the Ojibwa's skull with a dull thud. The sentry moaned and then fell forward into the bushes. He would not know who it was who had struck him. Kenonranon checked to see if he was still breathing. The man lived, but he would be unconscious for some time.

Kenonranon stepped over his body and waded into the stream. The water was frigid and his feet were soon numb with the cold. He walked until he reached the waters of the lake. He turned south in the water to hide his footprints. He would warn the English because that was what his mother, Johnson, and his uncle Joseph would want of him.

Captain Etherington had only recently taken possession of the fort at Michilinackinac from the French. He had thirty-five men and several officers under his command. It was his first independent command and he was determined to do well. He had followed the commanding general's instructions to give up the French practice of bribing the tribes with gifts, and he had personally removed the warriors who lolled about the fort's parade ground, drinking and carrying on. An English fort should be strictly run, like a proper military base. The slovenly Canadians who still ran the trading posts and stores very much wanted to continue the old ways, but he was a British officer and he knew the meaning of discipline. Tomorrow, June 4, 1763, was the King's birthday. He would open the gates and allow the redmen and their squaws to enter. Then he would awe them with a parade and fireworks and fire his cannon in honor of the King. The Ojibwa had invited his men to watch a ball game they would play against their cousins the Saux from Wisconsin. Normally Etherington would not have allowed it, but he knew the diversion would be good for the morale of his men, who had so little to do in the middle of this godforsaken wilderness.

There was a knock on the door and Corporal Davies entered.

"There's a young Indian outside to see you, sir."

"How did he enter the fort?"

"I don't know, sir. All I know is that he's here. He

speaks English. Claims to be from Sir William Johnson."

"Oh, Christ, that crowd," said Etherington, shaking his head in disgust. "Johnson just pours gifts onto these flea-bitten wastrels, while they sit around trying to figure out ways to stay neutral. If the bugger is looking for a handout, throw him out on his arse."

"He won't say what he wants, sir," said Davies. "Only that he must see the captain."

"All right, send him in."

Kenonranon walked into Etherington's office before the corporal could turn around.

"Captain," he said in his best school English, just as his uncle had taught him. "This fort is in jeopardy. The Ojibwa plan to destroy it tomorrow."

"How do they plan to do that?" asked Etherington rather sarcastically.

"I don't know," said Kenonranon, "but you will be attacked tomorrow in force. The plan is to destroy you."

"How much rum have you imbibed this evening, young man?" said the British officer.

Kenonranon looked at him without comprehension.

"You're drunk! Just like all you bloody savages. You can't keep away from the firewater—poor bastards."

"I've not tasted whiskey," said Kenonranon, "not ever."

"Davies, get this lying savage out of my office. No telling what kind of vermin he has tracked in with him."

The corporal grasped Kenonranon's arm. But the Indian, with one turn of his powerful shoulders, twisted out of his grasp.

"Don't touch me again," said Kenonranon. "I came here to warn you as I have been trained to do. And yet you insult me and call me foul names. I don't agree with the sentiments of my Ojibwa cousins, but I understand their feelings better than you do. Captain, you need training in the way to treat Indians from my father, Johnson." He turned around and walked from the room without looking back. He had done what his family and his clan would have expected of him. It was not his fault that the English chief was a fool.

The next day was the King's birthday. The British garrison, except for those with sentry duty, was placed on a holiday standing. The great wooden gates of the stockade were opened wide. The Indians encamped about the fort strolled in. They stopped at the trading post to purchase blankets and kettles, powder and shot and—for the lucky few who knew a Canadian trader who would bend the rules—some whiskey. All the goods were paid for with the richest beaver furs to be found in the region of the lakes.

Kenonranon strolled along the parade ground to the fort. He could feel the tension in the air, even if the British were oblivious to it. The Canadian shopkeepers had opened their stores, but nowhere could one see the white women and children. They had been carefully hidden away in cellars or in locked rooms on the second-floor living quarters above the shops. But Kenonranon noted the presence of large numbers of Ojibwa squaws inside the fort, and it did not escape his notice that all were wrapped in heavy woolen blankets on a hot June day. Minavavana came into the fort, dressed in his finest eagle feathers and a European coat frayed at the sleeves and elbows. The coat had been a gift from an earlier commandant of what had then been a French fort at the Straits of Mackinaw. Minavavana called Etherington in a loud voice. The captain came to the front porch of his headquarters building.

"Etherington," said the Ojibwa in French. "My people play a game against the men of our cousins from the west, the Saux. We invite all to watch."

Etherington waited until Lieutenant Leslie, his second in command, translated. He then nodded to the chief. "My men celebrate the birthday of our father the King. It pleases me that our brothers should choose this day as a day of celebration."

Minavavana stared at Etherington while his words were turned into a poorly accented French by Leslie. And then he turned and walked out of the fort without comment.

Kenonranon joined the Ojibwa. He met a friend from last night's council. The man was stripped to his loincloth, and his hair was tied in a knot. He carried two wooden sticks curved at the bottom into clublike instruments.

"Are the Mohawk familiar with our game, Baggataway?" he asked.

Kenonranon knew of the game by a different name, but he had never played it.

The Ojibwa handed him one of the bats. "Strip," he said. "And join us. You're strong and can run. You can play."

Kenonranon took off his shirt and leggings and laid them in a pile with the clothing of the other players. A large field in front of the fort had been marked off, and a goal stake had been driven into the ground at each end. Kenonranon joined the Ojibwa in front of their stake. They numbered about a hundred. An equal number of Saux stood at the opposite end. Minavavana walked into the field. He held a wooden ball in his hand. With a great yell he hurled it high into the sky. From two hundred throats came a cheer as all ran screaming toward the spot they thought the ball would land. Kenonranon raced ahead, holding his bat with both hands. He was a fast runner and soon reached the front of the Ojibwa line. The ball hit the ground and rolled in the direction of the charging Saux.

The leading opponent, a man with a crest of upright hair on his otherwise shaven skull, smashed the ball backward toward a line of Saux players. As Kenonranon rushed by the first Saux, he felt the smash of a bat against his shins. He doubled over in pain and fell face first on the ground. His Ojibwa friend came up behind him and helped him to his feet. Kenonranon put his weight gingerly on his leg and found that it was numb. He looked about in anger for his assailant, but the man was gone.

The Saux had cleverly pushed the ball toward the rear of their line, where their faster runners were now trying to outrace the Ojibwa on their right flank. The onlookers cheered their team. Kenonranon could now feel a throb of pain in his leg, but he placed more and more pressure on it and found that he could run, not fast, but he would leave that to others.

The Ojibwa were not without skills at this ball game. Their fastest runners had cut off the Saux, and in the mad melée of bodies falling on each other, most of the players had lost sight of the ball. Kenonranon ran toward the pile of bodies. Players were plucking at each other and pulling each other's hair in their efforts to reach the ball. Finally there was a yell, and one of the Saux pulled away from the pile and smacked the ball back toward his own goal. Kenonranon saw that he was the closest opponent and that, in fact, the Saux had made an error in strategy. Kenonranon was closer to the ball than the Saux himself. Kenonranon began to race for the ball. He cursed the pain in his leg, but the faster he ran the more excited he became and the less he felt the pain.

The path to the Saux goal was clear. No one had lingered behind to defend it. Kenonranon held the bat in his right hand and dived forward toward the ball. He felt the Saux coming up behind him. He knew that the Saux would attempt to hit him with his bat before he could reach the ball. His opponent's bat squeezed between his legs, forcing him to fall just as his own bat struck the ball and sent it whirling toward the goal. Kenonranon, lying face forward on the ground, heard a cheer go up from the Ojibwa as the ball crossed the Saux goal line.

His new friends crowded around Kenonranon and pounded him on the back. There were some who would have preferred the goal to have been scored by one of their own rather than by a visitor from the Six Nations, but a goal was a goal.

As the Ojibwa walked back toward their own goal line, Kenonranon could see that most of the British soldiers had left the fort and were standing outside the stockade to get a better view of the game.

The game began again. Once again the Saux tried an outflanking tactic. This time the same man who had first slammed Kenonranon with his stick gave a great yell and smashed the ball with all of his might. The ball rose high in the air and sailed over the heads of the Ojibwa defenders and beyond the Ojibwa goal. As it began to roll toward the open gate of the fort, two hundred screaming, naked players began to race after it. Kenonranon, still limping, could not keep up with the rest.

But he stopped dead in his tracks when he realized that

the players were ignoring the ball altogether. They raced toward the English soldiers, who stood or lounged on the ground, weaponless. Some ran past the soldiers into the fort, where Ojibwa and Saux squaws opened their blankets and handed their men muskets and tomahawks and knives. Others began to smash the soldiers with their bats, knocking them senseless. The slaughter began. An Ojibwa holding a living, conscious English soldier between his knees tore off the scalp of his screaming prisoner with his scalping knife.

Kenonranon stopped in the field. From within the fort the screams of the soldiers could be heard, and every soldier outside who was not already dead would, he knew, face an even more horrible fate that night in the fires. The stores of the Canadians remained untouched; the wives and children of the traders remained safe, if frightened, in the security of their homes. Minavavana was true to his word. The children of his father, the awakening King of France, were unharmed. But the English had paid a horrible price for ignoring the warnings of a son of the Six Nations of the Iroquois.

I

SUMMER 1765

William Vaughan was almost sixty years old and looked every bit his age. His hair was mostly white, and his belly protruded over the top of his breeches. Climbing a flight of stairs left him breathless. His left heel constantly pained him, and every old scar in his body was the seat of agony in the damp, chilly sea winds of Boston.

He lay on top of the covers in the giant bed in his rooms in the Cromwell's Head, an inn in the north end of Boston. He had been drunk the night before and the night before that. He rubbed his hand on his chin and felt the growth of whiskers. It was clear to him that he had been drunk for several nights prior to the last two as well.

His head lay propped against the carved oak backboard of his bed. His fine linen shirt was opened to just above his navel. He stared down at his chest and rounded belly. The hair on his chest had turned white as well. He knew that the white descended even further and that that part of him didn't work anymore. He wondered if the white on his head indicated that his brain had gone soft as well.

He raised his hand to his forehead and groaned. "Damn belly! It looks like I'm seven months gone," he said half aloud.

He remembered that last night—or was it the night before?—there had been a girl, a pretty young thing from the taproom below. He didn't want to remember, but vaguely he recalled the embarrassment of not being able to perform. He had paid her well anyway. Maybe that would keep her mouth shut.

1

He had a lot of money now, thanks to Stephen Nowell. The firm founded by Sarah Nowell and destroyed by Daniel Pierce had been reborn. Stephen, Sarah's son, was at the helm. He chuckled at the thought of Stephen at the helm. The man couldn't go below deck on any one of the ships he owned—even in harbor—without turning green. Besides, with only one arm, he would have trouble holding a course in a gale.

He closed his eyes briefly. The images of white water and a reef off Cape Ann flooded into his head, as did the screams of his crew as they dived overboard into the raging sea. He shook his head and pulled up his arm and covered his eyes with it. That had been so many years ago. He had lost his crew and cargo. Some, who said he had been drunk, made sure he never sailed again. A drunken ship's master was supposed to stay in port. And he *had* turned to drink. As long as he was accused of sin, he might as well enjoy the sin's pleasure along with the public condemnation.

But Sarah had found him. Even now, almost twenty years later, the thought of her overwhelmed him. Although her face and black hair were harder to remember, except when he looked at her son, he recalled vividly her strength of character—the driving will that had created Breed, Nowell and Pierce and made it the most powerful mercantile house in Boston, even in the face of the deceit and treachery of Daniel Pierce, her Aunt Breed's husband. And he remembered the love they had shared, a love that had raised him from the floors of Boston's taprooms and placed him back at the helm of his ship—or rather her ship. And he remembered the devastation that had consumed him when she disappeared from the deck of the *Betsy* off Cape Breton.

But now he owned a fleet of ships of his own, the gifts of Sarah's son Stephen. Vaughan had taken Stephen under his protection when Stephen, a mere boy, arrived in Boston, a fugitive from Jesuit villainy. Hope of revenge had kept Vaughan functioning, despite lapses, until that day in 1758 when he had kicked the ladder beneath the feet of Daniel Pierce on the gallows at the captured fort of Louisbourg.

With Pierce dead, Vaughan had lost his goal. He had sunk low. He and Stephen had gone to Quebec with Wolfe in 1759 to try to find Stephen's wife and child. But even then he had been drunk most of the time. When Stephen came into possession of his mother's trust fund and his grandfather's estate and became one of Boston's wealthiest men, his generosity to William Vaughan had known only those limits that Vaughan himself placed on him.

There was a soft knocking at the door.

"Go away," croaked Vaughan.

"Mr. Vaughan, sir, are you up?"

It was Josiah, the black man who once had been casual help to the ferry man and kitchen help in the inn, but who now ran the ferry between Charlestown and Boston, again thanks to Stephen Nowell, who had procured control of the ferry company.

Josiah had taken care of Vaughan for years when he had served the owner of the Cromwell's Head, and he couldn't seem to get out of the habit.

"Mr. Vaughan?"

"Go away, you busy old woman. My head hurts."

The door opened and the gray-haired, large-muscled black man stepped into the room.

"You've been drunk for five days straight, Mr. Vaughan. It's no wonder your head hurts."

Vaughan glared at him angrily and made an obscene sound with his mouth.

"I came because Mr. Nowell's returned from New York. He spent the night at the house in Charlestown, and I brought him over to Boston this morning. He's sure to be here at the inn just as soon as he comes back from the warehouses, and sure as I'm standing here, he's going to want to see you, and you ain't in no condition to be seen or smelled."

Josiah went over to the windows, which looked out on the waters of the strait between the Charlestown and

3

Boston peninsulas. He threw open the window. The breeze blew warm, fresh air into the room.

Vaughan pulled up the quilt.

"Damn it, Josiah," he yelled. "It's still bloody night out there. You'll be the death of me. God knows what diseases are lurking out in the night air."

"It's broad daylight, Mr. Vaughan, and it's August. Nothing but pleasant air blowing through that window."

He went to the cupboard and pulled out Vaughan's razor and shaving mug. "I've left your things out. I'll be back with hot water in a few minutes."

The black man walked to the door and turned to look at Vaughan, who still lay on the bed wrapped in the patchwork quilt. Vaughan didn't move, and Josiah left, shaking his head.

The room was quiet for a few moments, and again there was a knock at the door.

"Shit," yelled Vaughan. "What is this place—Fanueil Hall Marketplace?"

The door opened and Stephen Nowell entered. "You seem in fine spirits, Willie," said the younger man.

Nowell had fair skin and jet black hair that had begun to turn gray at the temples. His eyes seemed to dominate his entire face. They were a piercing steel blue. He was barely forty years old, yet his face was drawn and showed signs of past suffering. A thin scar ran through his eyebrow and could be seen faintly even on the eyelid. On his forehead was one deep worry line that was usually not seen, since his unruly locks normally fell into his eyes and covered his whole forehead. Frequently, though, he would brush back the hair off his forehead with his right hand and then absentmindedly rub the scar that ran through the eyebrow. But the extent of his physical suffering was best exemplified by the empty left sleeve, which was pinned up against his shoulder.

As a boy Stephen Nowell had been wounded and kidnapped by Indians. He had been raised by French Jesuits at Louisbourg in Cape Breton. He had studied in Paris; he had been a missionary among the Iroquois in central New

4

York. Later he had turned on the French and joined the English in their assault on his former home in Cape Breton. He had sought his family, only to find his father, mother and grandfather dead and the entire family fortune in the hands of his murderous uncle, Daniel Pierce. Only William Vaughan, his mother's lover, had defended him.

Vaughan opened his eyes and glared at Stephen. Then he yawned and scratched his armpit. "I haven't seen much of you in recent weeks, my boy," he said.

"You haven't seen much of anything or anyone. You've been too drunk, or so says Josiah."

"You know, your mother was just about your age when she died. But she looked a hell of a lot better."

"I should hope so," quipped Stephen.

Vaughan placed his flat palm on his ample belly and rubbed it slowly. "But Sarah was never the prig you turned out to be."

"It must be something in my background," answered Stephen.

Vaughan smiled, although he had meant what he said. He resented Nowell's tendency to moralize, especially since Vaughan always thought himself to be the chief object of his protegé's comments. But he could not help but like Stephen. He was Sarah's son. He had been hurt so often and had been the victim of so much evil.

"I visited the graveyard in Charlestown today," said Stephen. "I ordered a fine stone cut for Aunt Betsy."

"For all her silliness she had the good heart of your grandfather. She was a true Breed."

Stephen nodded. "She's buried on the other side of my grandfather." He came and sat on the bed next to Vaughan. "I'm going to miss her. She was the only member of my family left in the house. They're all gone now—my father, my mother, my grandfather and now Betsy, his sister. All I have left now are the servants, Hannah and George—and you, you old sot."

"You've heard nothing from your wife, Katherine?"

"You mean my ex-wife. No, nothing."

"I'll never understand you, Stephen Nowell, not as long

as I live. There's something perverse in you. You loved that woman and it was clear to me that she worshipped you."

"She made her choice. I asked her to come here with the children. She chose to stay in Canada."

"The woman was confused, Stephen. She had lost a man she loved."

Stephen bristled at the remark, and Vaughan realized that he had made a mistake in mentioning Karl Stiegler. In 1755, Stephen's wife, Katherine Schuyler, had taken their daughter and gone to Canada with his best friend, Karl Stiegler. Stiegler was dead now, killed at the battle on the Plains of Abraham, but Katherine, who had borne Stiegler a child, had refused to return to New England with Stephen. She had remained behind at the Stiegler homestead on Isle d'Orleans in the St. Lawrence with Amy Nowell and Louis Joseph Stiegler, her children.

Stephen rose from the bed and turned his back on Vaughan. He walked to the open window and looked across the straits to the farmhouse atop Breed's Hill. The wind was whipping up the whitecaps on the water, and Stephen could smell the fresh scent of the sea.

Vaughan sat up and stared at Stephen's back. "Well, what are you going to do about her?"

"As you well know, I've divorced her," Stephen said softly.

"What?"

"I've divorced her," said Stephen more loudly and, turning to face the bed, he said, "She deserted me and I've rid myself of her. Moreover, I plan to remarry."

Vaughan looked thunderstruck. "Who? When?"

"Her name is Abigail Hibbins. Her father is Edward Hibbins. He has a firm here in Boston and a fine house in the South End. She's quite a catch. Her father has provided a very large dowry."

"I know Edward Hibbins, and his daughter is a little girl."

"She's nineteen, Willie."

"As I said, she's a little girl."

6

"When I was nineteen I helped you to conquer Louisbourg."

"Stephen, she's the pampered daughter of a wealthy merchant."

"The marriage will bring the two largest merchant houses in Boston into alliance. Governor Bernard and Lieutenant Governor Hutchinson were delighted when they heard the news. Hibbins has always straddled the fence in their battles with Otis and Adams and the other radicals. They hope a union between our two houses will bring Hibbins into the governor's orbit. So everyone benefits. The firm grows stronger, and the governor's cause, which of course is His Majesty's cause, grows stronger."

"I can remember days not so long ago, Stephen Nowell, when you were not so anxious to aid the governor's cause or the King's cause."

"William, don't tell me you're going to start that business about the stamps."

"There'll be no Stamp Acts in Massachusetts, Stephen. The King's ministers will not bleed us dry with their bloody taxes. No right-thinking New Englander will pay them. Newspapers, attorney's licenses, even college diplomas. Do you know that to get the stamp on their diploma the boys at Harvard will have to pay an amount equal to half a year's tuition?"

"Willie, they pay more in England than we are being asked to pay. It's simply necessary to clear off a war debt. Even you must admit we benefited from the war. The French are gone; the Indians are finally routed; that scoundrel Pontiac and his allies are scattered. Someone has to pay for it all."

"Let it be the English. They at least have the right to vote those bloody robbers of Westminster into office."

"You know as well as I, Willie, that very few Englishmen can cast ballots. Besides, do you think the mob that destroyed Mr. Oliver's warehouses and his own home last week would run things any better? This ruffian MacIntosh and his South End bullies are only the tools of dangerous

7

men. The Sons of Liberty try to win arguments with clubs, bricks, not words. The very fabric of our society has been threatened by them, and Otis and Adams may rue the day when they turned to mob rule to overturn the King's justice."

Vaughan knew that it was hopeless to continue the argument. Stephen had become more and more conservative since the war. He was now thoroughly in Lieutenant Governor Hutchinson's camp. And besides, Vaughan agreed with Stephen about MacIntosh. He was a street rowdy who had led the annual bully boy riots on Guy Fawkes Day, when his mob from the South End fought against the North End group. Barrel staves and knives were their weapons. Last year a child had been run down by his drunken wagoners, who tore through the streets of Boston dragging an image of the Pope. But now he and his friends had turned to politics, intimidating the governor and his friends, all in the name of liberty.

Vaughan was silent for several more minutes. Finally he spoke. "It was not taxes or politics that got me started, Stephen. There was a day when it would not have been money or power that would have driven you to marry. You loved that Indian girl Molly when she could do little or nothing for you. And you married Katherine Schuyler when she was nothing but the disowned bastard of a dead New York aristocrat."

"Yes, and look how both those affairs turned out. Molly gave me a son who is running naked about the forest lifting scalps from innocent women and children—that is, if he hasn't perished already along with the rest of Pontiac's scum. And Katherine is living with the French, raising my daughter along with Karl's bastard."

Vaughan winced. "And you haven't done much better with your friends, have you, Stephen?" he said finally. "I'm nothing but an old drunk who plans to stay drunk for the next week and maybe the week after."

"That's why I'm here, Willie. You have to sober up."

"Why?"

"You're killing yourself."

"Life is dying, Stephen. I chose to die a less prolonged

death, helped over the pain by the god Bacchus. You didn't know I had such learning, did you?"

Stephen did not respond. Vaughan frustrated him. He loved the old man, but his drinking and his politics were getting on Stephen's nerves. In addition, Stephen had not expected Vaughan to oppose his marriage plan. He resented the fact that Vaughan had dared to air the very problems about his remarriage that had given him pause and that he had pushed from his mind unresolved. He did not love the girl. She *was* only a child. He was motivated solely by the desire to solidify his economic and political position, but none of his other colleagues would have had the nerve to state the truth.

"I'm giving a reception for Abigail and her father. I'd like you to attend. And I want you to be my best man. You're really the only one I have left."

"And," interrupted Vaughan, "you want me there fresh and clean."

"And sober."

"And sober," repeated Vaughan.

At that moment Josiah entered the room with the hot water. Stephen turned to the black man and smiled.

"Sober him up, Josiah," he said. "Get him shaved and get him on his feet." And with that he left.

Stephen rode in his carriage up the slope of Copp's Hill. From the top he could look out the window and view the grand panorama of the sea, the shrub-dotted islands of the bay filled with ships tied to wharves or waiting at anchor for wharf space to become available.

He rode down Fish Street and crossed the creek into the South End. Boston had not grown much in recent years. Both New York and Philadelphia had surpassed it as America's major cities, but the activity of the town hadn't really slackened. As he approached the Common, Stephen told George, his driver, to slow down so that he could savor the view as the carriage passed along the slope of Beacon Hill. To his left was Fanuiel Hall, alive with farmers selling produce, its red brick elegance contrasting sharply with the day-to-day activities it housed on its ground floor. Off to the North End one could see the spires of the Second Church of Boston—the North Church. And to the right of Fanuiel Hall was the ornate gilt and red brick of the seat of government—home of the general court, the governor and council of the Province of Massachusetts. Stephen loved this city of his birth. For all his travels to Paris, Versailles, and London and to New York and Quebec, he was content to spend the rest of his days here. As a youth growing up in Cape Breton, he had thought of himself as French, a *canadien*, but in recent years his attitudes and his way of life had become entirely those of a New Englander. And now his marriage to Abigail Hibbins would ensure his place in Boston society.

The Hibbins house was located on Oak Street in the South End. It was a wooden frame house of two storeys. The top floor, which projected over the first, was dominated by three great gables, like three great hooded eyes peering down at the carriages that plied their way on the busy street below. The house was painted a dark brown and was set back from the street under the shade of three giant oaks. A richly designed iron fence surrounded the property.

Stephen's carriage stopped in front of the house. As he climbed down, he balanced himself with a silver-headed walking stick, which he now frequently carried. He started to walk up the paved path when suddenly the front door was flung open and a girl dressed in a yellow gown came running down the path toward him. She threw herself against him and kissed his cheeks.

Stephen's face flushed with embarrassment, and he pulled back. His walking stick fell with a clatter to the path.

"Oh, now look what I've done, Mr. Nowell."

"Abigail!" called a voice from inside the shade of the house.

Stephen smiled at the girl. She was very young. Her hair was chestnut brown with streaks of gold. It was piled high on her head. Her nose had a slight upturn, and there were freckles on her prominent cheeks. Her eyes were a dark brown, and her lashes were long and curled.

"Abigail!" called Edward Hibbins again as he stepped

out the front door. "You disgrace me with your public show of emotion. I wish your mother were alive so that she could straighten these kinds of things out."

"Nonsense, Father," the girl called back over her shoulder. "You have given me to Mr. Nowell in marriage. All Boston knows it. There's no disgrace for me to proclaim it publicly."

Stephen took her hand in his. "Abby, let's placate your father and save hugs and kisses for inside."

"Provided you guarantee me that and promise to buy me some pretty things once we are married. Father's such a glum man, Mr. Nowell. He never wants me to have anything pretty." She pouted and looked up at Stephen. It dawned on him that she was serious. He would have to promise her "pretty things" before she would move.

"I'll get you whatever you want—and not from Boston but from New York or maybe Paris—if you behave yourself and come inside."

Abigail's father was a small man. He wore a brown wig to cover his bald head—a fact that Abigail had revealed to Stephen, much to her father's chagrin, at their first meeting. He wore spectacles set upon a nose that clearly marked him as the girl's father. He was richly dressed but his body was dumpy; even the best clothing seemed somehow shabby on him. As the two approached him he chastised his daughter.

"Abigail, you embarrass me and Mr. Nowell. Stephen, I must apologize for my daughter's behavior which, as usual, is outrageous." This last he said raising his tone and attempting to look at his daughter sternly.

Abby paid no attention to him whatsoever. She had picked up Stephen's cane for him and now set it in the stand by the door.

"I've made tea, Mr. Nowell," she said. "I actually did myself, not the servants. Come into the parlor. Will you join us, Father?"

"Of course. I can't leave you two alone unchaperoned."

Abby started to laugh. "Do you think Mr. Nowell would try to take advantage of me in my own parlor? What kind of a man have you given me away to, Father?"

"Damn it, girl," Hibbins blustered. "You can't talk like that."

"Let's have some tea," interrupted Stephen, leading the girl by the arm toward the parlor. "Don't you think that since we are to be married soon, you should stop calling me Mr. Nowell and start calling me Stephen?"

"No," she responded, "not yet."

"When?" asked Stephen, stopping in his tracks and looking at her quizzically.

"I'll tell you when the time comes," she responded.

The Hibbins parlor was dark, as was the whole house. The wooden furniture was of dark hue except for one cream-colored upholstered chair, which sat next to a small candlestick table in front of the leaded glass window. Across the room the clock chimed. It stood from floor to ceiling, and above the hour and minute hands a balance wheel turned to the left, moving a small plate on which was depicted a ship on the high seas. Each tick sent a wave against the bow of the endlessly battered vessel, which would see the end of the storm only if the master of the house grew negligent and forgot to turn the key. A silver tea service was set on the tray on a low table. Abby waved Stephen into the upholstered chair. Her father sat down in the straight-backed wooden captain's chair directly across from the clock. She poured tea for them all and placed herself on the floor at Stephen's feet. Her father looked at Stephen and was amazed by the amused look in his eyes. He had intended to say something about his daughter's behavior, but changed his mind.

"Stephen, I gather the governor has decided to make us toe the line and use the stamps," Hibbins said instead.

Stephen looked away from Abby, startled by the fact that a question had been asked of him. "I didn't hear you, Edward."

"The stamps—Governor Bernard has stored them at Castle William and has ordered Hutchinson to bring them into Boston. That's the word going around town."

"It's not true. The radicals are at it again. Bernard lost control when he moved to the castle in the face of the riots. Hutchinson has assumed control and is now in charge. I've known Tom Hutchinson since I was a boy. He's Boston born. His family has been here as long as yours or mine."

Abby started to laugh. "His is almost as notorious as ours—maybe even worse. His ancestors were banished as heretics. Mine were only hanged as witches."

"Abigail, would you please not mention that unfortunate incident again in public."

"Why not? Ann Hibbins was hanged as a witch and I feel close to her. She lives in this very house. Her ghost is said to haunt these rooms. Neighbors have seen her conjuring in the windows in the gables."

"That's pure nonsense. The woman was innocent—a scold hanged by ignorant neighbors. She was no witch. And that all took place over a hundred years ago, and this house is not even half that age. You exaggerate, to put it mildly, my daughter."

Abby pouted for a few seconds. "Well, I don't care. It's a good story, and if it's not true then it should be." She looked up at Stephen, who placed his hand on her head and stroked her hair. Her father looked on uncomfortably.

"Tom Hutchinson has written the Board of Trade and the Ministry and even the King to advise against taxing the Colonies directly," said Stephen. "He knows how jealously New Englanders, and especially the people of Massachusetts, guard their right to tax themselves. He has warned England that it is bad policy. But he believes in law and order, and he believes Parliament and the King have the right to tax. It may be bad policy, but it is law and law must be enforced."

"I'm telling you right now, Nowell, if Hutchinson attempts to enforce the law and take those stamps off the ships in the harbor and use them on newspapers or the like here in Boston, law and order will break down."

Stephen grimaced. Hibbins was right and he knew it. So did the lieutenant governor. "Hutchinson is not prepared to risk riots, Edward. I think Boston will see no stamps."

"That step would convince me to support Hutchinson in council, Stephen. It would prove to me that he's a man of moderation, and damn it, we need moderation above all right now."

"Too much politics," interrupted Abby. "I want to talk about my party. Mr. Nowell, tell me all about it."

Again Stephen smiled at his bride-to-be. "It will be at my house in Charlestown tomorrow evening. It will be a small gathering of friends of your family and mine. My aunt's death last month prevents us from celebrating too much. I'm still in mourning for her."

"Who is to be there besides Father, you and me?"

"My partner Mr. Vaughan for one."

Hibbins made a face clearly indicating his disgust. "Has he sobered up?"

"I'm sure he'll be fine," said Stephen defensively. "And members of the council and the lieutenant governor have promised to come, along with Mr. Oliver."

"But not Mr. Otis or Mr. Adams or any of that crowd."

"That's a different circle," said Stephen. "And one in which I do not travel."

"Will they bring their ladies, and will I look more lovely than anyone else?" Abby asked, grinning.

"You are the prettiest girl in Boston."

"Only that?" she asked, laughing. "The party will be in Charlestown. That could leave me not even the prettiest girl at my own engagement party."

"You're too clever for me, Abby," said Stephen. "I promise you, you will be the prettiest girl in all Massachusetts tomorrow and every night. And now I must go. The party needs some preparation. Hannah, my servant, can't do everything."

"But you'll be back tomorrow to fetch me?"

"I will not," said Stephen finally. "You know very well we all agreed last week that you would travel with your father."

"But Father is a terrible swimmer. Suppose the ferry should capsize. Who would rescue me?"

Stephen laughed out loud. "If you must depend on a forty-year-old, one-armed knight errant, my lady, you are in grave trouble."

14

"No matter," said Abby. "I'm an excellent swimmer. I could rescue you both."

Stephen rose from his chair. He had more than a party to prepare. He had promised the lieutenant governor that he would visit his residence on Garden Court Street that afternoon. But he knew that if he told Abby that, she would only pout. The girl was quickly becoming dear to him. Best she know only that he left to prepare something beautiful for her.

Thomas Hutchinson had aged noticeably in the twenty years since Stephen Nowell had first met him. At that time he had been counselor to Governor Shirley during the first Louisbourg expedition in 1745. Now he was chief justice and lieutenant governor of the colony and clearly the most important politician in Massachusetts. Governor Bernard had left Province House and fled to the castle on the island in Boston harbor during the last week's rioting. But although the mob had forced Hutchinson's kinsmen Mr. Oliver to resign his post as stamp revenue collector for Boston port and had destroyed his property, Hutchinson himself had remained calm and was attempting to win over to his side the conservative forces of the town.

Stephen stepped into Hutchinson's study unannounced. The majority of the lieutenant governor's servants had been sent to his country home in Milton for safety, and his doorman had been forced to help Stephen's servant George with the Nowell carriage. Hutchinson was working at his desk on his history. Stephen had seen him there many times before, pouring over hundred-year-old documents relating to the origins of Massachusetts.

"Thomas," Stephen called softly.

The lieutenant governor looked up startled. When he saw Stephen, a thin smile appeared on his face.

"Ah, Nowell, I didn't hear your carriage. Come over here; I have something that will interest you. These are documents signed by the court of assistance—the first rulers of the Bay Colony. One of the signatures is that of an Increase Nowell of Charlestown. No doubt your progenitor."

Stephen picked up the old paper with care. It was cracked and yellowed with age. "I've known that my family went back to 1630 but I didn't know any names."

"Well, he was a very strict fellow. He condemned Mistress Ann Hutchinson and her family as radical disturbers of the peace and good order of society and agreed with her banishment. It is indeed ironic that it should fall to me—a Hutchinson—to defend the peace and good order of that same state four generations later."

"I'm amazed that you have time for your history, what with the calamitous events of the past week."

Hutchinson merely smiled. "It keeps me sane. Tomorrow we will face another of those nights. Word is out that that fellow MacIntosh has called for a bonfire meeting on King Street. They say he threatens the custom house."

"Can't something be done?"

Hutchinson chuckled. "Governor Bernard has called on the colonel of militia to order his drummers to beat the alarm. The colonel, however, responded that his drummers would probably find their drums around their ears at the first roll."

"Well then, law and order have broken down. We must call on the crown to provide troops."

"Not yet, Stephen. This damn tax business was a wrongheaded policy from the beginning. Grenville was a fool to push it through Parliament. It will bring him down in the long run and we will have a more sensible ministry shortly. Bring in troops now and we give Adams and his friends in the general court another weapon. I'm hoping that the good people of this town will reject the bullies and realize that it is their property that the mob threatens."

Stephen put down Hutchinson's document and sat in the leather-back straight chair opposite the lieutenant governor's desk. "I assume with trouble brewing tomorrow night you'll not be coming to the engagement party."

"You assume incorrectly, my friend. Your engagement to Hibbins' daughter may be a matter of love for you, but it is

16

a matter of high politics for me. You and that pretty young lady are going to have to bring Edward Hibbins into line on the most important issues. But there is the issue of protecting this house. Most of my people are at Milton, at my country estate. I hate to leave this house with only my steward in residence."

"I can offer you the services of my man, if that would make a difference to you. Old George will enjoy the night off. I'll send him midday so that he can learn the premises."

"That would put my mind at ease, Nowell," said Hutchinson. And I'll be able to help celebrate the coming nuptials. You're a lucky man, Nowell."

Stephen wished he could believe Hutchinson. He desperately wanted this marriage to work, and he wanted to have children who would be with him as he grew older. But he could not be terribly sanguine. All his other attempts to establish a family had ended in utter disaster.

The Breed house on top of the hill was alive with lighted candles. The leaded glass windows shimmered in the flickering light and welcomed a select group of Boston and Charlestown's elite as their carriages struggled up the winding road. Stephen and Abigail stood together before the studded oak door and greeted their guests one by one. Some passed through the door and turned to the right into the dining room. There the great oak table was laden with platters of broiled fresh fish and smoked fish. There was also a great cured ham from the Breeds' larder. Hannah, George's wife, had spent the early hours of the morning making loaves of fresh whole wheat and corn bread which were now piled high on the table.

The lowboy, which had been moved from old man Breed's bedroom to the dining room years before, was covered with jugs of cider and several decanters of rich dessert wines from Spain and Portugal.

Except for the wines, the food Stephen offered his guests was the coarse fare of the country. There was none of the delicate cuisine from London and Paris, which had recently become popular in Boston. Nowell was wealthy, but he fancied himself more a country squire, like his grandfather Jonathan Breed, than a man of the city, and he played the role to the hilt.

Those guests who had turned to the left entered the parlor, where a small string orchestra played local country melodies. There would be dancing later in the evening.

When all the guests had arrived, Stephen and Abby left the front door and joined Abby's father in front of the central fireplace. Abby's father was speaking to a large, buxom woman, the wife of one of the governor's counselors.

Suddenly Stephen heard his name being called loudly from the doorway. He turned and saw William Vaughan in a black coat and breeches with silver buttons and a white-powdered wig. His face was shaved and his shoe buckles and coat buttons had been shined until they shone in the reflected candlelight. He looked ten years younger than he had the day before.

"Stephen," he shouted. "Where is the young lady? Ah, there she is." He walked over to Abby, bowed and raised her hand to his lips. "You are, my young lady, every bit as beautiful as I have been told and as I have seen from a distance. I am your servant, William Vaughan. The scoundrel you are about to marry was like a son to me." He glanced at Stephen and then said conspiratorially to Abigail, "Actually, he's now more like a father to me. But in either case we are very close."

"Mr. Vaughan," said Abigail, "I've heard so much about you from Mr. Nowell."

"Believe all of it. I'm every bit as bad as he says. Worse, in fact. I drink too much, I'm lazy, and I do other things that I can't mention in polite company."

Abigail laughed and took Vaughan by the arm. "Come to the window seat, Mr. Vaughan. I have to talk to you. I need to learn something about the man I am marrying, and you know him better than anyone alive."

Apprehensively, Stephen watched them walk away. God alone knew what Vaughan would tell the girl to frighten her out of the marriage. He was about to follow when the buxom woman grabbed his arm and dragged him into the conversation she was having with Hibbins.

The night was hot, almost sultry. George sat with Asa in the kitchen of the Hutchinson mansion. George was over seventy and was not strong. For years he had worked at Squire Breed's side on his farm. But after Breed died and Pierce had expelled George and Hannah, his wife, from his house, his strength had broken. Stephen, Breed's grandson, had found him, and together they had traveled to the Mohawk Valley, where again the work had been hard. Now, back in Boston, George knew that it was Nowell who took care of him and protected him. He was pleased to have an opportunity to be useful and to work, even if he was only asked to babysit a house.

He did not, however, enjoy the company of Asa Wallace, Thomas Hutchinson's steward. Wallace was a mean-minded man. George was sure he pinched every shilling that came into Hutchinson's coffers, not out of loyalty to his employer, but to guarantee that his own portion, something Hutchinson would know nothing of, was as large as possible.

Asa was working on his books. Suddenly he looked up. "Did you hear something?" he asked George.

"My hearing is not so good anymore," responded George.

"Well, I heard something," said Wallace, as he rose from his chair.

Then George heard it too. At first it was like a murmur, but it gradually grew louder and louder until the two men recognized it as the roar of angry men.

George and Asa hurried from the kitchen into the front hallway of the mansion. Through the windows in the darkened house they saw the flickering light of torches. George crept to the side of the parlor window and cautiously peered around the curtain. Outside the Sons of Liberty had assembled. George recognized the man known as MacIntosh, who led the group and carried a barrel stave over his shoulder. The man beside MacIntosh was dragging an effigy meant to depict Thomas Hutchinson. This straw man was lifted high in the air and a torch was thrust

19

into its belly. Soon the figure was consumed in flames. A roar went up from the crowd.

"Bring out the real man," yelled MacIntosh and the crowd picked up the chant.

George looked over at Asa. Even in the darkness he could see Hutchinson's servant almost shrink with fear.

"I'm getting out of here," said Asa.

"Your duty is to protect this house, and since Mr. Nowell assigned me to take on the task of assisting you, it is my duty, too."

"You have to be crazy or dumb or both to stay and face that mindless mob. I saw what they did over at Oliver's."

"That mob ain't mindless," said George. "That fellow MacIntosh, he's in charge. He's calling the shots. They want Hutchinson and he's not here. If we convince them of that, maybe they'll go away."

"And maybe the King is Irish," said Asa. He gave one more furtive look at George and then bolted back toward the kitchen and the rear door of the house.

George was frightened. Stephen had told him to help Asa Wallace. He didn't think his employer would expect him to try to fight off a mob, but, on the other hand, he couldn't just leave, as Asa had done. He had never run from a responsibility in his life. He took a deep breath and wiped his sweating forehead on his shirtsleeve. He went to the door and threw it open.

A hush fell over the crowd when they saw George. A man from the back of the crowd yelled out: "Who the hell is he? He's not Hutchinson."

"No," shouted another man, "Hutchinson is too busy licking the King's ass to see us plain folk of Boston."

The crowd broke into laughter.

"The lieutenant governor is not at home," George shouted over the noise. "He's over at Charlestown and he won't be home tonight."

"Horseshit," yelled that same voice. "Let's go inside and find him." There were several murmurs of approval and the crowd surged toward the door.

George looked at MacIntosh, but the mob leader did nothing to stop the crowd. George stepped quickly back into the house, slammed the door shut, and threw the bolt across it.

The window in the parlor gave way, shattering broken glass on the hardwood floor. Someone began to break away the jagged edges of the glass with a club. Soon they would begin to enter through it.

George realized he could do nothing but follow Asa. He moved down the corridor toward the kitchen. The back door of the house was wide open. George stepped through it, right into the arms of a burly giant of a man. Off to his left he caught sight of Asa Wallace, bound hand and foot and thrown like a sack of horse feed into the alley.

"You didn't think we was so dumb that we wouldn't cover the back way, did you?" laughed the giant.

George struggled in the man's grasp but it was no use. He was held firmly. A few moments later MacIntosh appeared in the doorway.

"Good," he said. "The old one was telling the truth, though. There is no one in the house as far as we can tell. I guess we'll just have to give our little warning to the governor's things and servants since he is not here."

George's eyes widened with astonishment as he witnessed what happened next. Every window in the house was broken. Room by room, furniture was tossed out the windows and picked up by members of the street mob. Each piece was smashed against the side of the house. Dresser drawers were emptied out the upstairs window, and clothing was strewn about the yard. MacIntosh came running out of Hutchinson's study with an armload of papers—the precious documents for Hutchinson's history of the province. He ran toward the carriage house and tossed them into a small heap of horse manure. Then he went back into the house. Soon hundreds of books were being hurled into the street from out of the broken study window.

The gutting of the Hutchinson house continued for an hour until almost nothing inside remained untouched. Jugs of rum were passed around to lighten the workload of the looters. There were several who were already drunk, and they soon were joined by a majority of the mob.

When the house had been cleared of the lieutenant governor's belongings, the men began to push against the interior walls, forcing them, by the sheer mass of pressure on them, to part from the ceilings and to collapse. The floors of the second storey began to sag as structural walls were cut away with axes. The second floor finally collapsed onto the crowded rooms below. Several of the looters were knocked unconscious and others were cut and bleeding, but their pain was numbed by the rum they had consumed.

The bloodied and plaster-covered mob fell out of the devastated mansion onto the street, laughing and exhausted.

Asa and George, with their hands bound behind them, were hustled onto a horse cart and driven back toward the King Street bonfire like trophies of war.

They reached King Street with little difficulty. Most of the residents of the South End had locked their houses and doused their lights as they always did when MacIntosh's mob was loose at night. The streets were practically empty. And no one offered to interfere with the agents of the "Sons of Liberty."

When they arrived at the bonfire site, off Boston Common, Asa began to moan. There was a large pot of simmering pitch. The acrid smell identified it immediately. The two men were hauled off the cart, and their clothes were ripped from their bodies.

Asa began to scream for pity. "I'm just a working man like you. Have pity! Don't tar me! I was in the house taking an inventory. I have nothing to do with Hutchinson; I am one of you. Fuck the stamps. Fuck the Parliament."

Someone grabbed him and was about to stuff a cloth in his mouth to shut him up, when MacIntosh shouted, "We'll spare you only if you're willing to help us with your friend here."

George looked at Asa and knew what his answer would be. George did not see what happened to Asa next, however. Rather, he felt rough hands grab his own naked body and drag him toward the foul-smelling tar. The giant who had first captured him approached him carrying a large, coarse-haired brush dripping hot tar. George clenched his teeth as he felt the biting sting on his chest and his legs. From the rear someone else began to paint his back and buttocks. He turned in agony and saw that it was Asa. The searing pain brought tears to his eyes. Then he felt his body lifted high into the air.

A cheer went up from the crowd of men and someone shouted, "He's turned into a darky. The Governor only employs white folk. He has no slaves. We better turn him back to white or he'll be in the poorhouse and a burden on the taxpayers. Next thing you'll know Parliament will want a stamp tax to support darky servants."

The men holding George's arms began to run. The crowd cheered as he felt himself hurled through the air. He landed in a pile of softness. Suddenly he couldn't breathe. He was drowning in a sea of chicken feathers, which clung to him, glued to his body by the still-wet tar.

There were feathers everywhere, in his nose and his mouth. He struggled to stand, but his knees buckled beneath him. He fell on his face. A hand clutched his hair and began to pull him from the pile.

MacIntosh stood in front of him. He broke into a guffaw at the absurd, feather-covered creature in front of him.

"This one," shouted the leader, pointing at George, "said His Excellency was in Charlestown. I suggest we give him a little ride through Boston and place him on the ferry to get word to his boss about the accident that has taken place at Garden Court Street."

Again the crowd cheered.

A great log, originally intended for the bonfire, was lifted atop the shoulders of twenty men, ten on each end. George was hoisted up and was forced to straddle the log. He cried out in pain as his genitals were crushed by the weight of his own body. But no one could hear his complaint over the noise of the crowd. His legs were tied together beneath him to keep him from falling. He was in agony as the procession through Boston's darkened streets began. Some windows were thrown open and furious residents looked outside to discover the cause of the raucousness, but most immediately closed their windows and shutters when they saw what was afoot. As the crowd passed a tavern, revelers brought fresh drinks for the marchers and some even joined the procession, while others proposed toasts to MacIntosh and his men.

As they crossed into the North End, the march became more subdued. This was not MacIntosh's territory. Here he would not be toasted, only feared. Last November his South End bullies had routed the North Enders' own gang of artisans, apprentices and tavern folk in street fighting. Now he used his power for more than just winning fights. He and his boys were the enforcement arm of the radical political groupings in Massachusetts. The street fighter MacIntosh was now the strong right arm of James Otis and Samuel Adams.

The run down Copp's Hill to the ferry slip left George unconscious. When they arrived at the bottom, his legs were untied and he was unceremoniously dumped on the ground. The crowd of men jeered and then made their way toward the Cromwell's Head for one more celebration.

Josiah had built himself a small cottage next to the ferry slip when Stephen Nowell awarded him the ferry franchise. He had been asleep when the crowd first came charging down the hill. He had awakened instantly, but the sound instincts of a black man in a white man's world kept him from coming outside until the crowd had departed.

At first he did not recognize the pitiful feather-covered creature dumped beside the roadway. He picked up the frail body in his huge arms and carried him toward the house. George mumbled through his fevered lips. Josiah lowered his head and caught the name Nowell. He looked more carefully into George's face and recognized him.

Josiah immediately changed directions and went instead toward the ferryboat tied at the slip. There was a breeze, and he could make it to Charlestown quickly. Normally he did not operate the ferry after dark, but this old, feeble man had been terribly abused. He would need the kind of care that Mr. Nowell and Mr. Vaughan would know about, and they were in Charlestown.

Stephen and Abby had danced most of the evening. Stephen was beginning to feel the strain of it. The calves of his legs were aching. The girl was slight and frail, and he doubted she had ever done anything more strenuous than making tea, but the dancing seemed to invigorate rather than tire her. The orchestra took up the beat of another country jig. Stephen, the sweat beginning to soak through his jacket, turned to Abby and begged off.

"No more, girl; I've had enough."

She laughed at him. "Mr. Nowell, if you would marry a girl, you have to behave more like a boy."

"That, miss, is a prescription for widowhood." He took her hand and led her into the dining room. There they found William Vaughan and Thomas Hutchinson holding sway. Vaughan was more flamboyantly dressed than the lieutenant governor, and he was by far the more flamboyant personality. But Vaughan was no match for Hutchinson's quiet but penetrating mind.

"Ah, Stephen," yelled Vaughan, his face flushed. "Come over here and try to convince this doubting Thomas of a lieutenant governor that the stamps will never be used in Boston."

Stephen thought at first that Vaughan had been drinking again, but then he realized that it was anger and frustration that had colored his face. He had crossed wits with a master and he was losing.

Hutchinson, for his part, looked calm as ever. When he saw Stephen and Abby, he bowed graciously.

"Abigail," he said, "I haven't had the opportunity to offer my congratulations on your coming marriage."

Abby smiled and curtsied back. "Thank you, sir."

"I'm sure the young lady does not wish to be bored by any further debate, Vaughan. I suggest we discuss less tiresome matters."

"Tiresome!" thundered Vaughan. "The matter involved is hardly tiresome. Don't treat the girl as if she were witless. It involves her too. If she becomes a mother it will involve her children and her grandchildren."

"Really, Vaughan, you go too far," said Hutchinson, clearly offended.

"Not far enough. No one has. The matter is one of freedom or slavery. We're Englishmen, even those of us who call ourselves Americans. Englishmen pay taxes; they don't pay royal levies. A tax is a free grant of the Commons to the Crown. Only the Commons can vote it. The Commons represents the people. They elect the members."

"The Commons of England, sir," responded Hutchinson wearily, "has voted a tax, a stamp tax on its colonies, the revenues of which are to help retire the national debt incurred in the late war—a war, sir, I am sure you remember, that was fought vigorously here in America for the benefit of Americans. I see no damage to freedom in paying such a tax."

"Well, I do, and you don't have to remind me and Nowell here about the war fought in America. I was at Lake George, at Louisbourg, and at Quebec, and I have a few scars to prove it. One has merely to look at Stephen's empty sleeve to see the price he paid for the crown. But I don't remember voting for the members of the Commons that voted that tax you mentioned, sir."

"Vaughan, I get a feeling of déjà vu whenever I argue with you. I think we have been over all of this before. Every Englishman is represented by every member of Parliament."

"As a lady I once knew was wont to say, donkey dust, sir, donkey dust."

Stephen smiled. He knew that Vaughan referred to Margaret Schuyler Kip, his former wife's aunt, now the wife of his old friend Israel Kip.

"The general courts, sir," Vaughan went on, "which meets across the straits in Boston, your general courts, sir, are the Commons of Massachusetts. Unless it taxes us, which I think is highly unlikely, no good patriot is going to pay."

"Vaughan," said Hutchinson in exasperation, "you know we disagree on the rights of Parliament, but you also know that I don't believe the tax should have been voted by Parliament. It was bad politics to antagonize the taxpayers so. I have urged the governor to keep the stamps in the castle. The mob violence of these past days, and the silent approbation of the most law-abiding, have convinced me that the stamps will lead to civil disobedience. And *that* will lead to regular troops and possibly martial law in Boston. Surely none of us would want that for our town and our beloved colony of Massachusetts."

"Bring in troops, and the militia will fight them," yelled Vaughan.

Hutchinson threw up his hands in disgust. "The man merely emotes. He doesn't listen. I think his brain has gone soft with rum."

An angry red flush crossed Vaughan's face. Stephen moved toward his friend to prevent him from doing anything foolish, but he had moved only two steps when there was a woman's scream from the parlor.

Stephen turned and rushed across the hallway to the other room. He saw the large lady whom Hibbins had been talking to earlier in the evening crumpled on the floor. Her husband was attempting to fan her back to consciousness. But even more startling, he saw the large black figure of Josiah filling the front doorway, carrying a grotesque figure of a naked man covered in white feathers. Stephen recognized George instantly.

"I tried comin' in the kitchen way, Mr. Nowell, but it was locked and there was so much noise that no one could hear me."

Stephen turned to Abby. "Get Hannah. If she isn't in the kitchen, she is probably upstairs in her room."

Abby climbed the stairway two steps at a time. Stephen bent down and put his ear to George's naked chest. His heartbeat was faint. George started to mumble, and Stephen raised his ear to George's mouth.

"Mr. Stephen," he whispered, "it was the Sons of Liberty. They destroyed Mr. Hutchinson's house. I didn't know what to do."

"Don't worry about it. Thomas!" Stephen called to the lieutenant governor. "They've been at your place. I think we will end this party. I'll arrange for you to get back immediately." Then he turned to Vaughan. "Is this what the freedom-loving citizens of this colony mean when they call for us to resist tyranny? Well, if abusing old men is the alternative to tyranny, I'll take the abuse of paying the few pence on a newspaper to help pay for a war that *did* rid this continent of the French tyranny. So help me God, my friend, your Sons of Liberty are pigs."

George died the next morning. The doctor explained that his heart, which was weak to begin with, hadn't been able to stand the shock of the tarring and feathering. He slipped away in peace, with Hannah holding his hand. She wept bitterly at first and Abby held her. The girl seemed lost in the massive bosom of the woman.

Stephen Nowell and Abigail Hibbins were married before the Justice of the Peace about two weeks after George's death. Stephen would have preferred the Anglican church, as would the bride's father, since it was the family church. But the Church of England vicar frowned upon Stephen's divorce and would not grant a church wedding. Abby complained to Stephen and scolded him for having been married before, but by the time of the ceremony the bride had resigned herself to having a magistrate marry them in her own home. Since her father was a member of the ancient and honorable artillery company of Boston, founded over a hundred years before, her wedding reception was held in the upstairs meeting house of Fanueil Hall.

The company ship, the *Sarah*, bound for New York, was forced to wait well past the ideal tide because her passengers were late. Normally, Captain Maynard would have sailed without them, but not this time. The passengers were the owner and his new bride. When they finally came aboard, fresh from their reception, they made no apologies whatsoever for their lateness. Maynard had been forced to give up his cabin to them, and there wasn't even a thank-you for that. As soon as they were below and their trunks were stowed away, he gave the mate orders to set off and catch whatever was left of the tide. The only bright side of the situation was that Maynard doubted if he would see anything more of the newlyweds until they reached Sandy Hook in New Jersey.

Stephen lay in the captain's bed. He was sure that the child beside him was asleep. He could only think of her in those terms. He had not touched her, and he was sure that she was deeply disappointed. She had expected him to make love to her, although he knew that she had not the slightest idea of what it was all about. But she had known it was supposed to be done—especially on this night. He had intended to, but when the moment came, he shied away. He had long since gotten over his embarrassment about the stump of his left arm. It wasn't that that kept him from making love to his new wife; it was his thoughts about others who had left him, including Katherine, his first wife. Their marriage had also been plagued from the beginning by the memory of another, his first love—the Mohawk woman Molly Brant, the mother of his son. Yet she had left him and devoted her life to Sir William Johnson. The last he had heard, they were still together in Central New York. Aaron, his son, was surely by now a Mohawk warrior under the tutelage of Molly's brother Joseph. Even after all of these years, he still felt the pain of that separation. The boy had been stolen from him by his mother. She was as determined that he would be a Mohawk as Stephen had been that he would be white. Molly had won.

Katherine had given birth to his daughter Amy. But while he had been away, Karl, his friend and his blood brother, had taken his place when his wife had needed help. It was no wonder she had turned finally to Karl after he had saved her and Amy at Fort William Henry. She had gone to Canada with him, had had his child. All the while Stephen had been off in London with Manya.

He smiled when he thought of Manya, the Princess Wroblevska, the master French spy. He wondered where she was now. He owed her. It had been she who had convinced him that he could still be a man with one arm. He remembered their lovemaking, their fights, their making up. Katherine had never known about Manya. If she had, would she have been as harsh with him as he had been with her about Karl? He knew she would not have been.

But now there was this new wife. This Abby. She stirred at his side and turned to face him, looking directly into his eyes.

"Mr. Nowell," she said, "why are you still awake?"

Stephen smiled at her and tried to avoid answering the question. "I guess it's still not time for you to call me Stephen."

"No, it's not," she responded.

"What must I do?"

"You'll know when the moment comes. Now, answer my question."

"Abby, I'm a man of business. I frequently think of business concerns at night. You'll just have to get used to it."

"Will I have to get used to no intimacy also?"

Stephen looked down at her. He was surprised by her directness. "I'm sorry," he lied. "I thought you might be tired. Sometimes it is best to wait."

"Did you wait on your wedding night with Katherine?"

Stephen swung his feet over the edge of the bunk and sat up, his back turned to her. "I don't wish to discuss her with you."

"How about the Indian woman?"

Stephen turned to her in amazement. "Where did you hear of her?"

"Really, all of Boston knew about you and Sir William's . . . whatever. Did you really think the old gossips of the town wouldn't come rushing to me or my maids with their stories? I asked Hannah about it and she even told me about some mysterious woman in Europe."

"That old witch. I'll fire her."

"No, you'll not. She's taken me under her wing. After George died, she needed someone to care for and she decided it would be me. She's determined to make this marriage work for your good as well. She's tired of seeing you moping around. She told me everything so that I might win your soul. No one else has ever done that, Mr. Nowell."

"Not since God did it," he replied softly.

30

"And I know all about that, too. You were raised by Jesuits. You became one and you took special vows."

"And I broke them all," he said grimly.

"Just as well for me," she smiled, "but then again I'm not so sure." She placed her hand against his back.

He turned to look at her. She looked so very young and so very small, propped against the giant pillows of the captain's bunk. He leaned against the pillows and kissed her forehead. She placed her arm about his neck and pulled him toward her. She kissed him warmly on the lips. He opened his mouth and she responded to him.

He touched her small breasts and felt her arch her back and bring her body closer to him. He slipped back under the covers. His nightshirt was already above his waist. He stroked her body. He could feel it tremble. He saw fear in her eyes, and he knew that her turmoil was not from anticipated passion. He would go slowly with her and be gentle. She was so very fragile and so very young.

Afterwards, Stephen rose from the bed and fetched some clean linen for Abby to help her to stop the bleeding. It had frightened her, and he knew she had not enjoyed the actual lovemaking. That would come in time. Some moments later she really was asleep, and he lay awake. But the lovemaking had changed things. He could not think of her as a child. She was his wife and maybe the mother of his children. Children could replace the haunting faces of his dreams, of Aaron and of Amy.

II

1765

Amy Nowell corraled her half-brother Louis Joseph and
headed him in the direction of their farmhouse. When she
got close enough, she grabbed his ear. He screamed great
seven-year-old oaths. He was as wild as his father and
looked so much like Karl, the Swiss soldier, that Katherine
frequently thought that he was the real source of the vivid
memories that she had of his father.

Amy, at fifteen, was a proper combination of her parents. She had Katherine's brown and gold hair, high
cheekbones and pointy chin, but she looked like Stephen
Nowell about the eyes, even if hers were brown and his
were decidedly blue. She was already a beauty and was
deeply in love with the boy she had known most of her
life—Antoine Gingras.

Amy shoved the howling Louis through the doorway.

"He was heading toward Antoine's house when I caught
him," she said.

"Louis, you age me with your behavior," sighed Katherine.
"You heard me call. Why didn't you head home?"

The boy merely shrugged his shoulders. Katherine grew
angry and slapped his face. His face contorted and great
tears began to flow down his cheeks. Katherine regretted
her action instantly and ran to hug the boy and smothered
his face in kisses.

Amy looked on in disgust. She disapproved of both of
them. Katherine had struck the boy for very little cause,
and then she spoiled him at the first sign of any discomfort. Amy's mother had little control over her half-brother.

She walked to the table and picked up the ladle and began to distribute the stew onto the pewter plates.

"Mother," she said quizzically. "Are you expecting company? You set four places."

Katherine backed away from the sobbing boy. A strange, glazed look came to her eyes.

Amy stared at her for some moments, waiting for an answer. "Mother?" she said finally.

Katherine still seemed distant. "I don't know which one will be coming," she said finally. Then she shook herself. She walked over to the table and picked up the fourth plate. "I don't know what I could have been thinking of," she said gruffly. "I've gotten so absentminded."

It was still early when they finished eating. On these northern summer nights it sometimes did not get totally dark until almost ten. Both children rose from the table and left the house after clearing their places and rinsing their dishes in a tub of soapy water that Katherine kept in her kitchen lean-to. Katherine walked to her covered verandah to her favorite rocking chair. She hated it when Amy went off. She knew Amy was meeting Antoine. But Amy and Louis were her only ties with the past. Aunt Margaret had written, but after Stephen had divorced her Katherine had never written back. She could face none of her Schuyler relatives. They had always hated her, the bastard. Aunt Margaret hadn't, but her aunt had always warned her never to marry, never to place herself, her body, at the mercy of a man. Margaret was wrong, of course. It depended on the man. With Karl she had known such joy. He had worshipped her.

She sat on her chair on the verandah of the old house, looking at the river and the falls. The day had been hot, but she had not entered the coolness of the stone house. Instead she used a fan and stayed out in the heat. She loved to watch the river. Sometimes she expected to see Karl come up from the landing beach, his white uniform clinging to the great muscles of his handsome body. She had even dreamed it. He would come toward her, smiling.

33

But as he came closer and closer his features changed, his hair darkened until it was black, his body became slim, and there he stood before her—her husband, whom she had loved. In the dream she turned from him and ran into the house.

But he would not be coming up from the beach. No one would. This evening she had prepared a place for him, but he had not come. Why had Stephen divorced her? Why did Karl die? She never would have come with Karl if Stephen had not deserted her. She knew the strange glances that Amy had given her. Amy didn't believe that Stephen was coming. But he was. She would prepare a place for him again. She didn't care what her daughter thought.

Amy sat gazing across the river at the falls of Montmorency. She absentmindedly twisted the gold locket that she wore around her neck. It had belonged to her grandmother. The spray of water hitting rock seemed not to rise as high as usual. There seemed less of it in summer. In the river, a great English warship, its white ensign drooping and its sails lying flat against the masts, struggled to make headway against the slow current of the St. Lawrence. The harbor of Quebec was in view, but at its current rate, it would take the vessel hours to arrive. The river seemed barely to move in the heat of the summer day, and seagulls that had followed the sailing ship up the river were flocking along the shore, squawking against any intrusion into their domain. The trees were showing some red in their leaves. The last days of August were at hand. Even now the nights grew as chilly as the days were warm.

Amy stood up and walked the path along the river from her mother's farm toward the Gingras' pasture. Henri Gingras, Antoine's father, had died last fall. His other sons had fallen at the Plains of Abraham with Karl. Antoine had been just a boy then. But now he was a man, the only man in the Gingras household, with a mother and sisters to care for. Amy saw him coming toward her along the path. He waved and she waved back to him. She broke into a run and he stood in his tracks to await her. She leapt at him, laughing, as he caught her in his strong arms and swung her around with joy.

At twenty-four, Antoine was tall and strong. His hair was jet black, and he had large brown eyes and the sharp features of the French Canadians. He was handsome. Amy had always thought so, even when they had been children together. She had always intended to marry him, but she couldn't leave her mother and brother, and he had to provide for his family. They had wanted to make love but did not dare, although a few times they had come close to losing control. They were betrothed, and many a girl became pregnant before the wedding day. Many thought if you were to marry anyway it made little sense to wait, especially when your body ached for the body of the other. But neither Antoine nor Amy knew when they might marry, and she had remembered the words whispered about her mother and her brother. She would never forget the day when the curé had shouted "fornicator and bastard" from the pulpit.

Antoine held her in his arms and kissed her lips and then her eyes. He swept her off her feet again and hurried her into the underbrush down the path to the riverfront, where they would be out of the view of all passersby. He went to the river's edge and pulled out two sealed jugs that he had cooled in the river water.

"I've some fresh milk for you and some fresh beer for me," he said to her in his Quebec-accented French.

"And I have some fresh bread and fresh butter and fresh woman for you," she responded in an accent identical to his.

"The curé would not approve," he said jokingly.

"Since when did you listen to the curé? You certainly don't listen when he says we must stop dreaming of a return to French rule and must make our peace with the English. Or when he says that the English have given us our freedom and we should be grateful."

"What he meant was that the English plan to give the Catholic church its freedom here in Quebec. I'm not sure what that means for you and me. I think the Americans have the answer—rebel against English rule."

"The Americans are rebelling? How do you know?" she asked.

"Letters and information get passed on. Especially to some of the Americans in the city of Montreal who came after the Conquest. Canada must be ready to throw off the English yoke. The Americans will do it, and we must join them."

"Who says the Americans will not then conquer us and treat us worse than the English do? They are very intolerant people. They hate Catholics. My mother was an American. She tells me that she was raised to hate the French of Canada, to hate the Pope and all his followers."

"Your mother also believes you should not marry me. So that shows how much she knows."

"Oh, Antoine, don't judge her harshly. She has lost everything. She has only me and my brother. She's afraid of losing us, too, and being entirely alone. She never said a word, but when my father's letter arrived announcing his divorce plans, I know she was devastated. She really did love him. I think she still does."

"And she loved Lieutenant Stiegler too?"

"Yes, she did," said Amy. "And I'm frightened for her. I can't even bring myself to think of it. But something is happening to her. Tonight she set four places at the table. I asked her who our guest would be. She wouldn't answer me. But all through the meal she looked out the door as if she expected company at any moment."

"What are you getting at?"

"Antoine, I think she expected my father, or even worse, Uncle Karl, to come walking through the door to join us."

"It is all too much for me," said Antoine. "Your mother was my father's friend. My father told me that Karl Stiegler asked him, on the day Stiegler lay dying, to protect her and you and Louis. He did as he was asked and he passed that responsibility on to me. And I'm happy to continue that responsibility—especially when it comes to you. But I don't know what I can do to help your mother."

"Neither do I." She shuddered and started to cry.

36

He reached over and kissed her on the lips. She responded at first and then pushed him away. "I'm not even sure it is safe to leave her alone."

"Your brother is with her."

"He's only a boy, Antoine."

"You know there is really only one answer for us," he said. "You and I must marry. Then Louis Joseph and your mother could come to live at my farm. It's more than big enough. Your mother and mine are friends. It would be good for them both."

Amy looked at him longingly. But she shook her head. "It won't do," she said. "My mother would never leave her house, and I'm not sure that she should. I have no idea how it might affect her. She is on the line, Antoine, I know it. Anything could push her over. I'd never forgive myself if it were my desires that were the cause of her illness."

"But what about my desires?" Antoine demanded. His voice was hoarse, and he was struggling to control his emotions. "I'm a man. I have desires."

"You think I don't?" she responded heatedly. "But I've got to keep them in check—for my mother's sake."

Antoine reached over and grabbed her shoulders, drawing her to him. She struggled against him, but he was too strong for her. Besides, she was not sure she wanted to resist. His hand, calloused from the work of the farm, reached for her breast. Yet he stroked her gently. She knew she should be resisting him more. His hand moved down her body, from her breast to her abdomen and lower. If she did not stop him now, it would be too late. She had to stop him. The motion of his hand was weaving a spell on her and her will to resist was dissolving.

Louis Joseph regarded himself as very important. Amy might be older and she might think herself more important, but he was going to grow to be a man, and everyone knew that men were more important than girls. He was going to be a soldier as his father had been. He wished his father were still alive. But he had been a hero of Canada and had died with Montcalm. His name, Karl Stiegler, was honored all over the island of Orleans, and Louis Joseph was proud to be his son. His own name was that of his godfather, the great Marquis de Montcalm.

He stopped at the parish churchyard every Sunday after mass, and he and his mother and his sister placed flowers on his father's grave. The people of the parish would pass on their wagons, returning to their farms, and the men would tip their hats in respect to his mother. Last month he had heard some women comment on how much he resembled his father, the blond Swiss. He had stuck out his chest in pride. His hair was fair, and he was big for his age, very big. None of the other boys dared to pick on him. Last year one boy had made some remarks about him and his parents. He didn't understand what the boy had meant, but he didn't wait to find out. The boy paid dearly for his remark.

He played this evening by the river's edge, finding stones worn flat by the motion of the river. He would skip them along the surface, counting the times they bounced.

At first his mother had been in view, sitting on the verandah, but as the evening progressed he had moved farther and farther west along the riverbank. He chased some frogs along the river's edge. He caught two but freed one, since he had no bucket with him and had to hold them in his hands. And he could hold no more than one at a time. If Antoine were with him or they had been fishing, the frogs would have been used as bait. But Antoine was always with Amy these days. He had little time for the boy. Louis liked being with Antoine. He understood about "men things."

When they went fishing in Antoine's boat, he didn't have to wash up, and he could go swimming naked off the shore. This last was something he was still working on. He was afraid of the water. Antoine was teaching him to swim, holding him about the belly and shouting at him to kick and to paddle. He would get the hang of the thing eventually, but now each time Antoine let go, Louis Joseph would sink like a bucket of sand. Then the man would grab him by his flaxen head and pull him up from the river bottom and begin all over.

He was far to the west of the house now. He stopped to listen. He could hear voices and noises coming from the beach upriver. He imagined it was in the days of the Iroquois raids. St. Pierre was in his hands. He could creep up on the enemy and warn the villge. Then he would be a hero like his father.

The bushes came right down to the river's edge, but then a small ridge of rocks extended out into the deeper water. He had traversed this spot many times, but never before under the requirements of a spy. He climbed on his belly on top of the first rock and pushed aside the bushes.

It was not Indians. It was Antoine and Amy. They were embracing. Antoine was kissing his sister and she was kissing him back.

Louis Joseph knew he was watching something that should not be seen, but he could not pull his eyes away. He had heard older boys talk of this, especially behind the schoolhouse when they showed themselves off and got hard. He couldn't help himself. He had to get closer to see. But then the frog in his hands made one more effort to get free. It slipped out of Louis Joseph's hand. Louis grabbed for him, missed, slipped on the edge of the rock, and plunged head first into the St. Lawrence. He screamed as he fell into the water and then sank.

Amy froze when she heard her brother's scream. All the passion in her disappeared. Antoine rose from her side instantly, and despite the awkwardness of his condition, he splashed quickly into the river toward the spot where Louis Joseph's hands were thrashing above the surface. When he got to the spot, he reached down and grabbed the blond head, as he had so often done, pulling Louis to the surface.

"You little shit," he yelled into the sputtering face of the boy. "You despicable little shit. You were spying on us."

Amy called to them from the beach. Antoine started to haul Louis Joseph back to his sister. The boy was coughing from all the water he had swallowed, and he was badly frightened. Antoine was still tempted to turn him over his knee and beat his bottom, but the look of terror in the

39

boy's eyes showed him that he should do nothing further to frighten him.

But Amy, her dress hastily rearranged, was not inclined to be merciful. As soon as the boy was in range she yelled at him, "You brat! How dare you spy on us!"

"I didn't," the boy cried.

"Enough, Amy," said Antoine. "Louis Joseph meant no harm."

Amy was still angry but she was also frightened. She had done nothing wrong, but once again she had been close to doing something wrong. Louis Joseph might run to her mother and tell her what he had seen.

"Send him home. He'll need to get dry clothes," said Antoine.

"I'll take him," said Amy reluctantly. "We can all go home together."

"No, I can't, Amy. I've a meeting in the village."

"Those men from the city, the Americans. Why do you insist on listening to them?"

Antoine shrugged his shoulders. "I've nothing to lose by listening to them."

"Yes, you do. They preach rebellion. You could lose everything."

"All *canadiens* lost everything when the English conquered us. We must throw them out."

"By inviting the *Bastonnais* in?"

He kissed her on the nose. "I'm going anyway. I'll stop by your farmhouse this evening. Louis Joseph, take care of your sister. And, by God, keep your mouth shut or I'll kick your butt."

The boy smiled at Antoine. If Antoine told him to be quiet, he would be quiet. He would do anything for Antoine.

Antoine Gingras thought it strange that Mario Albert's bakery should be darkened in the early evening. It was true that the baker went to sleep early, but not this early. His instructions had been to knock twice on the back door of the shop. He stopped in the alley between Albert's house and the priest's yard. The pungent aroma of skunk

40

filled the night air. Someone had been here earlier and frightened one of the striped night creatures.

Antoine knocked twice and waited. There was no response. He knocked once more. Again there was no response. Antoine looked up at the darkened sky. The stars were beginning to sparkle faintly.

Antoine grew fidgety. He had wasted his time coming here. No one was home. Suddenly the hinges on the door began to creak and the door swung slowly open. Antoine started to step forward to walk through, when the barrel of a dueling pistol was placed against the back of his head. Someone had come up behind him.

Antoine gave a start and began to turn. A voice, a soft but strong voice, instructed him to look straight ahead. When he did, he saw a redheaded man with freckles, a barrel chest, and a great pot belly, all placed on legs that seemed hardly capable of supporting the ponderous girth above.

"Looking for someone, sonny?" said the giant in English.

Antoine did not understand. "I was told to come to Mario Albert's," he responded in French.

"You ain't Albert. He's already here. Who the hell are you? You screwed up the signal. How do I know you're one of the invited guests?"

Just then, Albert, wearing his baker's apron, came into the room. "McCord, this is Antoine Gingras. He is a leader of the men on this island."

"Why the hell didn't he say so?"

"He doesn't speak English. I'll have to translate for him. Let's go get Walker."

McCord turned his back on Antoine and began to guffaw. "You can't miss Walker. Just follow your nose. He's been skunked. Smells worse than anything I can remember since the days back in New London when I was a kid and the whole town had beans on a Saturday night and came to church on a hot August Sunday morning."

They entered the back of the shop where the brick ovens were located. Antoine was nearly overwhelmed by the musk odor in the room. It came from a small, thin

41

man with black hair and black eyes and a razor-sharp face, who sat on the other side of the room.

"Hope you don't mind if I stay over here. I've had an accident. My name's Walker. Thomas Walker. Me and McCord invited you two fellows from the village because we heard you don't like the British. We was hoping that we could enlist you in our cause."

"Which cause is that?" asked Albert.

"The cause of freedom," laughed McCord. "We want you to help us plan for a free Quebec. Just like our friends to the south are calling for free Massachusetts and free Connecticut."

Albert translated the answers for Gingras.

"Freedom—what does that mean to you?" asked Antoine cautiously.

"Why, it means freedom to move across the mountains to new and fertile lands on the other side without no army saying we can't. It means not having to pay no taxes that your own assembly ain't voted."

Again Antoine waited for the words to be translated.

"As you know, monsieur, Canada has no assembly."

"That's one of the things that's got to change. The governor has been making laws without the consent of the free Englishmen living here."

"What about the free Frenchmen?" asked Antoine.

"That will come later," said McCord. "Once you French learn something about English law and once you learn our language, then you, too, will be ready to sit in and vote for a legislature."

"In the meantime?"

"Why, you raise the troops and get ready for the time when it comes."

Antoine waited for Albert to finish translating the last word and then he turned to leave the room.

"Where the hell is he going?" asked Walker.

Antoine turned around to face the two Americans. "After all these years in the countryside, I should have recognized a skunk when I smelled one. You, gentlemen, are hypocrites. You must think we Canadiens are stupid. You *Bastonnais* are as bad as the priests always claimed you were. You wish to use us French to fight your war and to put you in control of Canada in place of the English. Someday we French will regain our homeland. And if I have to fight alongside Americans to drive the English out, I will. But I don't intend to beat my brains out getting rid of the British master to replace him with an American one. We will have a free society here, Mr. McCord and Mr. Walker, and it will be *canadien*, not Yankee."

Antoine turned and started to leave. Another man, one he hadn't met, blocked his path. The man had a pistol tucked into his belt, and Antoine realized that this must be the man who had come up behind him. As soon as he began to speak Antoine realized that he was right. There was an almost velvety quality to his deep baritone voice and he spoke French.

"Please don't judge our cause by the efforts of these gentlemen, Monsieur Gingras. My name is Ethan Morin. I'd like the opportunity to discuss our proposal at greater length."

Antoine stood still. The man before him was about his age—in his mid-twenties. His face was thin and long. His forehead was very high, but he allowed his muddy blond hair to fall over it into his eyes. He was taller than Antoine.

"Why should I listen to you any more than to them?"

"Because they are greedy, self-interested merchants, living here in Canada. They plan to control the place after the English are chased out and to use the French to do a good deal of the hauling and hewing."

Antoine looked the newcomer over carefully. He seemed to exude confidence. "You're *Bastonnais*. How do you come to speak French?"

"My first name is biblical, but my last name is Morin—French Huguenot. My grandfather came from la Rochelle via England and South Carolina."

"Protestant?" asked Antoine in surprise. The only Protestants he had met were the few Americans he had encountered since the Conquest. But never had he encountered a French Protestant.

"Please don't hold it against me. If *le Vert Gallant* had

been a better one or had he loved Paris less, perhaps you too would be one of us."

Antoine did not know what the southerner with the strange, soft voice was talking about, but he had heard Walker and McCord, and he did not like what he had understood from them. "Why are you in Canada, monsieur?" asked Antoine.

"To arrange your liberation," said Morin softly.

"Will the Americans come to the aid of the French Canadians? My girl's family comes from Boston and New York. She tells me her mother was raised to hate us, to mock the Pope. Catholics cannot hold public office in the English colonies and they are persecuted."

"At least there are public offices to be held to the south. That's more than I can say for here in Quebec. Everything she said about us is true. But we are your only hope. You'll never be strong enough to drive out the English by yourselves."

"Maybe France will reconquer us."

"I wouldn't rely on it. A war with France now would drive the Americans right back into the arms of the British army and navy—especially if France should attempt to regain Canada. It would delay the inevitable American independence and leave you no better off than you were before. But you and I have a chance to liberate Canada."

"I know why I should be involved. But what's in it for you?"

Morin smiled. "I was wondering when you would get around to asking that question. I work for a group of men in Massachusetts who are convinced that our colonies will win freedom and who want to insure that Canada is a part of our new confederation. Our new land will be just as threatened by a British Canada as the British colonies were threatened by a French Canada until the last war. It is for our own security that we try to talk you into joining our fight. We must both be free—together."

"Your kind of freedom—not Walker's or McCord's?"

"My kind."

"Then I'm with you," said Antoine, holding out his hand.

Morin took it in his grasp.

They walked together out of the bakery and into the street.

"I have to meet my girl," said Antoine. "Come with me; I'd like you to meet her and help me talk some sense into her."

They walked through the streets of the village and out onto the pasture road.

"We must form our own organization," said the American. "Some men will be needed to spread the word of what happens in Virginia or in Boston, and some will be needed to become the nucleus of a Sons of Liberty organization. Nothing right now. I realize you don't have the clergy with you, and without them you won't have the people. But a few loyal souls that we can call on when the time comes—that's all we need."

They said very little more to each other as they walked down the rutted, dark road. They passed the Gingras farm and continued on until they came to the top of the knoll that looked down on the Stiegler place.

There was a light still burning in the living room of the house. Antoine broke into a trot on the way down and called Amy's name. Ethan followed him at a slower pace. Antoine called out again, but it was Katherine, sitting in the darkness on the verandah, who responded.

"Antoine, hush. Louis Joseph has fallen off to sleep. That is no small event in itself. I don't need someone waking him up—especially you. If he knew you were here, nothing, absolutely nothing, would keep him under the blankets."

"Madame Katherine," Antoine acknowledged. "I want you to meet a new friend of mine, Monsieur Morin. He's from South Carolina."

Morin went to Katherine's chair; he bowed, took her hand and raised it to his lips.

Katherine broke into English immediately. She had so few opportunities to use the language.

"Mister Morin, what brings you to Canada?"

"Business, madame," he said in his slow Southern drawl. "I'm working on a special deal for French Canada."

45

Amy came out of the house. She turned to Morin as Antoine introduced him, and her heart sank. Something about the man seemed dangerous and frightening. She shuddered when she heard his slow speech. He approached to kiss her hand as well, but she backed away.

"You must excuse the girl," said Katherine. "She's only fifteen."

"Amy, this American has come to discuss plans with me," said Antoine.

"Why you?" she asked.

"I'm going from district to district, miss," he said in English, "picking out potential leaders. I've been to Montreal three times already. Now I am at Quebec and Three Rivers."

Amy did not know how he knew to speak to her in English. Perhaps it was because Katherine had spoken to him in his own tongue.

"Monsieur Morin—" began Antoine.

"I'm called Ethan," the American interrupted.

"Ethan is going to help me to organize a committee of safety here on this island."

"Who will you be keeping us safe from?" asked Amy sarcastically.

"From the tyrants who would tax us without representatives and hem us behind the mountains and leave the best lands to the savages," replied Morin.

"I have a half-brother who is one of those savages, Mr. Morin. I'd appreciate it if you spoke of them and him more gently."

Antoine looked at Amy in amazement. He did not understand the English that had passed between them, but by its tone he knew it was hostile. He was bewildered. He turned to Katherine.

"May we use your kitchen for our meeting, Madame Katherine?" he asked. "It will be brief, even if it is the most significant thing to happen on this island since the city fell."

Katherine nodded and received a withering glance from her daughter in return.

Within the week Antoine was committed to even more

46

than the cause of reform. He was a founding member of a small group of French farmers who would await the day of revolt. Even the Americans like Walker and McCord did not realize that Morin and his supporters planned the future independence of America and of Quebec. Antoine had joined in alliance with the Americans, awaiting the day when their numbers would make it possible to throw over the hated British.

In the weeks that followed, Antoine spent less and less time with Amy and more and more time with his confreres, the farmers of the island. One night, when he failed to meet her as he had promised at their spot on the river shore, she went looking for him in the village. She knew his meetings took place in the shop of Albert the baker.

She entered the shop but only Albert's wife, Lise, was present. When she asked for Antoine, Lise merely shrugged her shoulders. No one had told her that the Englishwoman's daughter was to be included in the group.

The door of the shop opened, and Amy was surprised to see Morin enter. She thought he had left. Antoine had not mentioned him since the day they had met in her home.

"Miss Amy," he addressed her in his drawling English, "how good of you to decide to join us."

"I've decided nothing of the kind," she responded sharply. She was surprised when she stuttered over the unfamiliar words. She rarely had the opportunity to speak English except with her mother, and Katherine was growing more and more silent.

She started to pass him on her way out of the front door. But he stayed her with his hand.

"Why are you so hostile?"

Amy merely glared at him. "I resent you, Mr. Morin. Because of you Antoine is spending more time in the village at meetings than at his farm caring for his mother."

Morin smiled. "And more time with me than with you?"

Amy's face flushed with a combination of embarrassment and anger. "My relationship with Antoine is none of your business, sir."

"You're the one making it a contest, little girl. Why?"

Amy hesitated a moment and then the words came pouring out. "Because I hate everything you stand for. Because of men like you who plan battles and wars, my Uncle Karl is dead and my father has one arm and is not with my mother. And speaking of her, she's only thirty-seven, and yet she sits alone every night with her ghosts. I am terrified of you, Mister Morin. You'll rob me of the man I love before I've had a chance to love him."

She felt the panic grow within her—a mortal fear of life without Antoine—and she knew deep in her soul that if she lost Antoine it would be because of the man who stood in front of her. Maybe if she agreed to marry Antoine, she would keep him, but she knew she could never leave her mother.

Antoine entered the shop from the back room of the bakery. He was surprised to see Amy and then he looked chagrined.

"I stood you up," he said softly, smacking his head gently with the palm of his hand. "I'm so sorry, Amy."

"No harm," she said casually. "We can walk home together."

"I wish we could, but Ethan and I have a whole month's work to consolidate tonight. If we succeed, at least on this island we'll be prepared when the time comes."

"This island will become a base to spread our aims throughout Quebec," said Morin.

Amy felt a calm come over her. She knew that if Antoine refused to join her now, he would always leave her when the cause called.

"Antoine, I'm frightened to go home alone. My mother and I need you. Please come."

"But, Amy, this is important. You're behaving like a baby. You're not frightened to walk home alone. You've never been frightened as long as I've known you."

She looked at him, her eyes pleading with him.

Morin intervened. "Talk to her," he said, patting Antoine on the shoulder. "I'll wait for you in back." He left and Lise followed.

Antoine waited for them to leave. "Now what's wrong?" he asked her.

"I don't know. I'm frightened for you, for us. And I'm frightened of that man."

"Ethan? Why?"

"Don't ask. Just take me home."

"I have a meeting."

"Damn your meetings."

"Well, they're a damn sight better than sitting home alone listening to my mother complain about life without my father, or listening to unmarried sisters swoon over this one or that one."

"You don't have to be at home, or for that matter alone. You can be with me."

"No, I can't," said Antoine in exasperation. "When I'm with you, I want you. I'm tired of going home after being with you so sore that I can barely walk. I want to make love to you, Amy; I want to marry you. But you don't want me."

"I do want you. I can't leave my mother."

"You want everything your way, Amy. Only your way."

Amy was silent for some moments. Antoine turned and started to leave. "I have a meeting to go to," he said.

"Why can't we just keep on with the way we have been going?"

"I told you why. It's too damn frustrating."

"Don't do this to me, Antoine. Don't put me under this pressure. We can't get married. We both have too many responsibilities. But I will not sleep with you. I'll not end up like my mother—denounced in the church by the curé. I'll not be your whore."

Antoine stared at her. "As I said earlier, I have a meeting to attend," he said finally.

"Please take me home."

"All right," he said with considerable disgust. "You wait here. Morin and I will push this thing through faster."

Amy stood alone in the shop after he had left. Fifteen minutes passed. Then thirty, and finally forty-five. Amy's shoulders seemed to sag more with each passing minute. Finally, tears pouring down her cheeks, she bolted out of the shop and ran down the road out of the village toward her home.

49

When Stephen and Abby returned from New York, they settled into the old Breed house high on the slope overlooking the village of Charlestown. Every morning Stephen made his pilgrimage to the company offices in the village and across the straits to Boston with Josiah to visit his teeming molasses warehouses, his shipyards and his distilleries.

But the Sunday after their return, Abby convinced him to walk the farm boundaries with her. He wore his woolen coat, but the heat of the day soon forced him to remove it; he threw it over his arm. This in turn made using his walking stick difficult, and he placed it under the stump of his left arm and held on to Abby for support. Together they proceeded along the path, he in his white shirt and knee breeches and Abby in her favorite dress, white with tiny embroidered pink roses.

He led her to the top of the hill. The view of Charlestown below and Boston beyond was spectacular. They could see the ocean and the harbor, Back Bay, the rivers Charles and Mystic. The ocean breezes cooled them. Stephen spread his coat on the ground. They sat down.

"What's the name of the hill behind us?" asked Abby.

"It's called Bunker's Hill," responded Stephen. "Mr. Hutchinson tells me there were Bunkers and Breeds along with Nowells in early Charlestown. I suspect it's named after the first Bunker. No one by that name owns the land any longer."

"It's so cool and beautiful up here, Mr. Nowell. I don't think I want to go back to our home. It is too dark and too hot."

"Shall I build you a castle atop this mountain, my lady fair?" joked Stephen.

"A keep for me and my children," she responded. "A keep that will resist the troops of any evil lords who would appear before them and me. But, alas, my master builder, I have no children to protect."

"That might be a situation I could alter if you would only encourage me."

"You needed no encouragement at sea or in New York."

"Seriously, Abby, I am much older than you. Twenty-one

years older than you, to be exact. If anything should happen to me, you would have to face a major portion of our child's upbringing alone. But what frightens me more is that childbearing might endanger your health. I overheard your Uncle Taylor berating your father for allowing you to marry. He says you are too frail. He's worried about you."

Abby stared beyond him toward the harbor waters and the islands of the harbor. "Mr. Nowell, you and I will have one child at a time. Don't ever treat me as an invalid, and never, ever use my frailty as an excuse to run away from your own feelings."

Stephen turned toward her sharply. "What do you mean by that?"

"Just that you never possess if you don't risk. And you're not a taker of risks and so you are a poor man."

Stephen wanted to jest and recommend that she check the books in the counting house in Charlestown if she thought him poor. But her eyes halted him. He felt very vulnerable. She had seen so deeply into him. How could she, so young, see things in him of which he himself was unaware?

"You're a remarkable girl, Abby," he said finally.

She was quiet. The breeze blew her hair into a pleasant disarray.

"Do you love me, Mr. Nowell?"

"I married you," he said, smiling.

But she would not be put off. "That's not an answer. Never mind. You will love me before it is over," she said. "Did you love the Indian woman or the French woman?"

"What a question to ask!" He was angry, and his anger displayed itself by a slight throbbing in his scarred eyelid.

"I know you loved your first wife and that you still think of her."

"Abby," said Stephen angrily, "let's change the subject."

"I don't mind if you loved Katherine or the Indian woman or the French woman, just so long as you love me more. You don't now, I know, but I have time and they don't."

Stephen smiled and shook his head. She looked so

beautiful sitting there, and framed by the waters of the sea, with the sunlight shining on her freckled face. He leaned over and kissed her gently. She relaxed and allowed her body to come close to his. She felt almost completely enveloped by him. He laid her down easily atop his coat. He caressed her body.

"Please make love to me," she whispered in his ear as she gently bit-the lobe. His senses were filled with the taste and smell of the sea breeze and of Abigail, his wife.

When they had finished, they lay quietly together. He turned to her.

"There was no French girl," he said.

She smiled and looked slightly relieved.

"She was Polish," he said and started to laugh.

"You're a hateful man," she laughed and playfully pounded his back with her clenched fist.

Abby was annoyed that the house had no holly decorations. Hannah absolutely refused to get the plant from the garden; it was a job that George had always willingly undertaken at Christmas time. Abby had slipped from her room fully determined to attack the tangle of wild plants that were growing behind the summer vegetable plot. She wore heavy leather gloves to prevent thorn pricks, which would surely betray her to her husband. He would never approve of her working in the garden.

Most of the crops of the garden had been harvested at least two months earlier. She found the holly bushes and went to work. Every few minutes she would glance up and look to the back of the house to assure herself that no one was watching her. She nearly jumped out of her skin when a hand touched her back. She gulped down a scream and turned to see Dr. John Taylor, her uncle and one of the leading physicians of Boston, staring down at her angrily.

"And what, may I ask, is the daughter of Edward Hibbins doing working in the fields like a woman under indenture?"

"My God, Uncle John, you frightened the devil out of me. At least you could have given me some warning."

"How was I to know that the figure bent in half and digging in the dirt was my patient?"

"Potential patient, Uncle. Only potential."

"We'll see about that. Now get yourself indoors to your room and have your maid assist you. What could you have been thinking of?"

An hour later John Taylor sat in the parlor window seat, sipping a glass of Stephen's best madeira. Abby sat opposite him; her young face was flushed with excitement and some anxiety.

"I wish your husband were present for this," Taylor said with some annoyance.

"Uncle John, I've told you I don't wish to frighten my husband if your answer is negative. Nor do I wish to ruin my surprise if the answer is yes."

"Well, your answer is yes on both counts."

Abby looked at him uncomprehendingly.

"I don't mean to speak in riddles, girl. Yes, you are with child, and yes, he should be frightened. I wish someone had come to me to check you over before all of this. You're not a strong woman. You're frail. You eat less than a bird. You weren't meant for childbearing. I don't mean to scare you, but I doubt if you'll carry this child to full term. And if you do, it will be hard on you—too hard. Your husband should know these things."

"I'm glad he doesn't, and if you ever tell him I'll blast it all over Boston that Dr. John Taylor doesn't keep a confidence."

Taylor looked at her with annoyance. "Why shouldn't he know?"

"Because, Uncle, he'll withdraw from me. I'll lose him. I've come to know Stephen Nowell. He is a man who has rarely loved. He flees from those who love him for fear that either they'll be torn from him or they will desert him. He protects himself by feigning indifference. I think I am finally beginning to reach him. All he needs to know is that our love puts him in jeopardy once again and he'll leave me just as readily as he left his first wife—in fear. I'll not be left, Uncle John."

"You're a feisty girl," said the doctor, smiling. "I'll keep your confidence. Although I admire your spunk, I think you ought to show a bit more concern about yourself. You have to take care or you'll leave *him*, whether you want to or not."

Abby waved aside his remark.

"I'm serious, niece. Don't put me off that way. There's not a better doctor in Boston, no matter what the unethical radical Joseph Warren claims for himself."

Abby poured him a second glass of madeira. When he had finished, she set him on the path to Boston. Now that she knew she bore Stephen's child, she must set her house in order. And she had little time for the concerns of uncles.

The winter winds hurled their fury from out of the Atlantic against the shoreline of Massachusetts Bay. The ferry to Boston seemed almost to fly across the straits. Hannah held on to her bonnet with both hands in fear that it would fly off her graying head into the green, gray waves that cracked against the bow, sending spray in all directions.

Abby insisted on standing near the bow, and already her cloak was wet. Hannah clucked like an old hen in distress, wishing the young woman would come out of the wet wind.

"It's beautiful, Hannah," Abby insisted. "It fills you with a joy of being alive."

"The doctor would be furious if he could see you, Miss Abby. Please step to the back of the boat."

Abby saw how disturbed Hannah had become. Not wishing to cause the still-grieving woman any further pain, she took one more deep breath of the ocean air and allowed one more wave's spray to wet her face. Then reluctantly she followed Hannah to the tamer stern.

A few moments later the ferry entered the calmer waters before the slip. Then with a more forceful crash than usual, the ferryboat came to rest on the Boston shore. The boat rocked up and down in the slip, and Josiah had to hand out each passenger to his helper on the dock. Hannah howled, half in laughter and half in fear, as she was passed over to the helper's firm grip. Abby went over with no discernible change in expression. She had her eyes set straight ahead on the Cromwell's Head.

Hannah began to berate Abby as they walked toward the inn. "I can't imagine what has gotten into you. Why have you insisted on this meeting with Mr. Vaughan?"

"Because he is my secret lover, Hannah. Don't give me away to Mr. Nowell. God knows what he would do to me."

Hannah looked at Abby in shock. "How can you say such an awful thing? You're a young lady of proper upbringing—the best tutoring and all the things a young lady is supposed to know."

"Just like my husband's mother."

Hannah stopped in her tracks. "My Sarah was different. She was raised a proper lady by her father with no little assistance from me. She was forced to do the things she did."

"Don't apologize for her, Hannah. My father speaks of her with awe. She caused a scandal, but she was a successful merchant. Tell me, though, is it true the stories I've heard about her and William Vaughan?"

Hannah blushed. "I don't spread stories about them that's gone. Especially when they were as dear to me as my Sarah."

Abby was sorry that she had teased the old woman. But she was determined to speak with her husband's best friend, now that she knew that she carried a young Nowell in her womb.

They continued up the walk to the inn. Once they entered the foyer, they were forced to wait for the innkeeper, who was nowhere in sight. It was totally improper for women alone to enter the noisy male world of the taproom.

Abby paced up and down before the innkeeper's desk, growing more and more impatient. The front door opened again and an elegantly dressed young man entered the foyer. He looked toward Hannah and Abby.

"Ladies," he acknowledged. He had not the same hesitation as the two women. He stuck his head into the taproom and yelled, "Keeper! You've business out here too."

The harried innkeeper came scurrying from the busy and noisy tables of the taproom.

"Dr. Warren, may I be of assistance to you?"

"These ladies were here prior to me," he said, bowing and smiling at Abby.

The innkeeper then turned to her. "Mrs. Nowell, isn't it?"

Abby nodded. "I've come to see Mr. Vaughan."

Dr. Warren looked at Abigail with renewed interest.

A large, muscular man came stumbling out of the taproom. Beer splashed from a mug he held in his hand, and he nearly crashed into Abby. The doctor grabbed him by the shirtsleeve and the shoulder.

"Hold up, MacIntosh. We've ladies here."

"Bring them in," said the drunken street fighter. "We'll screw the fine one prettier than we do the whores."

Warren's fist came crashing into MacIntosh's jaw, snapping his head backward. As the street fighter fell forward onto his face, the doctor rubbed his knuckles and turned to Hannah and Abby.

"I regret the necessity of this piece of violence. The man has received such notoriety that he seems to have forgotten his place." He stepped over the body of the leader of the Sons of Liberty and entered the taproom.

Hannah was shaking. "I should have known better than to let you talk me into taking you here."

Abby ignored her.

William Vaughan, looking a bit haggard and staggering slightly, came out of the taproom, from which he had been fetched by the innkeeper. He took a puzzled look at the unconscious McIntosh; then he turned to Abby and smiled.

"You carry quite a punch, madam," he said and bowed at the waist.

"Miss Abby," said Hannah. "Mr. Vaughan is clearly under the weather. I believe we should leave."

Vaughan drew himself up in mock indignation. "My good woman, you cut me to the core of my besotten self." Then he reached over and pinched Hannah's cheek. "You've been known to take a little nip yourself, haven't you, Hannah?"

"Never!" she practically shouted.

"Ssh, not out loud; someone will think I've threatened your honor." He looked up and down and thought a moment. Then he shouted, "Never!"

Abigail started to laugh. She knew that Vaughan was just tipsy, not really drunk. She thought him very funny in that condition.

"Mr. Vaughan, I need to speak with you on serious matters," she said.

"I'd invite you to my rooms if it would not be a compromising suggestion to a lady. But then most of the ladies invited to my room are no ladies."

"Hannah, you can accompany us and chaperone."

"I'll lead the way then," said Vaughan.

They walked down the corridors to the suite of rooms that Vaughan had occupied in the Cromwell's Head ever since Sarah Nowell had found him there so many years before.

He dropped into his easy chair and motioned Abby and Hannah to the two chairs before the fire. He poured two glasses of a rich red port and offered them to his guests. Hannah ostentatiously refused hers. From the cupboard, he pulled out a bottle of rum. He returned to his chair, tankard in hand, and raised it to Hannah and Abby.

"To Stephen," he offered.

Abby smiled at the older man and had a good sip of wine.

Vaughan looked her over carefully. "I like you, mistress," he said. "I thought you'd be a spoiled young thing, but you're not. You're a fine lady." His voice trailed off a bit and an almost distracted look came into his eyes.

"Mr. Vaughan," said Abby.

He shook his head. "Nothing, I was just reminiscing. What can I do for you? What brings you to an old lecher's den?"

Hannah stirred uncomfortably in her chair.

"Hannah's nervous. She thinks I am going to make a move for her," he whispered conspicuously to Abby.

"Mr. Vaughan," said Abby loudly, "I want you to be one of the first to know that I am pregnant."

Vaughan blinked and stared at her. "The last woman to say that to me said it accusatorily."

Hannah clucked her disapproval.

"Mr. Vaughan," Abby said, somewhat exasperated by Vaughan's flippant attitude.

"My apologies. You're Stephen's wife. I'm not so far gone that I can't have a serious talk with the wife of the man who is like a son to me. What ails you, missy? Lots of women have babies. Even my mother had one."

"I'm not sure just why I've come to you. I suppose it's to do with Mr. Nowell. I'm afraid for him. My uncle, Dr. Taylor, says I run some risk having this child. My mother died in childbirth. I suppose I'm also afraid for myself."

Vaughan grew serious as he listened to her. Finally he interrupted. "Come, child, all women fear the rigors of labor. They'd have to be unnatural not to be afraid. My god, I've witnessed a birth. It was a terrifying experience and I was only watching."

"You bolster my courage," said Abby.

"I'm sorry, lass," said Vaughan. "I'm an old fool. Why would you come to an old fool with your troubles?"

"I want a promise from you. Of all the people in the world, my husband loves the three of us in this room most. Only the three of us have never left him or betrayed him, in his view. I don't think he has the strength to take any more losses. But if I should have to leave him, against my will, I want your promise, Mr. Vaughan, and yours, Hannah, that you'll stand by him through the worst."

"You came all the way to Boston and risked the ruffians in the tavern to ask me what you could have rested assured that I would do?"

"No, I couldn't have rested assured. You and my husband have done nothing but argue politics as long as I've known you."

"Well, the man's dense in politics. He's in so thick with the worst of people, betrayers of the people's liberty, Hutchinsons, Winslows and Olivers."

58

"See what I mean?" smiled Abby wanly.

Vaughan smiled back. "That's politics. That doesn't come between friends."

"I'm not sure that will always be so. Things get worse. Fellows like MacIntosh and his new henchman, Asa Wallace, grow bolder every day."

"You sound like a Tory, Mrs. Nowell," laughed Vaughan.

"I don't plan to leave my husband, Mr. Vaughan. Not if I can help it. But I do plan to give him this child I carry. If I die doing it, I want you and Hannah, who love him, to help him and my child. I've no one else to turn to."

Vaughan looked at her. For the first time he realized just how important his response was to her.

"Abigail Nowell, you need not have asked. You have my solemn word, by the love I shared with Stephen's mother, that I'll always care for him and his. That goes for you and all the children you'll ever have. You haven't known the lady who accompanies you as long as I have, but there never was a more loyal person in anyone's service."

Hannah squirmed in her chair. She was embarrassed by the praise, especially coming from a man whom she had always regarded as indecent. A vague concern that perhaps she had always misjudged him entered her mind for the first time.

"I needed to hear you say that, Mr. Vaughan," Abby replied. "I am still afraid but I'll have more courage now, knowing that I have you two behind me and behind my husband."

Vaughan started to raise his tankard to his lips, then stopped. "Oh my God," he sighed, "this means you want me to endure another period of sobriety."

She looked at him solemnly.

He lowered the tankard. He rose unsteadily from his chair and walked to the window of his sitting room. "I'm too old to be sober again," he complained. But he raised his arm and hurled the tankard and its contents far out into the night. Off in the distance the pewter mug could be heard crashing into a building below and then rolling slowly down the slope toward the straits.

Winter closed in on Boston. The wind turned from the northeast and the rain came. For five days straight it soaked the town. The streets were flooded and the drainage systems failed. All summer and fall, mud had collected in the gutters, and now the mud and the rain combined to create enormous brown ponds where once streets had been. After the rains ceased, the winds shifted again and the cold of the mountains to the north descended on the town, covering everything with a mud-brown ice.

Across the straits in Charlestown, Abby chafed under the forced idleness brought on by the combination of her condition and the tempestuous winter. She spent the days in her bedroom on the second floor. In the evening after Stephen returned home, he and Abby would eat the meal Hannah had prepared for them alone in the large dining room and then sit before the fire in the parlor.

As each day passed Stephen felt a bit more uneasy about his wife's health. As she grew larger in the belly, her body seemed to compensate for it by thinning the flesh on the rest of her. Despite the obviousness of her pregnancy, she seemed to grow smaller and more frail.

Yet there could be no doubt that she was happy. He could see it in the way her eyes seemed to sparkle when they sat before the fire and he read to her aloud.

He loved to read to her. But rarely could he get through more than one page in an evening. She was filled with questions as her mind, for the first time, came to grips with difficult subjects. In her father's house, a woman was taught to read so that she might find grace in the Good Book. Her father had no other book in the house but the Bible.

They read a great deal of poetry. Stephen was fond of Milton, but Abby was not. He read *The Merchant of Venice*, and she concluded that Shylock had been badly treated and sympathized with him, especially over the loss of his daughter. Stephen found that his grandfather had left some books by New England writers in his room. One book was entitled *The Tenth Muse* by Mistress Bradstreet of Andover, Massachusetts. Another was a strange history— hagiography of the colony of Massachusetts by Cotton

Mather, called *Magnalia Christi Americana*, which, despite its title, was written in English.

Abby knew little Calvinist theology, and continuously challenged Mather's assumptions. Nowell, raised a Roman Catholic, could do little to debate her. But both were direct descendants of persons written about by Mather, and they were fascinated to learn about the first days of New England.

When they had finished reading, Stephen would restore the book to the shelf, carefully marking the place. Then he would take his wife's hand and help her up from the chair. Together they would climb the stairway to their bedroom. She would undress quickly in the chill and climb up into their huge bed. Stephen would cover her and bundle her with a huge feather quilt that she had brought from her father's house. She would chatter her teeth together deliberately—a clear signal to him that she would not be content until he rested at her side.

Stephen would then undress quickly also and throw his nightshirt over his head, a trick he had learned over the years surviving as a one-armed man. She held the quilt open as he climbed into the bed next to her. She would seek his body with hers and then cuddle up, fidgeting until his body heat began to warm her.

He teased her as the months progressed. He could barely reach her with his arm, so big was her belly. She pouted the first time he said it; then her eyes sparkled and she turned her back to him. "You snuggle next to me from now on," she ordered. He laughed and moved closer to her.

The baby came in mid-April.

The pain took Abby by surprise. She was not due, according to Uncle John and her own reckoning, for more than two weeks. But there was no doubt in her mind, despite the fact that this was her first, that the baby was coming. She called to Hannah from her bedroom. The old woman was by her side in a flash, puffing mightily from climbing the stairs from the kitchen two at a time.

In an instant Hannah had sent the two boys Stephen

had paid to sit in the kitchen in case of emergency running off—one to Boston to fetch Dr. Taylor and the other to Stephen's offices in Charlestown. Then she placed Abby in her great bed.

Since the pains were coming about ten minutes apart, Hannah was not unduly worried. But the trip to and from Boston could be tricky. Dr. Taylor had planned to move into the Nowell home during the last week, but it had all started too soon. Hannah knew she would feel a great deal better once the doctor arrived.

Stephen came rushing into the house within half an hour. His face was flushed and he was breathing heavily. He had not waited for a carriage but had run up the path from the village to his home.

Abby smiled at him when he entered their bedroom. He sat next to her on the bed, reached over and kissed her on the forehead. It was damp with sweat, and her face was drawn and very pale.

"You're taking us all by surprise, wife," he whispered into her ear.

She smiled, but before she could respond, another contraction racked her body. She tensed and strained in pain. Stephen sat by her side, holding her hand until the pain subsided.

When she could speak again, she pulled him down and kissed him repeatedly, all the while talking to him of her joy that he was by her side and that their child was about to be born.

Stephen sat with her through four more contractions. They were not coming any faster, but they seemed to last longer and each was considerably more painful than the one that had preceded it.

A sense of panic began to grow in Stephen's mind, but he could not allow Abby to see his distress. Where the hell was Taylor? Why was it taking so long to get help from Boston? Why hadn't he arranged for the doctor to be in the home before this?

Hannah came rushing back into the room with fresh linen and warm water. The front door downstairs was thrown open with a loud bang.

"Who's home?" a familiar voice rang out.

"By God," said Stephen, "it's William. I'd hoped it would be Dr. Taylor."

Abby smiled. She was happy that Vaughan had arrived.

The older man climbed the stairs in response to Stephen's call.

"What have we here?" he said as he entered the room. "A new Nowell is about to descend upon us. Good God, given the trouble this one's given me," he said, pointing to Stephen, "I'm really disappointed in you, young lady, blessing me with another one."

Abby laughed but Stephen merely turned and looked out the window. This was no time for joking.

"Stephen, not so glum. The doctor and Mr. Hibbins were aboard the same ferry as I. They'll be here in minutes." He turned to Abby and winked at her. "They are just not in the same good shape I'm in. It'll take them a while to make it up here."

Abby was exhausted, but she laughed nevertheless at Vaughan's bragging. She knew also that he was sending her a reassuring signal. He had remained sober and he was taking care of himself for her sake, for her child's sake and for Stephen's sake, as he had promised her in the fall.

Dr. Taylor and Abby's father arrived ten minutes later. The first thing the doctor did on walking into the bedroom was to chase everyone but Hannah out.

"Damn it, a childbirth is no place for men. Get yourselves downstairs and hold yourselves ready to do whatever Hannah asks of you."

But Stephen refused to leave. Instead, he went back to the bed and held Abby's hand. She was content to have him there but the doctor was furious. "Mr. Nowell, I've delivered many babies in my career, through the strong and courageous hard work of hundreds of mothers. But I've never, in all of my career, ever received anything but grief and interference from a father. I want you to get the hell out of this room or I'll not be responsible for the consequences."

Just then Abby was struck by another contraction. The doctor began to pull Stephen's sleeve.

"Go," Abby groaned. "Let's allow Uncle John free reign to get this baby born and get this thing over with." She gasped then and finally yelled.

Stephen was horror-stricken. He had never been this close to a birth before. He did not wish to leave, but Abby's words, the doctor's tug, and Hibbins and Vaughan at the open door all combined to force him to stand up. At the door he turned to look at her, but his view was already blocked by Taylor as he bent over his patient.

Stephen sat in the window seat in the parlor. Edward Hibbins sat opposite him. It was William Vaughan who paced the floor like an expectant father. The hours passed with little or no word from the upstairs bedroom.

Abby's groans and later her screams could be heard throughout the house. Each time Stephen's face went whiter and whiter, and he became more and more silent, withdrawing deeper within himself. Hibbins had been through all of this once before—when Abby was born. Then all had ended in tragedy. Stark fear showed on his face.

"My God," said Vaughan in disgust, "why does this take so long?" He fell into a chair before the fireplace.

Just then Hannah came downstairs on the run. All three men jumped to their feet in anticipation.

"The baby is coming," yelled Hannah. "The doctor wants heated water and more fresh linen."

"I'll help," volunteered Vaughan. He hurried off after Hannah down the central hallway toward the kitchen.

Stephen walked to the foot of the stairs and hesitated a moment. Then he bounded up. Hibbins called for him to wait, but Stephen was past hearing anything but Abby's pitiful cries.

He entered their bedroom and saw her writhing on the bed. The lower half of her body was uncovered, and Dr. Taylor was trying to force her to lie still and bear down. He crossed the room and grabbed his wife's shoulders before Taylor realized that he was there.

She felt feverish to him. He gathered her to him and held her. He bent his head and whispered into her ear.

"Abby, my love, hold on to me." She opened her eyes and recognized his face. Even through the pain, he saw in her eyes her love for him.

Taylor looked up. He opened his mouth to yell at Stephen, but then he noticed that Abby had grown much calmer. He bent down to his work again without saying another word.

Stephen kissed his wife's eyes, wiped sweat off her forehead with his hand and held her head to his chest. When the pains came on her, he held her and allowed her to hold on to him as if holding on to life itself. Her grip was viselike.

Finally Taylor let out a yelp. "Keep pushing. Push, girl, push."

Abby's whole body seemed to turn into a large contraction, and the tenseness of her muscles lifted her body off the bed. She screamed with an explosion of air from her lungs.

"That's it," said Taylor. "I'll take it the rest of the way. Good girl. Fine-looking child. A little more, now. It's a boy, Abby. You have a son."

She collapsed back onto the bed. She had lost consciousness. She did not hear a word that he said.

Hannah reentered the room with a large pan of heated water. Taylor had cut the cord, and he handed the boy to Hannah for a bath. She took his tiny blood- and mucous-covered body into her arms and carried the baby over to the basin. She lowered the boy into the water. He sucked air into his lungs and began to give forth with his first cries. They sounded so puny that Stephen looked up from Abby with concern on his face. But Hannah only made a cooing sound as she washed the boy.

Dr. Taylor continued to work on Abby. The afterbirth had been expelled, and now he was using linens, trying to stop the flow of blood.

Abby opened her eyes and looked up at Stephen.

"It's all over," he said to her. "We have a son."

Her pale face broke into a beautiful smile. The freckles on her nose and high cheekbones seemed even more pronounced against the pallor of her skin.

"We'll have to name him. I haven't given any thought to names," Stephen said.

"Matthew," whispered Abby.

"What?"

"His name is to be Matthew. It is a strong name, a very masculine name, and my son is going to be a strong man," she said.

"Matthew Nowell it is," responded Stephen. At that moment Hannah brought the baby over to Abby and placed him in the crook of her arm. She smiled at her son adoringly and then looked up at the father.

"He's serious like you," she said. "It'll be hard to make him smile. I'll have to work on him just as I worked on you."

She closed her eyes and seemed to drift off for some moments.

Stephen turned to look at Dr. Taylor. He froze in place. The doctor had the stricken look of a condemned man on his face. His arms were covered with blood.

"She's hemorrhaged," he cried. "I can't stop the flow."

Hannah's hand flew to her mouth in alarm. She ran out of the room, leaving the door ajar. Soon she returned with William Vaughan. His face went into contortions at the sight of the blood. Edward Hibbins, behind Vaughan, started to weep. "Same as her mother," he cried.

Stephen bent low, placing his ear on Abby's chest. He could hear her heart and feel her breathing.

"Damn it," he yelled at Taylor, "do something. Don't let her die."

Taylor merely stood helplessly before him.

Abby's eyes fluttered open. She smiled faintly at her husband. "Stephen," she said. "I feel so weak. Help me."

"It's all right, Abby." He clutched her hand in his. But she could see tears flowing down his cheek and knew he lied. She was slipping away again. She struggled, but she was becoming enveloped in a greyness and could only make out moving forms. She saw someone approach her from the opposite side of the bed. She knew it was Vaughan.

"You promised me," she said hoarsely, and she felt him squeeze her other hand.

She turned to where she knew her husband sat. "Stephen, you loved me. Don't stop loving or you'll die, too," she cried and then she slipped away.

Hannah was weeping almost uncontrollably. She bent over Stephen and picked Matthew up from his dead mother's arms. Stephen continued to sit, holding Abby's hand in his. He stared down at her. The tears that had flowed so freely while she lived had stopped. But he could not pull himself away from her.

Taylor, who had washed up, approached him and grasped his shoulders. He wanted to cover Abby with the bed linens. Stephen shook himself loose from the doctor's grip. Vaughan walked around the bed to comfort Stephen, but Stephen rose and tore out of the room. He raced down the stairway and out the back door of the kitchen into the night.

He was already puffing from the exertion, but he didn't notice it. He ran up the slope at the back of the house toward the top of Breed's Hill, to their special spot. When he arrived at the summit he fell to his knees and began to sob. His whole body was torn by sobs.

He was enveloped in the night. There was no moon, and clouds covered the stars. Everything was pitch black. Stephen began to curse under his breath. Then he screamed obscenities at the black sky. Finally, he slumped onto the ground. His whole body sagged. He pulled his knees up into his belly and began a soft weeping.

He started when he felt a hand touch his shoulder.

"Stephen, it's me, William."

"Go away," said Stephen.

"I'm not likely to," said the older man. "You do what you have to do. I'll sit here by you until you're finished."

For the next half hour Stephen alternated between sobbing and quiet. Finally he sat up and held his head in his hands.

"Why did this happen, William? My God, how I had come to love her. She was such joy. So alive. I just don't understand how this could happen."

"I've been where you are now, Stephen. After your mother died, I couldn't face it. I couldn't face life. There is no answer. There is no answer to anything. There is just living and dying. You grab all you can while you're living. Some preacher type will tell you that she is happy now with her Maker. If you can believe that, you're lucky. You can make some meaning out of it all. If you're like me, and like I think you are, all you can do is to hang on to the memories and grit your teeth."

Stephen stared off into the darkness while his friend spoke. Then he started to cry again. "I just realized it," he said. "She finally called me Stephen, and I didn't notice it until just now." He covered his face with his hand.

"Come on home now, Stephen," said Vaughan. "The days that follow will be hard, but you'll have to face them. What comes after is even harder, but you won't have to face life all alone, as I had to without your mother."

"I can't face life without Abby," cried Stephen. "Everything I love dies. So help me, everything."

Vaughan put his arm on Stephen's shoulder and helped him to his feet. They began the long walk back down the hillside toward the darkened house.

III

1775

It was Stephen Nowell's fiftieth birthday and he was angry.
He looked across the straits at his native town, knowing he
could not return to it. The rebels had chased him, along
with his ten-year-old son, out of his ancestral home in
Charlestown. They now lived in rented rooms at the
Cromwell's Head in Boston.

Thanks to William Vaughan, his partner, his company
property in Charlestown was safe. Vaughan had friends
high up in the rebel cause—Dr. Warren and General
Ward. He also knew Israel Putnam and Samuel Adams.
Vaughan, now well into his seventies, had also accepted
the responsibility of caring for the Nowell house. He had
left his rooms in Boston and moved into the old house to
keep the rebel hordes out of it.

Stephen thought about how quickly his and Vaughan's
positions had reversed. Stephen's friends—the Hutchinsons,
the Olivers, the Winslows—had either fled Massachusetts
or had been bottled up on the Boston peninsula under the
protection of the British army. After the Tea Party in '73
the King had removed Stephen's friend Thomas Hutchinson
as governor and had all but declared martial law.
Now Thomas Gage, a British general, was the Royal
Governor of Massachusetts. On the other hand, Vaughan's
friends ruled all of Massachusetts outside Boston. John
and Samuel Adams attended the Continental Congress in
Philadelphia, and Joseph Warren was president of the
Provincial Congress.

Despite their political differences, Vaughan still remained
Stephen's closest friend. He was godfather, and at times

second father, to Stephen's son, Matthew. The boy had grown. He was brown-haired and freckled like his mother. Stephen winced at the thought of her—his Abby. Even after nine years he was not reconciled to her death. Hannah had cared for Matthew in those early years while Stephen busied himself in the overseas trade. He had accumulated a large fortune for himself and his partners.

When Hannah had grown too old and feeble to carry out her tasks, Stephen had hired young girls from Charlestown as maids to work under Hannah's supervision. She had liked none of them. No one could please her. And in 1770 she had died in her sleep. Stephen laid her to rest beside her husband George in the Charlestown family graveyard.

With Hannah gone, Stephen tried to look after Matthew himself, but he did not know how to care for a five-year-old. Yet, somehow or other, Vaughan did. Stephen never ceased to be amazed by the old man. He stepped straight into the boy's life, filling the void left by Hannah's death. The old man and the boy soon became practically inseparable. Stephen was grateful to William, but at the same time he was jealous. Each of his children—Aaron, Amy and now Matthew—was somehow or other estranged from him. Molly Brant had Aaron. Katherine had Amy, and now Vaughan had stolen the affection of Abby's son. *Stolen*, he corrected himself, was not the right word. He had been so stunned by Abby's death that he had abdicated the role of father. Others had stepped in to do the job he should have done himself.

In recent years he had stepped into Matthew's life more and more, guiding his education. Matthew attended the Boston Latin School now and was preparing for Harvard. The Latin School instructors were sound men who stood for law and order and had little sympathy with rebellion, but some of the youths came from families who were leading this mindless rabble toward their ultimate destruction. Stephen hoped his son would not be unduly influenced by the other boys, but only last night he and Matthew had argued about the legislation that had closed the port of Boston and placed Massachusetts government under royal tutelage. Stephen had explained to his son that the King had no alternative since private property had been wantonly destroyed and the King's laws flaunted.

He was shocked when Matthew challenged his interpretation and spewed forth the filthy rebel line that the King was attempting to enslave them all. In Quebec, the boy said, the King had denied an assembly to the citizens and had forced the people to accept the Catholic church. This was really what he wanted for Massachusetts as well.

Stephen had been shocked. He had silenced the boy with a look. He knew that Vaughan had never forced his rebel opinions on Matthew. He could only be learning this kind of nonsense at the new school.

The wind blew the curtains of the room aside. It would be a clear day. Stephen could even make out the pathway that led to his house from the village.

Matthew would be rising shortly. The boy loved to sleep late on Sundays. But soon the innkeeper would bring them some breakfast. Stephen had to go down to the warehouse today. He had moved his Charlestown office there shortly after leaving his home. The port of Boston might be closed, but loyal subjects of the crown who owned ships could expect favors if the right amounts were slipped into the right hands. He expected his entire fleet of ships to be at sea before the month was over.

He heard Matthew stir in the second bedroom. Stephen would have to get dressed himself. He threw off his nightshirt and washed quickly at the washstand on the dresser. Rather hurriedly, he dried himself and slipped on a white frilled shirt. He had never allowed the boy to see the stump of his left arm. It was an ugly sight, and he hoped to save Matthew from ugly sights.

Over his feet he slipped a pair of fine white stockings. He found this the most difficult part of getting dressed. His breeches were next.

The door to the next room opened and Matthew Nowell, sleepy-eyed, his hair standing straight up on one side and straight out in the back, walked into the room.

"Good morning, son," said Stephen.

The boy merely nodded. He was still half-asleep.

"Matthew, it is impolite not to respond to your father's

71

greetings. You must learn manners if you are to be a man of great affairs."

Matthew stiffened when he was corrected. "Yes, Father," he said. "But I may not become a man of business like you and Uncle Vaughan. I might become a doctor or a minister. Uncle Vaughan says your father went to Harvard and he was a minister."

"And he died a poor man," responded Stephen. "When your father and your Uncle Vaughan die, you'll be very rich."

The boy did not argue with his father. He was afraid of him. He was so stern. He rarely smiled, and he always seemed dissatisfied with everything that Matthew did. Uncle Vaughan told Matthew of his great-grandfather Breed, the country squire of Charlestown. His father never thought to tell him of these things. Matthew had complained once to Uncle Vaughan that his father did not love him. His uncle had corrected him. He told him of his father's grief over the death of his mother. Matthew then decided that his father's suffering was his fault. His mother had died giving him life. It was the same as killing her. Vaughan had scolded him for that. His mother had wanted him to live more than anything else, he explained. To blame himself for her death was to dishonor her memory.

Matthew loved the old man. Vaughan would always answer questions. When Matthew needed to cry, Vaughan allowed him to climb into his lap, put his face into his chest and weep. He couldn't do that with his father.

Last night he had hated his father for the first time. He had wanted so badly to discuss the new ideas he had heard that he had overcome his fear. He knew Johnny Adams, son of the rebel congressman John Adams and cousin of Sam Adams. They had talked about the King and the laws. But his father had no intention of listening to anyone else's ideas.

Today Matthew had every intention of waiting until his father went off to his business, as he did every day, whether it was the Sabbath or not. Then he would talk his friend Josiah the ferryman into taking him over to Charlestown. He wanted to visit Uncle Vaughan and to visit the old house he had been born in, which he loved.

The innkeeper had brought breakfast into the room.

"Matthew, have some tea and fish," Stephen called.

The boy moved slowly over to the table and sat opposite his father.

"What are your plans for today?" Stephen asked, more out of a desire to make conversation.

But Matthew froze. He was convinced that his father could read minds. He started to stammer.

"What's the matter with you, boy? You grow clumsier and stupider by the day," said Stephen in annoyance.

"I'm not stupid and I'm not clumsy," said Matthew angrily.

Stephen looked over at him, his own blue eyes bright with anger. "Don't you raise your voice to me."

Matthew was very angry now. Tears started to run down his cheeks.

Stephen lost his appetite. He rose in anger from the table. "I can't eat with all this blubbering going on. Boy, you stay in your room today until you learn a little respect. I've got to be off to work. I'll speak to you at dinner tonight."

Matthew rose from the table and walked quickly out the door to his own small room.

He threw himself on his bed. He missed his old bedroom in the Charlestown house. He had been forced to leave everything behind: his toys, his books. He desperately wanted to go back. He would go just as soon as he heard his father leave.

The door opened and Stephen entered. "I'm leaving now, Matt," he said. He had not expected the boy to remember that it was June 13, his birthday; with all the excitement, royal troops parading through the town, a rebel army gathered at Cambridge, he nearly forgot the event himself. But he did not want to leave the inn with hard feelings remaining between the boy and himself. He didn't normally do it anymore, but he bent down and kissed his son on top of his head. He didn't think physical affection between father and son after a certain age was good, but he loved the boy and he felt the need to express it. Matthew did not look up at him. Stephen shrugged his shoulders and left the room and the inn.

Matthew waited until he was sure his father had left. Then he rose from his bed and went to his dresser drawer and began to fill a sack with some stockings and linen. He was going home.

He found Josiah sitting alone in the ferry. He continued to operate it, but he was losing money. Very few were willing to make the trip back and forth across the straits. Boston was a city under siege. The rebels had left Charlestown a no man's land. Those who remained silent and did not express sentiments for the crown could remain behind and travel back and forth. But men like Stephen had to flee.

"Well, it's Master Matthew," said Josiah. "Where are you heading?"

"My father has a message for Mr. Vaughan. He wants me to deliver it. He gave me sixpence to pay you," lied Matthew.

Josiah had no desire to take the ferry out for sixpence, but he was not likely to find many more customers. If Mr. Stephen's son wanted a ride to Charlestown, he would take him there and see that he was safely delivered to the hands of Mr. Vaughan.

The sail across the straits was a slow one. The winds were contrary and Josiah had to make several tacks before touching the Charlestown slip. The village seemed very quiet on the hot afternoon. There was almost no one at the ferry slip, which in itself was very unusual. The ferry landing was normally one of the major events of the day in this sleepy town.

Josiah tied the ferry securely and then took the boy by the hand and led him up to the path above the village. Matthew broke away from Josiah and began to run ahead. He stopped halfway up. He could see the town below and School Hill off to his right. Behind Breed's Hill and his family home were the greater heights of Bunker's Hill.

Just as Josiah almost caught up with him, his chest heaving with exertion, Matthew turned again and raced the rest of the way up the hill. He reached the house and threw open the great oak door.

"Uncle Vaughan," he yelled at the top of his voice. The sound reverberated throughout the house.

"Who's that yelling below?" came Vaughan's voice. "Is it a mutiny? Where's the mate? Lock up the guns. There's mutiny below decks."

He appeared at the top of the landing, his belly larger, his hair almost totally white and thinning.

"Aye-aye, sir," shouted Matthew. They had played this game before.

"Mate, come to my cabin. We must discuss strategy."

Matthew ran up the stairs and into Vaughan's arms. "Uncle, it is so good to see you," he laughed.

"Aye, and it is good to see you, boy. And why are you here?"

"I ran away from Father. I had to see you."

"I heard that," said Josiah from the doorway. His black face was covered with sweat. "You told me you had a message for Mr. Vaughan from your father. You lied to me, boy."

"Never mind," said Vaughan. "I have him now. Josiah, you tell that stuffed shirt of a friend of mine that his boy is going to spend a brief vacation with me in his own home. You tell him that I'll return the boy on Wednesday. I am lonely over here. I need the company."

That night Vaughan cooked Matthew a supper. He had killed five passenger pigeons as they sat on a treelimb on the hill. He cleaned them and skewered them and placed them over the fire in the parlor.

Once Vaughan gave the word that the birds were done, he and Matthew each grabbed one and began to tear it apart with their hands.

"These are good," said Matthew, his mouth stuffed with meat.

"Don't talk with your mouth full," said Vaughan. Matthew

could barely understand him, since Vaughan himself had just jammed a pigeon leg into his mouth and was laughing at the same time.

When they had finished, the man and boy both wiped their hands on their clothes and lay down on pillows before the fire. Vaughan told the boy about his grandmother Nowell, about how she had built his father's firm. He told the boy about his great-grandfather Breed, and about how his father was kidnapped by Indians. He told him of the great Abenacki warrior, Socono, who had taught his father about the woods and nature.

"Is he alive?" asked Matthew. "Everyone in our family seems to be dead."

"The Abenacki is very lively indeed, and you have your grandfather Hibbins, but he's moved to London. Let me see; you have brothers and sisters."

"A half-brother and a half-sister. My father never speaks of them."

"Well, your oldest brother would be a grown man by now. He's probably in the West somewhere with the Iroquois. Your sister is in Canada, near Quebec."

"But we all have different mothers. Why is that?"

"You do ask difficult questions, boy," Vaughan laughed, tousling Matthew's hair. "Let me see how I can explain it. Your father's first, well, wife was an Indian woman, Molly Brant. The second one was a fine lady named Katherine Schuyler. She still lives with her daughter in Canada. She and your father had a big argument and they split up. Then your father married your mother. Katherine came from Albany. Lots of Schuylers there. They're your father's in-laws, so I guess they are your relatives too."

"Are they on our side?"

Vaughan looked at the boy quizzically. "What's our side?"

"The side of Congress, of liberty."

Vaughan started to laugh. "I'll be damned," he said. "Does your father know you think this way?"

"We had a big fight about it. That's why I came here. He called me stupid and lots of other bad things."

Vaughan reached over and patted the boy's shoulder.

"You're not stupid, Matthew. But you're going to have to learn to be forgiving of him. I know it's hard to do sometimes, but if you don't want to lose your father, you're going to have to learn to forgive. It is something I don't think he has ever learned to do."

"Doesn't he love anyone?"

"Oh, yes, he loves hard. He loves you and he loved your mother. I think he is still mad at your mother for dying."

"It wasn't her fault," said Matthew angrily.

"No, it wasn't anyone's fault. But your father loved your mother, and he couldn't bear losing her."

Matthew lay quietly for a few moments. Vaughan thought he had fallen asleep. He was about to stand and pick the boy up and carry him to bed, when Matthew said sleepily, "Uncle Vaughan, I'm glad I have you to come to when things are bad—otherwise I would have to go all the way to Albany to find good relatives."

Vaughan laughed and scooped Matthew into his great arms. He placed his face in Matthew's belly and made great rasping sounds with his cheeks and lips. Matthew started to laugh and then to squirm. He was frightfully ticklish and Uncle Vaughan knew his weaknesses.

The American army came to Charlestown three days later. Twelve hundred New Englanders marched boldly out across Charlestown Neck onto the peninsula. After some dispute by the generals concerning which was Bunker's Hill, they occupied Breed's Hill since it was closer to Boston and of far greater strategic importance. In order to satisfy their orders, however, they called it Bunker's Hill.

Vaughan had put Matthew to bed and was sitting before his fire. He had begun to doze and was awakened by a loud banging on the oak door.

"Who the hell is that at this time of night," he mumbled to himself. He opened the door and was instantly thrust aside by soldiers wearing homespun and carrying muskets.

An older man with the physique of a bull stepped into the house. Vaughan recognized him instantly.

"Seth Pomeroy, you old warhorse, the cause must be desperate if they've had to drag you all the way from

Northampton and out of retirement at your age and obvious decrepitude."

Pomeroy searched Vaughan's face. "Willie, Willie Vaughan? Is this your place? I was told it belonged to a Tory named Nowell." He paused a second, as his mind went back to 1745 to the siege of Louisbourg.

"It's him, isn't it? That boy you were looking after and training? His name was Nowell."

"Yes, and now he's my partner. Back when you, me and him took the Grand Battery and then blew the French out of their city with their own guns, I was looking after him. Now he looks after me. Or at least I let him think he does."

"Willie, I have orders from Colonel Prescott to occupy this house as an advance fort in case the British or the damned Tories try to stop us from fortifying the hill."

"Whose bright idea was it to do that?" asked Vaughan.

"Them other new generals, Artemus Ward and Dr. Warren, got the idea."

"What do you mean other new generals? Are you a general, Seth?"

"Not yet. I've been elected but I don't have the commission yet. Prescott is in charge and Israel Putnam is acting as his second. He's already a general from Connecticut, but this is Massachusetts. A Massachusetts colonel outranks a Connecticut general."

Vaughan merely smiled. "With logic like that, I don't see how we can lose the war. But I can't say much for your tactics. Christ, Seth, you've all walked into a trap. All the British would have to do is land a regiment on the Narrows neck and you'd be trapped. The whole army would be cut off. No help could come from the sea. Not with the royal navy out there."

"We had no choice. We've got captured documents that show that Howe's in Boston. We're not dealing with slow old Gage anymore. This is Sir William Howe, the man who led Wolfe's van on the climb up the cliffs to the Plains of Abraham. He's got some of the best troops—light infantry and grenadiers—some of the best in the whole British army. We got word that he was planning to seize these heights. We're preempting them. We're building a redoubt on the hill above here. By the time morning comes, there'll be nothing Howe can do about it. My boys can dig. They're farmers. Put them in trenches, protect their legs, and they'll fight like hell. No farmer can afford to take a ball in the leg. So we dig and we dig good."

Matthew, who had been awakened by the voices below, called to Vaughan from the top of the stairs.

"Go back to bed, boy," Vaughan called back.

But Matthew was down the stairs in a flash to see what was happening.

"Matthew Nowell, I want you to meet the man who in his day was the best damned smith in Massachusetts."

"Still am," interrupted Pomeroy.

"And the strongest man in New England."

"That, too," said the future general, shaking Matthew's hand, which seemed dwarfed in his huge mitt.

"The militia are occupying Charlestown peninsula, Matt. Seth and his fellows will be our guests for a while."

"Does that mean there is going to be a battle, Uncle Vaughan?"

"I don't see how one can be avoided. If I know William Howe, these troops will be like a canker sore he can't keep his tongue away from. We've got to wait and see if he's going to play it smart and trap these poor bastards out here on this damned neck of land, or if he is going to try to teach the Yankees a lesson and give them a taste of steel."

"I'm betting on the last," said Pomeroy. "Meanwhile, we're digging in."

The American army dug as few armies could. Before dawn they had completed their fort on the back side and highest point of Breed's Hill. It was placed to command the straits and part of the city of Boston with cannon, once they could secure cannon. Most of the Massachusetts men were sent into the fort. The Connecticut militia was sent to the other side of the peninsula beyond Breed's Hill and in front of Bunker's Hill. Here they were stationed in a depression of land behind a rail fence. They were badly exposed. They cut hay, and although there was not enough of it to stack for protection, they draped the hay over the fence, so that from a distance it looked like bales of hay, behind which riflemen and musketmen had placed themselves with relative security. When morning came, John Stark and his New Hampshire militia, Vaughan's friends and former neighbors, arrived on the field. Stark, without waiting for orders, led his men off the slopes of Bunker's Hill and joined the Connecticut men in the hay "fort".

Stephen was awakened in the morning on the seventeenth of June by gunfire from a ship in the straits. He rose from his bed and rushed to the window. Dawn had come, yet it was difficult to make out what the ship was firing at. He could hear the sound of troops marching up the slope toward Copp's Hill, overlooking the inn. There, the British had built a battery just in case the rebels should attempt to seize Charlestown.

Stephen's guess was that they had done just that. He panicked. Matthew was in Charlestown with William. Even if no battle was fought, there were sure to be cannonading and destruction from long distances. He had to get the boy back to Boston and to safety.

He dressed himself as quickly as possible and went downstairs to the taproom. The innkeeper was in a state of near collapse. Uniformed British soldiers were everywhere, clearing tables and chasing out early breakfasters.

Stephen stopped a corporal and asked what was happening.

"The Yanks are out," was the response. "The generals are meeting here for a council of war. Now be off with you. This is no place for a civilian."

Stephen pointed to his arm. "I wasn't a civilian when I lost this in the King's service. My son is over on the peninsula. I need information and I want to see whoever is in charge."

"Sorry, mate," said the corporal with considerable respect in his tone of voice. "I'll not be chasing *you* out. You stay. Just have your grub and stay out of the way. But once

Howe and Clinton and the others arrive, you had best be clearing out."

But Stephen had no intention of clearing out. He recognized Howe instantly when he entered with the officers of his staff.

"Sir William," he called out.

Howe looked in his direction but clearly didn't recognize him. "Sir, how did you manage to remain here? I left orders that all civilians were to be requested to leave."

"We have met before, sir, at the Plains of Abraham. My name is Stephen Nowell."

The empty sleeve pricked the general's memory. "Yes," he said finally. "I do recall. You were with that terrible drunk, what was his name?"

"William Vaughan."

"Ah, yes, Vaughan. Well, what can I do for you, Nowell?"

"I have a son, ten years old, over in Charlestown visiting our home. I am worried about his safety."

"As well you should, Nowell. There's going to be a major conflict over there. We are going to make the rebels run and then we're going to chase them all the way to the entrance of hell. That is, after we chase them from those hills and their base camp at Cambridge."

"I'd like to get to the boy before that happens. Or at least while it's happening. Once before, you let me accompany you even though I had no official capacity. Will you let me again?"

Howe looked disturbed. "Let me think about it. I certainly don't need civilians with me. But you were good luck last time. Perhaps you'll repeat that for me. Stick close and I'll let you know what I decide."

Stephen sat in the foyer of the inn while the council of war took place. He was terrified that Howe would change his mind and not allow him to come with him. There was no shouting as there had been at the councils he had attended while serving as a militia officer with his countrymen. The council was over quickly. Howe emerged smiling. He had obviously had his way and he was pleased. He gave a series of orders to his aides and then turned to Stephen.

"You *are* good luck, Nowell. I am to lead the troops in the field. We're going after them. Sir Henry Clinton wanted to take the easy way and to cut them off, but if we do that and capture them, they'll just raise another army. I know how to win this war. They can no more stand before British Regulars than the French could on the Plains of Abraham."

"May I accompany you then, sir?" asked Stephen.

"Why not?" said Howe, clasping him on the shoulder. "Maybe we'll be able to help you find that boy of yours."

The midday sun was hot. Yet the heat had not slowed the pace of the town. Bostonians from the North End had fled to Copp's Hill to see if they could get a view of the British assault across the straits. In the South End, some climbed to the summit of Beacon Hill to get their view.

Barges and navy longboats were lining the shore. Josiah, who knew the currents of the straits better than any man alive, was enlisted to instruct helmsmen about navigating to the Charlestown side.

All morning long, troops were marched to the embarkation sites. Each man toted a pack weighing over a hundred pounds. The red uniforms of the light infantry and grenadiers were soaked through with sweat. On the opposite shore, the American troops sat within their forts and trenches.

The boats were launched finally, and the navy ships opened fire on the American position. Soon the shots were falling into the village of Charlestown. Shortly after that, some wooden buildings caught fire, and before long Charlestown was ablaze.

From on board Howe's ship, Stephen saw the steeple of the church where Samuel Nowell had served so many years flame like a torch in the bright light of midday. He strained for a view of the Breed house. So far, to Stephen's relief, it seemed untouched.

The general intended at first to make a ship his command post. But he quickly gave up the idea when he found he had difficulty communicating with his shore commanders. He took to a small boat with his staff and soon landed on the Charlestown shore. He mounted a horse and ordered one commandeered for Stephen.

The entire British force had occupied Moulton's Hill and faced the rail fence camouflaged by hay.

"See that position directly in front, Nowell. That's the way we go," said Howe. "We'll take them on the flanks and then we'll approach the redoubt from the rear of Breed's Hill. They expect us to attack the redoubt first. We'll save that for later, after we've attained their rear as well."

"I know this ground," said Stephen. "If you have your men work their way around the stone fences between here and the rebel line, I think you can get close enough to blast them out of that line." He was grateful that Howe had picked the far side of Breed's Hill—away from his house—away from Matthew.

"We'll get close enough; don't worry about that. But the British army doesn't work its way up; it marches. Just watch."

Howe lifted his arm and then dropped it. A military band struck up a march. Each regiment unfurled its battle flag. The troops started down Moulton's Hill in columns. As soon as they reached the bottom, officers yelled commands and the columns swung with precision out into a long line, marching across the open fields toward the New Hampshire and Connecticut militia behind the rail fence.

Stephen was awed by the pageantry and by the long red line. Nothing could stand before this force. Howe would break the rebels. And he, Stephen, would gather up Matthew and return to his home and business in a saner world. Men like the Adamses and the Hancocks would be driven from the platforms from which they had inflamed the common folk. Howe and the beautiful red-coated soldiers moving across the meadow below had restored good order at last.

The troops marched on. Stephen was amazed when he saw their actions at the first low stone wall. They halted the march. The line was still strung out with exact precision across the width of the meadow at the foot of Breed's Hill. Another command was given. The soldiers broke ranks and climbed over the fence, their hundred-pound packs swaying on their backs as they clambered across. On the other side, they formed again and dressed ranks. With their muskets held in front of them, the soldiers moved forward until they reached the second fence, where they repeated the process. Not a sound was heard from the rebel line before them.

Howe and his staff looked on at the march of the light infantry and the grenadiers with obvious pride.

"There never was a prettier sight, my friend," the general said to Stephen. "You train them, you beat them, you scare the hell out of them, and you instill a pride in being part of this magnificent whole, and you get that kind of precision, that beautiful discipline. God, it's magnificent."

The British troops came closer and closer to the rail fence behind which the rebels hid. Suddenly, as one man, the rebels loosed a volley at the British line. Instantly, gaps appeared in the line, as soldiers fell, many writhing in pain from their wounds. Others fell dead in their tracks. Still the line moved forward. From its left flank, in hidden trenches dug along the base of Breed's Hill, a withering fire was loosed. This flanking fire unnerved the British. They were prepared to fight anything in front of them, but fire from the side frightened them. The New Hampshire and Connecticut men behind the fence also began an individual rapid firing, which, although not as immediately devastating, created more and more gaps in the line. The British officers ordered their men to close ranks to fill in the gaps. Defying all reason, the men obeyed the commands. But what was being asked of them was impossible. Whole companies were being wiped out by an enemy who could not even be seen. The line finally slowed and staggered as if hit in the belly, and then broke. Red-coated soldiers began to fall back, slowly at first, then more rapidly. Several American militiamen stood up and revealed themselves, as if to give chase, but the loud commands of their officers held them in check. American discipline had displayed itself as well.

As Howe watched the debacle evolve, his disappointment gave way to anguish. He kicked his mount viciously in the side and charged down the hill toward his retreating army. His staff followed at breakneck speed. Stephen, unsure on a horse, moved cautiously over the terrain until he came to the foot of Moulton's Hill. He found Howe talking to regiment commanders. The soldiers had collapsed on the ground, heaving. Those with minor wounds were being guided to surgeons' tents. Those who had been severely wounded lay on the ground groaning, blood soaking their uniforms.

"I'll send to Sir Henry for reinforcements," shouted Howe to his colonels, "and we'll land the Marines." Just then Howe's horse groaned and blood spewed from its mouth as it was hit by a sniper's ball. As the horse fell to its knees, Sir William slipped out of the saddle and landed safely on his feet. Stephen realized he would have to give up his horse. He dismounted and handed the reins to Howe's aide, who steadied the horse while the general got up into the saddle.

Howe turned back to his colonels. "We'll strike again, gentlemen, precisely the same way. We will feint at the left flank, but our real assault will be on the fence. We must roll up their flank. Get these men on their feet. Dress ranks. I want the flags flying and I want music. But most of all, gentlemen, I want to hear the sound of bayonets going into rebel guts. We must avenge our fallen comrades. No rebel can beat us. Never. Get them on their feet and get them moving forward."

Howe was shouting now. His face was flushed with anger and excitement. The aide who had helped him remount fell unceremoniously backward off his horse, his throat pierced by a sniper's ball. Howe glanced down at the young man. Stephen could see the distress in his eyes as he steeled his emotions and turned to a second aide.

"I suspect John is dead. See to him, will you, like a good fellow?" He turned his horse around to observe the second march.

One could hear a moan come from the British soldiers as they rose to their feet, dressed ranks, and formed the long line once again. The band struck up a cheerful tune and the flagbearers raised their standards high above their heads. Then this shorter red line moved forward across the meadow again. To their left fresh troops moved colorfully up the slope of Breed's Hill toward the redoubt.

Stephen watched in horrified fascination. Almost half the British force that had first attacked had become casualties. Most had been only wounded, although at least a hundred red-coated forms lay scattered over the meadow. The second wave of soldiers, after climbing over the low stone walls and regrouping once again, was faced with stepping over the bodies of their fallen comrades.

Again the Americans held their fire until the last moment. As before, the whole line behind the rail fence erupted at once in a volley of metal. The British line was torn apart. But still they marched on, closer to their hated objective, their bayonets now held low, looking for victims.

Stephen turned to watch Howe. His eyes flashed with excitement. He leaned forward in the saddle, as if to give his men that one last shove that would force them into the American position. But it was not to be. At least not this time. Again the line fell short of its goal. But this time, instead of breaking and running, the British soldiers stood fast and fired into the hay camouflage, hitting back at the tormenters at last. But the constant rebel fire was wreaking havoc among the exposed marchers. Gap after gap appeared as soldiers fell. But still the rank held, not moving forward or backward.

"My God, it's a slaughter," yelled Howe. "They're slaughtering my fine regiments. Get them to fall back. They're too proud to break. Order a retreat."

An aide galloped forward to obey Howe's orders but fell from his horse, a ball in his brain.

Howe himself galloped forward, leaving Stephen standing alone. When the general reached regimental commanders, he dismounted and gave the order to retreat. Reluctantly the line began to fall back. On the right flank the feint against the redoubt had met a similar fate. There were red-coated bodies lying all over the slopes of Breed's Hill.

The troops came staggering back across the meadow.

Their knapsacks, like giant weights, seemed to bend them in half. The sun beat down on them without mercy. The regiment had been decimated.

"We must attack again," said the general. "Or accept the worse defeat ever suffered by the British army. This time we'll not fail."

"It's too demoralizing," said a major of grenadiers. "I can't ask my men to step over their dead comrades again."

"You're right," said Howe. "We must change the focus of our attack. Clinton's reinforcements have arrived, along with Pitcairn's marines. We will attack the redoubt this time."

Howe walked forward into the ranks of the returning infantry. "Get those packs off," he shouted. "For once you are going to fight the way you are named—the light infantry."

The exhausted soldiers gave him a weak cheer and then collapsed on the ground. When Howe returned to his mount, Stephen saw that his leggings had been turned red merely by walking on the blood-stained grass of the meadow.

"This time it's the redoubt," said the general. "And, by God, we'll take it."

Stephen felt sick. The redoubt overlooked his house. With each assault death stalked his boy. And death was coming closer and closer.

At first Vaughan had hoped to have an opportunity to relax with his old friend Seth Pomeroy. But the British changed all that. First came the bombardment of the town, followed by the fire. Then it became obvious that the British were preparing the landing. As the day wore on, more and more militiamen crowded into the Nowell house and barn. The two buildings had become the right flank of the rebel position.

Vaughan's first thought was for Matthew's safety. He went looking for Seth and found him in front of the barn, watching the British battery of Copp's Hill through a field glass.

"Damn it, Willie, if we had some guns like we had at

Louisbourg back in 1745, we could have some fun here."

"Seth, I'm worried about the boy. I think I ought to get him to safety."

"There ain't no safety. Not in the middle of what looks to be shaping up as one helluva fight."

"Can't I get off the peninsula?"

"Not likely. The British gunships have moved in there. They are firing on everything that moves across the neck. If you're worried about the boy, I guess the redoubt would be the safest place to be once the fighting starts. If the British turn heavy guns on this house and barn, there'll be nothing left but splinters once they've finished with it."

"I'd stay with you, Seth—I'm not so old yet that I'd not enjoy one more good fight—but I've got to think of the boy."

"Off with you, you old warhorse."

Vaughan found Matthew hanging out the bedroom window, watching the fire in the town and the redcoats crossing the straits to Charlestown.

"We've got to go, Matt. Grab yourself some food from the larder and a set of clothes."

"I don't want to miss the battle, Uncle Vaughan."

"Well, I do. We're heading up to the redoubt."

Matthew was excited about climbing the hill and going into the new fort. It was built on the spot his father had often enjoyed visiting by himself. But Stephen would not have recognized it now. The earth bore a giant scar, made by pick and shovel. A great dugout, with dirt and dirt-filled barrels creating a barricade, had been created. The earthworks had been planned by an engineer with a redan for cannon facing toward Boston. But there were no cannon to fill the embrasures. The redoubt and its trenches had firing positions for about a hundred musketmen. It was a formidable fortification—especially since it had not existed at all some twenty-four hours earlier.

Matthew looked around wide-eyed when he entered the fort. Everything seemed in chaos. Soldiers with strange uniforms ran from place to place. Sweating work crews, stripped to the waist, put finishing touches on the earthwork. The noise was deafening. One man holding a sword seemed to be in charge. William Vaughan walked over to him.

"Are you Colonel Prescott?" he asked.

"Don't tell me you're another one of those generals," Prescott responded.

"Me? Why, I'm not even in the army."

"Then what the hell are you doing here?"

"One of your new generals, Seth Pomeroy, has taken over this lad's house and is using it as part of the defenses. We need a place to stay for protection."

"I say there," said a voice calling from the redoubt, "is that you, Vaughan? Over here; it's me, Joseph Warren."

"Another one of my generals," said Prescott in dismay. "I've got three goddamned generals serving under me— Putnam, Pomeroy and Warren—all of them deferring to me, a colonel. All of them telling me I'm in command. 'Pay no attention to me,' says Warren, 'my commission is not yet served. I've come to fight like any soldier. I hope to die up to my knees in British blood.' Well, I hope he doesn't get his wish. All I need is a dead general. Can you imagine all the inquiries we'll have to face back in Cambridge if he dies up here up to his knees in British blood? It will mean that Howe's attacked this fort in full force, and we're not strong enough to resist that."

"It is Vaughan," said Warren, coming up to him and grabbing his hand. "It's good to see you. We'll need every experienced hand we can get, won't we, Prescott?"

The colonel merely looked the other way and began to shout to his workmen.

"Here, take a musket," said Warren, handing his to Vaughan. "Who's the child? Why did you bring him?"

"This is my godchild, Matthew Nowell."

"The Tory's son?"

Vaughan bristled at Warren's words. "He may be a Tory, but he's also a friend and this boy's father. We do not agree politically, but there is much of that in every family. I understand Prescott's brother-in-law serves with Howe."

"Excuse me, Vaughan, I meant no insult, and you're right: this war will tear the heart out of many families. Well, let's see if we can keep one family safe. This is

89

certainly no place for a boy, no matter what his politics. You'll have to find a place for him. Some other boys have come with their fathers. They are helping load and carry powder and shot. They're older than young Nowell here, but he looks strong. I guess he can join them. Here, boy, see that dugout over the back of the fort? You go over there and join the others."

"Can't I stay with you, Uncle Vaughan?"

"Matthew, you can stay," Vaughan said, "but over there. You hear me? When all the fighting is done, I'll come for you and we'll go back home." He winked at the boy, who scurried away.

"That's if we still have a home," said Vaughan under his breath.

Matthew climbed down the steps into a dark, cavelike room filled with muskets, a keg of powder and pouches of musket balls. Three boys were loading muskets as fast as they could. It was unbearably hot and all three boys had stripped naked as they worked.

"Hey, look what we have here," said the smallest of the three boys. "A new helper. My name is Allen. The skinny fellow is Chris; his real name is Increase, but he likes to be called Chris. And the fat one on the other side is Micah. Here," he said, thrusting a musket at Matthew, "get to work. Start loading."

"I don't know how," answered Matthew.

All three boys stopped working and looked at Matthew.

"This kid's a baby," said Allen. "I'll bet he doesn't even have any hair on his balls yet."

"What do you mean?" said Chris. "Listen to his voice. He ain't even got balls."

The three started laughing.

Matthew was not frightened by the older boys. He had been forced to fight before and although he doubted he could hold off three older and stronger boys, he knew that if they came at him, they'd regret it as much as he.

Allen saw the look of defiance come into Matthew's face and, realizing where they were, he dropped the teasing.

"What's your name, kid?"

"Matthew Nowell—Matt."

"Well, Matt, I guess I'll have to teach you how to load a musket if you're to be of any use to us today."

Soon Matthew was loading one musket after another. After a while he took his clothes off as well. The air in the room was like that of a steambath and his clothes were soon sopping with perspiration.

The two other boys snickered when they saw him. But Allen had taken a liking to Matthew. "Shut up, you two," he said. "The kid has already loaded two guns to your one."

Matthew had never worked harder in his life. He was terrified of the noise of the British attack across the meadow to their left. They did not take a break; they kept loading guns. Then there was a lull in the fighting.

Finally Colonel Prescott stuck his nose into the dugout. "You, boy, start bringing out the loaded muskets. The British are heading up the hill toward us. And for God's sake, don't go running around out there like heathens. Put on your clothes like decent Christians."

"Shit," said Allen as he picked up his breeches. They were sopping wet. He had used them throughout the afternoon to wipe his sweating hands and face. "I can't stand the thought of putting these things on."

"Wait," said Matthew. He picked up the bundle that contained his food and extra clothes. "I have another pair and they're dry."

"Well, I'll be," said Allen. "You turned out to be a good fellow, twerp." He stuck his legs into Matthew's breeches. They were tight but they would do. Then he put Matt's white shirt on over his shoulders.

When the boys had dressed, they raced across the fort with as many loaded muskets as they could carry.

They could hear the bands playing as the British came closer and closer. Matthew ran back into the dugout for more muskets. Allen was ten steps ahead of him and already down into the hole. Suddenly there was an explosion in the dugout. A keg of powder had somehow been sparked. Matthew was thrown to the floor by the force of the explosion. He lay there for some moments, stunned. Chris and Micah came running back to where he lay. Chris ducked his head into the hole and almost immediately began to vomit. Matthew rose to his feet.

"Don't look in there," croaked Chris. "It's Allen. His head's been blown apart. He must have been hit face-first by the keg when it blew."

Suddenly the whole fort seemed to leap into the air with the force of the simultaneous firing of a hundred muskets. Each man brought his musket up to firing position and fired at will. Then each stepped back and the second line came forward to fire two volleys. Then it was each man for himself. The British line stopped and fell back.

Matthew, Chris and Micah forced themselves back into the dugout to reload armfuls of muskets brought back down to them. They had to step over Allen's bleeding and torn body.

"We need more powder," yelled Micah out of the dugout.

"So do we all," Prescott yelled back. "We have no more. Each man is to fire until he is out of powder or ball and then it is up to him what he does."

The British were coming again. This time they had taken the heavy packs off their backs. Their bayonets gleamed in the sun.

Vaughan stood in the line next to Dr. Warren. He felt glorious. Seventy-three years old and fighting next to a young pup like Warren—a general no less—even if he was a private soldier for the day. He hadn't felt so exhilarated in fifteen years. They had stopped the British on their last march. He had seen the major of Marines fall. He could have fired at the young officer who hauled Pitcairn away, but he had held his fire. Instead he had turned his musket on an infantry sergeant and caught him in the place where his white belts crossed. It was a fatal shot.

But now the British came on. Vaughan could hear Warren breathing heavily next to him. "I'm not running, Vaughan," he said. "I'll not be chased out of this fort. I'll die defending it."

"Warren, I think you're foolish. You're too valuable to the cause. You die here and you deny your countrymen the leadership they need." He knew Warren had not listened to him.

The British were almost upon them. Behind him he heard Prescott yell, "Fire."

Vaughan stood and took aim. His ball smashed the stomach of a soldier in red in front of him. The soldier was instantly replaced by another. He grabbed a second musket. He fired again, and again a redcoat fell. Vaughan stepped aside to allow the second line to step forward. But there was no one there. He turned to see men beginning to flee out the back of the fort.

"We've lost," he yelled at Warren.

The doctor stood up, his eyes glazed. He fired his musket. Now the redcoats were at the top of the embankment. They seemed to pause momentarily at the top. Then they came pouring into the fort, bayonets slashing and jabbing.

Vaughan turned to move away, but Warren stood his ground. British soldiers surrounded him. He went down, and Vaughan saw no more of him.

Vaughan had to find Matthew and get him out of the fort. He moved toward the dugout, where he had last seen the boy. He did not see the Marine who aimed at him. The ball struck him in the middle of his back, snapping his spine. He thought of the sea and Sarah and then all was black.

Matthew was terrified. The British were everywhere. He turned around and around, looking for Uncle Vaughan. Then he saw him lying face down in a pool of blood, his body trampled by soldiers. Tears started to flow. He knew Vaughan was dead. He was now even more terrified. He was alone. He saw men in militia uniforms running toward the back of the fort. He saw Prescott, his sword raised, walking deliberately in the same direction. He ran to get behind the colonel. He followed him out the back entry, out into the fresh air on the back of Breed's Hill. What should he do now? He could return to his home. He looked down the hill toward the Nowell house. He stared in amazement. There was almost nothing left of it. The side wall facing the streets of Boston was completely gone. The roof had collapsed from cannon fire. The barn was ablaze. No, he couldn't go home. If he returned to the fort, he would have to face the British. They would run him through with the terrible knives at the end of their guns.

For now he would flee with the American army. It was his only choice. Once they regrouped over on Bunker's Hill, he would be safe, and he could go home to his father's rooms at the Cromwell's Head.

First Stephen searched the ruins of his old home. He barely noticed the destruction. The pewterware had melted in the fire. His grandfather's and his own books were gone. Everything that he had loved had been in that house, and he had lost it. But not everyone he loved. Neither Vaughan nor Matthew had been trapped in the house. His hopes soared. He climbed up the hill and entered the sallyport of the fort just as Howe and Clinton entered over the embankment.

Both generals were deeply shaken. Howe walked over to Stephen. "Did you see the last attack, Nowell? I've never seen such courage. I can't believe there has been a more courageous army in all of history."

"A dear victory, Sir William," said a dour Henry Clinton. "We can ill afford any more victories like this one. Almost half our men are casualties, Sir William. That is the most I can remember in any battle I have ever been in. It may be the worst carnage in British military history."

Howe cared little for Clinton's critique. He knew that if his troops had not finally taken the hill and the fort, he might have gone down as the general who suffered the worst defeat in the military annals of the British Isles. But he had not lost. He turned to Clinton.

"We're not alone with our casualties, Sir Henry. Look about you."

Stephen started to walk the floor of the redoubt. He recognized Dr. Warren and called Howe over to view the body.

"Who is he?" asked Howe.

"Dr. Joseph Warren, president of the Provincial Congress of Massachusetts and one of their newly elected generals."

"Ah, one of the chief rebels. All we need do now is hang the Adamses and Hancock and we'll have some peace."

But Stephen was paying no attention to Howe. Instead he stared straight ahead of him toward the figure of a fallen man. He recognized him instantly. With a moan escaping from his lips, he reached across the floor of the fort until he reached Vaughan's side. He bent down and placed his head on Vaughan's chest, listening for a heartbeat, anything. It was hopeless. Vaughan had been killed almost instantly.

Stephen's eyes searched everywhere. He rose and ran from body to body like a crazy man. But they were all too large to be his son.

"There's another one down here. Looks like a kid," a marine sergeant called from the dugout.

Stephen's heart sank. He walked deliberately now, knowing in his heart what he would find. He climbed down into the dugout and stared. The sergeant had turned over the boy's body. His face and hair had been blown away.

"Jesus," said the Marine. "Couldn't have been more than twelve years old."

"He was ten," said Stephen as he recognized Matthew's clothes. He turned from the dugout and walked across the floor of the fort like a man in a trance. Tears streamed down his face. Now the cycle was completed, and once again he was alone.

Stephen buried William Vaughan and his son in the family plot in the churchyard in Boston. The burned-out church served as a backdrop for the ceremony. The town had been utterly destroyed. The Americans had escaped to the mainland when the tide had turned and prevented British warships from controlling Charlestown Neck. They now sat across Back Bay in Cambridge, awaiting their new commander, a General Washington from Virginia.

For Stephen, however, the war was over. He could no

95

longer live in a city of such memories. There they were, lined up in the family plot: Jonathan Breed; Betsy Breed; a memorial plaque for Samuel and Sarah Nowell; Richard Nowell, the older brother Stephen never knew; George and Hannah; and Abby, his darling Abby. And now his only link to her, their son, and last, his only real friend in life, William Vaughan. It was too much for him. All the mourners had left the churchyard. He stayed on, staring at the markers. The wind tore at his coat and blew his greying hair about. It rushed through the exposed, blackened beams of the church and made an eerie, moaning sound. It would rain soon.

Stephen turned from the graves finally and walked out of the churchyard. Josiah waited for him by his carriage. Two days later, Stephen Nowell, accompanied by Josiah, the ferry boatman, left Boston for England on one of his own ships.

IV

1775

For ten years Antoine Gingras had ridden the circuit from
Isle d'Orleans and Quebec City to Three Rivers and
Montreal and then back via St. Jean, Sorel and Point
Levis. He had built, with Ethan Morin's help, a hard core
of followers, ready to rise up and overthrow the British
conqueror. Until last year, events in Quebec had mirrored
those in the southern colonies. From 1767 to 1770 there
had been much interest in the movement. At that time,
the American colonies were convulsed with riots and
boycotts over the Townshend duties. Then from 1770 to
1774, Antoine had grown discouraged. Most of the rioting
to the south ceased with the repeal of the duties. The
quiet in the south convinced all but the most ardent of
Antoine's supporters that the cause was lost, that the
Americans would never break into open rebellion, never
come to their rescue. But all that had changed at the end
of 1773. The tea tax had rekindled the fires in Massachusetts. Sam Adams and his Sons of Liberty had struck and
dumped tea into Boston harbor. Britain had retaliated by
closing the port of Boston and removing the governor. Actual
fighting had erupted in New England.

But nothing similar had occurred in Quebec. In 1774
Britain had passed legislation for the future governance of
Quebec. It had proved devastating to Antoine's cause. The
Quebec Act extended the borders of British Quebec to the
Ohio River, depriving Virginia of most of her western
claims. More importantly, the act confirmed French civil
law in Quebec in most matters. What was most harmful to
Antoine was that the Catholic church was granted special

status. As it had always been in the past, the Catholic church was to be the church of Quebec. It was not just a tolerated religion; it was practically the established religion.

The Quebec Act won over to the British crown the clergy of Quebec. The church was protected, its future guaranteed. The bishops and curés could ask no more than this, since in some respects they were better off now under the English than they had been under the French. The church—and no other force—would dominate the French-speaking people of Quebec.

Over the decade Antoine had come to think of the clerics as obstacles to overcome. Their natural conservatism had thwarted many of his recruiting efforts. Now they were his out-and-out enemies. The Quebec Act had turned the clergy from cautious, slightly indifferent observers into sworn critics of any change. And the Americans had not helped. Antoine agreed with the Americans who called the governmental aspects of the act vicious—especially for not granting Quebec any legislative assembly. He was convinced it revealed Britain's true sentiments about self-government. The English would grant no legislature to Quebec and would strive to suppress them in the southern colonies in every way possible. But American criticism of the act had not been limited to this question. The overt intolerance of Catholicism, which existed throughout America, came to a head, and virulent attacks on the church, the Pope, on the Quebec clergy and on all Roman Catholics were circulated throughout the colonies. These attacks were duly reported to all who lived in Quebec by the Catholic clergy, aided by a more than willing British government.

At a time when fighting in Massachusetts promised that deliverance for Quebec was at hand, Antoine and Ethan had actually lost considerable ground to the pro-British sentiment in Quebec.

Over the years, Antoine had only occasionally visited Isle d'Orleans. On these visits, he met with Albert and his group of island patriots. The island had a strong and still-growing contingent. And he would come to the family farm. His mother had died eight years ago. His sister and her husband lived there now. Two years ago, Marie's Jean Guy had broken his leg. He had never really recovered from the accident. Antoine had hired Louis Joseph to come twice a week and help them out. He had ridden to the Stiegler farm to arrange it. There he had found a strange trio. Louis Joseph had grown into a fine lad with flaxen hair hanging in his eyes. He had his father's physique as well. He was built like a bull. He was overjoyed to see Antoine and followed him back to the Gingras farm willingly and then trailed after him all day like a puppy. Antoine had pitied Katherine. She was now almost totally removed from reality, sitting on her porch, talking to nonexistent shadows from her past. Her face had grown thin, and there were wrinkles about the eyes, but she was still a beautiful woman. Her chestnut hair was as brown as her daughter's—no grey whatever had appeared.

It was the daughter who had changed the most. Amy was no longer a young girl. She had adopted a very severe hairdo and manner of dress. There was no doubt who ran this little family. She was a cold and unloving woman.

Antoine's last visit had been two years ago. Now he rode the river road again. Jean Guy had lost his leg, and after terrible suffering, he had died. Marie had moved to Beauport and taken a second husband. Antoine had decided to return to the island and to the family farm.

He had been living there for a month, seeing only Louis Joseph, when a message from Ethan reached him. The new American commander, George Washington, had agreed to an assault on Canada. Two forces would be coming. One would strike north from Albany and Ticonderoga. Its target would be Montreal. The second was only rumored, but it was said that another force would come up the Kennebec River, over the mountains, and attack Quebec City. The Americans wished to capture the St. Lawrence and deprive the British of the best route into the heart of the thirteen colonies. To Antoine and his friends, it was far more than this; it meant freedom from the British yoke.

He reined his horse in as he descended the knoll to the house. Amy heard him coming and stepped out onto the verandah.

"Hello, Antoine," she said coldly. "Louis Joseph told me you had returned. Did you come to muster him for soldier-boying at Albert's tonight? That's where it's still done, isn't it?"

"The playing is over," he responded. "An army of liberation is on the move toward Montreal from Albany. I'm leaving tonight."

At first he thought he saw a fleeting look of pain cross her face, but it soon disappeared. The stone face returned.

Louis Joseph came charging out of the house. "Did I hear you right, Antoine?" he yelled. "They're coming at last?"

Antoine merely nodded. He winced when he saw the sarcastic glance Amy threw in Louis Joseph's direction.

"I'm going with you," said the boy.

"No, you're not," said Amy. "Your place is here with me. Besides, I need you to care for my farm."

The boy started to curse and shout loudly in protest.

"Shut up, you oaf," said Amy with venom in her voice.

The boy reacted as if he had been slapped. He was on the verge of striking back at her, but he didn't have the words, and he loved her too much to use physical power.

"You're not going, no matter what you shout, so give it up as a bad idea," she repeated. "You're too young and you're needed here."

"I'm taking no one from this island under twenty-one years," interrupted Antoine.

Louis Joseph knew Amy too well to continue the debate, and Antoine had put the final blow to his hopes. But that did not mean to him that he had lost the argument. He gave his half-hearted pledge to care for Antoine's farm while he was gone.

Amy entered the house. She was angry. She needed Louis Joseph. Antoine should have found other help. Antoine started to turn his horse as if to go home, but he swung back and dismounted and entered the house after her.

"Amy," he said softly as he had done in the past so long ago.

She had been standing with her back to the door when he entered and had not seen him. The words had touched her, but she hid it. When she turned around, she regained her composure.

"That was ten years ago," she said.

Her mother sat before the fire, staring. Amy walked over to her and sat at her feet, looking up into her blank face.

"I'm leaving tonight," Antoine said. "I felt I should say goodbye."

"Goodbye," Amy said without looking at him.

He grew angry. "Is that all you can say?"

"Why pick tonight to revive ancient history?" she said wearily. "I have to put my mother to bed. Poor woman can't even undress herself anymore. This is what your soldier-boy guns produce. The men die but they get off easy. The women have to bear the pain. Well, it isn't going to happen to me. I made up my mind to that ten years ago in the bakery. I've never regretted that decision and I'll never go back on it."

"But you loved me then."

"Oh, goddamnit, get out, Antoine. Get out of my life for good. It's taken you ten years to figure it out. I made my choice. It has been hard. But it's easier for me now. If I had come to you and become your wife and the mother of your children, where would I be right now? Right this moment? I'd be terrified. I'd be gathering my children about me, protecting them and trying to make them understand why their father had to go and leave them, why he had to leave me. They wouldn't understand. I never did and I still don't. My mother never understood."

Antoine grew angry. "What's the difference between that and what you're doing now? I'll tell you—ten years of happiness instead of ten years of bewilderment for me and pent-up anger for you."

"Goodbye, Antoine. I hope you come home safely. I hope you love someone and someone loves you back. At least one of us will have achieved that before we die."

"You've become hard. What happened to the young girl who loved me once and would have followed me anywhere?"

"Obviously she would not follow you anywhere. And she grew up. She had to care for her mother and had to come face to face with your priorities. First came Quebec and politics and then came me."

Antoine shook his head. "You rejected me."

"I was fifteen and frightened. All you could think about was your aching genitals. Now leave me be. I have my mother and my brother. I take care of them. That's my life now. Damn it, man, go away."

He left the room. She watched him go. And then she went to her mother to prepare her for bed.

That night Antoine left Isle d'Orleans with a small contingent of farmers who had agreed to join forces with the Americans to free Quebec. There were only a handful, but they hoped to be the van of a massive rebellion of French people, which would eventually lead to the expulsion of the British from their sacred land.

The next day Amy rose at dawn as she always did. Louis Joseph was already up. Normally she had to awaken him. But now he would be over at Antoine's place taking care of the Gingras livestock before he began to take care of their own. She would not have to awaken him for the next few weeks. He would always be willing to do Antoine's chores, even if she had to yell at him to do his own.

And she was tired of yelling, of being "hard," as Antoine had put it. But someone had to run things. Louis Joseph knew what to do, but he desperately needed someone to tell him when to do it.

She went to Katherine's room and found her mother already dressing herself.

"Good morning, Amy," she smiled.

It was to be one of her few lucid days, thought Amy. Well, count small blessings. At least today she would have someone to talk to.

Amy put some logs on the hearth on top of last evening's banked embers. She had a bucket of dry straw next to the poker. Before long she had a good fire going. The central room of the house would be cozy very shortly. She put on the kettle for some tea.

Katherine came from the bedroom and placed an apron about her waist. She stepped outside the front door and headed for the chicken coop. She returned with an apron full of fresh eggs.

"The cow needs milking," she said. "Don't tell me Louis Joseph is still in bed."

"No," said Amy. "He's probably gone to Gingras' to do the early morning chores."

"Why? Where's Guy?"

Amy did not wish a setback so early in what had started as a promising day. And so she lied that he had gone to Quebec on business.

The two women sat down and shared a breakfast of tea and boiled eggs. Katherine hummed happily, sitting back in her chair after she had finished.

For some reason which she could not explain, Katherine's contentment annoyed Amy.

"You're happy today, Mother," said Amy.

"Yes, I am, my dear."

"Why?"

"Oh, it's good to be alive with my children, or at least my child. Where is your brother? What's taking him so long? Lord, I've always had to be running after that boy. He's not steady like his father."

They were quiet for some moments. Amy sipped her tea and Katherine hummed. Finally Katherine broke the silence.

"Amy, I think you ought to marry Antoine."

Amy looked at her mother in surprise. In ten years she had acted as if she knew nothing of Amy's love for Antoine or her anger at him.

"Why raise that now, Mother? It's done with."

"No, you love him. He loves you. What else matters?"

"Fiddlesticks," said Amy. "I've barely seen the man these last ten years. I can get along without love. Besides, what does love get a woman? You loved my father."

"Yes, I truly did."

"What did that do for you?"

"It gave me you."

"And where is my father?" Amy regretted the words the moment they left her lips, but they seemed to have no effect on Katherine.

"Your father loved me, but he was afraid to express it. When I fell in love with your Uncle Karl, your father thought I had deserted him. And I had. But from the beginning your father had never been there when I needed him. God knows I learned to love dear Karl, but it could never have happened if I had felt certain of your father's affection. It's holding back the expression of love that destroys it. Amy, you're doing precisely what your father did."

Amy was growing annoyed. "I can't afford commitment and loss. He has his politics."

"Just like Stephen," Katherine mumbled.

Amy put down her teacup and rose from the table. "I'll milk the cow myself, Mother. Perhaps you could go in and make Louis Joseph's bed."

She walked into the yard and toward the barn, but she was only halfway there when she heard a frightful wail come from the farmhouse. She turned and ran back. She found Katherine sitting on Louis Joseph's bed, staring blankly. In her lap was a piece of paper. Amy picked it up. It was a note from Louis Joseph announcing that he would join Antoine's troop in Montreal.

She looked at Katherine. There was that old dullness in her eyes.

"I've lost you again," Amy said aloud, "but you lied to me, Mother. The pain and fear of losing is too much for you too."

At first she looked around hopelessly, but then her determination grew. She'd be damned before she'd lose her brother to Antoine's nonsense. No, a seventeen-year-old boy was not to be sacrificed to some elusive political goal. Certainly not her brother.

"Mother, I'm packing you a bag. We're off to visit our old friends at the convent. They'll take care of you until I get back. I'll give Albert's wife the milk from the Gingras and Stiegler cows for taking care of the farmhouses. I'm going to Montreal and I'll bring my brother back home."

Antoine's troop of men had paddled upriver from Quebec toward Montreal, traveling only at night. Fall had descended in the valley of the St. Lawrence and the nights were chilly. Antoine was grateful to be paddling. It kept him warm. He had instructions from Ethan Morin to join forces with a John Brown, who was in command of a troop of Canadians from the St. Jean-Iberville area. Brown was then to place his force under the command of General Phillip Schuyler of New York.

The night before they reached Sorel and the mouth of the Richelieu, Louis Joseph joined them. He had been following, waiting until they were too far to send him back. Now that they were close to Montreal, he felt secure.

Antoine ranted at him for twenty minutes. Louis Joseph sat before Antoine and looked properly grim, and eventually the older man cooled off. Antoine never had been able to stay mad at Louis for very long. The boy was strong and a good shot, and he had his own musket. They would need him.

Traveling by day now, the troop arrived quickly at Chambly. They had to leave the river there because the fort that guarded the rapids had a contingent of about eighty British soldiers manning it.

They arrived finally at the American camp, really more a sea of huts, with almost no reasonable military order. The camp encircled and besieged the British garrison in the village of St. Jean.

Ethan Morin was the first to greet the men from Isle d'Orleans.

"Antoine, the time has finally come after all these years of planning," he said. Then he saw Louis Joseph.

"Who's this one?"

"He's Amy's brother, Louis Joseph Stiegler."

Morin shook his head and then led Antoine by the elbow away from the others. "He's only a boy, Antoine."

"He followed without permission. He didn't join us until

105

yesterday. Besides, he is as strong as any of us. We will need his kind before it's over."

Morin reached into his coat pocket and handed Antoine a piece of paper.

"Here. This is your commission from the Congress. You are now a lieutenant in the Continental Army."

Antoine beamed as he took the paper. "And you?"

"Captain Ethan Morin at your service, sir."

"And what kind of army do we have?"

"Mostly New York and Connecticut militia. Then there are the New Hampshire Grants militia. They call themselves the Green Mountain Boys. They took Ticonderoga along with Major Arnold and his Connecticut forces. But now they are led by Seth Warner. Their colonel was Ethan Allen, but they got mad at him and un-elected him. All in all, we're about seventeen hundred, led by a Dutchman named Phillip Schuyler and a professional soldier from the British army—an Irishman, mind you—by the name of Richard Montgomery. He's the real soldier, but Schuyler is in command."

He hesitated a second. "Oh, Christ, speak of the devil and here he comes," moaned Morin, trying to turn Antoine away from the approaching figure.

"Hold there, Philistine," the stranger yelled. He was a huge man with a giant head and mane of hair. His muscles bulged through his homespun shirt and breeches.

"Namesake, don't try running away from me!"

Morin pulled up short. "It's Allen, Ethan Allen," he whispered to Antoine.

"I seen them new boys coming to camp. I want them Canadians for my plan."

"We all belong to Brown's contingent, Colonel."

"I know you do, and just as soon as I can convince Brown to move with me, we'll have Montreal in our hands. Why waste our time on this town?"

"Colonel Allen, I don't mean to argue with you, but the Richelieu leads from Lake Champlain. St. Jean commands the Richelieu. If the British control it, then the route to Champlain, Ticonderoga, Lake George and the Hudson lies wide open to them."

"Shit," yelled Allen. "There aren't five hundred British troops in all of Canada, and you're worried about them moving on Albany. Why can't someone pay attention to me?" He gazed up into the heavens and started a mock prayer. "Great Jehovah, god of hosts, who was with me when I took Ticonderoga, why have you abandoned me? Why have the Green Mountain Boys abandoned me? Are you listening, Jehovah, or are you drunk up there? Ah," he exclaimed, waving his arms in disgust, as if it were his form of amen.

Antoine, who spoke no English, hadn't the slightest idea what the man was saying or why he felt it was necessary to say it so loudly.

The stranger walked past Morin and grabbed Antoine. The Frenchman tried to pull away, but the man's strength was enormous. There was no loosening his grip. "You, heathen Papist, will you be with me when the time comes?" He let go of Antoine and moved toward the huts of the Vermont men. "Seth Warner," he yelled, "you son of a bitch, I want my boys back, or at least give me a drink."

"A dangerous man," said Morin.

"A crazy man," responded Antoine.

"Maybe a little of both. But he is right about how vulnerable the British are. We have this entire colony in our grasp. It will take only a little of Allen's type of boldness, tempered with Montgomery's skill, to achieve our goal. Who would have thought it after the response to the Quebec Act?"

"I think you are overly optimistic. The Americans have entered Canada not to liberate us, Ethan. They have come to take away the invasion route of the St. Lawrence and Lake Champlain from the British. If the going gets rough, they will desert us. If they do that before we have won over the minds of the people, the British will end up even more firmly in control than in the past. And even if you Americans should triumph, what guarantees have we Canadiens that you will treat us as equals?"

"You have the example of how I have treated you."

Antoine laughed. "I'm not sure that proves anything,

107

my friend. But enough of this talk. We have a revolution to win. Let's get on with it. We must drive the King's men from Quebec as you have driven them from the colonies to the south of us."

It took Amy three times as long to get to Sorel as it had taken Antoine and his men. After leaving her mother with the Ursulines, she had booked passage on a supply boat to Montreal with a stop at Sorel. She had to wait several days, sleeping in the woods at the edge of the town, before she could get a place on the *bateau* heading up the Richelieu to the British fort at Chambly. She was close to exhaustion when she reached the American encampment. She pretended to be the wife of one of the Canadian suppliers to the camp. No one tried to stop her from entering. Amy looked for the commander's quarters, but she could not be sure where it was. She stopped an officer.

"Where can I find the commander?"

Philip Schuyler was ill. He had never felt so poorly before. The fall rains were upon them, and the damp from the river marshes had caused fever and joint and muscle pain. He wanted to go home to Albany, to his wife and children. His wife was a meek woman, like most of the VanRenssalaers. Thank God, his mother had not insisted he marry a VanCortlandt like herself. He surprised himself. He rarely thought of his mother any longer. Cornelia Schuyler had died in Albany in 1762, thirteen years ago. He really could not say that he had missed her.

After she died, he had built a new Albany home, a showplace in the town, the finest Georgian red brick mansion in the city. The interior had been furnished directly from Europe. The house brought him closer to his Aunt Margaret. To his wife's horror, the old woman came down from Saratoga—from her house at the flats—to see the new townhouse with her strange frontiersman husband and his ancient Indian friend.

The three, especially the Indian, had looked so strange peering at the fine bone china and the Delft tiles on the mantelpiece. Margaret had, in turn, invited him to her house in the flats. It was really his house, but by decree of his grandfather's will, it was hers to use until her death. He had enjoyed his visit to Margaret. He had found that Kip, her husband, was a delightful man, full of stories about his colorful career as a fur trapper and Indian fighter and the liberator of the fortress at Louisbourg. The Indian, he said, lived in the woods near the abandoned fort at Fort Ann and came frequently. He did not show up during the three days he spent with Margaret and Israel Kip.

But now he had an army to command. And an army in serious trouble. Informants from behind British lines had warned him only last night of the trap Carleton had set for him here. He had to retreat.

An orderly lifted the flap of his tent and broke into his reverie. "We have a flag of truce from St. Jean, sir."

"Oh, damn, that means I'll have to get dressed. Can't Montgomery handle it?"

The soldier looked at the general in confusion.

"Oh, I forgot; he's left, hasn't he? Must be getting delirious. Well, send another officer, anyone but that idiot Ethan Allen. Send Brown, Warner, or that Connecticut fellow Wooster."

"Yes, sir, I'll see to it right away. But sir, which one is it to be?"

"Damn it, man, how should I know? I'm only a general. I was told it was you fellows who were the backbone of the army. Well, why not take a vote on which one to send? You Yankees take votes on everything else. Should the general be obeyed or not, you hold a goddamned referendum on it. God help us if we try it on the battlefield."

Schuyler went back to his field cot. He allowed his large body to fall backward. He hated this life. He had supposed that a general stayed behind the line and lived comfortably, enjoying the good things in life. He didn't mind getting the army organized. He was a merchant as well as a gentleman farmer. He did the organizing part well. But laying siege to a village like St. Jean—that was work for a professional like Montgomery.

Again the orderly entered. "Sir, it's your niece. She's here."

"Which one? I've dozens of nieces."

"This one is named Nowell, Amy Nowell, and she's come under truce from the British camp, compliments of Major André."

"Nowell? My sister Katherine married a Nowell. Yes, they had a daughter. Send her in right away."

He rose from the bunk and hurriedly arranged his clothes and his wig.

The young woman who entered behind the sentry was strikingly beautiful despite the soiled and bedraggled clothes.

"My child," said Schuyler, taking her by the hand and leading her to the camp stool. "You're certainly like your mother. I would have known you anywhere. How is your mother? Where is your mother? I've tried writing many times. Aunt Margaret has as well."

"My mother is not at all well. There are times when she doesn't know where she is. She lives with me on Isle d'Orleans downriver from Quebec City."

"That's far from here, girl. What brings you to seek me out after all these years?"

"My brother has joined your force. My mother needs him. I have come to bring him home."

"I can't have that, my dear. If I allowed everyone to go home, I wouldn't have an army."

"At least let me talk to him."

"That I can do. But you'll have to be quick about it. This army moves south to New York today. Orderly," he yelled. "Excuse me, my dear, I have much to do. You and I will get together later and we must discuss your mother. In the meanwhile I'll find you an officer's tent. You freshen up and we'll talk again, once we reach Isle aux Noix. We'll all be safe there."

Antoine could not believe his eyes when he saw Amy coming toward him. He was sitting in the hut he shared with Morin, attempting to shave. He saw her first reflected in the small piece of broken mirror he was holding in front of his face. He turned around just to prove to himself that the mirror lied. But it had not. She stood there looking down at him.

110

"My God, Amy, what are you doing here?"

Morin, who was dozing in the hut, stirred.

"I want Louis Joseph back. You may get yourself killed, but you'll not kill my brother."

"You'll kill him quicker than any redcoat if you, his big sister, drag him home. Besides, he can't go. He's enlisted in the Continental Army until December 31."

"There won't be any Continental Army in Canada after today. Schuyler is retreating."

Morin stuck his sharp features out of the sleeping hut. "Hello, Miss Amy. What's that you say? What about our retreating?"

Almost as if to answer his question, the drums started to beat the roll for retreat. Those who knew what it meant looked at each other in confusion. Morin began to curse.

"What's he frightened of? Damn it, we can't retreat."

"Where's Louis Joseph?" Amy asked.

Antoine pointed. Louis Joseph sat before his hut, searching his clothes for unwanted visitors.

"Put your breeches back on, brother. We're going home," she said gruffly.

He jumped in fright when he heard her voice. He turned around and stared in amazement.

"How? How did you find me?"

"I'm not the one who should be answering the questions. How could you abandon mother and me and leave us with no one to do the chores, no man on the farm? You had to go off and play soldier."

Several of Louis Joseph's comrades had come out of their huts and stood about smiling, as the boy, turning his back to his sister, hopped on one foot and then another to put on his breeches. Several hooted and started to laugh. Louis Joseph's face turned crimson red. One look at his powerful shoulders and biceps convinced most of the bystanders to find other things to do. One or two continued to jeer, but they made certain they were out of range.

Once he was covered, the boy faced his sister. He was so angry he began to cry, tears streaming down his cheeks.

"How dare you humiliate me in front of those men. I'll never regain their respect."

111

"Well, cheer up; you won't have to. This army is breaking up today. We're going home to Isle d'Orleans."

Amy was angry at Louis Joseph, but at the same time she couldn't help but feel sorry for him. She saw the look of confusion on his face. Officers were running through the ranks, giving word to break camp. They were heading south out of Canada to the tip of Lake Champlain, land claimed by both New York and New Hampshire.

She saw his shoulders sag and reached over and touched him. He pulled away from her violently.

"All right, stay angry with me," she said. "I only did what I had to do. I had to find you and bring you home."

"Why?" he spat out.

"Because, you big dolt, your mother can't face life without you. She idolizes you. To her, you are my father and your father rolled into one, and you're her son. And what do you do? You go to war and send her backward into a fog she may never come out of. The only chance I see for her is if you come home."

Louis Joseph's expression softened as Amy spoke of his mother. He hadn't thought of how his departure might affect her. Amy was right. She was always right. He shouldn't have come. He saw that now. Why hadn't he thought of it earlier?

Antoine came up behind Amy.

"Antoine," Louis Joseph called, "I have to be going home. My mother is ill."

The older man smiled. He could have objected and reminded Louis Joseph that he had enlisted for three months. He could have forced him to stay. If he did, however, he knew he would lose Amy forever.

"I'll arrange a furlough, Louis Joseph. You go home and see your mother."

It took them only two minutes to pack his sack. In the confusion of the retreat, no one on either side noted the young French-Canadian man and young woman walking the road toward Montreal. Once there, they could find river passage to Quebec and their island.

112

Molly Brant had heard the name Caugnawaga for four decades, but never before had she visited it. She didn't like it. The houses looked small and drab. She pulled her blanket about her more tightly and leaned closer to the hearth. True, the Catholic Iroquois who lived here dwelt in European-style houses, but she would have preferred a longhouse. Johnson Hall, Sir William's great new home, farther up the Mohawk, had spoiled her for any European-styled life but the most elegant.

But that was behind her now. Johnson was dead. Two years ago, he had gathered all the tribes at Johnson Hall: the Iroquois, even the Shawnee and Illinois from the west. He had addressed them and guaranteed their loyalty to the King. He then complained of a terrible pain across his stomach and chest. With Molly's help, he had crossed the estate to his house. Once in an easy chair in his bedroom, he had simply slipped away without warning and without farewell. She went to the open window of his bedroom and wailed her death lament, which was taken up by two thousand Indians on the grounds. Then his white son had come and taken control of his body and his estate. Sir John Johnson took over the hall, and Molly Brant had returned to her platform at Canajoharie. Johnson had rewarded his sons and daughters and her with tracts of land. They would be well off. But he had left nothing to her favorite, her first son, the blackrobe's son, Kenonranon.

He was a man now, but he still lived in her longhouse. He had moved to Canajoharie. He had taken no woman of his own, although she knew he slipped under the furs with many girls. They all hoped to snare him but none had been successful. And none would be, she knew, until she took another husband and chased her man-son out of her platform. But as long as she needed them, her son Kenonranon and her brother Joseph would be her supporters.

She missed Johnson. To everyone else he had been the diplomat supreme, the manipulator of Indian affairs, the source of peace in the Mohawk Valley and the valleys to the west. As long as he lived the Sons of Liberty had not

113

dared to enter the Mohawk. But now they were there, and Sir John Johnson and Colonel Guy Johnson could not handle them. To her, Johnson had been a sensuous, weak-willed man who had loved her passionately, had been faithful to her more often than not, and whom she, despite all his weaknesses and even because of them, had loved for twenty-eight years. His weakling white sons were now about to destroy everything. But Joseph and Aaron—she was amazed that more and more she used the white man's name for her son—would join with Johnson's sons by Molly, Peter and William, and they would restore all that Johnson had created.

But now the rebels threatened Montreal across the river from this Iroquois castle. Schuyler, the fat, lazy American general, and his army of rebels, New Englanders mostly, enemies of Sir William, now threatened the village of St. Jean on the Richelieu. Once it fell, they would move west on the road to Montreal and Caugnawaga. The Canajoharie Mohawks who harried the white army were led by her brother and her sons.

The door of the house creaked open, and Aaron Brant walked in. Molly rose from her fire to greet him. He dwarfed her in size; he was six feet tall now. With man-hood, his boyish muscles had broadened and hardened. He bent down and hugged her thin, wiry body.

"My son has won a victory at St. Jean. Surely it is not the chilly September night that brings him back to his mother's fire."

Aaron smiled at her. "My mother has the tongue of the bee—but unlike the bee, she stings again and again almost at will. I've returned because the Americans have retreated upriver to Isle aux Noix."

Molly's mouth broke into a smile of triumph.

"But the Canadians under the great giant mouth, Allen, will attempt an attack on Montreal tonight. Joseph has learned of it. We can stop them even with the handful General Carleton has, if you can convince the Caugnawagas to join us. No one in all the longhouses is more respected than you, Mother. They must listen to you."

Molly walked back to the fire. She really wanted to return to her home on the Mohawk River and forget all this. She wanted to be alone with her memories.

Aaron stepped up behind her. She turned toward him.

"Ask the chiefs for a council," she ordered. "We will drive the Americans and their French allies out of the north and we will drive them from the valley of our people. They will not deny my sons their birthright. I would not let Johnson's own white son deny them, and I have no intention of allowing men not fit to kiss the feet of Johnson or his sons do it either."

The nights were very cold in November on Isle d'Orleans, but not yet cold enough to freeze the river. The snows came in great, gray clouds out of the west. The drifts built up against the farmhouses and barns.

Amy sat spinning wool into yarn. The fire warmed the main room of the stone house. Katherine sat opposite Amy, reading. She had benefited from the time she spent with the nuns, but being returned to her own home in the company of her son had made the greatest improvement in her condition.

Louis Joseph had gone to Antoine's farm earlier in the day and had not yet returned. Since his return from his brief stint as a soldier, he had been careful of his mother's feelings and cold and hostile to Amy. A wedge had been driven between them. He resented her interference in his life, and she resented his carelessness with others' feelings and needs. He was always responsible with his chores about the farm, but he could never make responsible decisions. They were always left to her.

She leaned back in her chair and allowed the wheel to slow and finally stop. She stared across at Katherine, who sat smiling as she read. She was rereading *Gulliver's Travels*. God knew how many times she had read it already. But even she, abandoned by her men, alone in the wilderness with two children, even she had achieved some sort of contentment. Amy brushed her hair away from her eyes with her hand, then rubbed her eyes with the backs of her hands. They smarted. The chimney must not be drawing well enough. She would have to get Louis Joseph to clean it.

She was tired, not only of spinning the winter's wool—a task she hated—but of always being left with the responsibility of caring for others. She was tired of her empty bed at night. Surely she was the only unmarried twenty-five-year-old woman on the island. All the girls her age were long married and had children of their own. That was all Antoine's fault. The thought of him brought pangs of remorse. She had received no word from him. She grew angry and began to pump the foot pedal extra hard, and the wheel began to turn at a furious pace.

Katherine looked up from her reading. "Slow down, Amy. We have all winter to go and plenty of wool washed and ready for spinning. Besides, you'll break the pedal at the rate you're going. Stop for a while. Come over here and I'll read to you."

"I don't want to be read to, Mother."

Katherine looked hurt. The look of withdrawal that Amy so feared began to appear on her face. She moved quickly to her mother's side and kissed her cheek.

"It's not the book's fault. It is a good book and I know you love it. It's me."

Katherine looked at her in surprise. "You, dear? What could possibly be wrong with you? You're strong, you're healthy, you have a stout home, food and a brother who cares for his farm and for us."

"He cares for you, Mother. He hasn't forgiven me for dragging him home from the army."

"But you were right in what you did, Amy. Even Louis Joseph must come to see it that way one day."

"I really don't care what he comes to see. It's only Antoine who matters. I want him to see I was right. That I am right now and that I was right ten years ago."

"We've spoken of this before, child, and I told you to give in. You wouldn't listen."

There was a howl from the front yard as Louis Joseph drove the winter sled to a halt before the house. Amy ran to the door while Katherine remained seated. It was not the cry of a happy boy. It was the signal of distress and she froze at the sound of it. Amy threw open the door. She saw Louis Joseph climb down to stand next to another man who had already left the sled. It was Ethan Morin.

"I found him on the road to the farm," Louis Joseph yelled. "He knows where Antoine is. He's been captured at Montreal."

Morin came into the house. He stamped his feet to free them of the packed snow.

"Amy, get Monsieur Morin some tea," said Katherine from her chair.

"Is what Louis Joseph says true?" she asked, ignoring her mother's order.

Morin removed his coat. "Yes. He's in the chateau in Quebec City."

Amy walked over to the fire. She could not let anyone see her reaction. He was alive. Thank God for that. Next, however, he had to be with her. She turned to Morin. "How did it happen?"

"Plain stupidity and bullheadedness. We couldn't accept Schuyler's action. To retreat made no sense at all. All we had to do was to grab what was there for the asking. We fell into a trap. We paid attention to Ethan Allen. Antoine and I volunteered to join him in an attack on Montreal. The people were supposed to greet us with open arms. Allen said it was all arranged. Instead we were greeted by Indians. It seemed as if there were hundreds of them. And what was hardest for Antoine and me to bear, we had to fight the people of the town. The English and French rallied to Carleton and the British regulars. We were beaten by Canadians as well as Indians—after all these years of work.

"When the Indians broke our lines, I knew it was over. I slipped into the river and swam for it, since Allen hadn't brought enough boats for all of us to escape. But Antoine was with Allen himself. The British arrested both of them, after they surrendered. They were officers, but they were traitors also—especially Antoine. Allen has been sent to England for trial, but they'll leave Antoine to rot in the chateau's dungeon. Fine mess we have made of this

117

invasion. There's not an American soldier left in Canada—two months after it was begun."

Amy listened to the story with a growing conviction. When Ethan had finished, she spoke it. "You got Antoine into this useless war, Ethan Morin. He's given up ten years of his life to follow you and your harebrained schemes. I expect you to get him out now."

There was silence in the room for some moments. Ethan looked at her. Maybe she was right. Maybe if he hadn't come to Quebec, the lives of these people would have been happier. He doubted it, but as he looked into Amy's steadfast gaze, he found he had no argument to use against her. If she wanted Antoine Gingras back, he would do all he could to achieve that end.

Ethan sat up for most of the night, staring into the fire. On two occasions he rose and paced the floor of the farmhouse. In the morning he asked Louis Joseph to show him the way to the curé's house in St. Pierre.

Antoine paced the straw-covered floor of his cell. Water trickled down the sides of the stone walls of the basement. He was cold, frightfully cold, and he was lonely. No one had come to tell him what his fate would be. Colonel Allen had been removed from his cell across the hallway days before and had never returned. Rumors had it that he was being shipped to England.

Antoine's only contact with the world outside was a small runt of a sentry who spoke English with a coarse accent. When Antoine spoke to him in French, telling him how cold he was without a blanket and how inedible the food was, the sentry merely shrugged his shoulders.

"Why don't you people learn to talk human rather than frog?"

Antoine didn't understand the insult. But he knew he would get no blanket and would get no better food.

Three days later he came down with chills and a fever. Then the runt became alarmed. A physician was summoned from the town. The doctor ordered blankets and a cot and a dry cell. He received only the blankets.

Time seemed to stand still for him. The cold from the

floor and the water on the wall, which froze into ice every night, seeped into his bones. On the warmer days, the water dripped to the floor, forming puddles and then seeping through the cracks in the stones and escaping the chateau—something Antoine became convinced would never happen to him. He was still feverish, and he could not eat. He felt himself growing weaker and weaker. All was a blur. Day melted into night and then into day again. He lost track of time. He did not know how long he had been there, but he was sure if he did not get out soon he would die.

He thought of his incomplete life. If he died now he would have achieved nothing. Canada was still occupied. Canadiens had done their best to put him where he was now rotting. To hell with them. He had been as foolish as Allen, even more. He had given the cause ten years, while Ethan Allen had given it a bare ten hours. Which one of them was the bigger fool? Amy had been right. He had chosen the cause and Morin over her.

"Morin," he whispered through fever-cracked lips. "And where did you disappear to?"

If he died now, he would never have had the love of the woman he truly worshipped. That was a far greater loss than the loss of his country. He smiled to himself. He had come to that realization too late—too late to do anything about it.

He slipped away into a dream. Yet it was not a dream. He was still in the cell. The little runt leaned over him. His breath smelled of fish. He was trying to force something down Antoine's throat. Antoine struggled against it. It was hot. It warmed his mouth. God, they were torturing him. He tried to move his muscles but nothing would work. He tried to scream, but he heard only a feeble whimper escape his lips. Then he found he could focus his eyes again, and he could feel his limbs return to life. The runt was gone and, as if in answer to his earlier question, he stared into the face of Ethan Morin. But something was wrong. Ethan was wearing black. He, Antoine Gingras, must be dead. Ethan was in mourning. Then he saw Louis Joseph. The boy was still in his work clothes. He had no respect for his friend and teacher. But where was Amy? Couldn't even his death melt the ice maiden? Wouldn't she even attend his funeral? To the very end she was unforgiving. Then he remembered no more.

The simplest part of the plan had been stealing the priest's cassock. Ethan could not be faulted with driving too fast along the muddy streets of St. Pierre. It was not his fault that the curé came to the corner when he did. Had he not left the sled and tried to dry the curé off? Had he not offered to take the curé home and had he not agreed to bring the cassock back the next morning after his friend's mother had cleaned it for the priest?

It didn't fit. But few county priests were expected to dress richly. It was enough for any priest that he owned a cassock. The key to the plan was Governor Carleton's own desire to gain more and more Canadian support. Prisoners of war of Canadian origin could be paroled to the custody of their own curé if they would sign a promise not to take up arms against the King again. Ethan had prepared all sorts of arguments to use with his friend once he gained access to him. All proved unnecessary. Antoine was in no condition to argue when they found him. Neither was he in any condition to sign a parole. Ethan signed it for him and bribed the jailer with what little money he had left from his officer's pay.

Louis Joseph carried Antoine's limp form through the corridors of the chateau, the small and ugly British soldier leading the way and Morin bringing up the rear. At the guard gate they were halted. An officer sat slouched in a chair. His red jacket was thrown over the back and he smoked a pipe.

"Priest," he yelled. "What pile of garbage are you dragging out of here?" He rose from the chair and walked over to Ethan. Morin pretended not to understand English. But he could not ignore the prick of a sword in his back.

The British officer lifted Antoine's head as Louis Joseph also came to a halt. "Ah, Gingras. I'm surprised they let this one go," he said in a very educated French. "I'm told

120

he's important to the rebels around this frozen hellhole. He's a big catch for you, curé."

"And for you English as well. Gingras has signed a parole. That will just about finish the rebel cause in these parts," said Ethan, with more truth than he could have wished for.

Louis Joseph fidgeted, drawing the attention of the officer, who stared at him with pure contempt. "Who is this lout?"

"Just a village boy. He's not all there," said Morin, pointing to his head. "But he has muscles."

Louis Joseph broke into an enormous grin, confirming the curé's judgment to the officer. Then he went to the door and opened it, allowing a blast of arctic air into the guard house.

"Jesus, shut the damn door," the officer yelled at Louis Joseph.

"We'll be on our way then," said Morin, following Louis Joseph to the door and out into the cold night.

They climbed into the rented sled and threw a fur over Antoine's body.

"Get the hell out of here," whispered Ethan, "and don't stop this thing until we get to the boat. We've got to get him to the island quickly."

Amy threw open the door when she saw Louis Joseph and the figure of a curé carrying a third person.

"Hold the door," said the curé.

Amy realized from the soft tone of his voice, that smooth, chilling drawl, that it was no curé, but Ethan Morin, and that the body was that of the barely living Antoine.

Both Morin and Louis Joseph were exhausted. They had crossed the river in Antoine's own boat. The ride from the landing beach to the house had been at breakneck speed over an ice-rutted road.

Antoine was bundled off into Louis Joseph's bed. He had trouble breathing. His lungs were filled with fluid, and he was feverish and clearly in great pain. Every time he coughed, his whole body seemed to go into spasm.

Katherine sat by the fire without moving. It was clear that she was terrified. Amy put stones in the fire. When they were hot, she wrapped them in towels and placed them at Antoine's feet. His teeth chattered with his chill. She piled blanket after blanket on top of him. She got some hot tea down his throat and then sat by his bed and waited.

Louis Joseph sat keeping her company while Ethan tried to engage the staring Katherine in conversation.

Louis Joseph was overflowing with words. "We did it, Amy. Ethan said we could, and it was so bloody easy. Carleton from Montreal has issued a call to all Canadiens to join the cause and for all the misguided ones who took arms against the Crown to lay down their muskets and go home. Ethan walked right into the prison, claimed he had come to pledge the parole for a boy from St. Pierre who was held captive after the governor's call. The stupid jailers seemed awed by the priest. The English know the priests are on their side. They will do nothing to a priest. They handed Antoine over to us just like that," he said, snapping his fingers.

He said more than he had said to her in all the time since he had returned from Montreal with her. She listened to the story without comment. She didn't really care how they had managed to recover Antoine. What mattered was that they had succeeded. She looked down at his frightfully thin face. The emaciation exaggerated his features. His dark eyes were sunken. His cheeks had lost any roundness, and his nose appeared larger and sharper. He was dirty but she dared not wash him, not while he shivered with chill.

Ethan gave up staring back at Katherine and joined the group in the bedroom.

"Louis Joseph, try to talk to your mother. She needs some comforting. You can do that."

After the boy left them, Ethan and Amy sat, quietly listening to Antoine's labored breathing.

"Thank you," said Amy finally. "Thank you for getting him back."

"It was the least I could do for you. You love him, don't you?"

Amy did not respond.

"Maybe now you won't hate me so much and maybe you'll smile more. And don't worry, I'll not lead him off to war any longer."

"Don't tell me you're giving up on Canada," said Amy.

"I don't know why I began. It's not my country. If Canadiens don't want freedom, who am I to force it on them?"

"Don't misunderstand the French of this land, Monsieur Morin. They would like the English to leave them alone and go away from this river and this town. But the English have provided us with some sure benefits. We can't be sure the Americans will do the same. French Canadiens lost everything back in 1759. They'll stand aside now and let you and the English fight it out. When it's over, you'll find the people of Quebec on the winning side."

"And which side is that?"

"Why, the side that wins," answered Amy. "That's the only way French Canadiens will survive here."

"Well, I want to see you and Antoine survive. I don't want it on my conscience any longer that you're apart because I am here. You have him now. His parole is phony, but I'm sure the curé of St. Pierre, the real one, will back it up. It's a coup for him to get Antoine Gingras, the rebel leader of the island, to declare neutrality. And Antoine can't violate his word. Even if he doesn't remember giving it. We'll all tell him he did. He'll be out of it for the duration."

Ethan's words thrilled Amy. It was true. Antoine would be hers at last, if he lived, and she was determined that he would live.

V

1775

Antoine opened his eyes. They darted about the room. He recognized it instantly. On the other side of the bed, Amy sat in a straight-back wooden chair. She slept. He did not remember coming into her house, but he knew he had her to thank for being alive.

There was a thick frost on the inside of the windows. The sun struck it and sent the colors of the rainbow onto the opposite wall. The sunlight seemed incredibly bright as it struck the snow, which had drifted about the base of the stone house. He felt so weak he could barely speak. But he called to her. Her eyes fluttered open. She looked at him with concern. He smiled up at her and she smiled back.

"I'll never leave you again, Amy," he whispered.

"I know you won't," she responded, "because I'll never let you."

Antoine remained in bed for ten days more, but his strength returned quickly. Fifteen days after arriving at the Stiegler house half dead, he drove Amy in the sleigh to his own home.

He threw open the door to the house. It smelled musty and unlived in.

"How it's changed," he said.

"You sound as if you've been gone for years instead of weeks."

"No, I mean over the years, how it's changed. You weren't here the first time Karl came. The fête we had was magnificent. My father, brothers, the neighbors, Millards, my sisters making eyes at Karl, it was all so fine. And then when you and your mother arrived we had another fête, with music and food. The joy of it all still lingers here for me. But only in memory. It is now a sad, tired old house."

"Let's get a fire started," said Amy. "Once you get a warm fire you'll forget those old days and start to think of the future."

He turned and looked at her as she stooped to throw some dried tinder into the fireplace. He struck a flint, and soon little flames caught the straw and then the kindling, sending shadows across the darkened room.

"Let's get some light in here as well," she said, going from window to window and throwing open the shutters.

He stepped behind her and put his hand over her eyes.

"Antoine, stop your nonsense."

"It's a house of ghosts. You're seven and I'm sixteen and I call you 'Ugly' in English."

"And you inform me that my mother is living in sin."

"And my papa beats my fanny for it."

"Poor little thing."

He smiled at her, not knowing exactly what she referred to. "Now you're fifteen and I'm twenty-four. We're in love and I'm trying like blazes to get you into bed with me."

"And I was trying just as hard to keep out."

He lowered his hands from her eyes to her breasts. She gave a little gasp.

"Now you're twenty-five and I'm thirty-four. Don't you think it's time?"

She turned around and looked into his eyes. She said nothing, but merely nodded her head.

He picked her up in his arms and carried her into his mother and father's old bedroom and laid her down on the bed.

She was blushing now. He undid the buttons on the back of her dress and slipped it off her shoulders. He slipped the top of her chemise down as well. He bent down and kissed her breasts until her nipples were taut and swollen with pleasure. He slipped both the dress and the undergarment off her body and she lay on the bed totally naked. He kissed her eyes and her nose. When his

125

lips touched hers she opened her mouth hungrily. Her body was alive with passion, pent up for all of these years, waiting for this moment.

The Americans, led by Colonel Benedict Arnold, came out of the wilderness before Quebec early in the month of December. In the beginning they had numbered almost two thousand. They left Cambridge in Massachusetts, traveled up the Kennebeck River in Maine, across the height of land and down the Chaudière River to the St. Lawrence. By the time they reached Quebec, death and desertion left only six hundred ravenous, weary and almost helpless men. They poured out of the woods, desperately needing the help of the Canadians to survive. No one in the great fortress should have felt threatened by them, except there were almost no soldiers in Quebec to defend it. They were all with General Carleton, trying to defend Montreal against a renewed American thrust led by Generals Schuyler and Montgomery.

Then word came that the defenses upriver had collapsed. Montgomery had taken the field command from Schuyler, and the American army had returned to the Richelieu. Chambly, St. Jean and Montreal fell in rapid succession. Carleton escaped with a rather small force and sailed downriver to secure his capital, the great walled fortress town of Quebec.

"Antoine can keep my room," Louis Joseph said to his sister as they rode back from a pre-dawn visit to Antoine's farm. "I assume you two are planning to be married. Mother won't complain, but it's getting rough on me coming over to Antoine's farm and then traveling back home in this cold. I think I should either stay on at the Gingras farm or you and Antoine should take it over."

Amy thought for a moment. She pulled her fur about her more closely. The icy wind buffeted them as they sat in the sleigh. The horse put down its great head and trudged forward into the cold.

"I'm not sure that we can take over his farm. Not unless

you get yourself a wife, little brother. Someone has to look after you, Antoine and Mother, and there is only one of me."

"I can take care of Mother," said Louis Joseph, angered that any aspect of his competence should be questioned by his older sister.

The sleigh had reached the knoll above their home. The horse needed no urging to begin the trot down the hill. The house, light pouring from its windows and smoke rising from the chimney against a rosy dawn sky, seemed to call to the horse and the riders.

Amy jumped down from her seat as they pulled up to the front door. Louis Joseph clucked to the horse and continued on to the barn. Amy threw open the door and brought in a blast of cold air with her.

"My God, it feels good to get inside," she said as she walked over to the glowing warmth of the hearth.

Katherine was removing the tea kettle from the fire.

"We have a visitor," she said.

Amy froze in place. She's back at it again, she thought. What could have triggered it this time?

"Hello, Amy." It was the soft voice of Ethan Morin.

Amy turned. She looked so relieved that Morin misinterpreted it.

"If I'd known you were so anxious to see me, I'd have come a lot sooner."

"What's this?" said Antoine, coming from the bedroom. "Should I be jealous?"

"Oh, shut up, both of you," said Amy, laughing. She went to Katherine and hugged her. Katherine smiled but looked at her quizzically. Amy did not normally give affection freely.

When Louis Joseph returned from the barn, he greeted Morin warmly, throwing his arms around him. Then the five of them sat down to a breakfast of fresh eggs and yesterday's bread. Once they were all seated, Katherine spoke to Morin.

"What brings you back to us, Monsieur?"

"The American army. They are at Point Levis now. They await boats to cross. I've got to get some for them."

127

Amy looked at Antoine and her stomach sank. The look of pain in his eyes was wrenching.

"Are you looking for recruits?" asked Louis Joseph.

"Not here," said Morin, looking directly at Amy.

Again, she felt grateful to him. Tears started to form in her eyes.

"The men of this family have done their duty," continued Morin.

"Some more than others," said Louis Joseph in disgust.

Katherine patted her son's arm. "You've done your duty here," she said. Turning to Morin, she asked, "Is it true that the Americans turned cannibal rather than starve? That's what the curé said about them. He said they are horrible people."

"Mother," said Amy in surprise. "You're an American!"

"Oh, dear," laughed Katherine. "That's true. Sometimes I forget. I've been here twenty years. Almost as long as I lived there."

"I think someone is shaving a few years off," teased Louis Joseph.

"Not at all," said Katherine. "I'm forty-seven and proud of it."

"Well," laughed Morin. "There are no cannibals in the lot." He continued to chuckle. "Although one poor dog ended up in the stew pot along with leather, candle tallow and anything at all that might give even a modicum of nourishment."

After breakfast, Morin rose to leave. "I must be on my way, looking for boats."

"Take mine," said Antoine. "Louis Joseph, you show him where it is. Frankly, Ethan, I think the Americans should wait until the river freezes. A few more days of this cold and you'll have a solid bridge across the river. Then you won't need those boats."

"I don't think we have a few days to spare. You know how Carleton is able to stir the Canadiens. And Montgomery is on his way overland from Montreal. We must meet with him at Quebec, and we must attack. We have no time for a siege."

Antoine looked puzzled.

128

"It's the enlistments; they expire the first of the year. This whole bloody army is planning to go home on New Year's Day. And damn it, they'll do it."

The days continued cold but the snows held off. The Americans crossed the river and were now camped above Quebec on the St. Charles. The British remained locked behind their walls. They had few defenders, but the Americans had no siege guns and no time.

On Isle d'Orleans, it was as if the Americans and the British and the war did not exist. People whiled away the idle winter days with chores. Christmas was approaching and Katherine insisted that Amy help her prepare a great meal for all of the family. Amy protested that Antoine's sisters and their families did not live on the island. They would not come and the neighbors would be celebrating with their own families. There would only be four of them.

"No matter," insisted Katherine. "There is Mr. Morin. We'll invite him, and now that Louis Joseph lives at Antoine's, we'll have family coming for the celebration."

There was no dissuading her. They spent days making meat pies and preparing smoked hams. Christmas cookies of all descriptions were baked, along with sweet rolls and fresh breads. Even Antoine, almost fully recovered now, was drafted to knead the dough and to beat eggs and wash out cooking pans and pots so they could be reemployed.

Christmas Eve arrived, and Katherine waited by the window for her guests. The sun began to set almost at midafternoon at this time of year, its rays glistening on a crystal wall of ice and snow. The darkness arrived quickly, enveloping the brilliant world and reducing it to light and dark grey forms. Still no one came.

Amy went to the fire to check that the flames were ready to heat the food that had been so painstakingly prepared.

"Where can they be?" asked Katherine, half to herself.

Amy went to her bedroom. Antoine lay sleeping on the bed. He still needed more rest than he used to, but otherwise he had been restored to health.

She shook his shoulders gently to awaken him. He sat bolt upright in his bed, frightened.

"What's wrong?" he asked, clearly still half-asleep.

"It's my stupid brother. He was supposed to have been here two hours ago. Mother is nearly frantic. I hate to ask you, but could you go to your farm and return the dumb ox? He was supposed to get word to Ethan as well, so the two of them may be there. They can't have forgotten, but something may have held them up."

"Anything you ask, my love," he said, smiling and tweaking her cheek. She placed her hand on the bulge in his groin.

"You must have been having a good dream," she joked.

"Not as good as the reality. I hope tonight after our meal to drift off into the world of reality."

Antoine bundled himself in Louis Joseph's raccoon coat. It was too big for him. The young man just continued to grow taller and more muscular. The horse was reluctant to leave the barn, and it took some time to hitch up the sleigh.

He climbed into the seat. He waved at Amy and Katherine, who stood at the windows watching. "Christ," he mumbled, "it's cold. Seventeen or not, I'll whip that boy's ass for this trip."

The horse had some difficulty getting through the heavy snow that had drifted across the well-used road. Antoine had to get out and lead it through the drifts three times.

He arrived at the edge of his farm. The road was now clear. He came to the wooden gate that led to the farmyard. It was open. He turned the horse onto the trail. Now he was worried. He could hear his cow lowing. She sounded as if she needed both fodder and milking. There were no lights coming from the farmhouse and no smoke coming from the chimney. He tied the sleigh reins to the verandah post and entered the house.

It was pitch black, deserted. He went from room to room. No one was there. The bed was unmade, but Louis Joseph never made a bed. God knew when he had last slept here. He went to the hearth and felt the ashes with his hands. They were cold. He poked around in the charcoal pieces and found one at the bottom that still felt warm. It was possible that the boy had spent last night at the house.

He went back to the barn and checked the cow. It was clear she had been milked that morning.

Now Antoine was at a loss. He felt he had to go back to Amy and Katherine with some news. If Louis Joseph were hurt and lying out in the dark and cold, he would die if Antoine did not look for him.

He went back into the house and lit a fire. At least Louis Joseph, if he were aware that help was nearby, could call out.

The fire in the hearth cast eerie shadows about the room. Antoine stood up and saw a note lying on the great wooden family table. He walked over and picked it up. In Louis Joseph's primitive French spelling, he announced to his family he had gone off to fight for the cause of Canada against the British. He had gone looking for Morin. He was sure that Ethan would find a place for him.

Antoine sat down on the long bench by the table. He held his head in his hands. How could he tell Amy and Katherine? Katherine would be devastated again and Amy would surely blame him. Not so much for his present attitude, but for his attitudes in the past.

He would let the fire burn itself out. He would hitch the cow to the rear of the sleigh and bring her home. He realized that he now thought of the Stiegler farm as home. Home to him was where Amy was.

He left enough fodder in the barn to last the other animals for several days. He knew he would go after Louis Joseph, and there was no one else to care for them. But only the cow would need daily attention.

Katherine looked straight at Antoine when he told her the news.

"Bring him back" was all she said. Then she turned back to the fire and continued to make ready their meal.

Antoine looked at Amy. He could see anger in her eyes, but she was not angry with him. He had miscalculated her reaction. Her anger was directed at her absent brother.

"He's a boy," Antoine said in excuse.

"Well, he's chosen a man's trade. Let him have it. I'm tired of tracking him down and pulling him out of danger. I've spent my life doing it—and not for his sake but for hers," she said, pointing toward her mother.

Katherine turned to face Amy. "He's your brother and he's my baby and I want him back safely."

"Mother, let him be. Maybe he'll grow up and become a man, instead of playing at it."

Katherine began to moan.

Antoine seized Amy's arms. "You don't believe a word you're saying. It violates everything you always said to me. You don't believe that fighting makes a man. You believe it destroys him and those women and children who love him. Your mother is being destroyed before your eyes. Look at her."

"I don't care," Amy shouted. "It's you she wants to send after him. You're still sick. I won't have you go. I won't lose you again."

"I'm going to find your brother, not to fight a war."

"Don't go, Antoine," Amy pleaded.

He looked at her with a sadness in his eyes.

"I have no choice."

"Yes, you do. Let him be." She was weeping now. He took her into his arms and patted her soothingly on the back.

Katherine moved about the fire, preparing a travel pack of food for him. He would be gone for some days; she knew that for certain.

Antoine unhitched the sleigh and rode the horse bareback to the village of St. Pierre. The channel had frozen, and he was able to ride the horse across the river. He spent Christmas night in the village of Beauport, where his sister lived with her husband and two daughters. It was good to be with family on Christmas, even if his visit had been unexpected.

He left his sister's home on St. Stephen's Day. Allowing the old horse to pick its own way, he followed the shore road to the city. He was tired and didn't feel up to any exertion. He had just barely recovered from pneumonia, and he had no intention of rushing. He did not know where he would spend this night. Quebec was closed to the outside world. The Americans were camped on the Plains of Abraham and at the village of St. Roche across the St. Charles River on the Quebec side.

The Beauport road ran right to the edge of the St. Charles. The river was frozen, but the weather had turned warmer. He was worried about a thaw, but he had to get across. In the last war there had been a military bridge across the river at this spot. But it was gone now. He remembered when Karl Stiegler had sent him, a sixteen-year-old, across the bridge with a meaningless message to get him out of the way of an attack by the Scottish Highlanders—an attack that had cost the lives of his two elder brothers and then Stiegler himself.

He looked around anxiously. "The place is jinxed," he said aloud. The horse picked up its ears at the sound of his voice and stepped out on the ice.

Antoine guided the mount carefully. The ice groaned under the weight of the man and the horse. An occasional cracking sound frightened Antoine. He could feel a trickle of sweat run down his side.

The snow had drifted against jetties of ice, forced upward by the pressure of the river currents of the St. Charles and the St. Lawrence meeting. The route was not a straight one. Finally, the horse put its foot on the shore. Antoine whistled with a sigh of relief. Even the horse seemed to relax and shook its mane.

The road for St. Roche turned to the left, and Antoine took it. There were some military wagons on the road, but no one seemed disturbed by a single rider covered in fur from head to toe.

He arrived at St. Roche and stopped at the small village store. Soldiers in the vicinity were all New Englanders. He entered the shop. The room was filled with the smells of fresh-ground coffee, tobacco and cheese. There was a fire in the hearth. The storekeeper was about to close for the day.

"May I help you, Monsieur?" he said to Antoine. "We

133

are about to close but if your needs are simple, I would be pleased to serve you."

"The company of Canadiens—where do they camp?"

"That's a military question, Monsieur; I am a shopkeeper. I mind the store and I mind my business."

"And you sell goods to both sides," said Antoine, smiling.

"A man must feed his family," said the shopkeeper defensively.

"That attitude will keep us forever under the British yoke," replied Antoine, his demeanor changing to one of disgust.

The shopkeeper became nervous. "I'm closing, Monsieur. You must leave."

"Not until you tell me where the Canadien contingent can be found."

"Which one do you seek, Monsieur? The one that fights for the Americans or the one that fights for the British?"

"You make debater's points, shopkeeper. You must have attended the Jesuit college. But I'll fool you. I can respect both groups. They have the courage of their convictions. It is your kind—the kind that plays both sides and will come rushing to the cause of the obvious winner—it is your kind I despise."

"As I said earlier, I have a business to run."

"Tell me where I find the Canadiens in the American camp or I'll break your head."

The shopkeeper grew nervous again. "No need to threaten me. It is said that they camp on the plains above the city."

Antoine turned and walked out of the store. He was too late to make it that day to the camp on the Plains of Abraham. He would have to find lodging in the town.

The next day Antoine found the Canadian camp. Some of his compatriots from the St. Jean campaign were in the camp and greeted him warmly. Most thought he had returned to fight. But none complained when he told them he was merely searching for his betrothed's brother. None admitted to having seen Louis Joseph.

Antoine knew they were lying. The boy had probably warned them that someone would come after him.

"Where's Morin?" Antoine asked next.

"Now, there's something I can help you with," said a former fisherman from the Gaspé. "He's on General Montgomery's staff. Acts as liaison with the French-speaking troops."

"Where do I find Montgomery's headquarters?"

"Arnold and Montgomery are camped on the plains, Gingras. I'll lead you there."

Antoine found Ethan in Colonel Arnold's hut. Morin welcomed him warmly, clasping him in his arms.

"Antoine, I must introduce you to Colonel Benedict Arnold."

"It is a pleasure to meet you, Colonel," said Antoine in French, nodding his head.

Arnold rose from his camp desk and came around in front of it.

"My French, sir, is barely passable in a bordello in Cape François in the Indies, where I could use a good deal of sign language. I assume you greet me. Greetings back," he said, shaking hands with Antoine.

"Morin, translate for us."

"I am amazed, Colonel," said Antoine, "by your extraordinary accomplishment."

Morin translated.

Arnold looked first at him and then at his shoes.

"Good God, man, you mean the trek up the Kennebeck," said Arnold. "Morin is an idiot. He translated it that you were amazed by my feet, f-e-e-t, and you meant f-e-a-t. I'm an accomplished dancer and acrobat, you know."

"And comedian," said Morin, smiling.

"Enough teasing. Have you come to see me or Captain Morin, sir?"

"He wants me, Colonel," answered Ethan.

"Well, I've plenty to do. Be off with you both. Pleasure to meet you, Gingras."

"He's a strange man," said Antoine as they stepped outside.

"Brilliant soldier—but a moody man. You would never know it to listen to him go on, but he is vain, conceited, ambitious and too clever for his own good. But he is a helluva soldier. And he brought some good troops through the wilderness with him. Morgan's riflemen from Virginia, they're the best there is. But you didn't come all this way to discover my opinion of Benedict Arnold or Virginia riflemen." He looked at Antoine strangely. "You haven't changed your mind, have you?"

"No," said Antoine, "I'm looking for Louis Joseph. He's run away from home again. He left word that he was joining up with you."

"Honestly, Antoine, he has not come to me. I'd have sent him home."

"I knew that, but he is here. The men of my old company are covering for him. They've hidden him."

"Well, they can't hide him for long. There are fewer than a thousand of them here. You just keep looking."

Ethan was right. Three days later, Antoine caught sight of Louis Joseph sharing a meal with his mess partners.

Antoine walked up to Louis Joseph and sat down in the snow beside him. Louis Joseph glanced at him nervously. His blond head was wet with the heavy flakes.

"You want something to eat?" the boy asked him.

"I want you to come home with me. You've just about done your mother in."

"It's too late. I've enlisted."

"The American enlistments are up tomorrow. This army will just fade away with the new year."

"No, it won't. We'll spend New Year's Day in the wine cellar of the chateau." He laughed and looked at his mess mates for confirmation of his bravado.

"We just got word. We attack tonight," one of them said.

"You're crazy," said Antoine.

"Not me," Louis Joseph replied. "Maybe General Montgomery and Colonel Arnold are. I just take orders. I'm a private."

"A night attack in a snowstorm? It's madness."

"Mad enough that it might work," said the fisherman who had denied any knowledge of Louis Joseph a few days before.

The boy finished his meal of salt pork and biscuit. Then

he rose to his feet. He belched loudly, something he could never have gotten away with in Katherine Schuyler's home. He stretched.

"Time for some sleep before we take off," he said and crawled into the hut to the right. Within minutes he was snoring.

He is totally oblivious to the danger he faces, thought Antoine. He's a child. His mother is right. He may survive this night, but he'll have a far better chance with me at his side. I can't let the boy face the hell of war alone. Antoine took off his coat and crawled into the hut with Louis Joseph.

"Move over, stoopnagel, I'm coming in, too." He crowded next to the large frame of the boy and pulled the fur coat in after him, covering both of them with it.

Louis Joseph laughed. "Where did you pick up that expression? My mother used to call me that all the time. I don't think it is a compliment."

"You're right. It's no compliment and it is accurate."

But Louis Joseph had already fallen back to sleep.

When the dark had fallen, the officers rousted the men out of their huts and into ranks for the march. The snow was now blinding, hurled by winds that drowned out the shouted commands of the officers. Antoine got into line ahead of Louis Joseph. He had no musket but he had a knife and a tomahawk. Muskets would probably be of little use on a night like this, anyway. It would be impossible to keep the powder dry. Some of the men opened their shirts and placed their guns next to their bodies.

They marched down the sloping road that ran through the woods of the Cote St. Genevieve, where Antoine's brothers had died sixteen years before. Then they trudged along the snow-blocked road to St. Roche. Antoine wished he still had his horse, but he had given it to Ethan for safekeeping. He was already tired, and they still had a long way to go.

Louis Joseph moved ahead with the power and speed of the young. Antoine could not keep up with him. Yet he had to. That was the reason he was there. Since he could not bring Louis Joseph back to Katherine and Amy immediately, he had to protect him until he could.

The wind howled and the snow blew into his face. He peered ahead. The boy was still in view. He pulled his coat about him and took off his gloves and tied tighter the string holding the front of the coat together. He was glad to get the woolen mittens back on. His hands were wet and cold. The wind was warming up, and the snow was wet and heavy, not the dry, biting pellets of the midwinter Quebec blizzard.

They continued trudging past the turnoff to St. Roche. Now they approached the fortress by the Palais Gate.

Word had passed back through the ranks that Colonel Arnold was in the van. The men trusted him. If anyone could get them inside Quebec, it was Arnold.

They passed the Palais Gate unnoticed. And now they walked single file along the St. Charles shoals where that river joined the St. Lawrence. The shore was rocky and the path difficult to follow. Some of the men ventured out onto the shoals' ice, on which the wind-blown snow was piling in great drifts.

Antoine stopped dead in his tracks. He heard it off in the distance—the sound of gunfire. The fisherman who followed him crashed into him.

"Shit, friend, warn me if you're going to drop anchor."

"Listen," said Antoine.

Once again the thunder of cannon came from off in the distance.

"That will be Montgomery's column. They're attacking the 'pot ash' gate. So much for surprise attack."

Antoine hurried to catch up with Louis Joseph, who had disappeared into the blinding snow ahead of them. He let out a sigh of relief when he saw the boy's broad back and shoulders in front of him. They were now beneath the ramparts of the town, treading the narrow path between the cliffs and the river. Antoine knew Quebec well enough to know what Arnold's plan was. They would stay on this path until they came to the flat land along the river, on which had been built the Lower Town of Quebec. Once inside the Lower Town, they would have to fight their way up the streets and steps into the walled city above. It was desperate, but it was the only way.

There was the crack of a musket from above and a shout up ahead. Suddenly the world above them seemed alive with musket fire. Around him Antoine could hear the thud of musket balls pounding into the snow and striking the ice beneath.

Louis Joseph fell to the ground in front of him. Antoine dived on top of him, yelling in his ear, "Are you all right?" He looked into the dazed eyes beneath his face. The boy nodded. "Then get on your feet and keep moving forward. We have to get into the Lower Town."

The houses lining the shore of the flat part of the town acted as forts. But the street between them was their weakness. As the soldiers approached, a cry of distress went up from the ranks as they saw Colonel Arnold, helped by two officers, moving backward along the path. Blood was pouring from his leg and filling his boot.

"Keep moving forward, men," he shouted. "Dan Morgan's in charge. You can trust him. Take that town and Canada belongs to you."

The soldiers cheered him and all pressed forward.

The street between the houses was barricaded. There was a volley of fire from the barricades. The fisherman behind Antoine screamed and fell face forward, turning the grey snow of the night a darker shade.

Louis Joseph started to run forward. Antoine joined him. He heard a strange sound in his head and then realized he was shouting—no words—just noise.

The defenders of the barricades were not prepared for so large an assault force. They retreated. The Virginia Riflemen were the first to climb up and over into the town of Quebec. The Canadians followed behind.

"What do we do next?" shouted Louis Joseph. As if to answer his question, the giant form of Daniel Morgan loomed in front of them.

"That street," he shouted. "That leads to the Upper Town. We go up there."

The men turned to where he pointed. Some of the riflemen and some of the Canadians started to move forward. The street, like all of the streets of the Lower Town of Quebec, was steep and narrow. When they rounded the first twist, a second barricade loomed into view. It was massive, piled high with junk to the height of the second storeys of the houses on either side.

The men behind the barricade opened fire on the troops as they crowded into the street. Soldiers began to fall all about Antoine. He pulled at Louis Joseph. The two of them ducked into a narrow doorway. Fire from the barricade began again, this time with a devastating round of grape shot from a small swivel cannon atop the junk heap. Suddenly the windows on the second storey of the houses above them opened up with sniper fire. The houses were filled with British troops.

Morgan seemed untouchable. He stood in the middle of the street and raged. His riflemen, carrying what seemed like unusable long weapons, took their cue from him. Soon they began to take a deadly accurate aim on the snipers and the defenders of the barricade. Then Morgan shouted to his men to rush the barricade. The Virginians went dashing forward. Louis Joseph hung back. But Antoine was now caught up in the attack. His heart pounding in his chest, he joined the Virginians' rush. He heard Louis Joseph shout behind him and then heard the crunching of the boy's feet in the snow as he came up from the rear.

The Virginians began to pile furniture from the lower floors of the houses to make a platform to reach the top of the barricade. The Canadian troops to the rear had to halt their fire. Most of their muskets had failed to fire because of wet firing pans anyway.

Antoine reached the base of the barricade and jumped on an abandoned chest of drawers and started to pull himself up. He felt Louis Joseph's shoulder under his rump and felt himself lifted upward. He grabbed for the back of a chair that stuck out from the pile. He hauled himself upward. Above him he saw a British soldier looking down, no more than two feet away. He felt the pain of the bayonet as it thrust into his shoulder, piercing the heavy skin of his raccoon coat. He lost his grip and fell back

140

down on Louis Joseph, pulling both of them to the ground. Antoine was knocked senseless for the moment. Then he felt himself being hauled back toward the relative safety of the doorway. By the time he reached it, Antoine had regained his feet. He opened his coat and peered at his shoulder.

"Bad?" asked Louis Joseph.

"I don't think so. I won't be moving it much for a little while, but the coat took something from the thrust. It didn't go all the way through."

The street was littered with bodies. Morgan gave the order to his men to enter the houses for cover. Then began a bloody battle from floor to floor. The British kept control of many of the second floors while their opponents occupied the ground floors.

The house Antoine and Louis Joseph entered was empty of British troops. Either they had never been there or they had already fled.

Antoine took off his coat. His blood had soaked his shirt. Louis Joseph had removed his coat and shirt. He tied his shirt around Antoine's shoulders to stop the bleeding. He looked at the older man.

"I'm sorry I got you into this," he said softly.

"Don't make apologies, my boy. They don't do very much good. From now on, just think about the consequences of your decisions beforehand and you won't be forced to make many apologies. Promise?" He smiled at the boy.

"I promise," said Louis Joseph, smiling back.

"Now, let's see how we can get ourselves out of this mess. The attack has failed, in case you weren't aware of it. It didn't have much chance to begin with. But now we're in a trap. I think we had better look to the rear to get out of it."

"But isn't that desertion if Morgan doesn't order it?"

"You're absolutely right, my lad. It certainly is desertion. But I've already been paroled once. There's no way I'm going to get myself captured, which, I fear, is the sure fate of this army if Morgan doesn't retreat right now."

Antoine opened the door of the house. He could see

forms in the shadows of the buildings moving back toward the first barricade. He turned around to Louis Joseph.

"I think our countrymen have come to much the same conclusion as you and I. Get your coat on. Let's go."

They crept along the façade of the house to keep out of the line of fire. Down the street they came to the now all-but-removed first barricade. They were joined by several other Canadians.

"Montgomery's attack on the 'pot ash' gate has failed. Word is that Montgomery himself is dead. Carleton knows he has us trapped. He's sending troops along the riverfront path to trap us and cut us off from St. Roche."

On hearing this news, some of the Canadians fell back into the Lower Town. Some had relatives in Quebec. They would hide with them. Others discounted the news as rumor and started along the path back in the direction they had come. They would brave the fire from the ramparts above.

Antoine decided on neither course. He could not afford capture. He doubted he'd survive it. The snow had stopped and dawn would be upon them before they could pass the British fire.

He grabbed Louis Joseph's arm. "It's out on the ice for us," he said. "That way leads home."

The two men stepped out onto the ice of the St. Charles shoals. They had to move around even higher drifts and even taller projections of ice than Antoine had faced when he was mounted on his horse days before.

They walked and slid for almost fifteen minutes. From the Lower Town and from along the riverfront, they could hear the sounds and see the flash of musket shots. All about them the cracking sounds of ice under pressure rang louder than the muskets of the town.

Suddenly Antoine felt the ice give beneath him. He was plunged into the freezing waters of the river.

Louis Joseph shouted in dismay. The ice about him began to crack. He fell on his face in fear.

Antoine called out to him. "Louis Joseph, here, over here. Reach for me with your hand."

Louis Joseph crawled to the edge of the broken ice and

stretched his arm out. Antoine reached for the hand, but he had used his wounded arm to make the attempt. He screamed in agony.

"The coat," he yelled. "It's too heavy. It's dragging me under."

The ice about Louis Joseph's body began to give way. He scrambled backward in terror. He covered his ears with his hands. Antoine called to him, but he couldn't reach him. He heard one more feeble call of his name and then silence.

Louis Joseph was sobbing, both in terror and in shock. He crept on all fours along the ice and headed for the shore. He wished he had died back at the attack. He loathed himself. Terror-stricken, he heard the same cracking noise that had brought death to Antoine. Finally the shore loomed up in front of him. He crawled over the rocks sticking out of the ice and lay prone on the snow. He vomited, retching everything he had in his stomach until nothing more would come up.

Ethan found him there the next morning, sitting on the shore, staring out over the ice toward Beauport. "Where's Antoine?" he asked.

"Gone," said Louis Joseph, pointing with his hand out toward the ice. "I never learned how to swim. God, he tried to teach me but I never learned." Then he started to weep again.

It was Ethan Morin who brought the news of Antoine's death to Amy. He left Louis Joseph at Antoine's house and rode the horse back down the road from which Antoine had begun his journey.

Amy saw him come over the knoll. From the first sight of him she knew his news. She had known from the first time she met him that Ethan Morin would bring her bad news. She walked from the window to her room and sat on the bed.

Katherine opened the door. Amy heard some mumbled talk and then a crash as Katherine dropped the earthenware pitcher she had been holding. She heard Ethan help her mother into her chair and then she heard his steps approach the door of the room—their room. He opened the door.

Amy looked away from him as he entered.

"He's dead, isn't he?" she whispered. When she got no response, she looked at him. The expression on his face told her that even the faintest hope had been misplaced. Her world fell apart about her. She began to scream. All the hate that was in her rushed to the surface like blood to the skin. She ranted against her mother, her brother, Morin.

Ethan tried to hold her and calm her, but her rage gave her extraordinary strength. She broke away from his grasp and raced past him out into the main room of the house. There, she picked up the first thing that came into her hand and hurled it against the wall. She hurled plates, pewterware, anything she could grab. When nothing more was within her reach, she fell to the floor sobbing. All the while, her mother sat in her chair, not moving.

That night Amy lay in her bed alone, staring at nothing. She had made up her mind to leave. She could not live in the same house with her brother. Never again. Let him look after the invalid mother. She was tired of that, too. She had to flee from this place of death, from the killing and war. She would rise now and take some few things with her. She knew where she was going. Back to where she had been happy—back to Fort Vaughan, back to the Mohawk River and her girlhood home.

VI

1776–77

Matthew liked to watch the river traffic from his second-storey bedroom. Despite the ice floes, more and more *bateaux* and canoes traveled north and south, passing Saratoga to the great bend in the Hudson River to Fort Edward. He had arranged his bed so that he could lie in it and still see the river and its traffic.

The army had lost its chance to seize Quebec, but it continued to surround the fortress like Wolfe's army of old. American troops still occupied all the other major Quebec towns—Montreal, St. Jean, Sorel and Three Rivers. And this army of occupation had to be fed and supplied.

He had come to this place in the fall and had finally found peace. The time of terror still plagued his sleep, but in his waking hours it had begun to recede from his memory. But he would never forget the sight of his Uncle Vaughan, lying on the floor of the fortress, his back and mouth spewing blood. Even now he shook his head to clear it of that terrible vision.

He had retreated with the American army off Bunker's Hill toward Charlestown Neck. When the low tide forced the British gunboats away from their position commanding the narrow stretch of land, he crossed it and made it safely to the base camp at Cambridge. It was only then Matthew began to feel the loss of his uncle and the separation from his father. He did not know where to turn. He had to get back to Boston, but until then he had to eat and find a place to sleep.

He went to the camp area occupied by the Massachu-

145

setts militia, by far the biggest contingent in the army. They were his militia. But there were not many Boston or Charlestown men in the camp. Besides, there seemed so little order, he did not know where to turn. Tents were set up anywhere the campers decided to place them. Garbage was thrown outside and littered the area. Whenever a soldier had to relieve himself, he merely stepped outside his immediate vicinity, dropped his breeches and did his business. There was little or no concern for sanitation, and disease, the greatest foe of any army encampment, was surely stalking this victim with glee. A professional soldier's touch was desperately needed by this army of amateurs.

But Matthew was oblivious to all of this. All he knew was that he desperately wanted to see a familiar face. It had been almost twenty-four hours since he had last eaten. He smelled the stew brewing in the mess pot down the street that ran through the tents of the Massachusetts militia. He walked to the smell, timidly avoiding other campfires, about which sat unshaved, smelly and surly farmers from all over the Bay colony.

The mess pot was attended by a thin, grey-haired, fussy-looking man. As Matthew walked up to him, two large, burly men crawled out of their tent and sat themselves down before the pot.

"Asa, you dumb pisspot, ain't that food ready yet?"

The man called Asa looked over his shoulder. Fear crossed his ferretlike features.

"It's done now, Corporal, any time you're ready to eat."

"Goddamnit, it's about time."

Matthew was frightened by the looks of these men, but he was driven even more by his need to eat. He stepped in front of the man called Asa.

"Sir, can you help me?" he asked.

"Get lost, scum," said the cook.

"I'm hungry. Can you spare me some food?"

Asa picked up the ladle and, holding it as a weapon, got to his feet and moved toward Matthew.

The boy scurried out of his way. Asa did not pursue

him. Instead he went back to his stew and began to ladle it out into mess dishes.

The two large men accepted the food. One touched it with his fingers to test if it could be eaten in that manner without burning him. The other pulled a large spoon from his pack inside the tent and began to eat.

"Too bad we missed the fight over in Charlestown," said the larger man. "It would have gone over well in the pubs in Boston if we could proclaim you to be a hero of the battle of Bunker Hill, Colonel MacIntosh."

"Shit, you can do that anyway. Who the hell will know who was there and who wasn't?"

Matthew stayed within hearing distance of the men as they talked. He hoped they would grow tired, fall off to sleep and leave the pot unattended.

MacIntosh's shirt and chin were covered with droppings from his spoon. He wiped his chin on his sleeve. He looked up and caught sight of Matthew, who ducked behind a tent and out of sight.

MacIntosh elbowed the large man next to him. "There's a little kid over there who has his eyes on this stewpot. Let's get him in close and teach the little shit a lesson."

The other man smiled and nodded.

"Asa," MacIntosh whispered, "leave the pot alone and get into the tent."

MacIntosh rose from his spot on the ground and walked nonchalantly away from the campfire. His associate moved in the opposite direction to cut off any avenue of escape down the street.

Matthew saw the pot unattended. He moved toward it. He checked to his right and his left. No one was watching him. He picked up the abandoned ladle and dipped it into the stew and pulled it back up, filled to the brim with meat and gravy. Then, out of the corner of his eye, he saw a hand moving out of the tent and inching gradually toward his leg. He dropped the ladle and turned to run, bumping straight into the viselike grip of John MacIntosh, the Boston street fighter.

"You little snot-nosed thief," MacIntosh shouted into his

face. "We caught you dead to rights with your goddamned hand right in the pot. Didn't your daddy ever teach you it's wrong to steal? Asa, you and me and Corporal Dodd ought to have a Court Martial right here and now. Asa, how do you find this culprit?"

Asa's head was sticking out of the tent. He was grinning from ear to ear. "He's guilty as sin."

The corporal had rejoined the group. The huge man turned his thumbs down without saying a word.

"It's unanimous then—guilty. I sentence you to one spanking."

Other men had walked over to the mess when the commotion began. They started to laugh when MacIntosh began to remove Matthew's breeches. The boy kicked and fought. He screamed for help.

"Please don't hurt me," he shouted. "I was hungry. I haven't eaten since yesterday."

MacIntosh had the boy's breeches down around his knees. Asa Wallace grabbed Matthew's hands while Dodd pinned his feet. Then MacIntosh dragged him over his knees. He picked up a rough pine plank from the ground and slammed it against the boy's buttocks with all his might.

Matthew screamed in terror, and a huge red welt appeared instantly.

"Hey, Mac," called one of the soldiers, "that isn't funny. You'll hurt the kid."

"Shut your face or I'll let you take his place," said MacIntosh.

He brought the plank down on Matthew's rear with a vicious grunt. Again the boy screamed. He began a pitiful weeping noise. The third blow never reached its mark. MacIntosh's hand was caught in midair by a giant mitt. The Boston man looked up in surprise to see the huge form of General Seth Pomeroy standing over him.

"Drop the stick," said Pomeroy through clenched teeth.

For a fleeting moment MacIntosh looked as if he would disobey. Pomeroy truly wished he would. But the militiamen knew Pomeroy by sight and also by reputation. In addition, MacIntosh was sure he could be hanged for striking a general. MacIntosh had strong survival instincts. The plank hit the ground with a clatter.

Both Corporal Dodd and Asa Wallace let go of the boy. Matthew slid off MacIntosh's knees. He was still weeping and his behind felt as if it were on fire. He cried aloud when he bent down to pull up his breeches.

Pomeroy steadied him. Then he saw his face.

"You're the Nowell boy. You were with Vaughan. Where is that old reprobate?"

Matthew could not catch his breath from weeping. He finally managed to say, "Dead, in the fort."

A look of sadness crossed Pomeroy's face. He turned toward MacIntosh, Dodd and Wallace, only to find that all three had fled while he had questioned Matthew.

"Damn bullies," he cursed. "We don't need their type in the army. We'll take care of them." He looked at the boy's flushed face and tearful eyes. "But first we must get you back to your family in Boston."

For the next two weeks Matthew served as a messboy for General Pomeroy. Word was sent to the British authorities in Boston that Matthew Nowell was seeking his father. Much to Pomeroy's surprise, word returned that Matthew was dead and buried in the family plot in Charlestown, and that Stephen, his father, had left aboard one of his own ships for places unknown, probably England.

With this news, Pomeroy, at wit's end about what to do with the child he had inherited, took the boy by the hand to the tent of the new commander-in-chief. It was a meeting Matthew recalled vividly in later years. He never would forget the stern, haughty, unsmiling face of George Washington. The boy was in awe of him the moment he entered his quarters.

"It has come to my attention, young man," said the commander, looming above him like a giant, "that you have been disturbing the messes of this encampment and stealing food."

Matthew was terrified, but he had never stolen.

"That's not true," he said.

Washington looked at him, his eyes widening at the prospect of an accusation of falsehood.

"I never steal. I always ask."

"I see," said the general. "General Pomeroy has told me of your plight. You are a poor, Tory waif whose family has deserted you."

Matthew was about to correct the general again. He wasn't poor and he wasn't a Tory and he hadn't been deserted. But to correct George Washington twice in two minutes was beyond the capabilities of the ten-year-old. He shut up. When Washington inquired about other relatives, Matthew remembered Uncle Vaughan's telling him of his Schuyler relatives in Saratoga. No sooner had he said the words than Matthew found himself bundled off aboard a military transport wagon.

The trip to New York had followed the coastal road from Boston. He was sent by military wagon, and although the road was one of the best in America, the boy felt that the wheels of the wagon deliberately searched out ruts. Every bone and muscle in his body ached by the time they arrived at the Hudson. They did not enter New York City. Instead he was placed on a *bateau* that plied its way slowly up the Hudson to Albany.

A young lieutenant from Bradford, Massachusetts, was then assigned to deliver him to the city mansion house of General Phillip Schuyler.

The general was not at home, but his wife was. She heard the lieutenant's words of greeting from the commander-in-chief and then was handed a letter from Washington to Schuyler, telling him of the plight of his quasi-relative and asking his help. Mrs. Schuyler's face went absolutely pale as she read Washington's letter. She kept looking from the page to Matthew and then back again. She was near hysteria when she completed the reading.

"What am I to do with you, boy?" she said in great agitation. "The general is at Fort Edward. I can't take any waif in off the streets. I don't even see how you could be related to a Schuyler. Are you my husband's sister's child?"

Matthew did not know what to say. He did not know who this woman's husband was, much less whether or not the sister she mentioned was his mother. He looked to the Massachusetts lieutenant for help. But the officer merely shrugged his shoulders.

A man stepped from the kitchen into the hallway of the house. He was eating an enormous hunk of black bread smothered with fresh, sweet butter. He started to speak, but only gibberish escaped from his bread-filled mouth.

"Oh, Mr. Kip," exclaimed the general's wife. "What am I to do here? General Washington has deposited an orphan on us without any warning. What will General Schuyler say when I tell him that this Nowell boy has been left on our doorway?"

Kip's interest was pricked on Mrs. Schuyler's mention of the name Nowell. He swallowed the bread and walked toward Matthew, searching his features.

"Are you Stephen Nowell's boy?" he asked.

Matthew nodded yes.

"Well, I'll be. Won't the old witch be excited about this. If it be no trouble to you, ma'am," he said to the general's wife, "I'll take this boy to the general's aunt at Saratoga. She might be talked into taking him in, if he is Stephen Nowell's young'un."

Mrs. Schuyler gave an enormous sigh of relief. Within the hour Matthew found himself in the front of Kip's canoe, making his way upriver the few miles to Saratoga Flats—the home of the formidable Margaret Schuyler Kip.

He vaguely remembered William Vaughan's warning about Margaret Schuyler's temperament. When he was introduced to her as she sat on the verandah of her house, she scowled at him.

"I don't like children," she said testily. "And I don't like boys especially. So you're Stephen's son. What's your name, boy?"

"Matthew," he said.

"Matt," she shortened it. "I like it. What do you think, Israel?"

She need not have asked. She knew Israel's opinion already. She pretended to be hostile, but Israel could tell

151

she was intrigued. The meeting with the boy had solidified it. He was a handsome lad, looking a bit like his father, but Margaret, who never really liked Stephen, decided not to hold that against him. And he was brave, not afraid of her gruffness.

"I guess you can stay with us," she said.

The boy stepped forward and kissed her on the cheek.

"Bah," she exclaimed, wiping her cheek with her handkerchief. "Don't take liberties with me. Why, not even Mr. Kip is allowed such liberties with me." She got up from her chair and stormed into her house toward the kitchen, but halfway down the hallway her face broke into a broad smile.

All that had been six months ago. Since then Matthew had lived in the house of Margaret Schuyler, a woman deemed possessed by all of her neighbors. She shouted continuously, and frightened little children who strayed into her estates. Anyone—white, black, red—who had the nerve to trespass could also expect to be fired upon. She never hit anyone, so all assumed she was a terrible shot. In reality she was quite a good one.

Six months to the day, almost, after her first meeting with Matthew Nowell, she sat in her kitchen, about to wash her hair. She was seventy-six and as strong as ever. Her marriage to Israel Kip, the New Hampshire trapper, had been the happiest event in her life. She loved him dearly, but she never let him know it. No one in the Schuyler family had acknowledged that her marriage was legal. The preacher had been provided by that old scoundrel William Johnson. She was sure he was the same preacher who tied the knot whenever Johnson ran into a woman who continued to resist until benefit of clergy had been provided. She didn't care much. If Kip was her legal husband, so much the better. If not, what difference did it make? If it bothered her nephew Phillip, now a general, he could easily recall his departed mother's behavior and not judge his old aunt too harshly.

She was bent over a tub of warm water in the kitchen of her manor house. Her long grey hair was unbraided and hanging straight down to the middle of her back. She placed her hands in the back of her neck and swept the hair up forward and down over her face. She lowered her head toward the tub until her hair was completely immersed. Then she took a bar of brown soap and began to scrub, working up a lather all over her head.

She did not see the Indian enter the kitchen. He was bundled in furs to keep out the February cold. His hair was grey and his muscles sagged slightly. He was old, but he did not look as old as he really was. His face was unwrinkled except for an ugly scar that covered his left cheek. He stood watching her for some moments. Suddenly the old woman stopped scrubbing her scalp, wrinkling her nose.

"Does the white witch have lice? Is that why she launders her head?"

"If I do," she yelled blindly, her eyes closed for fear of getting soap in them, "I got them from you, you old bag of fart wind."

She dunked her whole head in the tub and rinsed the soap out. Then she reached for her towel, which was on the chair back. She missed the towel and it fell on the floor.

"Where the hell is my towel?" she yelled. "Did you take it, you fleabitten son of a bitch?"

"No," said Socono, but he made no effort to retrieve it for her. He stood there with an amused look on his face.

Finally Margaret felt the towel with her foot and, bending down, picked it up and wrapped it around her dripping head. She blinked once and then again, fixing her spectacle-less eyes on the old Indian.

"I knew it was you as soon as you came in. Even with my eyes closed. I smelled you. What brings you here in midwinter? I thought you'd be off in Maine or New Hampshire trapping. Wait here, don't leave this kitchen. I'll tell Kip you're here."

"How is he?"

"Suffers a bit from rheumatism in the cold, but other than that, he's well."

"I ask," said Socono, "because usually when you cage a wild animal it dies."

She looked annoyed at the old Indian. "He don't want to go winter trapping anymore. He's over sixty and it's not fitting or healthy to be freezing your tail off in the woods, when you could be sitting in a mansion house before a warm fire."

"Growing fat," interrupted Socono.

"He's put on a few pounds." She looked at the slimness of the Indian's middle. "You'd have a pot yourself if you ate proper."

"Like you?" said the Indian to the razor-thin old woman. "But I did not come here in the middle of winter to argue with the squaw who taught me English. I've come because Kip sent word to me of the boy."

The harsh features of the woman softened appreciably. "Matt? Yes, he's here. I think you should meet him. Kip, you scoundrel," she yelled, "you and Matt get down here."

Israel Kip was dozing before the fireplace in the parlor room of the manor house when Margaret's yell awoke him with a start. "What does she want now?" he mumbled to himself. "The woman's screech is more like an owl in heat."

Matthew Nowell, who had grown a few inches taller since summer, came noisily down the hardwood stairs from his room on the second floor. "Aunt Margaret called us, Uncle," said the boy.

"Called us is not quite the right word," Kip said slyly to the boy.

He had grown fond of Stephen's son, and he thought the boy had come to love him. He knew Matt adored the old lady. Never for a moment had he been frightened by her harsh tongue, and that instantly endeared him to her.

Kip walked with Matthew ahead of him. "Just in case she throws something," Kip said, but as soon as he entered the kitchen he ignored her shouts. He saw only Socono. He embraced him. "My friend, it's good to see you; it's been more than six months that you've been gone."

Socono smiled at Kip and returned the embrace. But then his eyes wandered over toward Matthew. The boy, his eyes wide at the sight of an Indian in his full regalia, had moved over where Aunt Margaret stood. She rested an arm on his slim shoulder.

"This would be Stephen's son," said Socono in his awkward and heavily accented English. He examined the boy slowly from head to toe. "He is Stephen's."

Kip walked over to Matthew. "I want you to greet the Abenacki chief, Socono. He was like a father to your father."

Matthew held out his hand to the Indian. Socono took the boy's forearm in his grasp.

"I've heard of you. You knew my father when he was a boy."

"I miss your father," the Indian said.

"All right, you've had your greetings," said Margaret. "Now get out of my kitchen. This Indian has vermin. I'm sure of it."

Matthew was shocked by her lack of respect for the great Socono.

"Trust an old woman to know vermin," said Socono, smiling. It had been a standing joke between them for twenty years.

Kip took two clay pipes from the wall rack and filled them with tobacco. He offered one to the Indian.

Margaret sighed with disgust. "Well, if you're not going to chase the Indian from the kitchen, Kip, the least you could do is fill a pipe for me as well."

The four of them sat about the walnut kitchen table, three of the four puffing away on some of Israel's best pipe tobacco and filling the room with columns and billows of white smoke. When they had finished, it was agreed among them that with the coming of spring Matthew would learn to plant, and that in midsummer he would go with Socono to be taught the Indian ways as his father had been. In the fall he would return for the harvest and school.

March winds blew across the Hudson Flats at Saratoga. The Adirondacks to the north were covered with snow, but the southern mountains on the other side of the Mohawk Valley were beginning to show signs of approaching spring. There was a faint greening to the willow tree branches, and the nights were shorter. In mid-March the second of Stephen's children arrived at Kip's doorway.

Amy Nowell had used the Schuyler name to make her journey to Sorel and then up the Richelieu to Isle aux Noix, down Lake Champlain to Ticonderoga, and from that fortress across the ice of Lake George to the site of Fort William Henry. Twenty years before, she had fled from this spot in terror of Indian slaughter, in the company of her mother and her Uncle Karl.

She traveled the overgrown wagon road from Lake George to Fort Edward. There she had confronted her Uncle Schuyler again. Knowing that his aunt had taken in one Nowell brat, he had immediately provided transportation for this one to Margaret's house in Saratoga.

Amy had no memory of Israel Kip. But when he opened the door in response to her knocking, Kip recognized her instantly.

"My God, it is Katherine's daughter," he exclaimed before she said who she was. "Margaret," he shouted for a change, "come quick. It's Miss Amy returned. It's Katherine's girl."

Margaret Schuyler was in the kitchen. She came to the hall and stopped dead in her tracks.

"Amy, child, it is you. Your mother, where is she? Is she with you?"

Amy shook her head. She had recognized her aunt instantly. Margaret rushed to her and swept her into her arms. She kissed the girl on both cheeks and squeezed her unmercifully. She backed away from her then, holding Amy at arm's length. She picked up the gold locket Amy wore about her neck.

"You still wear it."

"I've never taken it off," Amy said. The engraved Gothic *N* was only barely visible now.

"Well, child, come in. It's cold in the hallway here. Come into the parlor. Kip, go make some tea."

Margaret had enough money to have house servants, but she wouldn't have them in her home. At times like these, she put the burden on her husband.

Amy and Margaret sat before the hearth. Margaret rose

and took the poker and stirred up the fire. Sparks rose from the wood and flew up the chimney as flames rose from the logs. She sat back in her chair.

They were silent for some moments. It was Amy who broke the silence.

"I've left my mother and brother behind, Aunt Margaret."

"And how is my Katherine?"

"Not well." The story of Katherine's illness, of Antoine and Louis Joseph, all came spilling out of her. She cried and Margaret cried with her. Israel entered the room with two cups of tea and some soda biscuits. He sat in silence and listened to the two women.

Some twenty minutes later, the front door of the house burst open, and Matthew, out of breath from running along the mud flats, rushed into the room.

"Uncle Kip," he yelled and then stopped short at the sight of Amy.

Margaret rose from her chair and walked over to Matthew, placing her hand on his two shoulders.

"Amy, this is Matt Nowell, Stephen's son and your half-brother."

A look of shock crossed Amy's face. "Is my father here?" she asked.

"No," said Israel, "just Matthew. Best we can make out, your father thought this young one was killed when the Breed house was destroyed in the battle for Boston last June. He left for England. We're caring for him now."

Matthew left Aunt Margaret's side and walked over to where Amy was sitting.

"Are you my sister?"

"Yes, I guess I am."

"My father spoke of you." He offered her his hand.

She took it in hers and he smiled warmly at her. Amy took his hand tentatively. She was shocked to discover a brother that she did not even know she had. She looked at Margaret for some sort of confirmation. The old woman came over and placed her arm on Matthew's shoulders. "The boy is staying with us until your father can reclaim him."

Amy felt enormous relief. She could not handle any

more responsibility. She needed help herself. Even more now than when she fled. She needed a home, a place to be at rest, a place to be alone. She was destitute, without funds of any kind. She was prepared to tell her aunt of her troubles, but she was not willing to stay here.

They spoke late into the day. Margaret rose to make dinner. When she left, Amy turned to Israel Kip. "Mr. Kip, I would really like to return to my mother and father's old house on the Mohawk. Is that possible?"

"It is," said the man. "We rented the cabins on the tract of land to a group of Quakers from Pennsylvania. I've collected the rents for your father. He has never asked for the money. I think he meant me to keep it for our trouble, but we've never touched it. I'll spend it now, though, to care for his children. I'll take half for the upbringing of Matthew until after the war, when his father can come for him. And I'll give half to you to take care of yourself."

"If I move to Fort . . . I've forgotten what it's called."

"Fort Vaughan," Kip reminded her.

"If I move there, I'll have neighbors, other women?"

"Yes, but it will be hard for a woman living alone."

"That's precisely what I need. I need to live alone for a while."

When she came around the bend in the river with Kip and the old Indian paddling the canoe, Amy thought she remembered the site. The house stood on a rise above the Mohawk. Schoharie Creek ran by one side and the river marshes covered the ground to the other side of the garrison house.

They landed the canoe on a small landing beach that was still covered with patches of snow. The Indian steadied the canoe as she stepped out of it; then the three of them walked up the overgrown path to the house. The door to the house was bolted from the inside. Kip found an unlatched window and opened it. He looked at the Indian.

"Can you fit through?"

Socono looked at Kip with disdain. It was clear that he knew he could and that Kip's belly would prevent him.

"Kip, friend, the old white witch feeds you more than you can shit. It stays in you. You should beat her and then maybe she will stop stuffing your face."

"Damn you, Socono, your language in front of a lady should be a lot cleaner."

"What bad word have I used?"

Kip leaned over and whispered in his ear. A look of surprise crossed Socono's face.

"What other word is there?" he asked. "You never taught me any other word for that."

"Shut up and get through the window."

The Indian, whom Amy had heard was close to eighty, scampered through with ease. He came around the front and unlatched the door.

Amy walked into the house. It was like stepping into the past. Most of her mother and father's things were still there. She climbed the stairs and went into Katherine's bedroom. The precious mirror that Aunt Margaret had given Katherine was still over the small dressing table.

"I was born in this room," she said aloud to no one. The two men had remained downstairs. She crossed the hallway to what had been her bedroom. It too was the same as she had left it so many years ago. She walked to her own dresser. The top of it was covered with rag dolls, some of which dear Alte Karl had made for her. She ran her hand along the dresser top. There was no dust. How could a house remain so untouched and yet be clean?

She threw open the wooden shutters to allow more sunlight into the room. The sun's rays poured through the glass.

She went down the stairs, back to the main sitting room of the garrison house. Socono had begun a fire in the hearth. Kip had gone to the kitchen. They carried their own provisions and would eat those. But Kip wanted a kettle to boil water and make some tea.

The chimney did not draw well and the house soon was filled with smoke. They had to open the door and the windows.

The Indian noticed him first as he came trudging along

159

the riverfront from the west. He signaled to Kip and the two of them took their muskets and went to either side of the front door.

"Hello there," he called.

Amy looked out the window. She saw a man with blond hair approaching the house. He was older than she was, about forty years old, although his face had a boyish look about it and his long hair seemed full under the broad-brimmed black hat that he wore. He was dressed all in black. As he stepped up to the door, Kip and Socono pointed guns at his head.

"There's no need to be fearful of me. My name is Kurt Miller. I live on the farm up the Mohawk from here. I saw smoke from the chimney and came to investigate. I've been keeping a watch on this house for several years."

He entered the room but did not take off his hat, which struck Amy as very strange.

Kip and Socono lowered their weapons. They had nothing to fear from the Quaker.

Amy greeted her guest. "Mr. Miller, my name is Amy Nowell. This is my father's house. I've come here to live at Fort Vaughan for a while. Please take off your hat. I'll make some tea."

Miller seemed ill at ease. "No, thank thee," he said.

Amy looked at him. His strange speech pattern puzzled her. She had spoken French for almost twenty of her twenty-five years. In the last week she had spoken English exclusively, yet never before had she heard speech like this.

"I've just come to check that all is right. I best be going home. Please feel free to call on me if thou needest any assistance." He nodded to her and left.

"What an odd man," said Amy as she watched him walk away from the garrison house toward the river.

Socono put his fingers to his head. "The Friends have been touched by the madness of the Great Spirit," he said.

Kip stayed for two days at Fort Vaughan. Socono disappeared within an hour of their arrival. Amy walked with Israel to the landing beach as he prepared his canoe for departure. The Mohawk was high with the spring meltoff and flowed rapidly, gouging hunks of earth from the ancient embankments.

"Miss Amy, I'm not overjoyed at the prospect of leaving you alone here. Damn it, a woman needs a man on any farm, and she needs him twice as bad on a frontier farm."

"I'm not going to plant anything more than a small garden, Israel, and I've brought a healthy stock of supplies."

"Just the same, my Abenacki companion will be staying on in the vicinity throughout the summer."

"But he's old. Won't it be a hardship for him? What if the Iroquois discover him?"

"Horse dip! He's looking forward to a summer in the forest. In the old days he once lived for months right in the middle of Oneida country and they never knew he was there. He'll do all right here. There ain't many Mohawks left. Schoharie Castle is all but abandoned. The Mohawks have moved, mostly to the upper castle at Canajoharie, and that's quite a distance from here. He'll be safe enough, and with him around you'll be safe, too."

He climbed into the back of the canoe. Amy gave it a shove, and the boat pulled out into the river. The current grabbed it, and almost instantly Kip seemed to fly along the top of the stream. He dipped his paddle and steered the canoe toward midstream. He waved twice and then disappeared around the bend of the river.

The day after Kip left, Amy had a visit from other neighbors. Jonas Brinks and his wife Emma, trailing four youngsters, arrived at her front door.

Amy invited them in for tea. They occupied the cabin that George and Hannah had lived in downriver from the garrison house. It had also been the home of Amy's Uncle Karl. They were very impressed when they learned that it was the daughter of the landlord who now occupied the great house.

Amy formed an instant dislike for the couple. Jonas smelled of hard liquor and stale sweat. His shirt was dirty and he had not shaved in two or three days. His face was pockmarked and no beard would grow from the scar tissue. His facial hair grew in patches and made him appear even more unkempt than he actually was.

Emma Brinks also smelled as if she had not bathed in some time. Her tangled hair hung straight down her back. But what really annoyed Amy was her curiosity. She began poking her nose into chests and closets as soon as she entered the house. Her children all had runny noses and dirty clothes.

Amy did not like the way Jonas Brinks looked at her. She felt as if she had already been stripped by his eyes. She vowed to herself that she would never place herself in his presence without Emma being there as well.

Amy gave the Brinkses tea and biscuits. The children shoved the baked goods into their mouths with both hands. And as they left to return home, Emma requested a loan of a sack of flour. As they walked away down the treacherous path along the river to their cabin, Amy felt an enormous relief. She also knew she would never live long enough to receive payment for the flour.

The days that followed were blissful for Amy. Every morning she rose with the sun, made some tea and prepared the dough for her fresh bread. Before the sun grew too hot, she went outside to work in the garden, turning the turf and grading the plot to make it smoother. She had seeds that Kip had given to her. She was determined to feed herself from the garden and to preserve some of her crop for next winter.

Well before midday, she went back to her kitchen, kneaded her dough a second time, and set it aside to rise again. She made a small snack of Aunt Margaret's special cheese and some of her own bread. She carried her little picnic to the banks of the Mohawk. There was a giant pine whose base was covered with a brown blanket of old needles. She sat here in the shade of the tree and ate her lunch. Her belly grew more prominent with each passing day now. She had known she was with child since late winter. Sometimes in the past she had skipped a month, and she had told herself that this was what was occurring.

But by March, she could no longer delude herself. She carried Antoine's child. This was why she wanted solitude. The baby would come in mid-August.

The river continued to flow rapidly. One large rock, which in midsummer would stand almost free of the water, was now the source of the rippling noise. The rushing waters bounced off of it on their mad drive toward the falls at Cohoes near Albany.

Some warm afternoons found her asleep under the old tree. Other times she merely sat and watched the geese flying from the south on their way home to Canada. She still thought of Canada as her home. She missed her mother and spent long hours wondering how she might have handled everything better. But most afternoons she sat loaded with sorrow. Antoine, the father of her child, the boy driving the cows along the road bordering another river, crowded her mind. Antoine teasing her, calling her his pet name. Antoine, earnestly helping out Karl, getting them off Isle d'Orleans as the English under Wolfe came, burning and raping. Antoine, patriot of Canada after the death of his brothers at Quebec. And then Antoine, ill and weak after imprisonment, coming to her to restore him to health. And finally she recalled Antoine entering her with love so long delayed. She could not bring the vision to an end. She could not bring herself to envision Antoine cold and motionless under the ice of the St. Charles.

But gradually as the days passed, the work in the garden and the leisurely afternoons had begun to affect her, and a mending process was underway. When the sun grew lower in the western sky, she returned to her house. The dough would be very high on the breadboard. She would light her fire and bake her bread and cook some meat.

Once every week the Indian came. He made the sound of a squirrel before he appeared at her doorstep. It was his signal, though for the life of her, she could not figure out why he did it. Certainly it amused him. He would never stay. He frequently seemed to be checking the woods, which gave Amy the feeling that there were more of his kind out there. But she never saw anyone but Socono.

At the end of May, Kurt Miller paid a second visit. Amy was actually happy to see him. She had spoken to no one but Socono since the Brinkses had visited her.

He found her at her place under the pine. She was dozing lightly, and his arrival startled her.

"Don't be frightened, Miss Amy," he said. "I had hoped not to frighten thee that way. May I join thee?"

"Of course," she said. "What brings you to the garrison house?"

"I thought maybe I should check to see how thou art doing. I met Jonas Brinks at Fort Hunter. He told me he had been here. He said something I found disturbing, and so I thought thou might need a little company." A frown had formed on his handsome face as he spoke.

Amy decided on bluntness. "If he told you that I am pregnant, well then," she said, patting her prominent belly, "he's a keen observer. My husband was killed in the siege of Quebec. No, wait a minute, what's the point—he wasn't my husband. He was my betrothed. My child will be a fatherless bastard, Mr. Miller."

"That will make life difficult for thee and the child."

"I'm sure." She was silent for a moment. Finally she said, "I hope you will not mind my rudeness. Why do you speak that way? It sounds strange."

"Because I am a member of the Society of Friends," he responded.

"I don't think that is as self-evident an answer as you presume."

"Dost thou speak German?"

"No," said Amy, "only French and English."

"In many languages we find formal address in the plural rather than the singular. The English word *you* is plural—*thou* is singular. In our pride we have come to use the plural in all formal and informal address. It inflates the self-opinion and pride, as it does when the King uses *we* rather than *I* when he means only himself. It is a frightful pride that produces such speech. We Friends, or Quakers as some would call us, reject such pride. We attempt to be a humble people. Thus my plain black suit."

"And your hat?"

"Taking my hat off to another may be a source of inflated pride for him, which is the greatest of sins. Thus I keep my hat on and take it off to no man. That is God's will."

"And how do you know God's will?"

"Through the Holy Spirit, when it touches me or one of my neighbors. When we have the inner light of the spirit of God descend upon us and speak to us through the mouth of our fellow Friends."

"What will your inner light say about my outer belly?"

"I don't presume to know."

"I once heard a priest denounce my mother as a fornicator because she carried my brother, who was not the son of my father."

"We have no priests. And calling out names is not an act of brotherly love. We love each other as brothers and sisters. We do not judge."

"I find that difficult to believe."

"So did I. I joined the Society of Friends when my family moved from here before thou wert born. I had a terrifying experience. The Indians had me and planned to burn me. I was saved by Sir William Johnson and thy father. I was a boy then, sixteen or so. But I was within a hair's breath of dying horribly in the torture of the fire. When we moved south to Cherry Valley, I met some Quakers. My parents are Lutheran. They will never understand my conversion. I don't see them much anymore. I have even changed the spelling of my name. I anglicized it to Miller. They call themselves Mueller."

Amy stood. As she got to her feet, she stumbled slightly. Kurt caught her hand and steadied her. She brushed the pine needles from her skirt.

"Your religion sounds very idealistic and extraordinarily naive."

"Oh, thou art right," laughed Kurt. "We are very naive to do what God tells us to do. The world can never understand that."

They walked along the path back to the house. The sun was very low in the sky. Behind them the half-moon shone despite the continued presence of the sun.

"When is the child due?"

"In August or September," she responded.

"I'll talk to my neighbor women. Several of them have children. Thou willst need help."

He stopped suddenly and looked toward the river shore where Schoharie Creek joined the Mohawk. Amy started to ask what troubled him, but he quieted her by placing his fingers on his lips. Then he pointed to the undergrowth by the creek shore. Suddenly a sapling came crashing to the ground.

"Beaver," he whispered; "there are not too many left. Trappers have taken most of them."

Just then, the two round balls of fur that had felled the tree finally got their scent and went ambling down the creek and disappeared under the rippling waters.

"Maybe now that the trappers have moved west, nature can replenish itself," he said. "I often sit alone by myself trying to observe the animals."

Amy smiled at him. "So do I." She liked this warm and gentle man.

He came back two days later and found her working in the garden. Seeing her do manual labor in her condition clearly upset him. He took her hand and sat her on the steps of the back porch. Then he took off his black coat and hat and started to plant her seeds. She was annoyed with him. She liked the garden work. Besides, she was not sick; she was pregnant. As he worked he started to sweat heavily. His shirt stuck to his back. She went to a tub of fresh water she kept in the kitchen and filled the pitcher. She carried it to where he was bent in half, placing seeds and covering them lightly with dirt sifted through his left hand.

He straightened up and she held the pitcher to his mouth while he drank deeply of the cool waters of the creek. She removed her apron and wiped his brow and neck with it. His blond hair, which he wore tied loosely at the back, was already soaked.

"I could have done that work myself," she complained.

"No doubt," he responded as he bent down again,

placing seeds with one hand and covering them with the other.

"And I could have done it better than you."

He turned his head and looked up at her. "Miss Amy, if I have given thee offense, I will stop what I am doing. It was never my intention to force thee to give vent to prideful feelings."

"I am a good farmer. We learn that early in Quebec."

"God is the good farmer. We merely do the menial tasks like planting, weeding and harvesting. He must produce the sun and the river and, even more, that spark of life which is in the seed. That is his greatest creation, especially when that seed becomes a man."

He was looking at her as he spoke. She had to force herself not to tell him that his words filled her with pride. She had been embarrassed to be pregnant, although from the beginning she had been bold about announcing her condition. But for the first time someone had expressed what she felt deep down inside her about the life within her. She was not sure she agreed with him about God's authorship of life. Quite frankly, she thought of herself as having created that spark of life, she and Antoine, by their love. And of that she was proud—proud for them both.

He finished planting. With the pitchfork he began to turn over the sod to enlarge Amy's kitchen garden. The heat beat down on him more fiercely, and the sweat continued to pour off him. Amy went into the house to work on her bread and to cook some venison that the Indian had brought her yesterday.

When Kurt finished working, he called her. She stepped back onto the stoop.

"I'm very wet," he said, laughing and wrinkling his nose as he playfully smelled his armpits. "If thou has no objection, I'll go down to the river and wash up."

"I've some food preparing," she said, "so don't be too long."

Kurt walked down to the Mohawk landing beach. His canoe was pulled well up on the beach. He knew that Amy would be busy in the house and he need not fear that she would come down looking for him for some time. He took off his shirt and breeches and laid them carefully in the canoe to dry them. He sat down on the rocky beach gingerly and removed his stockings. He rose and stepped into the cold water. He was not the type to move gradually deeper and deeper. Instead he took a deep breath and dived head first into the water. The chill was numbing at first. But gradually his body adjusted to the temperature. He turned on his back and floated. The warm sun soon felt good.

Then he heard the scream. It was Amy. He swam madly for the shore. He heard the scream again. He felt his feet touch, but he tripped on a submerged rock and fell forward on his hands and knees. He pulled himself to his feet and started running up the path to the house. The front door was wide open. He raced inside. Again there was a loud shout and the sound of a man cursing.

He ran to the kitchen. She lay across the large oak table, her skirt up around her waist. Jonas Brinks, clearly drunk and inflamed with passion, was holding her down and attempting to push her skirt up even farther.

"You slut," he yelled, "you've let others in without much of a thought. Now you're going to get a real cock inside you."

"Jonas," Kurt said with an eerie quality to his voice.

Brinks looked up in surprise at the naked, dripping figure of Kurt Miller. At first he did not recognize him without his customary black costume. But then recognition dawned.

"Well, you damned hypocrite. You're going to tell me you were here first and you should get first licks. But Jonas Brinks is second to no man. You'll wait your turn, Blackbird."

"Jonas, don't lay another hand on her."

"What are you going to do about it?" He turned and faced Kurt. He was now even more belligerent and mean.

The Quaker walked toward the older, heavy-set man. He stepped between Amy and her assailant. Brinks smashed his fist into Kurt's bare stomach. Miller saw it coming and tensed his muscles to absorb the blow. He grunted but

Brinks did not possess great strength. His strongest punch only made Kurt wince.

Next he threw a punch at Kurt's face. But Kurt ducked and the punch went wild. Kurt moved away from Amy toward the kitchen door. Brinks stumbled drunkenly after him. Kurt stepped outside, drawing the other man with him. He maneuvered around as if he would finally challenge and attack him. But as soon as he had placed himself between Brinks and the door, he calmly turned his back and raced into the house, slamming the door and bolting it. He ran to the front door and did the same thing. Amy, realizing what he was doing, went from window to window, bolting the heavy wooden shutters of the garrison house. Soon there was no way for Brinks to enter the house.

It was only then, once they were safe, that Kurt became aware of his nakedness. His face went scarlet. Amy handed him her apron and he quickly covered himself with it. She sat on a stool by the table and started to laugh and to cry at the same time.

"I don't know how to feel," she said, tears streaming down her face. "That awful man, that dirty, smelly man who wanted to paw me. He terrified me. But what you did to him struck me as so funny I want to laugh, too. There he is," she said, peeking out the gunhole in the shutter. "He has nowhere to go." She started to laugh again.

Kurt was fearful that she was on the verge of hysteria and dared not leave her, but he felt absolutely ludicrous holding her apron in front of him to hide his nakedness.

"Are there a pair of breeches in this house?" he asked.

"Should there be?" she asked and started to laugh again.

He finally sat on the bench opposite her across the table, spreading her apron across his lap and knees.

She looked into his blushing face, heightened all the more by his fair complexion.

"I'll try to find you a pair," she volunteered finally. She rose and went up the stairs to her father's old room. She could not resist looking out the window for Brinks. She caught sight of him as he walked down the path to the river. She saw him tear Kurt's clothes to shreds and shove his canoe out into midstream. Then she searched her father's chest of drawers. It was empty. She went to the wall cupboard, where she found an old pair of work breeches. She returned to the kitchen and turned her back while Kurt put them on. They were too large. Amy concluded they had not been her father's but rather her Uncle Karl's.

"I hope he did not hurt thee," said Kurt as he slipped his legs into the breeches.

Amy shook her head. "But he did terrify me. I don't mean to criticize you, Kurt. Surely what you did was brave. But most men your size would merely have smashed him. You never touched him, as far as I could see."

Kurt sat down again. "Thou canst turn around. I could not hit him, Amy. It would be a terrible sin to strike a fellow man."

"But he was trying to rape me."

"I know, and I prevented it, but I could not hit him. It is wrong to do violence of any kind."

"But Kurt, old Brinks is one thing. What if he had been a British soldier with a bayonet or an Indian with tomahawk?"

"I guess I would have tried the same thing but without nearly the hope of success. It is part of my belief to reject all violence."

"That's hard to do when there's a war going on all about you."

"The war is meaningless to me. I'll not participate in it."

Amy was silent for a moment. "I called you and your people naive. But your naiveté is certainly a better answer than war. I think I could come to love your naiveté, Kurt."

He opened the shutters and allowed the sunlight to come back into the house.

"Dost thou think I can leave thee alone? Locked in until I can return from my farm with the proper clothing?"

"I have lived alone here thus far. The garrison house is a stout fort. Once it's locked up, no one gets in unless I allow them."

"I will be off then. I shall return just as soon as I can make arrangements for my livestock."

Kurt had been gone only an hour when Amy heard the sound of a squirrel. She reopened her shutters and saw the Indian walking gracefully across the open area of the garden toward her back door. She opened the door. This time he carried no food.

"Are you harmed?" he asked.

"I'm frightened but unharmed," she responded.

"I could have come to your rescue, but the crazy one was here. The one who wears black." His smile broadened. "Who wears black sometimes." He was almost laughing. "The crazy one arrived first."

"He saved me, Socono. He is a good man."

Socono nodded. "But now I will deal with the dirty one downriver."

"Don't hurt him, please, Socono."

The Indian looked at her strangely. "Are you adopting the religion of the crazy one?" he asked with a look of amusement on his ugly face.

"I think he would feel that it was his fault if anything happened to Brinks."

Socono nodded agreement and then returned to the woods. He gave the squirrel signal, and this time there was a response from the woods.

Matthew Nowell had never been happier than he was now. The old Indian had taught him so much already. But primarily he had taught him how to survive in the wilderness: where food could be found; which berries and nuts could be eaten and which could not; how to stalk game; how to use the bow; and how to handle a canoe. At night as he sat before the small fire that he himself had started, Socono told him stories of how he had taught these same skills to his father when his father had been a boy. Matthew found it difficult to imagine his father, who loved fine furniture, good food and good wine, living on berries and nuts and sleeping on the hard ground. And he could not even begin to think of his father as a small boy. He nevertheless listened to Socono's stories of how his father had rescued Socono from the Oneidas who wished to burn him, killing the Oneida chief Skenandon in his escape. He

171

was awed by Socono's tale of their escape along the frozen Mohawk in the dead of winter. The Indian clearly loved and respected Stephen. Matthew began to think of his father in a different light.

They had camped in the woods around his sister's house for some weeks. Today, Socono had allowed Matthew to come with him. Matthew had started toward the house at the sound of Amy's faint screams. But when they reached the clearing, Socono had held him back. They had remained in the woods. When Socono returned from speaking with Amy, he smiled at Matthew.

"Tonight, young one," he said, "we teach a pig to squeal."

They lay on the ground, observing the Brinks house for most of the night. The moon had risen and still they lay motionless. Matthew was growing tired. Initially he had felt a certain excitement at the prospect of stalking human game, but now it was becoming boring. He wondered how the older man could remain so quiet without moving or fidgeting. He decided to try to copy him.

Finally there was a stirring in the house, and a light flashed in the window. The front door of the cabin opened, and a naked Jonas Brinks came outside. He walked toward them, carefully trying to avoid rocks in the path of his bare feet, scratching his hanging belly and yawning. He passed Socono and Matthew, looking for the spot where he went to urinate, now that he had to get up in the middle of the night and his bitch of a wife complained if he used the chamber pot in summer.

Socono's whole body seemed to move in fluid motion. He was on his feet behind Brinks; his hand flashed out across Brinks' mouth. His other hand brought his scalping knife within view of the man's eyes; then it swung down low beneath Brinks' testicles, piercing the skin just deeply enough to draw blood. The farmer seemed to shrink several inches. His eyes flashed white in terror.

"Stay away from the Nowell woman, white pig," Socono whispered in Brinks' ear, "or they come off."

The man let loose what he had been storing in his bladder and then fainted.

Socono could not help himself. He started a squealing laughter and slapped his hand against his thigh. It was loud enough to awaken the Brinks household. Mrs. Brinks called out to her husband.

Socono, still laughing but more softly now, motioned to Matthew that they should withdraw into the blackness of the woods.

From that day forward Kurt came every afternoon to the garrison house. His own farm, which had occupied all his waking hours, no longer seemed enough for him. He still maintained it, rising an hour before dawn and working through lunch. But afterward, he would swim in the river, put on fresh clothes and join Amy at her spot on the riverbank or work in her garden with her.

He told her as soon as he received word that Jonas Brinks and his family had abandoned their farm and fled. They fled without paying the rent, but Amy was relieved to see them go. She was fairly sure who it was who had forced them to part in such haste, but she saw no need to tell Kurt of it.

The summer days passed slowly. Amy saw no one except Socono and, of course, Kurt. She had come to depend on the two of them. The Indian brought her food, the white man companionship. But by midsummer Kurt was aware that he thought of her as more than a companion.

He was over forty years old and had fallen in love. At least he thought he had fallen in love. He admired this woman, enjoyed her company. He did not feel an overpowering emotion toward her. He had always thought that when love struck, it would be with such force that it would overwhelm the senses. Yet he had a full appetite, slept well and kept his mind on his work. He knew he would miss her frightfully if she were not there. He knew he could be happy for the rest of his life with her at his side. Perhaps, he thought, the other aspect of love was for the very young.

173

For Amy there was no question of love. She had given herself finally and completely to Antoine Gingras and had no room for anyone else, even if that someone was living and Antoine was dead. But she had come to need Kurt. His quiet strength seemed to surround her, to protect her.

By mid-July she began to feel discomfort. She had slept on her stomach all her life. Now she could not. Her legs developed varicose veins and stretch marks appeared over her abdomen and her sides. Soon she was hardly sleeping at all, and dark patches began to appear under her eyes.

Kurt began to worry about her and to spend more and more time at the garrison house. When she couldn't bend over any longer, she gave up working in the garden. The midsummer sun was too hot for her, far hotter than she had been accustomed to in Canada.

It was cooler on the first floor of the house, and she had set up her sleeping quarters there. Kurt cooked her meals and cleaned the house for her as well. Finally he could keep silent no longer. They were sitting together under the shade of a maple tree that grew beside the garrison house facing the Mohawk. Kurt had moved a straight-back chair from out of the house for her to sit in. He sat on the ground, pulling at weeds, which covered the area under the tree.

"You're quiet," she said finally, after they had been sitting for fifteen minutes in silence.

He looked at her as she sat playing with the gold locket at her neck. "Wearest thou that trinket always?" he asked.

"Always," she responded. "It belonged to my grandmother. I never take it off."

"It is a vanity."

She grew annoyed with him. "Sometimes the greatest vanity is the ostentatious lack of vanity."

He looked at her in surprise. "Thou art very shrewd," he said. "It was wrong of me to criticize something that is precious to thee. I apologize if I hurt thee."

Her annoyance melted before his clear distress with himself.

"Amy, I think I must talk to thee seriously about us. I

174

want thee to marry me. I want thee to be my wife and thy child to be my child. I promise thee that I will take care of thee and thy child. I will work for you both. I love thee and I will love thy child with all my heart."

She had not expected him to speak to her in this way. "It's too soon for me, Kurt. I don't love you. At least not in the way I loved Antoine."

"I don't expect that from thee, Amy. At least not yet. It could be enough that thou carest for me."

She felt a sinking feeling in her stomach, and it was not the child moving. She wanted a husband. She wanted the security of a man's arms around her, and yes, damn it, she wanted her child to have a father—the father that she never had—and she wanted that child to have a name. She did not love Kurt Miller, but she knew she would marry him.

Kurt's Quaker neighbors gathered at the garrison house the next Sunday. Among them were two families whose farms had been carved out of the original rented lands of Herr Mueller, Kurt's father, and three families living on freehold farms south on the Schoharie and Mohawk lands. The six families met in the large parlor of the garrison house. The chairs had been arranged in a wide circle. The younger children were allowed to sit with the adults. There had been some talking when they first entered the house, but once they were seated, all was quiet. Amy sat next to Kurt. She had been greeted courteously by all the Friends at this meeting. None had questioned her or even seemed to notice what could not be ignored—that she was very pregnant.

Finally Kurt rose and began to speak.

"Friends, I wish to announce, before you and God, my love for this woman, Amy Nowell, and my desire to make her my wife. She is not one of us, although I feel she has the potential to become one of us. My parents are not of our Society either. And so I must turn to you, my friends, for your guidance and your blessing."

He sat down and placed his hand over Amy's.

175

Another man, who seemed very stern to Amy, although it was difficult to see his face in the shadow of the brim of the hat that covered his eyes, rose in his place.

"Friend Miller," he said softly, "it is our hope that the woman will become one of us. Before we consider this matter, we have a concern for thee. The woman is with child. Is the child thine?"

"No," said Kurt. He looked at Amy. She nodded her head for him to proceed. "The child," he continued, "is the child of her betrothed, who was killed fighting against the British."

"Thou knowest, friend Miller, that we have not taken sides in the conflict. All wars and all killings are equally obnoxious to us. Of what people is the woman?"

Amy stood now next to Kurt. "I am the daughter of Stephen and Katherine Nowell, who own this land. My betrothed was named Antoine Gingras. He was from Quebec and he was a Catholic."

Some of the Friends were shocked. Their indifferent mask was finally penetrated and a murmur ran through the room.

"Friend Miller," said the man from the shadows, after consulting with several neighbors, "thy beloved hath much pride. It is not seemly. Also she seems to have no remorse for her condition."

Amy interrupted him. "If you think me a sinner, old man, that is your privilege. I loved the man who fathered this child. I'll never be ashamed or repent of it."

The Quaker was silent. "I think it not possible to allow this union," he said finally.

But another voice interrupted him. It came from the woman who sat next to Kurt.

"The spirit visits me," she said. All now fell silent. "This woman, Amy Nowell, is proud but of good heart. The child she bears is our brother or sister. We must not place the sins of the parents on it. The child will be fatherless and rejected if our friend Miller is not allowed to protect it. Amy Nowell will be left an object of abuse and derision if our friend Miller does not take her to his breast. Charity, my brothers and sisters, love of each other and all

176

mankind, is our Lord's demand of us. Let us not become so strict in our observance of form that we lose the spirit of charity, for if we have not love, we have nothing. They must be allowed to join together and marry now." And then the woman looked at Amy's belly and smiled. "For next month's meeting may be too late."

The man from the shadows stood. "It is not the proper form, but the Lord has spoken. So be it," he said and then sat down.

The door of the house was suddenly flung open, and an ancient Indian dressed in his finest buckskins, his hair decorated with quills and feathers and shells, entered the room, his face painted to accentuate the terrible scar on his cheek. Behind him was a brown-haired, freckled-faced white boy, also dressed in skins. Several of the Quakers gasped.

"This is the giving of the bride, is it not?" said Socono. "Where are the gifts for the bride's family? I have brought her brother to receive them."

Amy stood and walked to Socono's side. She whispered in his ear.

"No gifts?" he said, his eyes wide in amazement. He looked at Matthew. "No gifts," he repeated. The boy also seemed disappointed.

Then Amy took Matthew by the hand. She felt at peace. She had found a community of loving people and she wished to share her peace with them all.

Kurt came to Amy's bed that night. It would not be possible for them to make love, he knew. She was very large and close to delivery. Nevertheless, it was the first wedding night for both of them. She had put on her mother's white nightgown with the lace and rosebud front. It was old now but still beautiful. She sat in her bed, her bed linen drawn up about her throat. She laughed when she saw the bulge of her belly.

Kurt came into the room. He had scrubbed his face and his hands, especially his fingernails, to remove the caked residue of farming. His nightshirt was the best he owned. It was a coarse linen and no match for Schuyler lace. But neither of them cared. He climbed into the bed next to his wife.

"I love thee, wife," he said as he kissed her on the lips. Then he bent down and kissed her stomach. "And I love thee, child."

The next day Kurt moved his personal belongings from his farm to the garrison house. He would have to return every day to his own place to work the farm, but from now on he would spend the nights with Amy. Socono allowed Matthew to spend some time with Kurt. The boy seemed to enjoy farming. Sadly Socono had concluded that Matthew had the white man's disease—the overwhelming desire to grovel in the dirt, doing woman's work with a hoe. But he would work on him. Maybe he could still make a warrior of him.

The baby came at the end of August. It was a difficult delivery and Amy had been frightened, but she came through it. Kurt had remained with her because she was so frightened. He sent Matthew to the neighbor's farm for Mrs. Parker, who was the community's only experienced midwife.

Matthew raced along the river's edge toward the Parker farm. He was terrified. He had never seen a baby born. He was not likely to see this birth, but neither had he heard a mother scream as Amy had screamed. The only thought that would come to his mind was the thought of his own mother at his birth—lying dead in a pool of blood.

He brought Mrs. Parker back. Amy did not die as Matthew had feared and as she herself feared on several occasions during the delivery. Instead she gave birth to a red-haired, fair-skinned girl.

The child screamed from the moment of birth, prompting Amy to call her Margaret. Kurt had never met Margaret Schuyler and did not understand the significance of the name, but Matthew laughed when Amy told him about it.

His sister was propped in her bed holding the angry, crying child in her arms. Kurt sat next to her on the bed, trying to soothe the child, to little or no avail.

"She should have been a boy," said Matthew.

Amy lay back against the pillows. Nothing this little brother said was going to offend her—not at this moment. "Why should she have been a boy?" she asked finally.

"So that he could help me and Kurt fight off the Iroquois if they should attack. Socono says that a lot of them still live around here and that they're snakes you can't trust."

Amy looked at Kurt and saw the expression of concern that came over his face.

"Matthew," he said softly. "The Iroquois are people like us. They leave us in peace because we are men and women of peace."

"Socono says they tried to burn him, and he was saved only because my father killed a chief."

"Socono is not a man of peace."

Amy sighed deeply. Holding her child in her arms, even an angry baby like Maggie—and surely she would be called Maggie—brought her a sense of the deep peace that Kurt had told her they must strive for. She had it already. The child and her life with her new husband brought it to her.

"What would you do," said Matthew defensively, "what would you do if the Indians or the Tories attacked?"

"They won't," answered Kurt. "They have not yet done so, and they have had more than ample opportunity."

"That's dumb," said Matthew.

"Matthew," said Amy with annoyance. "Watch your manners."

Kurt merely smiled at the boy and ruffled his hair. "He means no harm. He's just curious. It is natural for his age."

But Matthew was angry. Kurt had not answered his question. And it was Kurt's responsibility to see that his family was secure. Socono had told him it was a warrior's first responsibility—before he sought out his enemy—to make sure that the women and children were safe. He stepped aside to prevent Kurt from continuing to muss his hair. He did not like anyone to do that. He wasn't a baby to be played with. He walked out of the room without another word.

Amy dismissed him as a rude boy. All brothers seemed to possess the trait. Kurt leaned closer to her to get a better look at the baby. She was quiet now, and Amy offered her to him to hold. A look of terror crossed his face. He had never held a newborn in his life. But Amy insisted. He took the baby in his large, calloused hands.

"She won't break," Amy teased.

Kurt pulled the tiny form close to his body and began to rock her. Maggie ruined the moment by starting to scream again. Kurt practically tossed the baby back to Amy.

"Careful."

"Thou said she would not break," he teased back.

They sat together for some moments in silence. Amy's eyes began to smart and her lids began to droop. She had not slept in almost twenty-four hours. Kurt saw the signs of approaching slumber and stroked her forehead. He would place the baby in her cradle after Amy dropped off.

For Amy it had been a day she would never forget—the day she became a mother. Nothing could have ruined it for her, not even her petulant brother. She had not liked the way he had dismissed Kurt's arguments. But as she drifted off, she could not get rid of the boy's words. They had activated a deep-seated fear in her—what if the Iroquois should attack?

VII

1776–1777

Stephen had come to loathe London winters. He was always cold. The temperature did not come close to those he had experienced in the New York wilderness or in Nova Scotia or even in Boston. But here it seemed to seep into your bones with the fog and never leave you.

The thought of his home saddened him. He had left so much behind, but all those he had loved there were gone. He rose from his chair and walked to the window to look out. He had purchased this house off Fleet Street so he might be near the coffee houses where the other Americans gathered. He was far better off than most of them. He had liquidated assets over the years and placed them with his agents in London. His income in investments alone was nearly as large as his entire income from his companies in Boston had been, and he was still owner of five ships. They were all at sea and, with God's blessing, would return and increase his profits.

But like all the Americans, he still flocked to the coffee houses to hear the news and debate the strategies of the government, or the lack of strategies.

The number of Americans in London had grown last spring. In March, Sir William Howe, now commanding the King's armies in Boston, had determined the city could no longer be held. Indeed, he had decided it was not worth holding, since Massachusetts was lost to the rebellion. He turned instead to New York. The Americans in that loyal colony, he thought, would flock to the King's standard, should it be raised there. In March, with rebel cannon that had been dragged all the way from Ticonderoga surrounding Boston, from Cambridge to Dorchester Heights, Howe gave the word to evacuate. Hundreds of Loyalists in the town fled with him. The army retreated to Halifax, while Washington and his ragtag force marched through the streets of Boston.

Throughout that winter Americans besieged Quebec. But with spring, the relief armada had arrived, and the rebel force had fallen back to Three Rivers.

The news from Canada was good all summer. The British won a resounding victory over the Americans at Three Rivers, and the navy had forced itself upriver, passing Sorel, toward Montreal. The Americans evacuated that town and fled back down the Richelieu to Isle aux Noix, where it was reported that they died by the hundreds of smallpox. Finally the rebels retreated all the way to Crown Point and Ticonderoga. In the fall a naval battle had been fought in northern Lake Champlain, and a rebel fleet of row galleys and gunboats was defeated and sunk. In the spring, all expected Carleton to push on to Ticonderoga and beyond. Canada had been freed of rebel forces.

In midsummer General Howe struck at New York. He landed on Long Island and defeated Washington's forces at the Battle of Brooklyn Heights. But Washington escaped to Manhattan with his army intact. Howe struck again in late summer, landing in Kipp's Bay on Manhattan Island. Washington withdrew, this time to a strong position in Harlem Heights, from which he struck back at the British army and the German mercenaries who taunted him. Once more Washington retreated, this time to White Plains. The British followed. Washington finally crossed the Hudson and fled into New Jersey. The British dealt the rebel cause a disastrous blow, capturing the two Hudson River forts that the rebels had relied on to stop them— Fort Washington on the New York side and Fort Lee on the New Jersey side.

The rebels fled across New Jersey and did not stop until they crossed the Delaware into Pennsylvania. But for all their defeats they had not been beaten; Howe had failed to trap Washington and destroy his army. Stephen and every other Loyalist expected that to come in the following summer's campaign.

There was a knock on the door and Josiah entered. He made a terrible house servant. His familiar manner with Stephen was a scandal to most of Stephen's friends. Southern planters exiled from England could never accept the fact that Stephen loved Josiah as the only living link with his own past. The black man returned Stephen's feelings, even if he cursed Stephen daily as he dressed in the silly clothes he was forced to wear. Most of all, Josiah could not bear the white powdered wig Stephen wore on formal occasions. Whenever Stephen put it on and looked at himself in the glass, Josiah's face lit with an enormous grin, followed by a howl of mirth. But Stephen paid him well, very well, and he was putting money aside for himself.

"Some letters and an invitation from Governor Hutchinson, Mr. Stephen," Josiah announced.

"Not another," said Stephen in exasperation. "The Loyalist colony in London feeds on itself. I can't bear to spend another night with Thomas, weeping with him over his lost country place at Milton."

"It's sad for many of them," said Josiah.

"I've had my share of sorrows," said Stephen with some vehemence. "But I bear up better than Thomas, and he bears up better than most of the others."

He ripped open the wax seal of a letter and started to read disinterestedly. But his unconcern faded quickly. It was not an invitation to visit Hutchinson at all, but rather to spend a weekend at the estate of the Earl of Gilford in Oxfordshire. Gilford's son was the prime minister, Lord North. The weekend would include dinner with General John Burgoyne, who was scheduled to return to North America in the spring. Stephen was sure it was only superficially a social engagement. There were matters of strategy to be discussed, and Thomas Hutchinson had clearly convinced someone that the wealthy Mr. Nowell could be of some use.

"Josiah," Stephen called out. "Pack my trunk. We're leaving for Bambury next week."

Stephen picked up the second letter and broke its seal. Once again his attention was instantly seized. It was from Margaret Schuyler. As he read, the expression on his face went from incredulity to pure joy. He walked to the cabinet where he kept fine wine. He pulled out a decanter of his finest port and poured himself a glass. He lifted it to an imaginary companion.

"He lives," he whispered, "he lives and is safe with friends. Thank God." Then he ran to the door and opened it. "Josiah," he yelled. "It's Matthew. He's alive. Damn it, he's alive! He's with Margaret and Kip. He's safe." He didn't wait for the black man to respond. He went back to the cabinet for another drink.

The carriage ride through the countryside to northern Oxfordshire was difficult. Hutchinson had aged considerably and was even more self-contained than he had been in the past.

Stephen sat opposite him in the coach as it bounced over the ruts and through the puddles that were more frequent than the fine-graded sections of the road. He had given up trying to hold a conversation with his friend. Frankly, he wished he could be seated above with Josiah and Hutchinson's coachman.

They were finally at the village of Bambury. The earl's house—Wroxton Abbey—was three miles away. They would arrive shortly.

"Do you have any idea, Thomas, why the prime minister wishes me present at this conference? I understand his inviting you with your knowledge of colonial politics, but why me?"

"I rather think he's interested in you, not me. He has heard my views often enough. I think I have been invited so that I might make you at ease."

The carriage entered the front gate of the estate. They approached the house from the west down a long park road. As they rounded a curve, the old house appeared. It had originally been a medieval abbey, but the current house dated from the seventeenth century. It was constructed of yellow-orange stone, three storeys high. The first two storeys had huge windows that extended almost from floor to ceiling.

Stephen stuck his head out the carriage window to admire the house. To the right was a fine stable, constructed of the same color stone. Surrounding the house were formal English gardens of the modern sort. Something about this house struck Stephen as strange. It appeared imbalanced. The north wing protruded toward the visitor, and the house seemed to cry out for the addition of a matching south wing.

The carriage pulled up onto the graveled yard in front of the west front of the house. Liveried servants rushed out of the door and placed a stepping stool in the door of the carriage. They opened the door for the occupants. Hutchinson stepped out first. Then Stephen, steadying himself with his gold-headed walking stick, followed him.

The prime minister, son and heir to the estate of the first Earl of Gilford, greeted Hutchinson warmly. He was a plump man with a high, receding hairline and bulging eyes. Hutchinson turned and introduced Nowell.

"Lord North, I'd like you to meet my very good friend and companion in exile, Mr. Stephen Nowell of the late colony of Massachusetts."

"Sometimes, Thomas, you presume on my friendship. We will soon have regained control of your home and restored it to its proper allegiance to His Majesty."

"I despair of it," murmured Hutchinson.

"Mr. Nowell, let us ignore our despairing colleague."

"My lord," Stephen acknowledged, "your family estates are very beautiful."

"But you haven't seen the gardens yet. Quickly, come in and change your clothes and we will still have enough daylight for a tour of Mr. Miller's masterpiece. My father has turned an old-fashioned formal hedge garden into a lovely woodland pleasure ground."

They entered the front door and came upon the great hall of the house. It had a huge hearth in which a fire was burning, giving what little warmth such high-ceilinged rooms could maintain. At one end a carved wooden gallery loomed above the floor of the great hall below. Behind it,

185

light poured through stained-glass windows. Although the room could not have been here at the time of the old monastery, legend had it that the hall was built on the site of the old refectory. And Stephen had little difficulty imagining cowled, silent figures moving quietly about this setting.

"We will have dinner in the hall tonight. I've hired a quartet to play for us from the minstrel's gallery," said Lord North, pointing above.

They left the great hall. Servants led them up the stairs to individual bedrooms. Stephen's was small and had a beautiful view of the garden. He changed into a warm pair of breeches and a coat and threw his greatcoat over his shoulders. The prime minister was waiting for him at the foot of the stairs.

"Thomas has decided he is too weary to join us. We will have to walk alone."

They strolled out of the house and along a path past a recreation of a Greek temple set in the woods. Here North stopped and pointed to the southeast across a small pond, where an obelisk stood on a rise of land.

"My father had this view constructed in honor of the visit to the abbey of His Royal Highness Frederick, Prince of Wales—His Majesty's father. My father loves these grounds."

They continued along the path to the great pond.

"You've lived in the heart of the colony of New York, haven't you, Nowell?" said the prime minister.

"Yes, my lord. I own an estate in the Mohawk Valley, not far from the former estate of Sir William Johnson."

"Ah, Sir William, a great man. How I wish he had lived. Our problem would be so simple had that giant sat astride the Mohawk with all the tribes attached to him. His heirs are not of the same stature."

Stephen did not comment. He had heard that one of those heirs was his own son Aaron. But he knew that North referred to Johnson's white heirs, Sir John Johnson and Colonel Guy Johnson.

"I've been told that the people of the Mohawk will come

to the support of the King if they can be assured that royal troops will be at hand."

"I've not lived in the valley for almost twenty years, my lord," said Stephen. "I don't know if I'd be a good judge. The people, both white and red, did truly love Sir William. His loyalty to the crown was well known. There must be a residue of that loyalty left from his day."

"If we formed an army of Americans and Indians and sent it down the Mohawk, would the people rally to it and overthrow the rebels?"

"Not if you include Indians, my lord."

"Colonel Johnson tells me I must. His man Joseph Brant has the tribes following him. This Brant is the brother of Johnson's mistress."

"I know them all, my lord. If you must depend on Molly and Joseph Brant and their family to restore royal authority, then I must confess I find our cause in grave danger. The Brants will fight for the King if they feel that to do so is in the best interest of their-people—the Iroquois. And they will use Iroquois tactics—burning, torture, slaughter of women and children. Those tactics will turn the whole valley against us." He said this last through clenched teeth and with such vehemence that Lord North looked at him in surprise.

"I have a son, sir," said Stephen more calmly. "By an Iroquois woman. I suspect he is with the Brants. It is a matter of deep feeling with me."

"I understand," said North. He said it in a way to indicate that he would not pry. The matter was closed.

They had come to the end of the pond, where the water flowed over a cascade with a roar into a serpentine stream below. Above the stream was a hillock with another temple at its summit.

"From up there," said North, "you get a good view of the falls and the pond. Shall we climb it?"

Stephen nodded. He was grateful that he had brought his walking stick in case the footing became difficult.

The prime minister was in terrible shape, and his chest was heaving when they reached the summit. The trees,

187

free of leaves, could only partially obscure the view of the abbey from the spot.

"Your arm, sir. Did you lose it in the King's service?"

"Yes, my lord, in the last war against the French in the Battle of Lake George."

"My condolences. You have my admiration. I hope your King can someday repay you for your loyalty."

"He can do that by returning me to my homeland in peace."

The sun was setting behind the house, and shadows were lengthening.

"We must return from our walk while we have time, Mr. Nowell. I'm glad you were candid with me. Your advice on the use of Brant corresponds with what General Carleton has been writing me, but it will not be Carleton who commands next summer. The new commander will be at dinner tonight. I want you to speak with him."

When Stephen entered the great hall for dinner that night, he found the room transformed. A large table had been set up on a dais on the north end of the hall. Two great candelabra were set upon the table. The Guilfords' best china and silverware were set in five place settings. Two violins, a cello and a viola played gently in the background from the minstrel's gallery above them. The flames in the huge hearth leapt high and cast shadows on the opposite wall. But the room would have been too chilly for a meal had not several tiny enamel stoves been placed strategically throughout it.

Stephen sat opposite a British general, resplendent in his red and gold uniform. The earl, the prime minister's father, introduced himself to Stephen and Hutchinson and then introduced his guest as General John Burgoyne.

Lord North was the last to arrive. After he had been seated, the servants brought in a large silver tureen, which they set upon a buffet table. A hot lentil soup was served. After the soup the servant brought in grouse stuffed with chestnuts and finally the beef served in gravy.

"Have we met before?" Burgoyne asked Stephen. "I

seem to recall a gentleman with your handicap—an associate of Sir William Howe's."

"I served twice with Sir William. Once with Wolfe at Quebec and most recently in the Boston campaign at Breed's Hill."

"Pyrrhic victory if ever there was one," said the old earl. "Damn me, if we'd won a battle like that in my day, they'd have cashiered the general—maybe even shot him as they did Admiral Byng. This Howe fellow, I understand, is brother to Admiral Lord Howe. Some family— Irish peerage, isn't it? Upstarts, and what's worse, they're a bunch of Whigs. No concern of theirs that the King and my son are embarrassed. I'm sure this dandy here— gentleman Johnny Burgoyne, they call him—would put an end to that rebellion and hang the damned rebels on Tower Hill."

"They don't hang on Tower Hill anymore, Father."

"We'll make an exception for this Washington fellow and those fellows in the bloody congress. They declare themselves an independent, sovereign nation and then go consorting with the damned Frogs. They are the worst of traitors. This Franklin fellow, the one they sent to Versailles to court Louis and his clocks, he used to travel in the right circles here in England before the rebellion. Clever fellow, witty. I'd watch him; he's dangerous."

"His son," said Hutchinson, "is my former colleague, Sir William Franklin. He lives here in England. He was the royal governor of New Jersey before the war. The two men, father and son, have broken completely. They haven't spoken to each other since before the rebellion began."

"Well, next year," said the prime minister, "it ends— once and for all. General, I want you to outline your plan to these distinguished Americans. I think you should listen to their advice, particularly to Mr. Nowell's, who knows the terrain you will have to cross very well."

Burgoyne laid down his fork. He was about to attack his beef, but the mention of the campaign—his favorite topic— started him off.

"The strategy, gentlemen," he said, "is simple. Seize

189

the colony of New York and divide New England from Virginia. Separate the two cores of the rebellion from each other and then you will win New York and Pennsylvania back to the crown. At heart they are both still loyal. The rebellion will die of its own weight without the wealth of those two colonies.

"The tactics are more complex. We conquer New York by a three-pronged assault. Howe seizes the Hudson forts and approaches Albany from the south from his base in New York City. A force of Indians and Loyalists moves from Montreal to the Lakes at Oswego and comes down the Mohawk from the west. The only obstacle in its path is Fort Stanwix. But the most important force, a force of British Regulars and Brunswickers, will leave from Montreal via Lake Champlain and strike at Crown Point and Ticonderoga. Once they have been taken, the army will move south to Albany. All three forces converge on that town and *voilà*, New York Colony is ours."

Stephen looked at the prime minister. Lord North nodded to him, giving him permission to comment.

"It sounds reasonable enough," said Stephen. "I believe we have always known that a majority in New York, New Jersey and Pennsylvania has been opposed to the cause of the rebellion. But I wonder whether our aim should be capturing cities or capturing armies. As long as Mr. Washington, or my esteemed former brother-in-law Phillip Schuyler, is in the field, they keep the rebellion going."

"Schuyler is your brother-in-law?" asked Burgoyne. "I expect him to be my opponent in the push south. I will command the attack on Ticonderoga."

"I haven't spoken to him in twenty years," said Stephen. "My understanding is that he is a merchant who dabbles in war. But then so was Sir William Pepperell. Thirty years ago I was with him when he took Louisbourg—the Gibraltar of North America, it was called."

"Militia armies cannot beat professional armies," said Burgoyne haughtily.

"Strange," said Stephen, his voice dripping with sarcasm, "I could have sworn we'd begun this conversation with the mention of Breed's Hill. I could have sworn also that you'd said you were there. I warn you now, sir, you had better keep that battle in your memory. Don't let the militiamen dig in or fortify. If they do, they'll sting you as they did Howe in '75."

Burgoyne regarded his remarks as impertinent, and he ignored them. "Lord North said you knew the terrain, sir."

Stephen smiled. He knew Burgoyne was annoyed with him. "How can I be of service?" he said, switching his tone from that of the equal debater to that of useful subservience. He doubted if either role would make much of an impression upon the soldier sitting opposite him. The turn of his head, the polished manicure on his fingernails, forced Stephen to doubt if this dandy could lead an army through the wilderness and endure the hardship necessary to make it from Montreal to Albany. He remembered another meeting with another prime minister and another British general, Lord Howe, another brother of Sir William, thirty years ago. Howe had been charged with the same task in reverse, leading the British army from Albany to Montreal. He had been killed at Ticonderoga. There were those who said he could have done it, had he lived, but his successor, General Abercrombie, had failed miserably. Burgoyne reminded Stephen more of Abercrombie than he did of Howe.

Guilford interrupted. "Enough talk of war. Frederic," he called to the prime minister, "get the port."

Hutchinson leaned over to Stephen and whispered in his ear. "I think it's time you started demanding land grants in Canada as compensation for our lost homes. With these gentlemen in charge, we'll never see Massachusetts again."

Stephen went to his room soon after dinner. He had taken only one glass of port. He was disturbed that the campaign on which everything depended was to be led by a man whom he did not trust. Well, if Burgoyne made it to Albany, then he would fall under Howe's command.

He took off his clothes. He decided that he needed no

nightshirt and he crawled into bed naked. It had started to rain, and he could hear the splatter of the drops on the roof above him.

He thought back on the dinner conversation. To these men, America was a faraway land, territory to be won or lost. In the dark he saw the faces of his family—especially that of Matthew. His son was alive and safe. But for how long? The war went on and, judging from what he had learned tonight, it would come perilously close to the place where Matthew had sought refuge. He had to be sure the boy was safe.

He knew he couldn't go back to Boston, but there was another way—through Canada, where Katherine was. He shocked himself. He hadn't thought he wanted to see her again, ever.

His mind drifted back to the days on the Mohawk—to the garrison house. He remembered how she had defended his actions to Karl when Stephen had kidnapped his and Molly Brant's son and brought him to Fort Vaughan. It had been a foolish thing to do. And it had almost cost them all their lives. She had comforted him when he had been forced to give up Aaron. It was she who had nursed him back to health after he had lost his arm. She was always there when he needed her. And he was never there when she needed him. She had never abandoned him. He had abandoned her to Karl. And when she refused his offer of belated love, he had turned on her with pure hate. She had not deserved that.

Then came Abigail, beautiful young Abigail. God, how he had loved her, and he had suffered when he lost her. Their time together had been like a golden age—truly outside the normal course of his life. He had lost her, and the pain had overwhelmed him, blotting out an earlier pain and loss, a self-inflicted one. He had loved Katherine too. A sinking feeling hit him.

But of what use was love? He had hurt all whom he loved. But still he made up his mind that he'd return to the St. Lawrence to find Amy, and he would force his way to Albany with the British to reach Matthew. *And I will*

192

make it up to Katherine as well. He surprised even himself with the vehemence of this last conviction.

Molly threw another log on the fire. It almost smothered the weakening flame, and smoke started to rise. She was burning pine. It burned fast, but it was smoky. A tiny flicker caught, and tongues of fire began to lick at the new log. She looked about the large living room of her house. Many of the families of Canajoharie now lived in European-style houses. She always thought she would come back to this castle and live in a longhouse. But a few nights on a platform had sent her looking for Joseph and Aaron. They hired carpenters, and soon a new house stood on the site of the great Hendrick's longhouse, and old Brant's grand-daughter, chief clan mother of the Iroquois, lived in it.

A large kettle hung over the fire. Steam poured from it and rose to the low ceiling, where it condensed. Droplets fell from the ceiling onto the rough-hewn board floor. Molly went to the kettle and poured some water into the teapot. Drinking tea incessantly was another habit she had picked up from living with Johnson.

She thought it ironic that she should have difficulty living in a longhouse. She thought of Aaron's father and how she had faulted him for his aversion to the common life. But Johnson had influenced her in a way that the blackrobe, Nowell, never could. Johnson had accustomed her to the luxury of Johnson Hall. Now she had been forced to abandon the ways of her people and accept the ways of Johnson and of Nowell.

The door opened, letting in a blast of cold air and drawing some smoke out of the hearth. Molly's brother, the warrior chieftain Joseph Brant, stepped into the room. Her face broke into a broad grin. She had not seen him in more than a year. She walked to his side and, placing her arm about him, hugged him with all her might.

"The English have released you to me," she cried.

"Sister, you make it seem as if I have been a prisoner instead of a visitor to London."

"What was it like?"

193

"It was as he told me it would be. Johnson had been in America for forty years, but his memories of England and its city were very accurate. And he was right to tell us to tie our futures to the King. The English are wealthy and they are generous. Neutrality, argued by the Oneida and the Tuscarora and even the Onondaga, as well as by many Mohawks, will destroy us in the end."

"Even Corn Planter of the Seneca says we must observe neutrality with the Americans or the league will be destroyed," said Molly in disgust. "But if we take sides, the Oneida and the Tuscarora will join the Americans. The Seneca and the Cayuga will fight for the King. The long-house will be destroyed."

"That is the way it has been argued in the council, sister."

"Not by me!"

Joseph smiled. He had heard that Molly had insisted on bringing clan mothers to every council so that the warriors would not get carried away and make decisions without consulting the women.

"I have to conclude, Molly," he said to her in English, "that if the British do not win this war, if they fail to keep the Americans on the coast, then we have lost our lands forever. It is the rebels who farm, tearing up the trees and chasing out the game. In the long run it will be they who destroy us. We must unite and defeat them with the aid of the British. It is the only hope for the Iroquois, or for any Indian nation, for that matter. Neutrality may help the Confederation of the Six Nations from splitting, but the cost will be the total destruction of all of our people by the Americans. Of that I have become convinced."

"I know you are right, Joseph," said Molly. "You will be our leader in this war."

"I'm not a sachem."

"But a war leader who inspires can always undermine the sachems and lead the people. It is settled then. Our people will join with the British and their American friends who are loyal to the King against the rebels."

Joseph pulled a straight-backed leather chair in front of the hearth. Molly poured him some tea. He tasted it.

"It's good. As good as any served in England, Molly."

"I know it is," she said smiling. "Johnson always said I made the best tea."

"Johnson was Irish," said Joseph. They both laughed. At first Molly had not understood the difference between English and Irish. When she had called him English, he had bellowed at her. It was their first fight, but hardly their last.

"London is a great city. I met all the best people. They seemed amazed that I am Mohawk but did not stand naked before them, fiendishly checking over their scalps. I think I might have farted in the King's boudoir and they would have forgiven me."

She laughed loudly at his joke.

"But the adventures did not happen there in London. On the way home, your stepson Sir John and I were attacked aboard our packet by an American privateer. We fought them off. I got several of the sharpshooters on the American ship myself."

Again the door opened with the same effect as before— smoke filled the room. Joseph stood and raised his hand to the newcomer, his nephew Aaron. The two men came together and embraced. Then Aaron bent down and kissed his mother's cheek.

"It is good that you're back, Uncle," said the younger man. "The tribes are divided. We need your leadership."

"And I'll need your strength, Aaron. Our survival depends on it."

Aaron nodded at him.

"Ssh, no politics," Molly said. "Joseph was telling me of his travels."

"Well," continued Joseph Brant, "we arrived in Staten Island, our rigging shot to pieces. I joined Howe's landing at Brooklyn and fought with the British at Brooklyn Heights. Howe generaled brilliantly, and defeated the Americans. But then he let that fox Washington escape. I could not wait for Howe to push up the Hudson, if he ever does. I disguised myself and passed through the rebel lines and here I am."

Aaron looked in awe at his uncle. He was so close to

him in age and yet Joseph had been through so much, much more than any other Indian of his day. He could read and write in English as well as Aaron could. He was a devout Christian and a member of the Anglican church, and he belonged to a white man's secret society called the Masons. He was a handsome man with strong features. He had married and had had children. Aaron had done none of these things. All he had done was to learn to become a good warrior, and he had cared for his mother, especially in these years of her widowhood.

"Aaron," said Joseph, suddenly remembering, "I caught sight of your father in London. He's one of us, a Loyalist. He was forced to leave Boston for England."

Aaron looked at his uncle in surprise. He had not thought of his father in years. He remembered the last time he had seen him, propped on his pillow, feeble with fever after losing his arm. He remembered walking up to his father's white squaw after saying goodbye to him and giving her the golden talisman his father had given to him.

Molly started to chuckle. "Poor Stephen," she said. "He was such a *Bastonnais*. Now he lives in London. He left me because I tried to make him live in the longhouse. Now I live in a fine European house. He could have been comfortable with me in this house."

"You may live in this house, Mother," said Aaron solemnly, "but you are the great clan mother. You are Iroquois."

Molly reached up and patted his cheek. "Before you arrived your uncle and I were talking about our next step."

Aaron's eyes sparkled with excitement.

"There will be a campaign this spring and summer," said Joseph. "Regular troops will push down the lake of the Iroquois toward Albany. A second attack—and this is the one that concerns us—will be manned by Loyalists and ourselves. It will liberate our valley from the rebels. Once we've seized Fort Stanwix, the way will be clear from Oswego to Albany."

Molly poured herself another cup of tea.

"This is our moment," she said. "The Loyalists, like Guy Johnson or Sir John and the Butlers, will never have a better chance than this. Destroy the rebel fort and the

Loyalists of the valley will rise. Our people must be convinced to join them. The whites surround the Mohawk castles. And they push far into Oneida country. This chance is our last. The fate of the Loyalists and the fate of the Iroquois are tied together. They will rise and fall together."

"Precisely," said Joseph. "And we must guarantee that we do not fall. For if we do, it will be our last fall. I'm off to Fort Oswego. St. Leger, the British commander, will be there with regulars. Sister, you ought to stay here and send word of any rebel reinforcements traveling west along the river. And nephew, I give you a very different task. John and Walter Butler are at Niagara. They talk of creating regiments of white Loyalists. But so far they have used only influence with the Seneca. It is essential that the Seneca come to the war with us. First they must be made to realize this, and secondly they must be weaned from the Butlers and be made more willing to cooperate with St. Leger. I don't trust the Butlers. They have white interests at heart. Claus will be made commander of the Indian troops in this campaign, but neither John Butler nor his son Walter must know this until they have joined us at Oswego. Claus is our kinsman. He can be trusted."

"I don't think any of Johnson's sons or sons-in-law like Claus are to be implicitly trusted either. They tried to take an inheritance from your nephews, Joseph," Molly interrupted. "We still have ties of blood with the Johnsons and Claus. We have nothing with the Butlers."

The Lower Town of Quebec showed none of the scars of the fighting of 1776. The barricades were gone, and the Americans, who had no siege guns, did very little damage. In fact, it seemed as if the war had just passed the old fortress by. All the activity was upriver—at Sorel and at Montreal.

Stephen walked to the waterfront of the Lower Town, looking for someone who could take him to Isle d'Orleans. He was shocked by the amount of French he had forgotten. For years it had been his first language and practically his only language. Now he had to stop and think of the right word. He had spoken English almost exclusively for the past twenty years.

He walked out on a jetty. In the channel, a man of war dipped its flag and began its salute to the capital city of Canada, but it made no attempt to enter Quebec harbor. It would sail straight to Montreal—toward Burgoyne, who was outfitting his army for the trip down the lakes to Albany, or toward St. Leger, who would lead American Loyalists and Indians into the Mohawk.

An old fisherman sat at a boat tied at the jetty. He watched the man of war disappear. He was dressed in dark breeches and a light brown shirt of homespun. A pipe was jammed into his mouth, but no smoke rose from it. His face was bright red, bearing the mark of the sun and wind on the river.

Stephen approached him and greeted him in his best Acadian. "How much to take me to the island?" he asked, pointing upriver toward Isle d'Orleans.

"Nothing," said the fisherman.

Stephen looked at him in astonishment. Perhaps he had been in Europe too long. He had forgotten about neighborliness and helping another person out.

"Ah, you were planning to go there yourself?"

"No," said the fisherman.

Stephen was still puzzled. "Then why aren't you charging me to take me there?"

"Because I'm not taking you there." He cackled, revealing brown-stained, crooked teeth.

"Look, old fellow," Stephen said. "Do you see this empty sleeve? This means I can't row a boat by myself. I wish to get to the island. What do you suggest I do?"

"Why, get someone to row you there."

"Do you have anyone in mind?"

"Yes, me!"

Stephen was now truly exasperated. "What made you change your mind?"

"Nothing, monsieur. But I will determine when I will row. You're a rich Englishman, although your accent is almost good enough to fool most. Rich Englishmen expect everyone to drop everything they are doing and do what the Englishmen want, simply for money. You will have trouble with us French over that. I must first go home. I have been fishing since before dawn. I must sell my catch, have my dinner, make love to my wife—and at my age that is no quick accomplishment. Then I will rest—at my age equally important. And I will take you to the island before sunset. Unless, of course, you can find someone who can take you sooner."

Stephen truly regretted his decision to leave Josiah in charge of his London house. But he saw no other boatmen on the jetty, and he had little choice but to accept the old man's offer.

"How much?" he asked for the second time.

"An English silver crown."

"My God, man, that is outrageous."

"I know, monsieur, but what else can a one-armed man do? Too bad you aren't a frog. I hear they can regrow their limbs."

Stephen decided he had little choice. In the meanwhile he would have his own dinner. He smiled bitterly to himself. He had no catch to sell. No wife to make love to. There was a tavern at the far end of the jetty.

"I'll be waiting for you here before sunset, old man. I want to be on that island before dark."

The shadows cast by the bluffs of the Upper Town had covered most of Lower Quebec by the time the old man arrived back at the jetty. He saw Stephen pacing impatiently by his boat. He began to rub his belly in contentment and then patted his crotch.

"A successful afternoon, monsieur. I hope you used yours well."

Stephen handed him the coin and slipped over the side of the jetty after the fisherman, who steadied the boat against the dock.

"It will be dark before I even get there," said Stephen. "And I have no place to stay."

The old man shook his head. "A man of your age and with your infirmities should do one of two things. Stay at home or stop complaining. Once we get out onto the river, away from the bluffs, the sun will be in the sky. When we get to the village of St. Pierre, see the curé. He sometimes puts up travelers."

Stephen was annoyed with the fisherman. He was not accustomed to receiving lectures. But then he started to laugh to himself. It was true. He was becoming a fussy old Englishman, demanding instant attention. His money brought him that. It was refreshing to meet someone who would not cater to him.

The current in the channel drove the boat toward the island. And as the boatman had promised, before the sun disappeared from the western sky in a haze of rose and purple, the boat bottom scraped the gravel of the St. Pierre landing beach. Stephen climbed out and walked a few feet up to the village.

"Where does the curé live?" asked Stephen, turning to the boatman.

The boat was already several feet offshore on its return journey.

"Look for the largest house," called the fisherman. "They always live in the largest house." He chuckled.

The curé was a nosy man. He provided Stephen shelter for the night, but the price he tried to extract was information. Since he got little from Stephen, he in turn decided to inform Stephen all about the island. Most of it bored Stephen. He found the story of the island Sons of Liberty rushing off to aid the Americans mildly interesting. The tragedy of the drowning of their leader, Antoine Gingras, at the attack on Quebec made little impression on him until the priest mentioned the Stiegler boy.

"What was that?" Stephen interrupted his flow.

"What?"

"You mentioned the Stiegler boy. What happened to him?"

"Nothing," said the curé. "He still lives here on the island with his mother. Poor woman. She has lost so much. Two husbands. I'm being generous about the second. Far be it from me to condemn her. That was years ago, and one of my predecessors from the parish . . . what was his name? No matter, we will soon all be forgotten. Nevertheless, this curé condemned her as a wanton woman. The Swiss, Stiegler, he cursed the priest. But it was a double curse. He said he would die in peace if he could see the priest die with blood in his mouth. The priest was later shot in front of Stiegler. Those who were present say the blood literally pumped out of his mouth. Before the summer was out, Stiegler was dead. They say his death was peaceful. But the woman never quite recovered from her loss. And now her daughter has left."

Stephen sat quietly, listening to the priest tell of Amy's love for Gingras and how she had abandoned her mother and brother after his death and fled to New York, where she might find her father. He grieved for her. She had already suffered too much for one so young. And now he had missed her. But Katherine was still here. Poor Katherine; she had suffered even more.

"The woman, Katherine, is she well?"

"Physically, yes. But they say she never speaks. She just sits and stares."

Stephen, too, simply stared. God, how he had hurt her. How her children had hurt her.

In the morning Stephen thanked the curé and set out on the road along the island's north shore. He had asked for no breakfast and the curé had offered him none. The curé was truly disappointed in this traveler. A visitor to the island was a rare event, and it was irritating when one came and offered no news.

The road along the river was deeply rutted. It had rained overnight, and the ruts were filled with water. Stephen's fine London shoes would soon be destroyed by the mud. He remembered once, years ago, following a mud path that led to Karl Stiegler. That had been in the Port Royale campaign, just after he had met William Vaughan, thirty years before, and now he followed another path that would lead him to Karl's son and his own wife, the boy's mother. That last time, he had removed his shoes and walked in the icy mud until the sun warmed it up. Now he could afford to ruin the shoes.

The traffic on the river was heavy this morning as well.

All of it was passing upriver toward the campaign. There were Canadian geese along the shore. Pairs of adults preened themselves and darted their heads into the water, looking for food. The younger ones, not yet paired off, looked awkward and still a bit fuzzy. They seemed to stay closer to the shoreline, perhaps frightened by the *bateaux*, gunboats, and merchant vessels that crowded the channel.

Stephen had walked this route before—the last time he had come looking for Katherine. The next farm would be that of her neighbor. Stephen rounded the bend in the road. There it was. The yard was overgrown with weeds, and the place was now clearly abandoned. Stephen continued along the road. The ground was higher here, and there was not so much mud. The sun had come up. It was barely nine o'clock in the morning and he was sweating. It was to be one of those unbearably hot St. Lawrence Valley June days.

He wiped his forehead with his sleeve. He felt the scar on his eyelid throb. A jumping nerve there frequently bothered him. The same thing often occurred in the muscle of his arm.

He wondered what she would look like. He had changed. He knew it. He was thicker in the middle, and his hair had started to turn white on the sides. This last he didn't mind. He hoped his whole head turned white. Then perhaps he could give up the silly wig he had to wear on formal occasions.

He was puffing now. The road climbed a sloping hill. When he reached the top, he could see a lovely farm. The house looked out onto the river. Its verandah had a beautiful view of the river and Montmorency Falls. Smoke rose slowly from the chimney. Stephen began the walk down the slope toward the house.

Katherine had changed very little, he thought. There were some strands of white in her brown hair, and she had the beginnings of a second chin. She was plumper than before. But even if she looked much as she had years before, she was not the same person.

She sat on the verandah with her hands in her lap, staring out at the falls across the river. He walked up to the steps. He called her name. She did not respond.

"Katherine," he called again.

"Can I do something for you?" a voice said from behind him. He turned around and looked into the face of Karl Stiegler.

Of course, it was not Karl. Karl had died in his arms at the Plains of Abraham. And this face was young—young as Karl's had been thirty-five years ago.

"Can I do something for you?" the young man repeated.

"You must be Monsieur Stiegler," said Stephen.

The blond-haired youth nodded.

"I'm Stephen Nowell."

The boy looked confused at first, but then Stephen noticed a hardening of his features. It was clear that the name Nowell would be greeted with hostility.

"What do you want here?"

"I'd like to speak to your mother."

"She don't talk. And she don't talk especially to you, since you were the one who originally put her in this shape."

Stephen turned back to Katherine. He took her hand in his. She still had that faraway look in her eyes.

"Katherine? It's me, Stephen," he said.

She made no response.

"Speak to me, Katrina," he said, reverting to her old Schuyler Dutch name. Staring into her eyes was like staring into deep, empty wells. He put her hand down and turned to Louis Joseph, who was still standing with hands on hips and fists clenched.

"Why did you come back here? Haven't you done enough to her already? She left you. She loved my father. You divorced her. Now leave her be."

"I might ask you the same question. Why did you come back here?" responded Stephen. "It seems to me you've done your bit as well. The curé told me that Amy had left, and he told me why she left. Was my wife like this all of these years since the divorce? Could it be that you contributed to some of this?"

The look of anguish that crossed the young man's face was his answer.

"Just go away, Nowell," Louis Joseph shouted. "I've taken care of her for these months. Look at her. She's fed; she's clean. I set her out here in this chair and sometimes she even rocks. I think deep down she knows I'm here and that I love her." He was crying now. "That's more than she can say about you. You Nowells, you and Amy—you both deserted her."

The tears of grief were mixed with tears of anger. He made a move toward Stephen. But he realized that the man was middle-aged and disabled, and he was embarrassed. In addition, Nowell made no move either to protect himself or to run away. Louis Joseph jammed his fist instead into the verandah post, splitting the wood and forcing it away from the roof. The roof sagged slightly. His knuckles were split. He shook his hand and put it in his mouth to stop the bleeding.

Stephen turned his back on Louis Joseph to spare the boy's feelings. He knelt down beside Katherine's chair and began to speak to her.

"Katrina, it's me, Stephen. I've come back. I don't expect you to forgive me for what I did. I never loved you enough when I was a young man. God knows, after your childhood, you desperately needed love. I failed you, and Karl gave you what you needed—love, protection, security. He was there. I wasn't. I wish I had understood then as I now do. I would never have left you. I failed you and I'm sorry. I can't undo what I did—that's a hopeless route to travel."

Katherine stared straight ahead.

Stephen patted her hand and then stood up.

Louis Joseph was in control of himself again. "You leaving now? Now that you got that off of your conscience?"

"I'm going back to make arrangements to stay in the village."

"What for? I'm taking care of her."

"Physically, you've done the best you can," responded Stephen. "But I'm going to work on her head. From what the curé told me, she got this way gradually. Well, what's done gradually can only be undone gradually. I'm staying. Every day I'll come to speak to her and to help her."

"Like hell you will," said the boy. "I'll kick your ass right off my property if you set foot on it again."

"We'll see," said Stephen. He stepped off the verandah and started up the road to the knoll above the farm. When he was halfway up, Louis Joseph yelled at him.

"Don't come back here, do you hear me?"

Stephen ignored him and kept on walking.

The young man went back to his garden to pull weeds. But he was still angry and worried. He walked around front again and climbed up onto the verandah.

"Son of a bitch," he mumbled under his breath. He knew she wouldn't hear him, but he could not bring himself to swear aloud in her presence. He walked over to her and pulled up another chair.

"It's all right, Mother. He won't be back to bother you. I promise."

She moved her eyes and looked at him. Louis Joseph was startled. It was the first time she had recognized his existence since Amy had left them. Then she moved her lips. He rose from the chair and placed his ear next to her mouth. He barely caught the sound that came from her. She was repeating her own name over and over again in a whisper.

"Katrina, Katrina, Katrina."

Something wet fell on Louis Joseph's cheek. He pulled away and saw that tears flowed from her eyes. He knew immediately what had caused it all, and he knew what he had to do. He went to the barn and saddled his horse.

Nowell did not have that much of a head start. Louis Joseph climbed into the saddle and kicked the horse's sides while still in the barn and rode out the door at breakneck speed. He rode up the slope. When he reached the top he reined in the horse. He saw Nowell walking far ahead of him. He kicked the horse again and tore down the road.

Stephen heard him coming well before he was upon him. He turned and faced the boy, fully expecting him to attack. He had only his walking stick with which to defend himself.

"Monsieur Nowell, would you please hold still?" Louis Joseph yelled.

Stephen relaxed. If the boy were still enraged, he would not be so polite.

Again the young man pulled in on the reins and the horse reared. Louis Joseph jumped from its back and steadied it.

"I . . . I . . . need to ask you to pardon my behavior back there," he said. "Something has happened to her. She spoke and she cried. I think that maybe if you come back it would help. You achieved more in a few moments than I did in months. Please, sir, come back and help my mother."

Stephen took the reins of the horse from Louis Joseph's hands. The boy surrendered them without a word.

"Climb up," said Stephen. The boy placed his feet in the stirrups and with one fluid motion was astride the horse.

Stephen gave Louis Joseph his hand. After placing his left foot in the empty stirrup, Stephen was awkwardly hauled up behind the rider. He placed his arm about the young man's middle for support.

"Now let's get the hell back to your mother. She's been alone long enough."

Stephen knew where he would spend his days and nights for the foreseeable future. He would look for his son later. For now Burgoyne's campaign and St. Leger's campaign were of no importance. Now it was only Katherine who mattered.

VIII

SUMMER 1777

Just eighteen months before, Joseph Brant had dined with nobility. It was hard to imagine what the lords and ladies would think of their guest now as he crawled on his hands and knees through the underbrush. He was dressed in buckskins and his face was painted in zigzagged white streaks on each cheek. Behind him his nephew, Aaron, followed his path, careful to avoid stepping on branches or disturbing the underbrush. There was no breeze, and any movement in the underbrush would be a signal to an alert sentry.

A daylight reconnoiter was dangerous but essential. Ahead of them stood Fort Stanwix, or Fort Schuyler, as the rebels now termed it. It was the key to the whole campaign. Nothing but frontier blockhouses stood between Stanwix and Albany. If the fort fell, the road was clear. The fort stood astride the portage between the bend of the Mohawk near its headwaters and Wood Creek—the water route to Lake Oneida, the Oswego River and Lake Ontario. At Fort Oswego on Lake Ontario, St. Leger and his force now awaited Brant's report.

Joseph signaled Aaron with his hand. The two men crawled several more feet. Brant signaled a halt and motioned Aaron to join him. They had reached a small rise. Slightly ahead and slightly below them was the fort.

It was built of earth and timber and was almost, but not quite, square. At each corner there was a bastion. Surrounding the whole fortress was a deep ditch with a palisade made of sharp stakes. There were cannons mounted. Aaron counted thirteen. Joseph agreed.

"Three of them look to be heavy nine-pounders," Joseph whispered.

"This force does not look like the rabble we were told would be manning this fort," said Aaron.

"No, you have seen what they have done to Wood Creek by felling trees. It is all but impassable. St. Leger will have a devil of a time bringing siege guns here—even the few that he did not leave behind. We must get back to camp with this news. St. Leger must not come forward without his guns. This is not a simple, unfinished outpost."

The two men retraced their steps back down the rise and through the woods. They crossed a small brook, using a log that had fallen across it as a bridge. About five miles from the fort they came to the clearing where they had spent the night with three Seneca companions. The Senecas had returned. With them was a rebel militiaman, bound hand and foot.

Brant greeted Geyasada, the Seneca leader, with warmth.

"The Seneca have had great success," he praised them. "My brother Johnson and the British general will get good information from the prisoner."

Geyasada grimaced. "Will they read his bones? I did not know that the son of Johnson had become a shaman. We will prepare the prisoner for a quick fire. His screams will not be heard this far from the fort, and he will scream."

Joseph's face remained totally impassive. "It is my understanding," he said, "that Butler leads the Seneca from Niagara to Oswego. In the war that is coming, many of your people who are my brothers will be fighting. I would grieve if some of them were to die because this soldier was burned uselessly here in the woods instead of being brought to my brothers Claus and Johnson to give them the information they need."

"He knows nothing," insisted Geyasada.

The two other Seneca had joined the discussion in support of their leader.

"Why don't we let Butler decide?" suggested Brant, trying to win the life of the soldier without jeopardizing the friendship of the Senecas.

But Geyasada was in no mood to be placated. He

turned from Brant to the militiaman, who cringed in fear and turned away from the Seneca as much as the ropes would allow him.

The Indian pulled his razor-sharp scalping knife from its sheath at his side and brandished it in front of the soldier's eyes. The white man followed its motion as if mesmerized.

Brant turned his back on the scene and spoke to Aaron loudly enough for Geyasada to hear.

"We must inform the clan mother of this incident. Geyasada is brave but risks the safety of his brothers, his tribe, and his clan for personal satisfaction."

Geyasada had torn the white man's shirt from his chest. His knife stopped in midair. His face clouded with anger. Then the knife plunged into the chest and the heart of the soldier. The white man's body shuddered and then sagged at the knees. His eyes went blank and he fell to the ground.

"Tell Gonwatsijayenni about that, too, Englishman," he spat out, surprising even himself with his boldness.

Aaron started to make a move toward Geyasada, but Joseph held his arm.

"Be calm," he said in English. He turned to the Seneca and smiled. "Be at peace, Geyasada. I will tell my sister at Canajoharie that the war leader Geyasada acted bravely and gave up the pleasure of torturing a prisoner and killed him quickly so as not to encumber himself and so that we five could return to our respective camps with our news." He stepped over the body of the American as if it were a newly fallen log. "Geyasada, you must tell Corn Planter and Butler that they must join St. Leger immediately. The rebels grow stronger at the fort daily. We must strike quickly. We have no time for any delay."

Geyasada listened to Joseph and then he knelt down and deftly removed the scalp from his victim, stuffing the grisly trophy in his leather pouch. He motioned to his two colleagues, and the three moved silently from the clearing and disappeared in seconds.

Aaron stood watching them go. He was angered by what Geyasada had done.

"The man is a pig," he said angrily to Joseph.

The older man smiled. "You're right, but what's done is done. At least we spared the pour soul the pain of the fire."

"We should have saved him. Look at him. He's a boy."

Joseph stared at Aaron. "Nephew," he said, "this is war. Bad things happen in war, and they are done by both sides. Our people are villified by the rebels and the British alike as cruel and savage. Yet we do what we have always done. We kill males, even infants. They will grow to be men and kill us in turn. Sometimes our people torture. Sometimes they adopt. It is part of our culture. We bring honor to ourselves and to our prisoner. The whites do not understand this. If we are to survive in a world dominated by them, if our Indian people are to have their own nation, away to the west, away from the white farms, then we must give over these aspects that the whites call cruel. We must adapt our culture to theirs or we are doomed to oblivion. But all that takes time."

Aaron picked up the body of the soldier, carried it to the edge of the clearing and dumped it under some honeysuckle bushes.

"We have already drunk much," said Aaron. "And I chose that word deliberately. Rum, muskets, steel knives and tomahawks, sewing needles, even houses and mills. All have become essential to our way of life. Building a longhouse is practically a lost art among the Mohawk. We are corrupted by the whites. They hate our torturing. They hate our killing the helpless. So do I. But I hate their rum, their knives that never break, their muskets that kill without a test of strength. I hate all of that as much as I hate what in our culture is brutal and cruel."

"Why, nephew, you're a reformer. A Mohawk puritan. I had not believed you had that in you. I thought you, Molly Brant's son, were at heart a pragmatist like her and me. We do what is best for our people to make an Indian nation."

"Don't mock me, Joseph," warned Aaron. "I'm not a boy or even a new warrior. I can take care of Mother. I love her and I love you. I've given my life to you and our people. I do not always think your way has been the right way."

"You've been very slow to say it."

"That's true," responded Aaron. "I am not a talker."

"Well, this is not the time for talk. We must get to Daniel Claus and to St. Leger at Oswego. We'll need everybody we can get if this campaign is to succeed."

Barry St. Leger stood in full view of the American fortress, not far from where the Brants had stood days before. He had rushed his little army of British regulars and loyal Americans, Canadians and Indians to the outskirts of Fort Stanwix. Somehow he had to take it and force his way downriver to Albany and Burgoyne. The flooding and blocking of Wood Creek had forced him to leave what little artillery he had back at Lake Oneida. Now he realized the full import of leaving the siege guns behind at Montreal. Even if he had brought his guns forward from the lake, they would have been of no more use than popguns against this formidable fortress. Now he was reduced to two options—surprise attack or siege. This last would be difficult. He had not nearly enough men to carry it out. The former also had little chance of success. An easy amble up the Mohawk by his force of whites and Indians seemed less and less likely.

Daniel Claus, commander of Indian forces and son-in-law of the great Sir William Johnson, joined St. Leger.

"Your reports were right, Daniel. Brant and the other scouts told us it was strong. Damn it, I wish I had siege guns. I could make short work of it."

Claus' thin face broke into a weak smile. "My estimate is that it will take over a week to clear the creek and bring our small guns into place."

"You rule out surprise?" asked St. Leger.

"The Oneida know we're here. They'll have told Colonel Gansevoort. There'll be no surprising the rebels."

"What do you know about my opponent?"

"I know he's twenty-eight and he's inexperienced. I'd be more worried about that old goat, my former neighbor

211

Nicholas Herkimer. He commands the rebel militia in the valley. He's a shrewd old bastard."

"I've heard the name Herkimer before."

"Joost Herkimer, our overseer of *bateaux*, is his brother."

St. Leger shook his head. "This war has torn you Yankees apart, hasn't it?"

"Yes, and it's even worse in New York. This is a strange place. Listen to our American names—Claus, Herkimer, Gansevoort, Schuyler, VanCortlandt, Delancey. We English in this colony are a feisty lot," he said with a broad smile.

St. Leger broke into an ironic grin. "My name's not exactly Anglo-Saxon, and for that matter, the King's only second-generation. Well, Claus, siege it is, then. Though God alone knows how we will pull it off without siege guns."

Joseph Brant sat with a small contingent of Mohawks in the woods beyond the range of the camp of the fort, watching a group of Royal Yorkers and regular army artillerymen prepare to move out into the fields in front of the fort after dark. They were to prepare a breastwork with gun emplacements. This was work that the whites understood and the Iroquois avoided.

The whites had decided on a siege. It was not the way the Iroquois fought best. There was already grumbling among the Seneca. They complained that the Ranger leader, John Butler, was not in charge and that they had not received the gifts that he had promised them at Niagara. All had gone to Brant's men because of his relationship with Claus. It was true that Brant disliked Butler and was disgusted by his tactics. Rum was his great persuader. Brant preferred the honored tradition of oratory. But he knew that he and Butler shared the same immediate goals—the conquest of the Mohawk Valley and the restoration of the King's peace. From there on they differed. Few whites, other than his sister's husband Johnson, shared his view of a great Indian nation under royal tutelage. Both rebel and Loyalist expected the Indians to

212

give way to white settlement as it pushed farther west. Ultimately, after this war was won, it might be necessary to persuade England to limit settlement. Otherwise the next war would be one of white against red man.

Brant heard the bushes behind him sway with the breeze. But the noise lasted just a bit longer than the wind could have caused. It was Aaron's signal. His nephew had been east, visiting his mother at Canajoharie. The news he brought from Molly must indeed be important if other Mohawks were to be kept from hearing it.

Brant rose, commenting that last night's venison must have gone bad. He held his belly and started to amble off to the rear to find a secluded spot. A Fort Hunter Mohawk teased him and demanded that if that were the case, he should pity them all and find a spot downwind.

Brant made an obscene gesture back and guffawed.

Once out of view and hearing, he stood absolutely still and waited for Aaron to contact him. He felt the hand on his shoulder before he heard or saw anything. He thought himself a good woodsman, but Aaron always impressed him with his skills.

"How is my sister, the clan mother?" Brant said without turning around.

"My mother sends urgent word to you and to Claus. Herkimer marches this way with the rebel militia, one thousand strong."

"Come with me," Joseph said. The two men walked quickly through the camp of the recently arrived Seneca and Cayuga. Claus' tent was not far from St. Leger's and Sir John Johnson's. A sentry saluted Brant as he pushed back the flap, to find all of the commanders in conference. He and Aaron entered. The three whites saw the look of concern on his face and did not waste time with greetings.

"Herkimer is on his way with the militia to relieve the fortress."

Johnson stood up in consternation. "How many men has he?" asked St. Leger.

Aaron answered. "About a thousand, all of them local militia."

"Worth about a hundred of our boys," said Johnson.

"Your boys are their former neighbors," said the British general. "If we are to disparage the enemy, let's do it after a fight."

He turned to Aaron. "You, sir," he said, "I'm sorry I don't know your name."

"Aaron Brant, sir."

"My nephew and the revered Molly's son," said Joseph Brant.

St. Leger decided he was treading dangerous ground. The Brants, Johnsons, and Clauses were all interrelated, with their own internal feuds. Was it possible that this Indian was another of Sir John's half-brothers? But the others bore the name Johnson and not Brant, and Sir John had offered no introduction. Strange lot.

"Mr. Brant, that is, Mr. Aaron Brant, my assumption is that their troops are farmers, not woodsmen."

"Correct."

"Good; then my solution is that we set a warm greeting for them."

The hot August sun beat down on the men as they marched along the river trail west. They had camped at Oriska, an Oneida village, the night before. Israel Kip didn't much approve of all of this marching, and Socono was decidedly hostile. The Indian, as usual, had disappeared along with the Christian Oneida. They had all showed up in camp at night. They came the same distance, but their way. Kip was furious that Socono, who was decidedly older than he was, always seemed fresh at the end of the day, while Kip felt exhausted.

Kip wasn't even sure why he had come on this expedition. If Margaret learned of it, she would surely kill him, but not until she had worked him over slowly in a fashion that would put a Mohawk to shame. He had gone to Fort Vaughan to look in on Amy, only to find her married and delivered of a daughter. The old woman would be furious that he had kept this news from her. But Israel also knew that Amy's decision to call the baby Margaret would more than make up for it. Israel was not much on counting, so there was no need for him to give any details about when the baby was born and how much she weighed. A little fudging and a little prematurity would, in years to come, cloud the issue until no one could remember exactly what had happened.

He and Socono and Matthew had stayed in Socono's lodge in the woods until word came that the militia was out. He couldn't understand how a daughter of Stephen Nowell and a niece of Margaret Schuyler could take up with a "thee" and "thou" fellow, but he knew that someone in the family was going to have to represent them in the militia. Sure as hell no Quaker was going to do his duty. So, without further ado, Socono and Kip had taken Kurt Miller's place. Matthew had begged to come along and bragged he was a veteran of Bunker Hill, but Socono had merely looked at the boy with disdain and had silenced him. Kip thought a boot in the ass just as effective, but Socono had clearly done a job on the boy. He obeyed his elders, did what he was told and had developed a dignity reminiscent of the Indian's. None of that had been there before.

"Damn the sun," Kip cursed. He wished he was with Socono off in the woods now. He didn't like the way the column was moving. Some of these ground-chopping farmers had wanted to rush right into Stanwix. Herkimer wanted a cautious approach. The idea was to relieve the fort, not to provide hairy lodge-pole decorations for the Iroquois. But farmers associated with sheep and chickens too much. They thought like sheep and chickens, which meant that they didn't think much at all. They called old Herk a coward and reminded him that he had a brother with the Tories. The old, fat general's Teuton face had gone red with rage. He yelled and shouted and then sent word to all to push on to the fort, and push on they did. Word was that Herkimer had sent messengers to Stanwix to warn them that he was coming. He wanted a sortie from the fort to fight a path for him to enter.

Kip heard a squirrel chirp. He stopped, and the man behind him stepped on his heel.

"*Gott in himmel,*" said the man from the rear. "Watch where you stop."

Kip hopped about on his foot, cursing. Then he sat down on the ground and began to rub his heel. His militia unit proceeded forward without him, then continued down the road into a ravine.

Ahead of them was Oriskiny Creek. The men at the head of the column had already crossed it and were proceeding farther along the path to Stanwix.

Suddenly the van was staggered by a volley of musketry. A roar came from hundreds of throats as the green-coated Johnson's Loyal Americans poured out of the woods on both sides of the road in front of the column.

Even more terrifying, however, came the dreaded cries of the Iroquois, Seneca, Mohawk, Cayuga and Onondaga, as they leapt out of the underbrush on both flanks, wielding axes and spears.

Kip watched as the German soldier who had stepped on him was cut down, a lance thrust through his belly and out his back. Socono appeared from out of the woods at Kip's side. The signal had been his, and Kip had recognized it instantly.

The Indians had sprung the trap too soon. The rear of the rebel column had not entered the ravine and was not under attack. Nevertheless, all around him Kip saw men dropping whatever they carried to flee madly down the path away from the ambush.

"The Mohawks are working their way down to try to cut us off," said Socono. "We must either flee or turn to fight them. This is your battle, my friend. I'll join you, no matter what you decide."

"I ain't never run from a fight in my life. But you're right: this is my fight. You go. I'll catch up with you later."

"An Abenacki never misses a chance to take an Iroquois scalp. It's a fight for both of us."

The two men raced forward toward the embattled center of the American column. Kip stopped, aimed his musket and fired. An Indian seemed almost to leap into the air from the force of Kip's ball. He fell forward, the tomahawk he held in his raised arm falling harmlessly to the ground.

Socono gave off a piercing yell and threw his tomahawk.

It split the skull of an Indian who had bent low to remove the scalp from a screaming, still-living militiaman.

The Iroquois had wreaked havoc among the American forces. The bodies of the slain were everywhere. Their supply wagons had been set on fire, and dozens of smoke columns blackened the white, hazy August afternoon.

Some of the rebels had rallied and moved out of the ravine to a wooded plateau west of the road. Kip pointed out the spot to Socono. The Indian nodded in acknowledgment and the two men moved toward the new rebel line. Socono crouched low and moved with incredible speed for a man of his age. Kip started to follow. A young Mohawk came racing from behind the cover of some trees in his eagerness to make his first kill. Kip did not see him coming. But he heard him. He dropped to the ground and the young brave tripped, falling forward over his body. The Mohawk flipped from the ground onto his feet and stood now between Kip and the comparative safety of the plateau. Then he approached Kip slowly, his eyes watching Kip's hands to see if the white man would attempt to grab either his knife or his tomahawk, which hung harmlessly from his belt. Kip's musket was empty.

The young Mohawk stood straight up. A look of surprise crossed his face, then blankness. He fell forward, and Kip saw Socono's knife protruding from his back.

The old man came back down the slope. He pulled out his knife and removed the boy's scalp with several deft cuts. Kip had seen it all before, but he still felt sorrow for one so young.

Socono offered Kip his hand, which was covered with blood. "Kip grows too old to fight?" he asked with his eyebrows arched.

"There are two things I'll never be too old for, you old bug-eating scarface, and one of them is fighting." He brushed aside Socono's hand, and the two men began anew the climb to the plateau. The regrouped rebel forces had rallied about their general. Herkimer had been carried to this place by his men. His leg had been shattered by a musket ball. He was propped against his saddle, smoking a pipe.

Socono and Kip came before him. The general looked at Socono.

"Be you one of ours?" he said, pointing his pistol at the Abenacki.

"He's with us," said Kip.

The general sighed, mostly with pain. "And who is us?" he asked no one in particular. "Find yourselves a tree and get behind it. I want two behind every tree. One fires. The Indian attacks, thinking you're reloading. Your companion kills him. It's that simple. If you do it well, you live to see the morrow. If not, you join me." He looked down at his smashed leg with resignation.

Aaron had become separated from Brant and the Mohawk almost at the very beginning of the ambush. He found himself among Butler's Seneca. He was furious with them. It had been their impatience that had allowed the rear of the American column to escape. He had killed three rebel militiamen in the first rush. But now the rebels had established a position on high ground out of the ravine. The easy slaughter of the first ambush was now over. The rebels could stay where they were unless they were driven out.

Aaron looked to his left and saw four Seneca crouched in the gully. He recognized Geyasada.

A platoon of Sir John Johnson's greencoats filled the gap in the line and poured into the gully on Aaron's right. Most of his new neighbors were boys, nineteen or twenty years old. They chattered away excitedly and paid no attention to the Indians, whom they assumed spoke little or no English.

A blond boy, lying prone next to Aaron, called to another down the line.

"Andrew! I got me a Dutchman right at the beginning. I got me Joost VanRiper. Damn near took his head off. Imagine that. I used to court VanRiper's cousin. Tried to make her on the family back porch. Her old man kicked me in the ass and sent me scurrying before I could get my breeches up. Fixed them all, the sons of bitches."

Andrew apparently did not hear or had ignored the

blond boy. He turned his head and looked anew at Aaron. He shook his head and mumbled.

"The King's got damned strange friends."

"Agreed," said Aaron, looking straight ahead toward the plateau where the Americans had grouped.

The blond boy looked again in surprise. "Are you one of them praying Indians?"

"No."

"Good. I can't stand them even worse than Dutchmen."

"I'm glad I failed in spirit, considering what you do to Dutchmen."

"It's a goddamned war out there," said the boy. "Maybe you haven't noticed. I killed Joost before he could kill me."

"I make war on my enemies, not on my friends," said Aaron.

"There are some of your kind on their side, mister, and I suspect if one of them comes at you with a gun, you'd blow his head off just as I blew off VanRiper's."

"I hope I don't have to face that."

"Well, that's the kind of war we got here in the valley, neighbor against neighbor, father against son, brother against brother. Their general is supposed to be old Herk. My daddy and him smoked many a pipe and downed a few beers together at Fort Hunter in the past. But these rebel bastards drove us out because we wouldn't fight against our King, God bless him. No one drives us Nortons from our farm. My pappy and me left Mom with the kids and we headed for Niagara. The rebels have been abusing my mom ever since, and VanRipers are big shots on the Committee of Safety. That's one who is paid off for making my Mom eat slops and fear for herself and her kids every time someone knocks at the front door, snooping to see if Pa and me is back."

The boy ducked as a musket ball rattled through the limbs of a maple tree above their heads.

A green-coated lieutenant came to the back of the Loyalist line. He stuck his fingers in his mouth and gave off a shrill whistle. The whole line moved forward, each soldier bending low to take advantage of whatever cover he could get from the underbrush.

Aaron moved forward with the Loyalists. On his left he saw several Seneca moving as well. He saw Geyasada and his companions of a few days before. They were creeping on all fours. The Indian glared at Aaron and grimaced. He recalled the encounter over the militiaman with annoyance. It was a bad omen to meet a Brant as they entered battle.

The lieutenant whistled a second time, and his Loyalist rangers rose from their cover and, with a scream, began a headlong rush against the rebel position.

Aaron rose and charged. He gave his war yell and traced a zigzag rather than a straight line toward a clump of birch. He could see the figure of a man, outlined by sunlight pouring through the limbs and leaves. Aaron dived to the ground. The musket ball passed over his head, nipping the top of his feather and removing it as neatly as a scissor. He rolled over to his right and crashed into the side of the boy.

"Shit, Indian, watch where you move."

"Shoot at the birch," yelled Aaron.

"I see him." The boy fired his musket. The man in the birch clump screamed. The boy rose to charge the position. Aaron caught sight of the second musket being lowered to replace the first that had fallen harmlessly to the ground. He grabbed the boy's ankle as he started to run by him. The boy tripped and fell forward. The ball intended for him lodged itself in the trees beyond them.

The blond youth sat on the ground, holding his ankle.

"You shithead," he yelled at Aaron. "You've broken my goddamned foot." He rolled on the ground in agony, holding his ankle.

"There was another rebel in that same position. You got the one; another was about to get you. Stay put here. At least you're alive."

The boy looked at Aaron with gratitude mixed with anger. The Indian rose and ran forward, closing up the line. Many of the Loyalist rangers were on the ground, dead or wounded, fallen victim to Herkimer's tactics.

On Aaron's left Geyasada came charging up the plateau. When he was about even with Aaron, he stood, gave his war cry and glanced over at Aaron, as if to challenge him. Aaron took up the challenge. He rose, towering over the hurt boy at his side. He gave his cry. Together Geyasada and Kenonranon, Iroquois warriors, attacked their enemy.

The Seneca was met head-on by an Abenacki. Aaron stopped dead in place. The Abenacki was an old man with grey hair. He flipped the Seneca over his back and onto the ground with a thud. It took a moment for Geyasada to catch his breath. A second Seneca had followed his war chief into the battle. The old Indian grabbed the newcomer's wrist, bending it backward and breaking it with a resounding crack. The Seneca screamed.

The shadow of a man fell on Aaron, drawing his attention away from the old Indian. Aaron rolled onto the ground and grabbed his knife from its sheath. The rebel who came at him held a wood axe high over his head and was about to split Aaron's skull open like a log of pine. Aaron had no time to fend him off. He threw his knife, knowing that it might be ineffective at such close range. The axe fell harmlessly to the ground with a thud. The eyes of the white man bulged from his face and seemed to stare down incredulously at the hilt of the knife protruding from his throat. Then he followed the axe.

Aaron retrieved his knife with a yank. Blood poured out onto the leaf-covered ground. Then he turned back again toward Geyasada and the old Indian. The young Seneca lay flat on the ground, his hand under him and his wrist and his neck twisted in an impossible position. Geyasada stood facing the Indian; his back was now toward Aaron. The Seneca expected the Mohawk to come to his aid. They were the guardians of the eastern and western doors of the longhouse, and the enemy was within. Yet Aaron could not bring himself to attack an old man, even if he seemed more than capable of defending himself. Geyasada signaled him with his eyes, a movement not lost on the old man.

Geyasada feinted with his knife. The Abenacki's foot flashed out, striking Geyasada's wrist and sending the knife flying from his hand into the bushes. Now the Seneca was weaponless. A shrill whistle sounded in the woods, calling the rangers back to their lines to regroup.

Geyasada heard the whistle. If he remained here, he would be trapped in the rebel lines. Without further effort, he turned and raced away, back toward the lower levels and safety.

Aaron now stood alone, facing the old man, whose chest heaved in and out from exertion. The two men looked at each other. The old man's eyes widened with surprise as he stared into Aaron's face. His muscles were still tensed, but a certain resiliency seemed to leave him. Aaron circled the man. He knew his position was becoming more and more difficult, but he could not flee battle as Geyasada had. The man before him was an Abenacki, enemy of his people, even if he was old. He had not fled, so neither could the Mohawk warrior Kenonranon.

A white man carrying a musket came running down the slope toward where the two Indians faced each other. He raised his musket. The Abenacki held up his hand for him to halt.

"No, Kip," he yelled.

Aaron was startled by the old man's English words, but the Abenacki had been among the whites for as long as the Mohawk. He moved with all of his swiftness against the left arm of the Abenacki, which held the tomahawk. The old man, with incredible speed, switched the weapon to his right hand. Aaron saw the switch and at the last moment went for the Indian's legs. The old man fell backward. Aaron jumped on him, hoping to knock the wind out of him, but again at the last moment the Abenacki rolled away and jumped to his feet. Aaron crouched on the ground. He moved his knife from right to left hand alternately, but the old man's eyes never left his. Aaron sprang forward. He felt his wrist grabbed, and the two men stood chest to chest in a test of strength.

"If all Abenacki, old one, fight as well as you, you should have left the young at home, and the Mohawk could never have beaten you as often as we have."

Aaron said this with an explosion of air from his chest. The old man was strong, yet he seemed to hold back from the offensive, and damn it, thought Aaron, he's smiling at me. The old one has been touched by the Great Spirit. He's mad.

The old man backed away and broke contact. Both were now covered with sweat and breathing deeply, as if they would never regain their breath.

"Break it off," yelled the white man.

Aaron stood straight, to see if the old Indian would do the same, but he did not. Aaron crouched low again. He felt his strength fading from exhaustion and wondered how the old man felt. He must be even more tired. Aaron started to play with his knife from hand to hand again. The Abenacki was exhausted. His concentration was gone. He was following Aaron's hands, not his eyes. Aaron made a motion to switch hands, feinted with his left hand and lunged with his right. Too late he realized that he had been suckered in. The Abenacki's tomahawk flashed out at his exposed chest, but at the last moment it seemed to turn in midair. The flat of the tomahawk struck him a numbing blow on the chest. He heard several ribs crack, but still he lunged, even as the pain crawled from his chest down into his arm. He felt his blade enter the taut muscles of the old man's belly and sink to the hilt.

The old man groaned, a look of surprise on his face. Aaron yanked out his knife.

The white man shouted to the Abenacki to get out of the way. He had his musket to his shoulder. But the old man stood motionless and stepped back. Incredibly, he was still smiling.

"You are a worthy opponent, Kenonranon. Our fight is over. Go." He called to Kip to lower his musket.

The sweat on Aaron's face was stinging his eyes. His chest was heaving in and out. Pain racked his chest every time he breathed. But he stood tall before the old man.

"You are a great teacher, grandfather," he said. Turning his back on the Abenacki and his white friend, he walked to the low ravine.

The old man held his belly. Blood poured through his fingers.

223

"Goddamnit," yelled Kip. "Why did you keep on fighting? Let me see that. Let's get you up onto the plateau again. I want the doctors to look at it."

Socono looked down at the wound. "I shall die from it," he said calmly.

"No, you won't," said Kip. "I'll take you back to the old witch. She won't let you go."

"That was Stephen's son," said the old man. "He did not recognize me, but I remembered him immediately. He's a fine warrior—the best. Stephen can be as proud of him as I am of Stephen." And then, as if a joke had been played on him, he started to laugh. "I said to Stephen when we last saw this lad that I should put a tomahawk into his skull to save my people. I joked then, but I could not have known that to have done so would have been to save myself."

The hand-to-hand fighting lasted all afternoon and into the early evening. The rebel militia had been battered by the ambush, and the rear guard had been routed. But after the initial slaughter, the local militia had started to fight their kind of fight. The Loyalists and their Indian allies were killed in high numbers as they attacked again and again. The Loyal Greens fought with the ferocity of men denied their land. They saw this fight as their last chance to go home again. The slaughter was staggering. But at the end of daylight the rebels held their position on the plateau. A relief column from the fort had attacked an unguarded Loyalist encampment and taken their supplies. The Indians lost their presents and medicine bundles.

The next morning Herkimer and his men limped back toward the Mohawk settlements. Five hundred of their original thousand lay dead in the woods and plateau of Oriskiny.

When Aaron came back to the camp that was besieging Fort Stanwix, he found Joseph Brant, sweating and bloody from the fighting. His uncle threw his arms around him. Aaron cringed with pain.

"I feared for you, Aaron."

"You feared rightly," said the younger man. He then told him of his fight with the Abenacki. "I should not have come out of that fight alive. I believe the old man could have killed me."

Geyasada, the Seneca, interrupted their talk. He was in a rage.

"Brant," he called to Joseph. "Tell Claus and his redcoats that my men and I are leaving this place."

Brant looked at him, puzzled.

"We have suffered losses greater than our people have ever suffered because of you and your white friends," Geyasada explained. "Seventeen Seneca are dead and sixteen have serious wounds. Some will not survive them. Your war has destroyed us."

Brant said nothing. He let Geyasada go.

Aaron spit on the ground, a habit not common with him. He wanted to show his disrespect.

"Geyasada is a coward. He fled from the Abenacki and now he flees from the white rebels."

"Not all great Iroquois are brave warriors, Aaron," said his uncle. "Geyasada argues a great war in council. Among our people the tongue is the mighty weapon. A great speaker can be forgiven almost anything. Cowardice may be termed wisdom if it is wise to withdraw when the odds against you are overwhelming. That way, you live to fight again, when the odds will be more to your liking. I will not fault Geyasada," said Brant, a weariness creeping into his voice. "Seventeen dead for us is a greater tragedy than seventeen hundred for the whites. They are so many and we are so few."

"What will happen now?" asked Aaron.

"The Seneca will go home. The Cayuga and Onondaga will follow them. St. Leger will give up the siege and return to Oswego. Our Loyalist friends will have no choice but to go with him. I feel almost as sorry for Claus and Butler and Johnson and all of their old neighbors as I do for us. Deep down I fear they shall never go home again. Perhaps they should be looking for a new home. Perhaps all of us should be looking."

Socono's wounds were infected and smelled badly by the time Kip got him to Fort Vaughan. He told Matthew he would die, and the boy had run away to hide his grief. Kurt insisted on putting him to bed. The old Indian was weak but he resisted. He would not be put in a white man's bed. He wanted a lodge outside so that he might die properly.

Amy talked him into the bed by telling him that it had been her father's. He recalled seeing Stephen propped in it so many years before, but still he tried to leave the garrison house. He collapsed. Kip and Kurt carried him to bed.

Margaret Schuyler arrived the next day. The British army under Burgoyne had pushed as far south as their house at Saratoga. They had destroyed her beloved mansion. Margaret was crushed, but she would not turn to her nephew, whose dumb war had been responsible for all the suffering. Instead she journeyed to Fort Vaughan as she had years before when driven from her home. She went looking for Kip and for comfort in her sorrow.

She found even greater sorrow. She loved the old Indian. She found him in bed, too weak to move.

"What's a fleabag like you doing in a decent bed?" she yelled as she entered the room.

A smile crossed his pained face. "I must have done the Christian Jesus terrible harm in my life," he croaked. "Even in the face of my death he taunts me with the big voice from the great river."

She sat on the bed next to him. "I hear they have made it possible for you to fart from your stomach." She bent down to smell his wound. "It smells like you've been practicing," she exclaimed loudly.

"Witch," he said to her, "I'm dying. Get me onto the ground so that I may die like an Abenacki."

Margaret looked around. Kip sat in the chair across the room, asleep. He had been up all night with his friend. Amy and Kurt were in the kitchen. The old woman placed the Indian's limp arm about her shoulders. She hauled and pulled and tugged and finally got him half out of the bed. Then she slid him gently onto the floor. The thud of his body striking the wooden floor awakened Kip. He jumped up, thinking Socono had fallen out of bed. He was startled to see his wife sitting on the floor beside the Indian. She had found his blankets among his other things in the corner, and she was wrapping his body in them.

Kip knew he should argue with her, but he had never won a fight with her yet. He saw no reason to believe he could win this one.

The Indian was shaken with chills and he began to chant. His face had thinned remarkably, and the scar on his cheek was now even more pronounced. It seemed to dominate his whole face.

The words of his chant did not vary. He sang it over and over again. Amy heard the singing and rushed into the room. She was shocked to see her aged aunt sitting on the floor with the Indian's head in her lap. She was wiping the sweat from his face. Kip sat next to her, tears coming down his cheeks.

Then the Indian stopped. Kurt, carrying baby Margaret in his arms, joined his wife in the doorway. Matthew walked sheepishly behind Kurt. He had come back to face what he dreaded.

Socono raised his head off Margaret's lap.

"The circle is completed," he said to the room, to his lodge, to his only gods, Glooskap and Malsum. "I killed the blackrobe's father and now the blackrobe's son has killed me."

He lay back onto Margaret's lap and he died.

It was late October when word of Burgoyne's defeat by the American army and his surrender of his entire force at Saratoga reached Isle d'Orleans. Cold fear gripped Stephen's heart. He walked with Katherine along the shore of the river. She still did not say much, but he knew that she was content to have him there. But today he did not think of her immediate problems. Two days before, when Louis Joseph returned from Quebec with the news, Stephen realized that it meant he would not be returning to Boston or to his home in the Mohawk Valley. He could remain in Quebec, but it had bad memories for both of them.

Katherine looked at him quizzically. She did not want him to be distracted from her. She tugged on his empty sleeve.

"What? Oh, Katherine, I'm sorry. I've been thinking about where we might go. Would you be sorry to leave this place?"

She thought for a moment and then nodded. "Yes, I would be sad to leave."

Stephen looked about him. He resigned himself to spending his life here if that was what she wanted. He bent down and kissed her on the mouth. It was the first time he had done this since returning to the island. He rejoiced when she responded to his kiss.

They returned to the house to find Louis Joseph waiting on the verandah. He had moved to the Gingras farm shortly after Stephen had moved in. Stephen had hired several farm youngsters to help Louis Joseph keep the farms operating. A widow from St. Pierre came every morning to clean and cook. Stephen took care of Katherine. Here in Quebec they were still husband and wife, since the church did not recognize his divorce. The whole village agreed that Mistress Katherine had improved since her husband's return, and all approved of him as a result.

Louis Joseph gave him the letter addressed to him. It was from Kip.

Dear Steven,
    Last summer, I rote to you in England. They told me you wuz in Kebec. I'm glad to no that you are back on this side of the oshun but I got bad nuz.

Stephen deciphered the letter with growing anxiety. Normally Margaret corrected Kip's spelling and wrote the letters in her precise script. He feared for Matthew. Had the British armies harmed his friends?

Katherine looked at him anxiously.

Your frend, Socono, is dead—kilt. He wuz hert at Oriskiny and dyde at yur hous at Fort Vaun. Yu wuz on his lips at the end. I am sorry for him, for you and for me. He was my frend to. Mathu and Amy are safe.

Your servant,

I. Kip

Stephen folded the letter in two on his knee. He placed it in his coat pocket. Katherine looked at him with deep concern on her face. She could not yet take any bad news. He knew that. He would have to suffer this loss alone, as she had suffered many alone earlier.

"Matthew and Amy are together at Fort Vaughan. They are well," he said.

A look of relief crossed her face. She had known their whereabouts, but they had received so little information because of the war. Any word was welcome to her.

That night he rose from his bed after she had fallen asleep. He walked out on the verandah. The October night air was chilly. The moon rose over the horizon, a giant orange ball. It had been a long time since he had made the sound like the chirping of a squirrel. He made it now. It sounded strange to his ears. He listened for the response. The night was silent. Then he turned and went back to bed.

IX

1779

Kurt entered the bedroom he shared with Amy on the second floor of the garrison house. Amy was propped up on pillows. She held her newborns in the cradle of each arm.

"How art thou?" he asked, walking to the bed and sitting gingerly on the edge.

"Tired," she whispered.

"As well thou might be." He laughed now that he had assured himself that his wife had survived her ordeal. "But did thou not worry about what two sons would do to my feeble attempts at humility? How can I face our neighbors here? How can I go to Fort Hunter and tell all who ask that we have two children, not just the one we were expecting? How can I help but throw back my shoulders and stick my chest out with pride?"

"And thou wilt just have to endure it," she teased. She never used the archaic "thou" except to tease him. She was a good Quaker in all else, but she could not bring herself to use old-fashioned, and to her mind affected, forms of speech.

It hurt him to hear her use the formal forms, and she had developed elaborate schemes to avoid the second person, all of which ended in making her communication to him less direct.

The baby on her right yawned and stretched his tiny hand outward, fist clenched.

"I think this is the one who will give us trouble. I think we should name him after your father," said Kurt, still smiling at her. "Stephen Miller—it's a good name."

"What about this fellow over here?" said Amy, nodding with her chin.

"My grandfather was named Karl," said Kurt. "I was fond of him, but we are English now. Let's call him Charles."

Amy agreed. She had special reasons for loving the name Karl. The irony of two sons, one named Stephen and the other Charles, was not lost on her.

Margaret, a three-year-old with flaming red hair, pushed open the door of the room.

"Mama," she called. Her face broke into a great smile when she saw her mother. It disappeared and was replaced by a look of bewilderment when she saw the babies.

Kurt rose from the bed and scooped her up in his arms. He kissed her cheeks and then he sat back down, balancing her gently in his lap.

"Maggie, my heart, these are your new brothers, Stephen and Charles."

"Can they play?" the little girl asked her father.

"When they get as big as thee, of course, but right now they're too small."

She asked a series of questions, all amounting to the same point, her demand that these two babies, her promised playmates, would be an enormous disappointment if they did not begin instantly to amuse her.

Amy listened to the conversation with only half an ear. She was comforted by the fact that Kurt loved her daughter as if she were his own. It was even more comforting to watch him display that love and patience now that she held the children of *their* bodies in her arms.

These years at Fort Vaughan had been the happiest of her life. Her husband and his way of life had brought her peace in the midst of chaos. The war continued on; the regular English army had moved to campaigns in the south after the loss at Saratoga and Fort Stanwix. But in New York Colony, Indian and Loyalist raids had gone on without halt. In retaliation, Loyalist farms were burned; women and children of known Loyalist soldiers were harassed out of the valley and driven into the cold. Some had come to find shelter at Fort Vaughan. Amy and Kurt had clothed them, given them food and sent them on their long trail westward to Canada and to freedom.

After Oriskiny, the local populace had turned on the Mohawk castles, burning out Canajoharie and driving out the arch-Tory Molly Brant, whom all knew had given the news of Herkimer's march to her relations. She escaped and fled to Niagara. The rich farms of the Iroquois at Fort Hunter, Schoharie and Canajoharie were burned and looted. The Oneida, loyal to the rebel cause, joined in the looting of their brothers. In retaliation, Joseph Brant and his followers burned the Oneida castles at Oriska and Kanowalohale.

The horrors of war were everywhere about them, but Kurt created an oasis for Amy, for Maggie and now for their two sons. The war passed them by or stayed its distance.

Margaret Schuyler and Israel Kip had remained for several months after Socono died. But then Margaret had insisted on going back to the ruins of her home at Saratoga Flats. She would rebuild. Margaret and Kip had taken Matthew with them.

Last year, just about the time Amy began to suspect that she was pregnant, she received a letter from her father in Quebec, telling her of his reconciliation with her mother and Louis Joseph's acceptance of their renewed love. He gave Amy formal title to the lands at Fort Vaughan, with the right to collect the rents. He had also requested that she send Matthew to him. Amy had discussed the matter with Margaret Schuyler, who had insisted that the boy return to her and the relative security of Saratoga. Amy smiled as she recalled Margaret's arguments. She knew that her aunt had become fond of the boy and was only using the dangers of the unsettled border as an excuse to keep Matthew with her.

Stephen, however, had accepted the fact that his son would be safe in Saratoga, certainly safer than he would be trying to travel in these uncertain times. Amy had not told him that Matthew had seemed relieved when told he would be remaining with Margaret and Kip. She suspected that his relationship with his father had not been a close one, but she had never questioned him about it.

Baby Stephen began to fuss and woke his brother.

"Maybe he is ready to try a little nourishment," said Amy.

She opened her gown and offered the baby her breast.

Maggie stared at the privileged baby with awe and envy mixed in equal parts.

"I want that," she cried.

"That's for the baby," said Kurt patiently.

"I'm a baby," whined Maggie.

"You're not," interrupted Amy. "Besides, you have teeth. You'd hurt Mama."

"No, I won't."

Kurt put Maggie down on the floor and, taking her hand, started to walk away from Amy. The little girl began to wail loudly.

"There's only one way to resolve this," said Amy. She took a disappointed Stephen from her breast and called Maggie to her. The little girl leapt onto the bed and hungrily went for Amy's breast.

"Yuk. That tastes terrible," she complained. Then she sank her teeth into her mother.

Amy yelled in pain, and Kurt grabbed the child by the scuff of the neck. He took her into his arms. He leaned over to Amy.

"Art thou all right?" he asked.

She nodded, but there were tears of pain in her eyes.

"I don't know what's gotten into her," said Amy. "She is always so gentle and loving."

"I think I know," he said. "Let me handle it."

He walked out of the room, holding Maggie's hand. They went down the flight of stairs to the kitchen. Kurt took a piece of shortbread from a metal box and retrieved some fresh milk from the root cellar, where it had been chilling. Maggie grabbed both hungrily from him.

"Thou likest this food?"

The little girl nodded.

"The other food, the babies' food, is not for little girls.

The babies do not mean that thy mama and I love thee any less, child. Thou art our oldest, our most loved child. But thy brothers are not as big as thee. Thy mama will need thy help in caring for them."

The girl pulled at her red curls for some moments and then frowned.

"Did I hurt Mama bad?" she asked.

Kurt nodded.

A worried look crossed Maggie's face. She rose from the table and began an unsteady climb back up the stairs.

Kurt followed behind her. She walked back into Amy's bedroom. The midwife had placed one baby in the cradle that had been Maggie's. The other found himself in a hastily improvised bed made from an old tool crate. Amy was dozing.

Maggie ran to her, tears flowing freely down her cheeks.

"Mama," she cried, "please, I didn't mean to hurt thee."

Amy awoke immediately and lifted the child to her heart. She stroked the back of the weeping child's head. She looked over to the doorway and saw Kurt standing there, smiling. She smiled back at him. She was totally exhausted but happy.

The summer in the Mohawk Valley was a time of heavy work. Kurt Miller had spent the whole spring planting his fields with Indian corn and wheat and barley. In the late summer and early fall he would harvest. Midsummer was the time he cleared new fields, the heaviest of all work.

He was stripped to the waist, working on a tree stump. His farm horse was in harness and attached to the remains of an old maple. He had dug and chopped out as much of the root system he could. His sweat, mixed with dirt, had formed a strange pattern of stripes of darker hue on his fair skin.

He grunted as he leaned on the stump. Then he clucked to the horse, which moved forward and then halted as it felt the pull on the gear. Kurt urged the horse forward and leaned even harder. His muscles strained and the veins in his arms seemed ready to burst through his skin. The stump began to inch forward. There was a loud popping sound as the roots were torn out of the ground; the stump moved with sudden jerks and finally pulled free.

Kurt fell to the ground, but still held the reins and kept the horse in check. He rose to his feet and guided the horse to a large pile of refuse. He would have to start burning this week, before the pile became too large.

Jack Tice, the son of a neighbor hired out to him for the summer, came strolling out of the woods carrying an axe. He too was sweating freely. It had soaked his shirt, which was stuck to his chest and back.

"Mr. Miller," he called across the clearing, "can we break? It's almost time for lunch."

"We stop when Mrs. Miller arrives with our lunch," Kurt called back.

The boy gave a weary shrug of his shoulders and set out toward the woods and his half-finished tree.

Despite this exchange, Kurt was grateful to have Jack. He was a hard worker. His desire to break off stemmed from the insatiable hunger of a growing boy rather than any laziness.

Amy would be coming any moment now with lunch.

About a month after Amy delivered the twins, Mrs. Brinks had come wearily back to her abandoned cabin with her children in tow. There was no sign of Jonas. Kurt had worried about her. She was a woman of known loose morals. If she had no visible means of support, he was concerned about what might develop. He voiced his concern at the monthly meeting and was shocked when Amy came forward with a solution. She needed help at home. Kurt could hire Mrs. Brinks as a maid. Her children could attend the local school during the day, and she would return to them at night in her own cabin, which would remain rent-free while she remained employed with the Millers.

Kurt was delighted with Amy's suggestion. Jonas Brinks had attempted to rape her. That she could consider such kindness to his wife was a sign of her growing sense of brotherly love.

She deflated this notion by pointing out that she received cheap and relatively steady service in return for her act of charity. A woman with three children and a great house to care for could only hope for more opportunities for "charity."

Amy entered the clearing, carrying a bundle. Kurt waved to her. He pulled the horse's reins over its head and allowed them to fall freely to the ground. The horse immediately lowered its head and began to feed on the grass.

Kurt greeted his wife with an arm's-length kiss.

"I'm sweaty and smelly," he said to her. "Thou won't want to be too close to me."

She wrinkled her nose. "My nose agrees," she said, handing him her bundle.

He sat down on the ground and spread it out. He gave a yell and very quickly Jack came out of the woods and trotted to where they sat.

The cloth wrapping the food served as their picnic cloth. There was a ham bone with at least several inches of meat still clinging to it. Amy had also brought this morning's fresh cornbread with sweet butter and a flask of homemade beer. Kurt took his knife and cut several pieces of meat from the ham bone. Jack grabbed his and downed it almost immediately.

"Slow down, boy," said Amy. "It lasts longer that way."

"Yes, ma'am," he said, reaching for his second piece.

"Mrs. Brinks was by this morning. She said she couldn't stay. She wanted to be home with her kids. Rumor has it that the Butlers and the Brants will be entering the valley again from Canada."

"They tried that before. Fort Stanwix still blocks their path," said Kurt.

"But there will be raids, not formal campaigns. They can slip by the fort and attack settlements and be gone without any way for the Americans to stop them."

"They've done it before, and they've left this community in peace. The Iroquois know us as Quakers, peaceful people, who have done them no harm and take no sides in the war. We have given succor to the families of our Loyalist neighbors. They hold no grudges against us."

"One would hope that that is so, Kurt, but this is a civil

war. Neighbor against neighbor. I hope logic such as yours prevails and not the hatred we see all about us."

"It is not hatred I see all about us," he said, "it's trees. Jack, thy belly is a bit sated and thy muscles grow soft from the chatter. Get thee off to the woods. Chop me more maple trees. I want cords piled before the garrison house by fall and I want more land plantable by next spring. Off with thee, boy."

"Can I have me the last piece of cornbread, Mrs. Miller?" the boy asked.

"My word," said Kurt. "The boy will eat us out of food. His appetite exceeds what little advantage I get from his services."

Jack blushed but smiled when Amy handed him the bread. Then he ran off to the woods.

He liked these Quakers. They were good and generous people. His family were newcomers to Fort Vaughan. They had been burned out of the Wyoming Valley earlier. He feared the Butlers and Brants more than he feared anything else in the world. His sleep was still interrupted by the memories of the Indian screams and the shouts of the greencoated Loyalists. He hadn't seen any, but he had heard stories of the atrocities. How Joseph Brant had personally thrown children into the flames, holding them down with a pitchfork so that they could not scramble out of the fire. He hadn't seen it and he wasn't sure who it was supposed to have been done to. But it must be true. The local Committee of Safety had published the account. And they were all men of honor. They wouldn't lie about such things.

He had to agree with Mr. Miller that it was wrong for the Fort Hunter, Stone Arabia, and German Flats Loyalist families to be driven from their homes. Their goods had been taken and their farms confiscated. But you couldn't trust a Tory except to be sure that he'd stab you in the back. Quakers were peculiar. They didn't understand the realities. But they were nice.

Jack found the tree he had been working on before lunch. He spit on his hands and lifted his axe up over his shoulder. He brought it down with a resounding thud

237

neatly into the wedge he had created in the trunk earlier. If the Indians and Tories came again, he thought it would be good to be in the Millers' garrison house at the time.

Amy left Kurt and walked back over the fields to the site of her house. She had left the three children napping while she brought her husband his food. She was suddenly aware of how dependent she had become on Mrs. Brinks. She was nervous about leaving her children unattended even for a brief visit in the fields.

She entered her kitchen through the back door. She looked in on the two cradles and the bed in the second-floor bedrooms. The children slept peacefully.

She went back to the kitchen and wiped her brow on her sleeve. She spent so many hours in this room, before this fire, she thought. Lunch was over and it was time to prepare supper. She looked at the pot of beans that had been soaking overnight. They would be about ready for baking with some salt pork and maple syrup.

The crack of a musket broke the silence of the afternoon. Amy left the kitchen and moved toward the front of the house. She opened her door. Off to the right she could see downriver. There were boats landing on the beach. She saw the black coats and hats of her Quaker neighbors mixed with the homespun of her tenants. She ran down the path to the creek.

"Mistress Miller," said Jeremiah Parker, the man who had once objected to her marriage. "It is the savages. They are loose and have been sighted just west of here. It's the Brants, we are told. The alarm is out. We are all to seek haven."

Amy led the group of about twenty back to the house. She ordered the men to fill barrels of water from the creek and carry them into the house. The women loaded all they had carried with them into the root cellar.

Kurt arrived with Jack just as the last household wares had been stored. The house now contained the winter's store of salt pork, potatoes, apples and dried vegetables. With their water barrels filled, they could hold out longer than any Indian band could risk staying in the field.

Mr. Abel Tice, Jack's father, was a militia noncommissioned officer and should have assumed command. But Kurt Miller was master of Fort Vaughan and all deferred to him, Quaker or not.

"Jack," said Kurt. "I want thee to go down by the creek. If the savages come this way, they'll have to cross it there at the fording place. If thou seest any signs of them, thou art to come back here—fast. Relief will be sent to thee in two hours. Off with thee."

Jack took his musket, but Kurt grabbed it away from him.

"Thou will need no weapon to give us a warning."

Jack exchanged a glance of distress with his father. If the Indians attacked, would the Quakers insist on no weapons? It was a clear route to a slaughter, especially if some of the white Tory devils were present to drive the savages on.

Jack disappeared out the front door. Kurt gave orders to fill every empty bottle and flask in the house with water and to move the kegs filled earlier to the second-floor traps in the garrison house overhang.

The whole of the Fort Vaughan community, men, women and children, Quaker and non-Quaker, lay huddled together for two days, waiting. They saw no sign of the Indians, but neither did they receive an all-clear from the militia commanders upriver. They tried to keep their daylight hours busy by working in the house and taking in enough fresh vegetables to feed the community and preserve their siege stores. But at night it was different. They lay in rows, men in one room, women in the other, sleeping on the floor or listening to the lonely sounds of the night: the chirping of crickets; the rummaging in the underbrush of predators; the whirling, beating sound of great owl wings; or the squeal of a trapped mouse. All of these signs disturbed their rest and left both young and old restless and sleepless.

On the third day they came. Sergeant Tice, who had hidden his musket under his coat, was on watch. He saw the white man enter the meadow by the opposite shore of the Mohawk. The man looked up the river and down. Then he turned to the woods and signaled with his hand. About fifteen warriors came out of the wood, bearing two canoes, probably hidden there days, maybe even months, before.

Tice took aim and fired across the river at the white man. He missed, as he knew he must at this range with a musket.

The Indians let loose with war whoops, and Abel Tice retreated as fast as his feet could carry him back to the garrison house. He arrived to find the entire group inside, all accounted for. The door was slammed and bolted. Each shutter was slammed into place. The men took their positions. Women and children went calmly into the root cellar through the trap door in the kitchen floor.

Amy took Maggie from Mrs. Brinks so that she might concern herself with her own youngsters. The Brinks' oldest, Elaine, would be placed in charge of all the children, especially if the women were needed to aid the men. Amy herself went upstairs to complete the feeding of the garrison house community. They would eat, whether Indians surrounded them or not.

Kurt stood by the front window. It was shuttered closed and allowed only slits of light to enter. He put his face to the gun slit. Then he pulled it back.

"The white man has a white flag. He wants to talk."

"Don't trust him," said Tice. "They learned that from Pontiac and his devils after the last war."

The Quaker group agreed with Tice that they should not trust the Indians, although several argued that not to trust them was to display a lack of charity. Kurt argued for compromise and he prevailed. He went to the window and opened the shutter.

"What dost thou wish of us, sir?" he called out to the white man.

"Surrender, and you all go free."

"If thou wouldst go away, we would be free without surrendering. We are peaceful farmers. Many of us are members of the Society of Friends and have taken no part in this war, other than to minister to the suffering. Why dost thou descend upon us in this manner?"

"You man a fort; that's reason enough. Surrender or you'll all die in there."

Kurt returned to the men. Several of the Quakers moved off into a corner of the room. Tice spoke to the non-Quaker group.

"We're going to fight. I don't trust them buggers. They'll murder us all," he said.

Jeremiah interrupted. "We have met and it is our opinion that to surrender is the only option consistent with our profession of faith. Friend Miller, thou must surrender this house to them."

Kurt's shoulders seemed to sag with the responsibility. At the same time, fear gripped Amy. The Indians had come, and Matthew's question of what would happen could no longer be avoided. But in her heart Amy knew what her answer would be. She would fight for her children. Her decision shocked her. For the first time she understood Antoine Gingras and even Louis Joseph. They had had the conviction that they must fight for what they believed in. Amy would not have fought for a free Quebec, but she would fight for Maggie, Stephen and Charles.

Parker repeated himself. "Thou must surrender this house."

"No," said Amy sharply. "This is my house. No one will turn it over to anyone else." She turned to Kurt. "Husband," she said, in a softer voice, "I love the Society of Friends. Its people have most of the answers about war and violence that I have been looking for all my life. But these people will be slaughtered if they surrender. If that happens, evil will have prevailed over good. Kurt, don't let that happen."

He looked at her. Her eyes pleaded with him. He looked at the calm confidence in Jeremiah's face, and he saw the beginnings of panic in Tice. He turned his back on all three. He heard Maggie let out a howl from the root cellar. Elaine had her hands full down there. He turned around once again.

241

"We will not surrender."

Tice exhaled loudly. "Thata boy!" he exclaimed, grabbing his musket.

Amy walked to Kurt and placed her arm around his waist. He hugged her.

Jeremiah stood before him dumbfounded.

"Hold on, Tice," said Miller. "We're not fighting either. We're going to stay put and leave them to sit outside."

"That will never work," said Tice. "They'll attack."

"Unless they have cannon, that won't do much good."

Now Jeremiah understood. He nodded solemnly. "It is allowable," he said.

Kurt moved Amy out of any line of fire and reopened the window.

"We reject thy offer, sir," he yelled.

The Loyalist yelled back, "It's on your head."

Kurt closed the window and barred the shutter. The Indians opened fire with muskets. The balls smacked harmlessly against the heavy log walls of the garrison house.

"Keep away from the firing holes," yelled Kurt. "Stay low and no one will be hurt."

Kurt ran to the second floor. He opened the hatch over the overhang. He put his eye to the firing hole in the wall. He could see several Indians pulling logs from his woodpile. Others pulled hay from the barn. They ran toward the door of the garrison house and hurled their combustibles against it. At first they ran low and zigzagged, but once they realized they drew no fire, they became bolder and openly came up to the door, placing firewood and kindling. Then the white officer, bearing a torch, walked up to the front door and shoved his torch into the pile of materials.

The flames caught, then sputtered. The hay from the barn was not dry enough yet to catch quickly.

Kurt walked down the stairs. He motioned to Jeremiah to pass a large keg of water to him. Then Jeremiah opened the front door and Kurt doused the kindling with his keg. The whole mess began to smolder and gave off a column of grey smoke.

Kurt slammed the door shut. Tice howled with laughter. But the howl that came from outside was one of anger.

The Indians found the hay wagon in the barn. This time they set it aflame. When they had a roaring fire going, they pushed it against the front door. Soon the flames from the wagon reached the bottom of the overhang.

Kurt returned to his post by the overhang hatch near the front door. He began to pour water through the opening down into the burning hay. The smoke began to rise again. His keg was almost empty. He yelled down the stairs, and Jack Tice, his broad shoulders and arms staggering under the load, came up the stairs with a great barrel of water.

Kurt took smaller buckets and poured bucketful after bucketful into the burning wagon beneath. Gradually the flame got smaller and more and more smoke rose from the smoldering hay. Kurt's eyes were running and he could barely see. Jack had to leave the second floor, he was coughing so badly. Kurt continued to pour water and to make smoke. He could not afford to stop and give the flames a chance to get started again. Finally the hay was so soaked that even Kurt had to admit to himself that there was little danger.

The mood in the garrison house had changed remarkably. Twice the raiders had been thwarted. Everyone's confidence began to build. Amy had served a stew and beans to all. She came over to Kurt and handed him his bowl. He was soaking wet from spilled water and sweat, and he smelled of smoke.

"What will they try next?" she asked, almost rhetorically.

He shrugged his shoulders. He seemed relaxed, but she knew that Indians terrified him as almost nothing else could. He had never recovered from the ordeal he had undergone at their hands as a boy.

She placed his hand in hers and she squeezed it. He looked into her eyes and smiled. He took some stew meat in his fingers and popped it into his mouth.

The musket fire from the Indians had stopped. Jack Tice and his father, each keeping a musket out of sight, went to the second floor to keep watch.

"There are none of the bastards in sight," called Abel Tice.

The Quakers clapped their hands together. "The Lord has delivered us," said Jeremiah.

"Don't be sure of the Lord," said Amy. "That's presumption. He has a way for making one pay dearly for that sin."

As if to punctuate her words, there was a splatter of musket balls hitting the walls of the garrison house. The Indians had taken cover in the woods and settled down for a siege.

After sunset the firing from the woods ceased. Kurt wanted Amy to go down to the root cellar, but she refused. He spent the night on the second floor in their bedroom with her by his side. He kept the shutters open. It gave him a clearer view, and as long as no light shone in the house, the raiders would not be able to spy on them.

"It's practically impossible to see anything out there," he whispered to her.

"Be careful, Kurt," she warned. "Close the shutters. It frightens me to see them open."

He patted her hand. "Don't be frightened."

"I can't help it. No matter where I turn, Kurt, this awful war comes to haunt me. When will it end? When will all the killing stop?"

"I don't know."

"If they enter this house—"

"They'll not," he interrupted. "We have only to keep it locked up."

"But if they do, I don't want to survive."

"We will follow God's will, my love. And if it be that we die, I want thou to know that thou hast made me the happiest of God's creatures."

"Thou hast done the same for me," she said solemnly.

He noticed immediately that she had addressed him as a Friend, and he leaned over and kissed her mouth.

Just before dawn the darkness was shattered by a streak of light that rose into the air and descended in a great arc. It fell short of the house and went out. It was followed by a second flaming arrow. It struck the second-floor wall near the window in what was Maggie's room. Kurt raced down the hall. He opened Maggie's shutter and doused the flames with water that sat by the window in a bucket. A third and fourth flame descended on the house. Both struck the roof with a thud. Now Kurt became frightened. The roof was made of wooden bark shingles—highly flammable.

He called to Amy to get more water. He grabbed two glass flasks and dunked them in the water barrel, filling them to the brim. He shoved the flasks into the waistband of his breeches. He threw open the shutters at the second-floor hallway closest to where the fire arrows had struck. He thrust his leg out of the window and grabbed the roof. He almost lost his grip and had to grab the second row of shingles for a hand hold. He hauled himself upward. His whole summer of clearing the forest had left him stronger than he had ever been before in his life. He pulled his body up onto the sloped roof. The shingles had caught and were burning wildly. He rose to his feet and grabbed the flask at his side. Knowing he was outlined in the flames, he bent as low as he could. He poured the flask of water onto the flames. The fire diminished. He poured out the second flask, and the fire went out. Another arrow had struck the roof, but its flames extinguished itself. He crawled slowly back to the window. He saw an arm holding a water bucket. He grabbed the bucket. He knew without seeing her it was Amy there, aiding him. He saw four more arcs of flame rise into the sky. But he was on the roof and he had water.

Amy kept passing the water bucket to Kurt, but she knew that time was running out. Soon it would be daylight and the man on the roof would be a pretty target for any musket bearer. But without his efforts the house would be in ruins already.

Amy leaned out of the window and called to Kurt to reenter. Abel Tice came up behind her. She turned to the militiaman.

"Someone will pick him off," she cried.

Tice nodded. "They will, but they'll have to come out in

the open to get any accurate shot at him. The woods are too far. If they leave cover to shoot him, I'll get them," he said, patting his musket.

Amy called to Kurt again. But he insisted upon staying atop the roof as long as the Indians aimed fire arrows at the house.

The sun's first rays struck the east side of the house. Now Kurt was in full view. Amy pleaded and Kurt relented. He backed his way down the sloped roof and hung his feet over the side, lowering himself inch by inch. Tice and Amy reached for his legs.

Amy saw him first and screamed. An Indian bearing a musket had raced from the woods. He raised the gun to his shoulder to fire. Tice let go of Kurt's legs and grabbed his own musket. He was quick. He fired, and the Indian's musket flew into the air; he fell face forward. The report of Tice's gun, however, startled Kurt. He lost his grip and he fell down the two stories to the ground below.

"Shit," yelled Tice. He and Amy stared at Kurt's prone form on the ground below. Then Tice raced from the room, down the stairs to the front door. But Amy watched in horror as Kurt rose to his feet and began to limp away from the door toward the fallen Indian. She screamed again as the raiders poured out of the woods and dragged Kurt away into the shadows of the forest.

Jack Tice crawled over to where his father was seated, looking out the half-opened shutters toward the woods.

"Papa, can you see or hear anything?" he asked anxiously.

"Not since that commotion right after they got Miller. But they're still out there," said Abel. "Frankly, I'm surprised. I thought they'd take Miller and go. An eye for an eye. But they know we've got Blackbirds here. They must think we're easy pickings. I'm sorry it was Miller, though. He was a genuinely brave man and saved all our lives this morning."

"I don't like the way the Quakers get together and talk in small groups," said Jack.

"If we're lucky, Jack, the Indians will leave us be. But if they attack, I have every intention of using this weapon."

Amy came into the front room. She had been weeping, but her eyes were dry now.

"Mr. Tice," she addressed him.

Tice nodded his acknowledgment. There was a note of panic in her voice that concerned him.

"The Quaker leaders have determined to surrender. They claim my husband's act was a clear sign of what God wants for all of us. I will survive what happened to Kurt," she said, trying now in vain to hold back her tears, "but the Indians will not get my children. You and your son are armed. You must stop them."

Abel Tice looked beyond Amy. The Quaker Jeremiah had followed her into the room.

"Sister," he said, "thou must not thwart the will of God."

Tice raised his musket and pointed it at Jeremiah. "Maybe she must not, but I've got no reason not to save my ass, Blackbird. You try to open that door and you're dead."

When Kurt reached the body of the Indian, he knew he was dead without touching him. And he knew that the Indian's death was his fault. If he had not attempted to place himself between the will of God and those he loved, then maybe no evil would have befallen any of them. He felt a hand grab him. But he didn't care anymore.

He was dragged through the underbrush. His arms were jerked behind him and tied with rawhide. He was led before a white man in a green coat.

"My name is Captain Walter Butler. What's yours?"

"I am Kurt Miller."

"Mr. Miller, you are in grave danger. Your people have resisted an offer of surrender. And now you have killed one of my Onondaga warriors. You were captured by Seneca. They are currently arranging a trade for you. The Onondaga could adopt you to replace the dead warrior, or they could torture you and burn you to placate his spirit and his clan. I hope for your sake you are adopted."

"Is there anything thou canst do for me?"

"You're a Quaker. My God, how did you end up killing someone?"

Kurt did not attempt to defend himself. He merely shrugged his shoulders. He truly regarded himself as responsible for the Indian's death.

A warrior, his face painted vermillion, and naked except for his loincloth and moccasins, came to Butler and addressed him in a strange language.

Butler looked at Kurt with sorrow in his eyes.

"I am truly sorry, Mr. Miller. There is nothing I can do."

The Indians grabbed Kurt's shoulders and shoved him forward. Then the captor, leaning his head back, let out a wild yell. From all over the camp there were responding whoops. The Seneca and Onondaga came forward. Kurt was still numb. He offered no resistance as his clothes were torn from his body.

The Indians had formed two lines and wanted him to run between them. But he was still in a state of shock, and at first he could not comprehend what was required of him. He stood watching the angry warriors. Maybe if he refused to run, they would make quick work of him. Whatever God decided. He stood still. A warrior approached him from behind with a burning torch. He thrust it between Kurt's legs, singeing his buttocks. Kurt shuddered with the pain and began to walk forward. The first blows landed on his back. Then the flat of a tomahawk took his breath away and sent him falling onto his face. He did not scream until they showed him the torture stake. The fate he had escaped at sixteen and that had been his constant nightmare ever since had become his fate once more.

Jack Tice was scared and bored at the same time. The Indians scared him and the Quakers bored him. The Quakers had been talking for at least an hour. One after the other would stand and say something silly and then sit again, to be followed after some silence by another. He wished they would be as quiet out there. Night had descended again. His father had assured him that the Iroquois would come to attack again. Especially now that there were more of them.

Just before sunset his father had seen a whole new group arrive. There were twice as many of them out there now. There was another big commotion after the newcomers arrived, but now all had settled down.

He heard his father's whistle sound once. It was their signal to each other that all was well. He put his fingers to his mouth and signaled back.

It seemed like ages since he had had lunch with Mr. Miller and his wife. In reality it had been less than a week ago. Now Miller was taken and probably dead.

Jack's mind went back to this morning's events. Mrs. Miller had come up from the root cellar, where she cared for the children along with the other women. He admired her. She carried on despite her grief. She saw to it they were fed, and she had reinforced his father's decision to keep on with the defense of the garrison house. Sooner or later a militia force would arrive. All they had to do was to hold out. Mrs. Miller saw that, and she was determined to force the Quakers to see it too. She had argued with Jeremiah, using his own arguments against him and accusing him of a frightening pride in claiming to know the will of God.

Jeremiah's face had clouded at her charge, and his air of assurance had left him. He had gone scurrying back to the group, and they had been at it ever since.

The quiet was shattered by two whistles in quick succession. His father's distress signal. Jack crowded to the gun hole and peered out. His eyes had adjusted to the dark, since all lights had been doused in the garrison house at nightfall. He could see nothing. He continued to stare. Damn it, there it was. His father had incredible night vision. There was a slight movement in the dark. Someone was crawling toward the house.

Jack stuck his musket through the gun loop, ready to fire on the next signal from his father. But it never came. Instead, Jeremiah and the Quakers, their bodies quivering, set up a terrible howling. Some fell to the floor. Jeremiah himself walked to the door of the house, lifted the bolt and called out into the night.

"Our brothers, we are all children of Christ. This bloodshed and violence must . . ." He never finished the sentence. An arrow slammed into his chest with such force that he was shoved backward into the room. Jack dropped his musket and raced for the door. But just as he reached it, it was slammed back with overwhelming force, and the naked, painted bodies of Iroquois came pouring into the house.

Jack ran back for his musket. A tomahawk slashed into his skull, piercing it and sending bone splinters deep into his brain.

Amy saw the Indians enter and ran to the root cellar door, pulling it closed behind her. The women and children were huddled together behind some barrels of potatoes. Several were screaming. Amy went to them.

"Shut up," she whispered. "If we have any chance whatever, it will come from silence. Mrs. Brinks, keep Maggie still. Elaine, quiet your brother."

The Quaker women were praying. "Hush," Amy said to them.

The noise from upstairs was deafening and horrible. The war cries of the Indians were mingled with the screaming of the victims and the dull thud of bodies falling on the floor above their heads. After some time the cries stopped, yet the noise continued. It sounded as if the whole house was being torn apart. Drawers were emptied onto the floor; chests of drawers were overturned with a crash; iron pots were hurled across the room, breaking the glass of the windows. Some liquid had been spilled on the floor above and had seeped through the cracks in the floorboards and dripped down below. One drop at a time splattered on top of the hogshead filled with pickled cucumbers.

Amy crept back toward the stairway. She wanted advance notice if the Indians put the house to the torch. If they did, all would have to make a run for it. Inadvertently she placed her hand on the barrel top. A drop of the liquid struck her wrist. It was warm. Then she realized what it was. Her hand rested in a puddle of warm blood. A scream rose in her throat but she checked it. Screams would be distinguished from the noise above, whereas they could not have been before.

The lives of this group depended on her. She continued to walk toward the trap door. She stood at the foot of it when suddenly the door swung open, revealing her in the full light of a torch. She was forced to back off and shield her eyes. She saw an Indian, dressed in leggings and a loincloth, his face covered with war paint. The Indian came toward her. She backed off farther, but realizing she might save the others if she distracted him, she tried to run by him and escape. He reached for her and caught her by the gold locket and chain she wore about her neck. It held her in check for only a moment and then it broke. He grabbed her with both hands to prevent her escape. The Indian glanced at the locket in his hand and then at Amy. A strange look came onto his face. He pulled her body close to his, blocking her from the view of the other Iroquois, who came racing downstairs into the root cellar. They gave cries of joy at the discovery of the women and children.

The cellar was now in chaos. Women screamed and children cried. Mrs. Brinks tried to crawl behind a bin of potatoes, but one Indian saw her and grabbed her by the legs and began to haul her out. A flash of red hair caught Amy's eyes. An Indian with a hideously painted face had grabbed Maggie by the hair and was dragging the child, kicking and screaming, toward the stairway.

A large figure darkened the doorway, cutting off light from the torches from the main floor. He was tall and handsome, dressed partly as Indian and partly as a white man. He called out in Indian language. The red men stopped yelling. Only the women and children called out in despair for help.

"Quiet down there," said this same Indian in perfect English. "No one is to be hurt. Captain Butler and I have agreed to it. You are all prisoners of war. If you remain quiet and calm, no one will be hurt. My name is Joseph Brant. You will follow my comrades. If you do not, I can't protect you and you will be killed."

Amy searched the crowd below her for the sight of her children. She strained as far as she could in the Indian's grasp. She was shocked when he spoke to her.

"Do you have loved ones here?"

She turned and looked at him. She noticed his eyes immediately. They were blue.

Then she saw Maggie again. She pointed toward the child.

"She's mine, and I have babies. Twin boys."

A look of concern came into those blue eyes.

"Where?" he asked, pulling her down in the cellar behind him.

"Behind the barrel," she responded.

The Indian dragged her to the spot. The twins' cradle was empty. From out of the potato bin came a young Seneca, dragging two infants by the legs. Clearly Mrs. Brinks had not been trying to escape, but rather she had hoped to save the boys from slaughter.

Amy's captor intercepted the Seneca and began to speak in his language. The young man began to argue with him, but the older said several harsh words and then opened his hand. The younger man reached for a torch from his companion and held it above the hand. The gold locket with the gothic N reflected the glittering light of the torch. The blue-eyed man pried the locket open with his fingernail while speaking the harsh sounds of the Iroquois language. The young man sucked in his breath when he saw the cuttings of dark black hair inside the locket, mingled with light blonde. It was truly a magic talisman. He nodded to the older man and grabbed it from his hand.

Amy's captor turned to her. "Take the babies from him. They are to stay with you. If you can feed and care for them, they will stay alive. If anything happens to you, they will die as well," he said to her.

Amy merely nodded. Then she scooped up both the boys in her arms. They were both screaming with terror. She soothed them, kissing the tears off their wet cheeks.

"Let us get out of here," said the Indian.

"I have a daughter, the little girl with red hair. I must save her, too."

"I can do nothing about her. She is the prisoner of Geyasada, the Seneca sachem. I can only plead with my uncle and Captain Butler that he be made to keep her alive. He is fascinated by her hair color. You must convince him that the hair moving about and living is even more fascinating than it would be on a pole outside his house."

Amy started to groan.

"Stop it," said the Indian. "I tell you the blunt truth so that you tell yourself no lies. I want you to survive this. Now we must get out of this house. Butler and Brant have agreed to put it to the torch."

He led Amy out of the cellar to the first floor. She tried to look away from the slaughter. But her eyes caught sight of Jeremiah's body stretched across the kitchen table. He had been scalped and mutilated.

The contents of her stomach exploded out her mouth almost without warning. The Indian took the babies from her and allowed her to be sick. When the retching ceased, she wiped her mouth on her sleeve. The Indian merely stared at her. She took the boys from him without comment. Then she saw the white man in the green coat. Her anguish had been so great that she had little room for any other emotion. But now anger pushed everything else aside.

"Why?" she screamed at Butler. "Why have you done this to innocent people?"

Butler started to turn away. But she yelled again.

Now it was Butler's turn to be angry. "You could have surrendered immediately and avoided all this. I can't control the Iroquois way of making war, and this is war."

"War on simple farmers trying to scratch a living out of the soil? War on a loving, generous people like the Quakers? War on children?" she yelled at him, glancing down at her own babies.

Butler bristled. "I was a simple farmer. My family made its living from the same soil. You rebels drove us out. You hanged those too slow to get out. I was captured once. Because I was a 'Tory' I wasn't treated like a British prisoner of war. Instead I was sentenced to hang. We didn't even start the use of Iroquois raiders. It was your preachers among those snakes, the Oneidas, who started everything."

"I don't care who started it," Amy groaned. "Why in God's name continue it?"

"Because," said Butler, "this valley was my home and it still is. When this war is over I intend to be back, farming my father's lands. I want my birthright back."

"And I'll be here, too," said Amy, "and I'll tell them about this night—about Jeremiah the Quaker, about Jack Tice, just about old enough to think himself a man, about my dear Kurt. Oh my God, my dear Kurt," she wept. "I'll tell them about Kurt and you'll never live here in peace. Not in my lifetime."

Momentarily, the self-defeating nature of the Indian raids must have sunk into Butler's mind because he looked terribly distressed. But then he turned on his heel and left the house.

Amy would have followed him, but her captor restrained her.

"Butler can't be antagonized too much," said the Indian.

The chief who had identified himself as the hated and feared Joseph Brant joined them. The two Indians spoke rapidly. Brant looked at Amy with surprise. The Indian who had captured her child came up from the cellar, holding Maggie by her full head of hair. The girl was screaming in anger, and she kicked the Indian, but a look at the slaughter changed the anger to terror and she became quiet.

Amy's captor became very excited and continued to point at Maggie. But Brant kept shaking his head. Almost all the Indians had left the house by now. Brant reached for one of the torches. All the household goods had been piled in a great heap in the center of the room. Brant stuck the torch into the pile and watched the flames build. Then he gave the word for all to leave.

They began the trek to the west by canoe. Amy, her eyes always straining to get a glimpse of Maggie, was in the lead canoe, paddled by Brant and her captor. They moved rapidly by both day and night. They passed the site of Canajoharie, sacred to these Mohawks but now deserted. Before striking German Flats and possibly running into militia from the west, they left the Mohawk River and entered the woods. Some of the women who carried older children began to complain, but Butler threatened them with scalping if they did not shut up.

They followed a clear trail through the woods for hours. Finally they came to the headwaters of a small, clear stream that flowed south. They followed the stream until it opened into a large lake—Otsego Lake, the Iroquois called it. Here the parties split. Butler and the Seneca left.

Amy saw Geyasada leaving with Maggie in tow. She called out in anguish. The child heard her and started to wail. Her captor came running to her side and clamped his hand over her mouth. The Seneca set out overland to the west toward Niagara. They disappeared into the woods. Soon the only remnant of them was the fading sound of a child's cry.

Amy knew that her sanity hung in the balance. If she let go, it would be for her as it had been for her mother. The image of Katherine staring blankly at nothing, rocking in her chair on the verandah, saved her. She would not let that happen to her. Kurt was gone, Maggie was gone, but she still had her sons, and their continued existence depended on her.

"They will live, by God," she said aloud.

The Mohawks under Brant now uncovered a cache of canoes and loaded the remaining captives in them. They set out across the lake. All was quiet. The sun was setting in front of them off to the right. The winds had died down, and there was not even a ripple on the mirrorlike surface of the lake except those caused by their passing canoes. The faroff wail of a loon was the only noise, other than the sound of the canoe cutting through the water, propelled by strong, bare shoulders.

They reached the far shore of the lake, where the Susquehanna River flows from it, and finally made camp. There was little chance that the whites would follow them this far. Several hunters set out, and after some time returned with a variety of game. Some fires were lit and food prepared. Amy fed her sons at her breast. She wrapped them in an Indian blanket provided her by her captor and placed them between two logs in a kind of natural cradle.

Her state of shock had begun to recede, and more and more she found herself crying in grief. Then she would shake herself and try to get control. She began to think of the strange man who had captured her. She did not know what to make of him. He had kept her alive when he could have killed her. It was clear to her that he had preserved Charles and Stephen from a sure sentence of death. Why? Yet at the same time he was one of the persons whose very existence she despised. He was the murderer of Kurt and the abductor of Maggie. He and the others had destroyed a beautiful world of peace and contentment.

As she thought of these things, the Indian with the blue eyes came and sat beside her. He looked behind him to where the two babies slept, as if to check that they were safe. Then he looked at Amy. He reached into the pouch at his side and withdrew some dried beef.

"It will be a while before the meal is ready," he said, offering her his food. "Are you hungry?"

She shook her head.

Then he reached into his pouch again and pulled out her gold locket and handed it back to her.

"I thought you had given it away for the boys," she exclaimed.

"I did," he responded. "But I went back to the Seneca later. I told him you were a witch and whoever wore the locket carried your curse with him for life. You've never seen anything taken off quicker. I told him I was sorry for giving him bad medicine and I gave him my musket as compensation. He wasn't much interested in the babies by then. I buried the locket with much ritual. As soon as the

Senecas left, I dug it up again. It means much to you, I know. Here."

"How do you know that it means much to me?"

"Because it meant much to me when I wore it."

She looked at him, sure she had not understood him correctly.

"You and I," he said "are both children of the blackrobe, Stephen Nowell."

Amy looked at her brother. Her eyes wide with shock.

"I am Aaron Brant, your brother. Your sons are my nephews. By Iroquois custom and culture, they are dearer to me than my own sons."

"If that is true," said Amy, suddenly angry, "how could you let them do to me and to my family what they did?"

"I didn't know, sister. My Uncle Joseph and we Mohawks arrived near the end of the siege. There were Onondaga present at the beginning. I know they took a captive." He sighed deeply and then continued. "They planned to burn him."

Amy started to weep again for Kurt, gentle Kurt, who could not hurt anyone and gave only love. He had died in the manner that had brought terror to him so often.

"My Uncle Joseph and I had all we could do to hold the Senecas in check. Butler had lost control of them."

They were silent for some moments. Only the sound of the fire and the sizzling of the roasting meat broke the quiet.

Finally Amy turned to Aaron. She sobbed bitterly. "If you are my brother, you must help me and my sons. I have to know what happened to my husband, and I must get my daughter back."

Aaron looked at her with pity.

"I will bring you and the boys to a safe place and I will protect you. I will make inquiries among the Onondaga, and I will not rest until the one with the flaming hair is back in your bosom."

Then he took the locket from her. He placed it about her neck and tied the chain in a knot to replace the broken catch. That night, for the first time since she had left Fort Vaughan, she did not awaken screaming.

Israel Kip kicked the piece of charred wood with his foot. The house that Stephen and Karl had built was gone. Only a mass of burned-out timbers remained. He turned toward Matthew, who had come with him all the way from Saratoga. The boy had been sick to his stomach when he first smelled the stench of rotting corpses that came from the ruins.

A contingent of regular army troops had been sent from Fort Stanwix to aid them. General Schuyler's niece had been abducted by Indians—the army would have to be involved. The major in charge was a soft-spoken man from the South. He seemed especially interested in the case. When Israel commented on the fact, he explained that he had known Amy for years and would do everything he could to help them.

But it was Matthew who made the most important discovery. He found Abel Tice, delirious but alive, in the woods. When Tice regained consciousness in Major Morin's tent, he told them the whole story. He himself had escaped the second floor by going out the window onto the roof as Kurt had done. Once all the Indians were in the house, he had jumped to the ground. Although he had broken his ankle in the fall, he had crawled to the safety of the woods. Helplessly he had watched the slaughter proceed and had seen the women and children led off. He could not walk and had expected to die of starvation or thirst. He had lost consciousness and recalled nothing until the boy had discovered him. He wept when he was told his own son was dead.

Morin clapped him on the shoulder and rose from the edge of Tice's cot. He walked over to Matthew and Kip. "Your sister and her children appear to have survived and are imprisoned," he said to the boy in his soft manner. "I intend to get her back and to punish those Tories and their savages once and for all."

Matthew nodded in agreement with Morin. He had been sickened by the slaughter, but his anger had been tempered by his fear for his sister, his brother-in-law, and their children—his only real flesh and blood. Now, although externally calm, the boy was consumed with a burning rage. He hated all Indians. Socono had been different, but even he had been killed by an Indian. But even more he hated the Tories—the white traitors, like his father, who turned on their own kind and urged the slaughter. He vowed revenge on all of them.

X
1779–1780

The river flowed quickly and silently by the village, which consisted of longhouses mixed with European cottages. A few miles downstream from Onaquaga, the Brant headquarters, it crossed the Pennsylvania line. Here the Mohawk mingled with Cayuga, Onondaga, and a few Seneca. Occasionally even an Oneida would find his way into the Brant village, even though these last were now a despised people for making war on their own nation. Most of these Oneida were Brant's in-laws. Joseph had once been married to an Oneida woman.

Molly stirred the stewpot as it simmered over the fire in her hearth. The blackrobe's grandchildren stirred in their joint cradle. She bent over to check on them. Their mother was out working and harvesting the corn with the other women.

Molly was pleased with her. This Amy was a hard worker who asked her son for no special treatment merely because she was his half-sister. Molly would have beaten her if she had tried. But it was not necessary. And Stephen's daughter was a good mother who cared for her sons as Molly had cared for hers.

The babies were sleeping, but they would soon be awake and crying. The Nowell girl was blessed to have had two sons at one time. Yet it was said that their father was one of the Blackbirds—men without gonads. When she laughed about this, Aaron looked sternly at her and recounted to her the feats of his nephews' father. He took his role as uncle seriously. Not even his mother was allowed to mock his nephews' father.

She raised the ladle to her lips and sampled the stew. It burned her tongue and she cursed. She remembered, like a flash from the past, the old clan mother at Kanowanohole when she had first met the blackrobe, Stephen. That was almost thirty-five summers ago. Now *she* was the clan mother guarding the cooking fire. But the Iroquois were different. The Mohawk, her people, were dispersed. Schoharie and Canajoharie were gone. Most of the Mohawk were followers of her brother and lived here at Onaquaga, far from the eastern door of the longhouse. Their successors as guardians were the traitors—the Oneida. Not only did they not guard the door and keep out the enemy, it was said they now led the rebel armies into the heart of the house. The Tuscarora followed the Oneida in all things. The Cayuga had given up separate identity and lived with the Seneca. Only the Seneca and Onondaga occupied their own lands, and now they would be challenged by the Americans.

Joseph refused to believe her word, but he was sure she would be the last clan mother chosen by the council in the capital of Onondaga. The Six Nation confederacy was dead, killed by this war. Joseph and Aaron had brought warriors from all the tribes here to Onaquaga, turning it into a mini-federation. But they pursued a lost cause. She had followed Johnson's advice. He had warned her of the settlers. It was they who threatened the longhouse, and it was only the King who could protect them from the settlers. But now it was clear to her that even the King had been beaten. The rebels were triumphant everywhere and had made an alliance with King Louis of France. Soon a new Onontio would arrive to claim back his old lands in Canada. This must never happen. The Americans like Johnson's sons and Butler and even her blackrobe, Nowell, must all withdraw with the Iroquois into the new land— Canada. From these lands behind the lakes and rivers they would form a new longhouse, safe from the settlers. There, younger men like Aaron and even Joseph could adapt the Iroquois way of life to accommodate the white ways and white knowledge. In that way, they might survive as a people. Joseph and Aaron did not see the truth of

261

this yet. They were excited about this village. But all that would change. The Americans would come looking for them.

The door to the cabin opened. Amy, dressed in Indian buckskin, entered and went directly to the cradle. She unlaced the front of her dress and picked up one of her sons and placed him at her breast. He soon made hungry, sucking sounds—loud enough to awaken and anger his brother, who began to cry.

Molly left the pot and went to Amy's side. She picked up the remaining boy in her arms. His face turned to the softness of her covered breast.

"You will have dry fare there, little fellow," she said in English.

Amy smiled. "He'll have to wait his turn. I have enough for both," she said.

"How is the harvest going?" asked Molly. She was glad that her position now exempted her from the hardest work.

"Some of the women are angry that the men join in the tasks."

"Times change," said Molly wearily. "Our men must learn to give up hunting and roaming the woods. They must learn to farm like white men. And our women must learn to accept them. It will be part of the adjustment our people must make. Among your people, men farm and women care for the house and children."

Amy smiled softly. "Women do a bit of farming also," she said.

"Well, we do all of it. That must change."

The two women were silent. Only the sounds of the baby feeding filled the room. His twin had fallen back to sleep in Molly's arms.

The door opened again and Aaron entered. He walked to his mother and kissed her cheek. She liked to be kissed and demanded that she be treated that way by all her children. Johnson had kissed her whenever he came and went—and far better than that when they were alone together.

Aaron merely nodded to Amy. He sat on the stool next to her.

"My Uncle Joseph has made inquiries among the Onondaga and Seneca. I have no word about the fate of your husband. Geyasada the Seneca still has your daughter. She is alive and well. Geyasada's wife has adopted her as their child. You need not fear for her life."

Amy's shoulders sagged with relief.

"What about my release, and the release of my babies?"

"I had hoped to make you comfortable here—so comfortable that you might consider staying."

Molly started to laugh. "Kenonranon," she said in Mohawk, "she is a white woman. Marry your own wife; have your own children. Let this woman go after she is ransomed."

The warrior merely glared at his mother. "We will speak of your release at a later time when fewer ears are present," he said finally. He rose and angrily left the cabin.

The late August heat was almost unbearable. Amy had done farm work all of her life, but nothing as backbreaking as harvesting corn and squash. The storage bins in the longhouses and the barns in this mixed European and Iroquois village were filled to overflowing. Yet Amy had the feeling that the inhabitants were nervous and insecure.

Then in September, Aaron, Joseph and most of the warriors disappeared. The Americans, explained Molly, had moved through the country of the Delaware and advanced on the lands of the Seneca and Cayuga. Major Butler and remnants of his Rangers had joined the tribes that were trying to stop General Sullivan and his four thousand American regulars.

Amy went to the fields every day, despite Aaron's absence. She did not try to escape. She knew she could not have found her way out of this wilderness. And she had a healthy fear of Aaron's mother. She was convinced that if she tried to escape, even with the men gone, Molly by herself would lead a tracking party and she would be found. Although the work was hard, she suffered through it without complaint. She lived to keep her sons alive and to regain her daughter. All else, she concluded, was vanity.

She was picking beans when she heard the cry come from the village. It was like a wailing coming from many voices at once. She dropped the woven basket she carried at her side and followed the other women as they raced back to the village.

Joseph Brant was present. His foot was bandaged and his sister was trying to force him to sit down so that she might sniff the wound and care for it. She was sure from the look of it that it needed attention.

Brant spoke in Iroquois. Almost every word brought a gasp and further wailing from the crowd. Some of the women started to cut their hair and slash their bodies with knives. Amy caught sight of Aaron entering the village at the head of a band of warriors. It was clear Joseph had come ahead with the bad news. She ran to Aaron's side.

"Brother," she called to him, acknowledging their relationship for the first time. "What has happened?"

He took her by the arm and led her toward their house.

"It is good news for you and unhappy news for us. It would not be proper to make you share in our sorrow, but neither would it be appropriate for us to see your joy. We met the Americans in the land of the Delawares. They outnumbered us four to one and we were beaten badly. Our people ran. The Americans followed. They have burned most of the castles of the Seneca and Cayuga. Even the great Seneca castle on the Genesee, the largest of our people, is gone. Burned. The corn destroyed. Our nation lies in shambles."

Amy now understood the reaction of the women. This village was made up of Iroquois from many villages. Brant was reciting the names of the burned villages to the west.

"Now a smaller force heads this way," continued Aaron. "We will have to decide whether to run or to resist them."

Amy realized that Brant was telling her that her rescue

might be at hand, depending upon what he and Joseph decided to do.

That evening a great council of the village met. The council fire was set in the square formed by several longhouses interspersed with European cabins.

Joseph Brant presided. He was not the sachem. But as a war leader and captain in the British army, he was the most prestigious person present, bar one—his sister, clan mother of the Turtles, granddaughter of old Brant.

The council fire sent sparks up into the night blackness. Joseph rose and, in tones rich with anguish, told the whole village of the defeat at Chemung to the west.

"The Delawares and Seneca insisted on fighting there," he said, "even though Major Butler and I thought it better to retreat into the mountains and try to ambush them. But now we are defeated and followed."

A gasp went up from the listeners. To that point they had not realized that they were in danger.

"An American army comes up the Susquehanna toward our village. Now we must decide what to do."

Aaron rose and asked to speak. Joseph acknowledged him.

"My brothers," he began. "We must not allow the rebel troops to defeat us. If we retreat we give up our homes forever. We will have no corn or vegetables. All the food you have worked to plant and harvest, sisters," he said, pointing beyond the inner ring out toward where the women stood, "all that food is forfeit. We lose all freedom. With winter coming, we will either starve or be forced to flee to Niagara to have the King feed us. The King loves us, and I have no doubt he will feed us, but never again will we have the choice to say no to him. We will pass from being his children to being his slaves. But, worse, we will never again be free to live by the beautiful river or roam these beautiful mountains and lakes. If we flee now, we are finished as a people."

There were nods of approval and grunts of agreement with Aaron. Then to the surprise of all, Joseph acknowledged his sister, the clan mother.

Molly paused for some minutes before she began to speak. She looked about the council fire and then at her son, aware that with these words she might place a distance between them.

"My son speaks out of his great love for his people and his great love for this land. I love my son. I love him more than his love for us and our land. But I must speak against it. My son is half white. I hold him up as a model of what you must become if we are to survive as a people. Johnson taught me, and who would deny that he was wise? He taught me that all must become like the whites. We must keep our Iroquois spirit, but we must farm like the whites and live like them and think like them. These white men—the rebels—they are the most evil of the white men. They are greedy devourers of land. They will never give us the time to learn to become like them. They will chew us up and spit us out. But across the lakes and rivers behind the British forts, there are not so many whites. Those who are there have come to know us and respect us, as the Johnsons, the Butlers and even, I hear, Aaron's father the blackrobe of Kanowalohale, have done. These men will allow us to come and live among them. We should go now. We must have no more bloodshed. We must cross the rivers and lakes to Canada."

A cry went up from the majority of the council when Molly had finished. Joseph rose and stood by his sister's side, signaling that he had decided to go. Soon most of the council members stood with her. All eyes turned toward Aaron.

He was clearly in agony. He loved his mother and uncle dearly. But he loved this land. He rose, and all were quiet. Only the noise of the council fire was heard. He turned his back on the council and began to walk away. Molly called out to him, but he would not look back. About fifty warriors, mostly young men, followed him. The village of Onaquaga, like the confederation of the Six Nations itself, was split.

The next morning Molly Brant and her brother left the site of Onaquaga and retreated to the north up the

Susquehanna. Their path would lead to the west eventually—toward the haven of Fort Niagara.

Aaron watched his mother go. He had not spoken to her since the council. He was sure that she had expected him to come around and join her and his uncle, but he had not. Nor had he allowed Amy and her sons to go. They were his prisoners and no one could take them from him.

As soon as the Brant party had left, Aaron ordered his warriors to set up a breastwork along the river extending to the woods. They could be flanked only by woodsmen coming through on their right. Regular soldiers would never attempt that.

Aaron had no delusions about winning. Even if his force could not be outflanked, it could be overwhelmed by a frontal assault. He stood only because he could run no more, because he could no longer watch his people being nibbled away. It was too much for him to bear.

Amy stayed in her cabin and took over the care of Molly's fire. At midday, Aaron came, and she served him a meal of cornbread and venison stew. He ate in silence. When he had finished, he turned to her.

"The rebel army will be here this afternoon," he said. "I will send a white flag out to them and turn you and your sons over to them. I would not want anything to happen to you in the fighting."

Amy was deeply grateful for his gesture. She had come to respect him. At first she had clung to him in terror. He had saved her and her children. She resented his people for destroying her life and her home, but she knew that others in other times had destroyed Iroquois lives and Iroquois homes. She had hated neither the Americans nor the British after Antoine's death. She had turned her ire on violence and war. She could not now blame the Iroquois for Kurt or for Maggie.

"Why must you fight this last fight, Aaron?" she asked.

"Because I cannot bring myself to give up these rivers and lakes. My people have lived and died here for centuries."

"And now our father's people—my people—will come to

267

live here and come to love these rivers and these lakes."

He looked at her with anger.

"Don't be angry with me, brother," she said. "Before the Iroquois were here someone else was. You took it from them. Now it is taken from you. But I do not believe that the loss of any lake is worth dying for, any more than the loss of my lover or my husband. There is always someone else—my sons, my daughter. They needed me and I continued to live. For you there is another place, another land. Why did you refuse your mother's advice to go to Canada?"

"I wish to talk no more about it," he said, rising from his seat and placing his bowl down on the table with a thud. "It is time to return you to the rebels."

The drum rattle of the approaching rebel force had begun to unnerve the warriors behind their breastwork. The front line of the march came into view. Then, on command, the rebels, who had come far in four years of fighting British regulars, swung from a column into a line stretching from the river to the edge of the woods.

Aaron took a white cloth and raised it on a pole, which he then placed above the top of a breastwork.

There was a stirring within the American ranks. Within a few minutes, an officer, also carrying a white flag, stepped to the front and waited.

Aaron took Amy by the arm. She carried Charles in her arm, and Aaron carried his twin brother Stephen.

She climbed over the breastwork. Once on the other side, she waited for Aaron. He jumped down beside her. The babies were both disturbed by their leaps and began to fuss.

The small party walked across the open field and halted before a Yankee captain. His hostility toward them was obvious in his eyes. From his alertness, Amy was sure he expected some sort of Indian trick.

"Stay there," he said when they were about twenty feet from him. "We can talk at this distance. What do you want, Indian, other than to have us spare you, even though you've been slaughtering in this colony for over two years?".

Aaron ignored him.

"I bring you a captive white woman—Amy Miller of Fort Vaughan in the Mohawk Valley and her two sons, who were captured earlier this summer. She wishes to return to her people, and I do not wish either her or her sons to be harmed in the fighting which will take place here today."

The captain was first surprised by the quality of Aaron's English. As Aaron spoke, his eyes went to Amy and her children. As soon as Aaron had finished, he gave Stephen to Amy and walked away from her and her sons. She called to him, but he did not turn around.

The captain rushed to her side.

"Mrs. Miller," he said, "let me assist you." He took the children from her and called to the ranks for assistance. Several privates broke rank and came to her and the captain.

The ranks parted and allowed Amy and her sons to pass through to safety. The captain found a camp chair for Amy to sit on. There was a scurrying in the rear of the ranks. The small group about Amy separated to let the commanding officer of the expedition up the Susquehanna enter.

"What's the commotion here?" he asked.

Amy recognized his voice immediately. It was the soft Southern drawl she had so hated in the past.

"Miss Amy," said Ethan in surprise when he saw her. He turned to his aide. "Tell the ensign to get over here immediately." He moved quickly to her side and touched her shoulder.

"Are you all right?"

"Yes, and so are my sons."

"We came to Fort Vaughan and found Abel Tice. He told us of your husband and how you and your children, along with the Quaker women, were taken. Most were recaptured in the Seneca campaign by General Sullivan. The Quakers told us you had gone with the Mohawks. So we set up this smaller force to look for you."

"My daughter?" Amy asked fearfully. "Was she recovered from the Seneca?"

Ethan shook his head. "We thought she might still be with you."

There was another commotion behind Amy, and a young officer, really still a boy, entered the group about the returned captive.

"Sister?"

Amy turned around and saw Matthew looking at her and her sons. She stood up and moved over to him, allowing him to hug her. She bent forward and kissed him. She was truly happy to see the boy.

"Well, now that I'm recovered, for God's sake let's all of us go home."

"Not without taking care of one further matter," said Morin, pointing toward the Indian breastwork behind which Aaron had disappeared.

Most of the young men who stayed behind with Aaron were Mohawk refugees from Schoharie castle. Only five of them had been in battle before. All were as resigned to die that day as Aaron. Aaron felt like a father to all of them. In fact, he was old enough to have been the father of most of them. It saddened him that this afternoon the flower of his people was to be picked. They were a small tribe to begin with—soon only the Caugnawaga would carry the blood of Hendrick and old Brant.

He told his men to eat their fill of the cornbread and meat the others had left behind. There was no sense in leaving it for the Americans.

The enemy lengthened its line and seemed to make preparations of some sort. Aaron's greatest fear was that they had brought field pieces with them. Artillery would make quick work of their rapidly built breastwork. But as the afternoon wore on, he became convinced that they had none.

He went from warrior to warrior along the breastwork, encouraging some who were clearly frightened but would die rather than show it, and joking with others who were too naive even to be scared.

As the sun grew less hot and began to move across the sky to the west, Aaron became puzzled. Why did the rebels wait? They should have attacked hours ago.

But then he heard the fife and drums. Just like the British, he thought, they could not march into battle without their strange music and their strange metallic-sounding drums. The rebel lines were moving. He climbed up higher on the breastwork to get a view. His signal for his warriors to rise up and fire their muskets was to be the fall of his arm. He raised his hand and climbed up farther. He reached the top and peered over. His arm never fell.

The rebel lines were moving, but in the opposite direction. The rebel patrol was withdrawing. They would not allow the Mohawks the dignity of a last fight.

On the second night of their return march to Fort Sullivan, as the post near Tioga was called, Matthew entered Amy's tent. He fussed a bit with the flap and then nervously inquired about the health of his nephews.

"What is it?" said Amy finally. "You're behaving like a bridegroom on the eve of the wedding."

When he didn't answer, she picked up a comb, which had been loaned to her by Major Morin, and began to work on her hair.

Matthew gave a fake cough and took a deep breath to screw up his courage.

"I have two important, or rather delicate, questions to ask of you, sister."

She turned to face him and stopped the combing.

"The Indian fellow who brought you to our lodge, I presume he was your captor."

"Yes?" said Amy with a question in her tone.

"Well, I have to know. Well, if he was your captor, did he . . . or did you try to . . ."

Amy smiled at the boy soldier. "No, Matthew. It was not likely. He is our brother."

Matthew's face went from relief to incredulity. "What?"

"Our father, Stephen Nowell, is a well-traveled man, Matthew. Aaron Brant is his son by the clan mother Molly Brant, the widow of Sir William Johnson."

271

Matthew was silent for some moments as he remembered his Uncle Vaughan telling him of his half-brother. Amy began to comb her hair again. Finally he spoke.

"That news makes my second question all the more important. Some of the men are saying that you tricked Major Morin into withdrawing. Some say there couldn't have been more than sixty men behind the flimsy breastwork."

"There were only fifty," she interrupted.

"And they're saying that you chased us off to save your . . . lover, but I knew that couldn't be true. But maybe you would trick us to save a brother."

"I would do anything to save a brother," she said, rising from her chair. She walked over and patted the ensign on his fuzzy cheeks. He was desperate to grow a beard and look older, but it was just not happening.

"There were fifty men in the barricade but hundreds more in the woods. I told Ethan that and no more. He decided to report back to General Sullivan for instructions. Yes, I saved a brother, but it turned out to be the young Matthew, not the older Aaron."

He blushed. He was relieved and reached over and kissed her. "Thank you, Amy," he said, and then he walked rapidly from the tent.

She went back to the stool and picked up her comb and began to run it through her hair again. It was good to get the tangles out. When she got to Fort Sullivan, maybe they could grant her the luxury of a bath so that she might get months of dirt from her body and hair.

Kurt would not have approved of what she had just done. She lied to the boy to assuage his feelings. Kurt would have called that a sin. But the other lie—the big lie to Ethan—somehow or other she felt he would have understood that.

The carriage drove down Pearl Street with an escort of mounted dragoons. Phillip Schuyler was the senior general officer of the now relatively quiet Northern Department. The Iroquois and the bloody Tories still raided, but they would never get their lands back. The French alliance was a success. The British were now driven from Philadelphia. In the north only New York City and Newport, Rhode Island, were still in their hands. No more British armies would be descending among them from Montreal. This was the kind of war he could appreciate. This was closer to the general's life he had anticipated from the beginning.

The carriage turned down a little alley at the end of the street and entered the mews and stable of his aunt's Albany house.

Normally the old lady lived in her Saratoga property, but it was victim to the war. His wife insisted that he should reclaim that property and he supposed that he should. The old lady was becoming more and more peculiar. His wife had been scandalized several times by her behavior, especially bringing that ruffian she claimed was her husband to family functions. Getting her out of town was his strongest desire at the moment, however. He still thought it preposterous that she would not answer the front door and that she insisted that guests enter from the rear. She said that the city dirt in the gutters was unhealthy. From the rear, guests more than likely would track in horse dung. When he pointed this out to her, she merely cackled and told him that real horse dung was something she had learned to cope with early in life, but that city dirt—never.

He descended from his carriage with the assistance of his aide. The young officer went to the back door and knocked. The door was swung open wide by Israel Kip.

"General, welcome. Margaret is expecting you."

General Schuyler nodded to Kip. He had always liked the man. It was his wife who was offended by him.

Margaret was seventy-nine now and beginning to look even thinner as she aged.

"Well, you finally got here," she said sarcastically, without any other greeting. "You're as slow visiting me as you're slow in giving me the money to finish my house. I'll be in a wooden box before I'll be in that house again."

"Aunt Margaret, please," pleaded the general. "There is a war on. I surely cannot commandeer items for my personal use that are necessary for the army."

"Fiddlesticks," she interrupted. "Everyone else does it. If that pussy-faced VanRenssalaer whom your mother, damn her, forced you to marry wanted a house, I'll bet you anything she'd have a house by now."

Amy walked into the kitchen and went over to the general.

"Uncle Phillip," she greeted him and kissed him on the cheek.

Matthew had risen to stand at attention, following Ethan's example.

"Gentlemen," Schuyler acknowledged the two junior officers. He returned Amy's kiss.

"Well, you didn't answer me. What about my house?" Margaret yelled.

"Glory be to God, woman, you're a worse scold than my mother was."

Margaret looked as if she had been slapped in the face. She was flabbergasted. She had despised Cornelia Schuyler, the general's mother, and never in her life had she been compared unfavorably to Cornelia.

"Aunt Margaret," said Amy, "we did not come together to badger Uncle Phillip."

But now Margaret was angry. "Why not?" she yelled. "I can't think of anything else I would rather do."

"Simmer down, Margaret," said Kip, placing his hand on her thin shoulder. To everyone's surprise, she looked at the man with obvious affection and shut up.

"I need your help again, general," said Amy. "I am desperate. I need to go through our lines to the lakes and cross over to the Niagara side. I'll need your help—a safe conduct, a letter of introduction to the British commander."

"My dear, you ask a great deal of me. We are still at war. At this moment a British army is operating, or I might say rampaging, through the Southern colonies. What makes you think the British would honor a safe conduct?"

"The British are honorable," laughed Amy, "even if General Arnold is on their side now."

"Tragedy, that," said Schuyler, shaking his head. "Arnold was a fine soldier. He saved us at Saratoga. I guess it was greed and the Congress. I have no greed, but Congress could make me switch sides."

"Will you help me, General?"

"Why do you feel you have to go to Niagara? Why now?"

Amy took a folded piece of paper from her dress pocket. She unfolded it and handed it to Schuyler. It was written in an almost childlike script, and it was dated from Niagara.

"It's from my brother," she said as Schuyler began to read.

Dearest Sister,

My Uncle Joseph, who is very literate, is helping me write this letter to you. I know I have you to thank that I am alive and reconciled with my mother and uncle. I thank you.

Now it is my turn to favor you. I have located your daughter with the red hair. She lives in the Buffalo Creek settlements with the Seneca, Geyasada. I have asked for her release, but the wife of Geyasada loves the child and will not give her up. I have told her of your anguish, and she has agreed that she could share the child with you if you could come here to live. I pass this word to you. If you come, you will be treated as the honored sister of a Mohawk sachem, since I have been raised to this dignity by the clan mother—my mother.

I regret that I have no further word on the fate of your husband. This seems not a good sign to me.

Your brother,
Aaron.

"Do you trust this man?" asked Schuyler after he had finished reading.

"Sir," interrupted Matthew, "you must not let her go. My sister cannot go over to live among the enemy."

"Why not?" said Schuyler. "I lived among them all my life until this damned war broke us all up." He turned to Amy. "I could write General Haldimand in Quebec and try to obtain the release of your daughter."

"You know that wouldn't work. Geyasada would simply move away and I would never find Maggie again. She would disappear like Kurt."

"Send the girl on her way, Phillip," said Aunt Margaret. "A woman needs her children. I know. I never had any children because I couldn't stand the little bastards, but a woman needs her children if she has them."

"Is that so, Margaret?" smiled the general. "I'll send her if you get off my back about the house," he said, winking at Amy.

"That badly she doesn't need her children," said the old woman, shouting again.

Schuyler laughed. "Major Morin, you are to arrange for my niece to travel to Niagara and you are to accompany her and remain as long as she needs you."

"Yes, sir," said Ethan.

Matthew started to protest. "But that's like turning Ethan over to the enemy."

"I suspect they will inter him for the rest of this bloody war. But they'll accept his parole and he will be free to move about within their lines. If I know the British, they'll regard his task as a romantic and noble one, and they'll honor him greatly. Bloody fools."

"But my sister, she is going to live with the Tories and the Indians."

"Those people of whom you speak so disdainfully, Matthew," said Amy, "include our father and our brother. We have just gone through a terrible civil war, which has split our families and our people. It is time for a reconciliation."

"I have no use for your brother and I hate your father," said Matthew angrily. "And I disown you. I'll have no Tory sister." He stormed out of the room.

Schuyler was about to call after him, but Aunt Margaret intervened.

"Let him be," she said. "He needs to do some more growing up before he can see the sense of what the girl says. If you run into that scalawag Stephen Nowell, you tell him to bring my Katherine to me as soon as he can. I want to see her again before my eyes fail me."

EPILOGUE

1784

The fog on the bay would be lifting soon. The heat of the sun was beginning to penetrate the cloud cover. Before long Stephen was sure they would see the rays reflecting brilliantly off the drops of water that hung suspended in the air. Katherine stood by his side. She was anxious for the fog to lift so that she might see the town that he had chosen for their new home.

He looked at her lovingly. These last years at Isle d'Orleans and in London had been happy. On the island he and Louis Joseph had worked together for over a year with her. By their love and care, she had gradually begun to accept reality again, and by their continued love, she had gradually been restored to health.

His attempts to get his son Matthew to join them had all been unsuccessful. He finally had to admit to himself that the boy didn't want to leave the home he had found with Margaret and Kip. So once again, as he had since Matthew had been born, he resigned himself to the fact that his son's upbringing would be in the hands of others. He knew now that he had only himself to blame for the rift that had developed between him and those he loved. At least he had partially been able to make it up to Katherine.

Once Katherine's health had improved, he also had to admit to himself that he had been away from his own business affairs too long. Stephen had broached the possibility of a trip to England with trepidation. The look in her eyes had terrified him. She had begun to cry. Suddenly her tears stopped and she turned on him with fear in her eyes.

278

"You'll never go anywhere without me again, Stephen Nowell, so help me God. I'll not be left behind again."

Stephen looked at her in amazement. "I had no intention of leaving you behind," he said. "I wanted us to go together."

"You just said that. You made it up just now."

"No," he argued.

"Then why all the caution?"

"I don't think Louis Joseph will be willing to come with us."

She smiled an enormous smile of relief. "I don't care," she said, laughing, "so long as I have you. I don't care what Louis Joseph does. He's a grown man. He'll marry. He'll have a house full of French babies and he'll be happy. But I am not ready to take on the role of grandmère. I am too young for it. I want to go to England with you."

Louis Joseph had argued with them bitterly, but finally he had reconciled himself to their leaving.

The farms would be his, both of them. The notary had arranged the purchase of the Gingras property from Antoine's sister. Stephen, in turn, had assigned it to Louis Joseph. The Stiegler property was already his by inheritance from his father. He would own the largest farm on the island, and he would have his pick of the island girls for a wife. Stephen teased him, but Louis Joseph had become a serious young man.

Katherine had said goodbye to her son with a great flow of tears. But she was happy to be away from the island. As much as she loved it and her house, her years there had been an imprisonment for her mind. When the ship sailed for England from Quebec City and passed the island in the north channel, she could actually see her farm. She shuddered and cuddled closer to Stephen on the deck.

England had been a whirl of business, parties, weekends with the prime minister at his estate, and entertaining Loyalist friends, some of them very indigent and others aloof, especially when they learned that Mrs. Nowell was the sister of a rebel general.

But she was happy when Stephen announced he had received compensation from the crown in the form of a land-grant farm—an estate really—on the Saint John River in that portion of Nova Scotia soon to become the province of New Brunswick. He would establish his business office at Saint John, a year-round port, and he would purchase a home in the town. They would develop a country estate later.

They had been in England almost four years. But now they were coming home. The war was over at last. The treaty ending it had been signed in Paris the year before. The thirteen colonies, their old home, would now be the United States of America. But they, as Loyalists, would not be welcome there. They would, like so many others who had been faithful to the King, turn their eyes to the north and establish a new land, where they would be free and not be punished for their loyalty. The sun finally broke through the clouds and the fog evaporated swiftly. A breeze came from the southeast, and Stephen's ship began to edge ahead slowly.

Stephen caught sight of the shore and pointed it out excitedly to Katherine.

"There it is," he called out.

Then both of them became quiet. Off in the distance, the harbor of Saint John was spread out before them. The warehouses and wharves were bustling with shipping.

Katherine squeezed Stephen's hand and looked up at him.

"Welcome home," he said to her.

The wind caught the ship's sails and it heeled to port. The shores of Canada seemed to rush toward them.

ABOUT THE AUTHOR

A Canadian citizen since 1976, ROBERT E. WALL draws on his love for Canada and his native United States in creating the saga of *THE CANADIANS*. He perceives the histories of the two nations as deeply entwined and, influenced by the writings of Kenneth Roberts, seeks to teach those histories through the historical novel. *Blackrobe*, the first in the series, is Wall's first novel, followed by *Bloodbrothers* and *Birthright*.

Robert Wall is married, has five children (one is an adopted Cree Indian, the most authentic Canadian in the family), and divides his time between New Jersey, where he is provost at Fairleigh Dickinson University, and Montreal, where his family lives.

THE PATRIOTS

BLACKROBE, BLOODBROTHERS,
BIRTHRIGHT
and now . . .

THE PATRIOTS

Volume IV of THE CANADIANS

By Robert E. Wall

*Read this special preview of the thrilling open-
ing pages of the next great novel in this sweep-
ing saga.*

THE PATRIOTS

1792

Rain soaked the streets of Albany, turning them into rivulets of muddy water. The old Dutch-style houses seemed to droop under the weight of the humidity. At the riverfront, the downspouts from the houses poured a flow of rainwater onto the banks. Once the soil had been thoroughly soaked, sections of the muddy bank crumbled into the river, turning the Hudson a darker brown.

The richly dressed black man waded across Pearl Street. He leaped the submerged curb onto the brick sidewalk and took refuge under the eaves of the Albany Inn. He ran his hand through his steely gray hair and tried to wring some of the water out. He stamped his feet to free his expensive leather boots of the brown muck that clung to them. The boots would have to be carefully dried and polished this very night if they were to be of any use to him in the future. He smiled. Stephen Nowell had turned Josiah the ferryman into Josiah Ferryman, a partner in the firm of Breed, Nowell and Vaughan; yet he still thought like a servant. He would never get used to the idea of someone else taking care of chores like muddy boots.

He swung open the inn's front door. His senses were overwhelmed by the rank stench of stale beer and day-old spilled rum, mixed with the pungent odor of burning pine in the hearth. Josiah surveyed the room until he caught sight of Nowell sitting alone by the fire. He too was richly dressed. His greatcoat was thrown over the back of his chair. It still dripped rain onto the bare hardwood floors of the taproom. But the cloak had served him well. His dark blue coat with polished silver buttons had been untouched by the downpour. His silver gray hair was almost exactly the same color as the breeches he wore. And he still wore breeches. He would have nothing to do with the new revolutionary radical style of pants. To him they were a symbol of the French Revolution and radical Jeffersonian democracy in America, both of which he detested. He had grown heavier over the years. His middle had thickened and there were unmistakable signs of a pot belly protruding over the edge of the waistband of his breeches. His face was chubbier, displaying a flabbiness about the jaw that in profile could only be described as a double chin. He looked every inch the wealthy, conservative merchant-gentleman he was.

But there were aspects of him that did not fit

the mold. A thin, white scar ran through his left eyebrow and lid, and his empty left sleeve was pinned against his shoulder. He had not always been a merchant. He held a silver-headed cane in his hand. The cane's tip was wedged in a broad space between the floorboards. He rested his hand on the silver head and his heavy chin on his hand, staring at the leaping flames of the hearth.

Josiah walked to his friend's table and sat down. Stephen looked up at his, startled by his sudden arrival. "Josiah, is everything taken care of?"

"We leave for Saratoga in the morning by hired coach."

"Have you any word on her condition?" Stephen asked.

"The old woman lives—although just barely. We can't waste any time getting there."

Stephen sat quietly for some minutes, lost in thought. "I'm glad we arrived in time," he said finally. "But I'm sorry Katherine could not be with us. She loves that old lady. But I couldn't take the chance."

Josiah nodded. "There is something else you ought to know," he said. "Major Nowell is living with Miss Margaret."

Stephen smiled wanly. "How many years has it been since we last saw him, Josiah? It was just before Bunker Hill. It's been seventeen years since I last saw my son. I don't know how many times I've tried to see him. When Katherine and I built the house in St. John, we asked him to come to Canada and join us. He never even responded to my letters, and when Katherine and I visited Israel and Margaret in Saratoga, we discovered he had been posted to Fort Pitt. I don't even know what the man looks like, Josiah. As a boy he favored Abigail."

Stephen grew silent and began to stare into the fire again. A sadness seem to descend upon him. Josiah had seen this happen whenever he mentioned the girl-wife, Major Nowell's mother, who had died so tragically almost thirty years before. But now he did not mention her often and never in the presence of his wife, Katherine.

"It's ironic," Stephen said suddenly. "The son I hoped would make up for the loss of the others is estranged. My daughter writes to me and her mother regularly from Upper Canada, and even Aaron—Molly Brant's wild Mohawk —acknowledges me as his father and has sought my help. But this youngest will have nothing to do with me."

Josiah said nothing. He knew from long experience that talk did little good when his friend was in this mood.

The door of the inn swung open again, and a heavyset man with a ruddy face half-hidden in his dripping cloak entered the taproom. He too searched the tables with his eyes and, catching sight of Josiah and Stephen, he came to their table.

"My esteemed brother-in-law, I presume," he said with a smile.

"Phillip?" Stephen responded. "I mean Senator Schuyler, or do you still prefer General Schuyler?"

"I prefer Phillip. Your associate," he said, glancing at Josiah and not sure just what their relationship entailed, "was at my home earlier making inquiries about Aunt Margaret. I simply could not let you slip out of Albany without greeting you."

Stephen laughed. "I wouldn't do that, Phillip. The word I received was that you were in Philadelphia trying to help your son-in-law, Secretary Hamilton, keep Jefferson from turning my unfortunate native land into a vile democracy."

Schuyler ignored his barb. "My sister is not with you, I gather."

"No," responded Stephen. "She's not really well. The doctors diagnosed a slight stroke last year. She has recovered from that. But she is not yet strong enough to travel. We have moved from the city to our country home in the St. John River valley. It is quiet and very beautiful there. She loves it very much."

"We've seen each other only twice since we were children. But I know she is happy in Canada—from her letters."

"It's our home now," said Stephen. "We are at peace—with a sensible and conservative government in New Brunswick."

"I'm happy for you both. It is important to have a place you can call home. My aunt has taught me how important that is. She nearly drove me to distraction for years until I rebuilt the mansion at Saratoga Flats. And she has lived there in peace and has given me my peace ever since." He hesitated a moment and then added with sadness, "until now."

"Will you come with us?" Stephen asked.

"No," responded Schuyler. "Margaret and I have taken leave of each other already. She finds goodbyes difficult. She wouldn't appreciate having to see me again. Just carry my love to her."

The coach followed the course of the Hudson north to Saratoga. The rain of the night before had given way to a smoky fall sun. The trees that grew along the riverbank were a blaze of reds, oranges and browns. The river beyond Albany was almost empty of traffic. Stephen recalled former days—days of invasion from the north or from the south, when the river was so busy it was difficult to reason how the *bateau* men avoided collisions. But with the peace of the past decade, no invasions disturbed the tranquility of the northern Hudson.

Josiah had fallen alsleep. They had risen early

to begin this journey, and the black man could not sleep at all the night before a trip—not that Josiah or Stephen traveled that much any longer. Stephen looked back at the river. He remembered this bend in the river road. The old Saratoga house had stood almost on this spot until it had been destroyed by Burgoyne's soldiers in 1777. That British invasion had gone no farther, and its members had reached their goal of Albany only as prisoners of war. And earlier, from this spot, the Abenacki sachem, Socono, Stephen's Indian father, had taken him across the Hudson and taught him to be a man again, saving him from the life of an invalid filled with self-pity. The new house would come into view any second now. Stephen would face two difficult tasks once he reached it. He would have to say goodbye to a lady whom he loved but whom he was not sure cared for him, and he would have to greet a son whom he loved but whom he was sure despised him.

The old lady lay propped in her bed. She was so thin and frail that Matthew was afraid to move her. She had asked him to bring her into the front bedroom, to give her a view of the river. He had moved the whole bed rather than hurt her by lifting her from it. At ninety-two, Margaret Schuyler demanded everything and got precisely what she wanted. Matthew saw to it. When Kip died the year before, at the age of seventy-six, Matthew asked for leave from his regiment to be with her. He was the only family she had left, and he was not even a blood relation. But this old lady had raised him since he was ten, and he loved her as much as he could have loved his own mother.

He was nervous this morning. Word had come from Albany that his father, a man he had not seen in seventeen years, was coming to Saratoga to visit the old lady. The last time his father and his father's wife visited, he had missed them by volunteering for service on the frontier. But there was no avoiding this visit, and for this meeting Aunt Margaret made him promise to be present.

Matthew sat looking out the window of her bedroom. The delicate lace curtains stirred slightly in the soft breeze. The day grew warmer as the morning wore on. They would be blessed with a few days of Indian summer before the cold came down out of the mountains to the north. He rose from his chair and walked over to the great fourposter bed. Margaret was dozing, but each breath was followed by a slight gurgling sound in her chest. He heard the noise of a carriage coming down the Albany road, and he went back to the window.

Matthew could not help but be curious about his father. His memory of him was so faint. The carriage stopped in front of the verandah, and a black man stepped out. Matthew recognized him instantly. It was the ferryman, Josiah. Then the other man climbed out. He did not immediately recognize his father. He had changed greatly, but Matthew knew him by his cane, which he carried to balance himself and compensate for his lost arm. Matthew left his aunt alone to go downstairs and greet the guests.

"Gentlemen," Matthew greeted them from the first landing.

Josiah smiled at Matthew. "Mr. Matt," he said. The black man would have preferred to go to Matthew and throw his arms about him, but he knew the father would not, and he could not embarrass his friend.

"Matthew," said Stephen, in a greeting rivaling his son's formality and coldness. "You've grown into a strong-looking and handsome man. Your mother would be proud."

"How is your wife, sir?" Matthew asked, trying to keep the conversation going.

"Not as well as I'd like. I had to leave her behind, much against her will. Gave me the devil for breaking a long-standing promise by not taking her with me. But she wasn't up to a long trip down to New York, and then the packet-boat ride to Albany would have done her in. How's Aunt Margaret?"

"I doubt if she'll last the week," said Matthew with some feeling. "Her birthday is coming up, and she insisted I send for you."

"She'll be disappointed that Katherine is not

with me. It couldn't be helped. Take me to her; I want to see her."

Matthew turned back up the stairs, and Stephen followed. They entered the old lady's room together. Margaret was still dozing and did not hear them enter. Matthew stood beside her and touched her frail shoulder. She awoke with a start.

"Aunt Margaret," he said, "Mr. Nowell is here."

She looked around. Stephen stepped into her view and she smiled. Her teeth were now completely gone, and he was shocked to see how truly frail she was. But then next week she would be ninety-two. No one in Albany or Saratoga could truthfully remember her as young. She had outlived all of her contemporaries and many born well after her.

"Where's Katherine?" asked Margaret.

"She couldn't come, Margaret. She's not well."

"You always were a disappointment to me, boy," she said.

Only Margaret could get away with calling a sixty-seven-year-old man a boy.

"But then you were no better and no worse than most men. I never liked men. That is, except for Kip. He died last year."

"I know," said Stephen sadly.

"I liked Kip," she continued. "The only man worth his weight in spit. I decided not to hate you as much as I really could and as much as you really deserved because you introduced me to Kip."

Stephen smiled.

"I called you here, Stephen, because I am dying. I'd rather have told this to my Katherine, face to face, but you'll have to do it. I'm leaving all of this," she said, waving her frail arm wearily, "my house and my lands, to Matthew. I want Katherine to know that I had not forgotten her. I always said I would leave it to her, but she's got so much from you, and your son has nothing."

"You know, Aunt Margaret, that I will provide for my own son."

"I can't be sure. The boy is almost as obnoxious as you are. You probably won't be able to stand him, and you'll probably disown him."

"I never would," said Stephen indignantly.

"Good. You hear that, Matthew; your father promised me on my deathbed that he'd never disown you, no matter what you did. Remind him of it when he tries to disown you." She cackled her familiar laugh, a much weaker sound than it had been in the past.

"Get out of here, now; I want to die in peace."

Stephen looked at her with some concern. But Matthew merely chuckled.

"You say that every day, old woman, but you never do it."

"One of these days," she said, holding up her hand, "one of these days." And she began to doze again.

The two men went down the stairs.

"You realize that it can never be," said Stephen to Matthew.

"What do you mean?"

"She couldn't leave you this house; she doesn't own it. She never did. It was willed in the Schuyler estate, and Cornelia Schuyler and then General Schuyler allowed her to live here. When she dies, it reverts to the Schuylers."

"I know that," said Matthew, "and she knows that. Why do you think she went through the charade of getting you to promise not to disown me? I know that was a sham too."

"Matthew, I meant what I said. When I die, you will receive your proper portion of my estate in Canada."

"I don't want any of your Tory loot."

"Oh, Matthew, the war has been over almost a decade. Why continue to fight old, tired battles?"

"If the war is over, why do you continue to hold the forts that were ceded to us in the treaty —Detroit, Niagara? No, sir, the war won't be over until our army enters Canada and drives the damned British and you damned Tories into the sea. There is room for only one nation on this continent, and that nation is going to be the United States. So help me God, I'll lead an army across the lakes and I'll take for us all that God intended for us to have—the whole continent."

Stephen was shocked by his son's outburst. Matthew was not really angry; he spoke in a cold and calculated tone. It sent a chill through the father. Stephen was suddenly frightened for the peace he had come to cherish in his new home, and he was suddenly frightened for Canada.

Read THE PATRIOTS, *on sale August 15, 1982, wherever paperbacks are sold.*

★ ★★★ ★★ ★★★

GREAT HISTORICAL SAGAS OF AMERICA'S FIRST FRONTIERS

The Producer of the KENT FAMILY CHRONICLES now brings you the WAGONS WEST and COLONIZATION OF AMERICA series. These books are full of the spectacular adventure and romance that followed America's first settlers as they struggled in a new land.

The highly acclaimed WAGONS WEST series by Dana Fuller Ross:

☐	20419	INDEPENDENCE!	$3.25
☐	20417	NEBRASKA!	$3.25
☐	20420	WYOMING!	$3.25
☐	20421	OREGON!	$3.25
☐	20422	TEXAS!	$3.25
☐	14260	CALIFORNIA!	$2.95
☐	14717	COLORADO!	$3.25

The thrilling COLONIZATION OF AMERICA series by Donald Clayton Porter:

☐	20349	WHITE INDIAN	$3.25
☐	20362	THE RENEGADE	$3.25
☐	20579	WAR CHIEF	$3.25
☐	20361	THE SACHEM	$3.25

The new SAGA OF THE SOUTHWEST series by Leigh Franklin Jones:

☐	20096	REVENGE OF THE HAWK	$3.25
☐	20556	HAWK OF THE DOVE	$3.25
☐	20635	WINGS OF THE HAWK	$3.25

★★★★★★★★★★★★★★★★★★★★★